Heave To

By Pete DeBoer

Rob

Enjoy. The Adventure
you might see a few
familiar faces in here

Pete

Aug 2016

This story is a work of fiction. Any references to historical places, persons or events are used fictitiously in the story. Other names places and events are purely a product of the author's imagination. Any resemblance of any character in this novel to any person living or dead is purely coincidental.

Community Relations Division.US Coast Guard Office of Public Affairs: "Using the names of cutters in a fiction work is not an issue for the Coast Guard."

Cover design and artwork by Diana Kingsley,
Kingston Cove Studio

Editing team, Betsy Curfman, Jennifer DeBoer, Pat Farquar, Cynthia McCurdy and Thomas Tearnen

ISBN: 9 781533 575081

Heaving to. (To Heave To and to be Hove to) is a way of slowing a vessel's forward progress, as well as fixing the helm and sail positions so the boat does not actively have to be steered. The term is also used in the context of vessels under power and refers to bringing the vessel to a complete stop. In waters over which the United States has jurisdiction, the U.S. Coast Guard may, under Title 14, United States Code, Section 89, demand that a vessel "Heave To" in order to enforce federal laws.

Dedicated to my mother Dorothy DeBoer who encouraged me to continue this project regardless of how long it took. She loved good stories and read three books a week. She was unable to join me at the finish line. She left us at the age of 93 on the morning of my 66th birthday

Mom, I finished!

Prologue

Oh Charleston!

The palm and oak-forested delta created by the confluence of the Ashley and Cooper Rivers in the low country of South Carolina has provided the world with countless sagas, legends and folklore. Wartime battles, tragedy, romances and piracy just to name a few. For decades in the late seventeenth and early eighteenth centuries, the region was the disembarkation point for slaves snatched from African prairies and villages for delivery to colonial plantations. It was the site of the very first naval canon shot igniting the great Civil War. Post World War II, Charleston emerged as a major East Coast mecca for arts and tourism.

The presence of Air Force Base Charleston, The Charleston Navy Yard and Navy Base Charleston, home to the Atlantic submarine, mine warfare and anti-submarine fleets along with the home porting of four Coast Guard Cutters and the Coast Guard Communication Center in the mid-eighties provided a cornucopia of military activity along the Carolina coast.

As Vince Lubar and his wife Denise squired her parents around Fort Sumter, that day would mark the beginning of a new story. This curious region once again found itself in the crosshairs of a new conflict.

In the post-Vietnam era, the use of recreational drugs expanded. The distribution system in North America and Western Europe evolved into a monumental industry. Federal and state agencies pooled resources and talents assembling forces to combat drug smuggling and distribution.

The interdiction of drug trafficking became the major focus of the Drug Enforcement Administration, Customs and the United States Coast Guard. With the Reagan administration on full throttle, and VP George H.W. Bush as the country's Drug Czar, so began America's New War on Drugs.

Coincidentally, the U.S. Coast Guard Cutter ESCAPE embarked on an unusual career. Never designed to serve the Coast Guard, she was built in 1943 as a 213' rescue and salvage vessel for the US Navy. She plied the oceans and harbors of the world salvaging vessels aground or damaged from their wartime activities. ESCAPE enjoyed a gallant history as a hard working naval ship bringing home dead and wounded sister ships of battle. Some ships she towed home were to be returned to the fleet. Others were relegated to the scrap heap or to Davy Jones' Locker. ARS 6 USS ESCAPE and her crews enjoyed adventures in the Mediterranean, the Caribbean and the Western Pacific. ESCAPE and the men who served in her labored hard. As the Korean Conflict wound down, she was preserved as a decommissioned "Ready Reserve" vessel to live out lifeless years shackled to a buoy chained to a fifteen-ton cement block on the bottom of Virginia's York River.

In 1980, Fidel Castro viewed his capitalist neighbors to the north as in need of diversion from a post-Watergate recovering economy. He allowed any Cuban desiring to do so to leave his island. Over 125,000 Cubans escaped his dictatorship, departing from the Port of Mariel on the north coast. They traveled by raft, boat, barge, inner tube or on logs. The warm and friendly current of the Gulf Stream quickly delivered them to southern Florida.

Castro also emptied his prisons. Filled with thugs, gangsters and other non-political inmates, they also drifted north as a gift to every judge, magistrate, officer of the court and law enforcement official in the southeastern United States.

Castro enjoyed the elimination of thousands of mouths to feed and prisoners to care for in his jails.

The men and women of the Coast Guard rescued thousands of refugees and retrieved bodies of the unfortunate ones. Only 27 persons perished during the exodus. The mission however, stretched East Coast resources of the Coast Guard to the brink of collapse.

Most cutters deploy for periods of three to eight weeks. They return to port for repair and replenishment for a few weeks then redeploy. Every cutter from Maine to Key West and along the gulf coast from Mobile Alabama to Galveston had been underway constantly for 6 months. Each ship and crew were in need of major repair and rest. Occasionally, unrelated events curiously stimulate others. As the Mariel Boat Lift was winding down and the ships of the Atlantic Area Fleet were returning home, bureaucratic maneuvering was breathing new life into the sleepy hull of USS ESCAPE and two of her sister ships. The Chief of Naval Operations signed over control and ownership of the USS ESCAPE, USS LIPAN and USS UTE to the Commandant of the U.S. Coast Guard.

The ships arrived in new homeports manned and re-commissioned through a massive and hurried shuffle of personnel and special appropriations. Designated as medium endurance Coast Guard Cutters, their names continued as ESCAPE, UTE and LIPAN. The ship designations were changed to conform to the standards of the Coast Guard. WMEC 6 USCGC ESCAPE, WMEC 11, USCGC UTE and WMEC 201, USCGC LIPAN were recommissioned and began careers as Medium Endurance Cutters.

The industry of illicit drug distribution in America is vast and complicated. Logistical records, normally part of ordinary business do not exist. Hundreds of young energetic, mostly male Americans and Canadians engage in moving product to the shores of the homeland.

They wholesale it to rookie distributors in small towns along the coasts. When successful, they earn a tidy profit. If they quit while they are ahead, they survive. Imports captured represent about thirty percent of the contraband destined for the States. Pursuing and apprehending these vagabonds account for about eighty percent of the expense and effort of the "War on Drugs."

Many successful pros in the business never see a marijuana cigarette or experience mind-altering jolts from that first snort of cocaine. They are planners and financial backers moving the bulk of the narcotics to the large cities in America. Many are successful business people in their own right. In their illegal operations, they employ the best people with experience, good judgment and a propensity for keeping out of trouble. As they become more successful, they take chances jeopardizing the safety of their employees and confidants. They have achieved comfortable lifestyles through hard work or inheritance. However, they find the thrill of successful crimes far surpasses the satisfaction of legitimate careers.

Occasionally through a series of unconnected events, the web holding a syndicate focused on importing contraband begins to unravel.

A bank robber, auto thief or extortionist generally has an escape plan. They remove themselves from a local environment starting anew elsewhere. In the case of criminals also engaged in successful legitimate commerce it is difficult to vanish for a while. Their talent and counsel are in demand. When things go sour, they employ desperate measures to conceal their subversive activities.

When a team of law enforcement professionals orchestrates the demise of a complex operation, it is akin to winning the Super Bowl or World Series.

Heave To

Heave To

Part One

Chapter One

The mid-September sunset on the Florida skyline painted an eerie mural of the launch gantry at the Kennedy Space Center on Cape Canaveral. Five months had passed since the shuttle Challenger exploded directly overhead. "I wonder how long it will be before they fly again," Rob Byrd asked his travelling companion Carl Peterson.

The two Americans and their Colombian crewmembers were looking forward to the end of the trip. It had been eleven days since they put to sea from Cartagena, Colombia. Rations were running light, the water onboard was nearly gone and the acrid heaviness of the stench of the marijuana was making everyone's eyes and skin itch.

"What a mess, I can't imagine they knew what hit them," Pearson, a six-foot-two blond haired Texan responded. "Wasn't a school teacher on board too?"

"Yeah, what a suck ass-deal for the program. Lots of dudes lost their jobs over there too," Rob added, pointing towards Titusville.

The steady drone of the GM diesel engine below decks would sing on in their brains for weeks. The voyage had gone off without a hitch. Later tonight, Chad Walgren, a local Narco team leader and a half dozen distributors from the southeast coast would meet them to offload the cargo. The Colombians would go ashore with the crew of the pickup boats and be back in Jamaica by noon tomorrow. A day later, they would be home in Bogotá with enough Yankee dollars to feed and dress their families in style for a year or so. Rob and Carl needed to return the tuna trawler Fanta Seas to the marina at Merit Island. Then they would take the briefcase full of money received from Chad at the time of the cargo transfer to Tom waiting in Atlanta. Next they needed to go to a UPS office and ship the suitcase containing the wireless facsimile receiver to Palm Beach.

The transit had been boring but the adrenalin rush in anticipation of a big payday kept everyone on track.

1

The Coast Guard had been busy on a Search and Rescue near the South Florida coast.

A small airplane belonging to some senator's son had gone missing. Every available cutter and aircraft was involved. No one noticed as the blue hulled Fanta Seas chugged quietly up the Straits of Florida. Of course, the twice-daily radio based facsimile information on the whereabouts of Coast Guard Cutters on patrol provided by Leon at Fort Sumter had been helpful and they successfully wove in and out of the Coast Guard patrol patterns.

Rob pondered often as to just how his friend Higgins and Leon were able to obtain such information and what it cost. Farther south in the Caribbean, they transited north smoothly and without a hitch. The Colombian Coast Guard, the Cubans and fellow scoundrels had not seen the vessel moving quietly north.

Friday afternoon, Rob, who was the captain and Carl would each divide $180,000. Rob would keep a hundred grand and go back to his farm in Montana. Carl would get the eighty. Being Rob's third trip it was the best paying one ever. It was also the first time the people in charge hired him as captain of the operation. Cory Higgins, the senior smuggling captain, convinced the leadership to trust him with the task. Higgins of course had been on the dock in Cartagena when the cargo was loaded and made all the logistics arrangements. As for who was in charge of the operation as a whole, Byrd didn't have a clue. Nor was he interested. For Rob, it seemed like a slick way to make a lot of quick tax-free money. And heck, he thought, even if he got busted Cory told him about a top notch attorney available to mitigate any punishment the feds could dish out for a first time offender.

As the trip neared the end, he could feel his heart pounding in his chest. He knew his superiors would be pleased and call on him for further assignments.

In Carl's case, it was his first adventure and he knew there would be more in his future. This one would solve all of his present financial woes, but in a year or two, he could see himself well set for life. All he needed to do for it was transport twenty-three thousand pounds of top grade Colombian marijuana and hashish to the eagerly awaiting wholesalers in Savannah. So far, the risks had seemed minimal when compared to the compensation. Rob however, was already starting to think of ways to retire before his luck ran out. He learned at the outset, in spite of the financial rewards, this was a difficult business to quit.

2

Carl peered into a cone covering the radar. "OK, it looks like three or four boats gathered together eight miles ahead."

"Great," Byrd replied and joked. "I hope they aren't Coast Guard boats. I will feel better when this stuff is gone."

"Me too."

The sun had set and the quarter moon rose on the eastern horizon.

Chapter Two

The Coast Guard Cutter ESCAPE was returning from her third law enforcement patrol in the Caribbean and the Gulf of Mexico. The first two trips lasted three weeks. Deployments began soon after the crew reported for duty and sufficient shake down training was accomplished to operate the ship safely. On the first patrol, Executive Officer Vince Lubar wondered if things would ever work on this old tub. After years of idleness, it would take a while to get all of the kinks out of the shipboard systems. Pump gaskets and valves failed in rapid-fire succession. The ability to distribute electricity from the generators was a perplexing problem for Engineering Officer Ed Tarzano and his electrical chief petty officer.

On this third patrol, many of the kinks were finally getting resolved. ESCAPE was becoming a viable Coast Guard Cutter. The last week of the trip had actually gone off without a single major machinery casualty.

As an added bonus, they scored a bust of forty-foot sail boat Sally Mae. Spotted northbound in the Windward Passage just east of Cuba, Sally Mae was an American Flag vessel.

Standard procedure at sea is to hail the vessel on the VHF radio and require them to stop and prepare for a visit by the United States Coast Guard. This is a provision in federal law many boaters do not agree with. Those finding solace and refuge on the high seas believe this authority is too invasive. All the same, it is the law and it is a good idea to play along with the game.

The standard command to hail a vessel prior to a boarding is: "CAPTAIN, HEAVE TO, PUT YOUR BEAM INTO THE WIND, STOP YOUR MOTORS. STAND BY FOR A BOARDING BY THE UNITED STATES COAST GUARD"

Once on board, the law enforcement party quickly discovered four thousand pounds of marijuana. The vessel was seized as authorized in Title 14, United States Code. The statute allows the Coast Guard to enforce America's domestic laws on the high seas. The crew of two Americans and one Colombian were arrested and brought to ESCAPE. They were detained in a small brig below decks. ESCAPE towed Sally Mae into Fort Lauderdale where the cargo was off loaded and custody of the boat transferred to the U.S. Customs Service. In a year or so, after all trials and appeals

4

were over the boat would be auctioned off to a new owner. One or two representative bales of contraband would remain with the U.S. Marshals until needed at trial. The rest was incinerated under careful supervision in one of South Florida's coal fired power plants.

U.S Marshals in Fort Lauderdale also took custody of the crew. At arraignment in federal court within 72 hours they would be charged with trafficking controlled substances. Their intent to smuggle contraband to the United States would be the job of the federal prosecutors to prove. Depending on who funded the voyage, great legal representation might appear, or if self-funded and not connected with a larger group, they would have to find their own counsel.

LT Phil Sutton, ESCAPE'S Operations Officer, sensed this was probably not the first voyage for the crew. The Colombian, Carlos Ortiz's name appeared on a list of people arrested in the late seventies. He denied being the same person.

The high grade Sensimillian Colombian pot had a street value on the east coast of $1,200 per kilo, making this and any other previously successful trips worth just about two and a half million dollars each.

With the dockside price of the stuff in Bogotá or Cartagena just $10,000 per ton, a handsome profit split two ways would allow the crew to obtain the right lawyers. If they were smart, a defense team would already be in place with a hefty retainer in the bank. The lone Colombian crewmember, hired from the dock in Bogotá unfortunately would be on his own. A public defender would handle his case.

While ESCAPE was pier side at Fort Lauderdale Coast Guard Station, a small plane on a trip from Baltimore to Miami went missing. For three days, the ship and crew joined forces with two other cutters and a C130 search plane from Jacksonville in an attempt to locate the downed aircraft. When it was discovered that the missing owner was the son of a U.S. Senator, the search intensified. Two helicopters joined, and another ship diverted from patrol in the Eastern Caribbean. About eighty hours into the search, the occupants of the plane walked out of the Everglades where the pilot had put the plane down after running out of fuel.

It was time for ESCAPE to return to Charleston.

In an effort to make the entrance to the Ashley River Channel at sunrise and catch the corresponding slack tide, the captain ordered the watches to slow the ship down as they passed

5

Jacksonville. The reduction in speed resulted in the ship missing by three hours the offloading of contraband from Fanta Seas two miles east of the Savannah River Entrance Buoy.

As ESCAPE entered the channel towards homeport, the deck force was busy painting the symbol of a marijuana leaf on the stack. These icons indicate to others, this ship had in fact made a bust. Many cutters in the Coast Guard sport dozens of such insignia to boast of their success. Had timing been slightly different, they would be half a day late getting home. To justify the delay, they would have been painting two symbols on the stack and towing Fanta Seas along with them. Such was not the case today.

Chapter Three

ESCAPE'S Executive Officer Lieutenant Commander Vince Lubar, a Coast Guard veteran of 15 years, began his career as an enlisted petty officer. Completing 4 years in the service, he decided he needed work that was more challenging. He applied for Officer Candidate School and soon was off to Yorktown Virginia for the seventeen-week training program.

One weekend while on liberty in Yorktown a dozen years earlier, he remembered a day he and two other classmates rented a sloop and sailed on the York River. Passing the Navy's strange and quiet graveyard of ships, he recalled noticing USS ESCAPE. He wondered what would ever become of those grand floating machines for which no one seemed to care. Little did he know at the time, destiny would provide the answer.

Not the top graduate in his class, he completed the training with honors and joined the crew of a cutter stationed in Seattle. He caught up with the ship on patrol in Alaska's Bering Sea. As a "green" ensign, he completed all training to become a qualified Deck Watch Officer and soon was part of a law enforcement team. He enjoyed five Bering Sea patrols and quickly discovered, much to the delight of his superiors, he had the talent to operate a large ship and the inquisitiveness and analytical skills to become an expert in interpreting and processing intelligence data.

In the Bering Sea and the Gulf of Alaska, law enforcement equaled fisheries law enforcement. Although this particular mission seems far less glamorous than drug interdiction, still the job is serious. The elements are very dangerous and oftentimes, the penalty for violation of an international fishing treaty is much harsher than sentences for smuggling drugs.

He met and married Denise Taggart while assigned to a Cutter in Coos Bay Oregon. Through the years, Vince, Denise and later young Jeffrey Lubar moved around to three more commands. At the time of the Mariel Boatlift, he was the Coast Guards' liaison officer assigned to the Navy Military Sealift Command Mediterranean COMSCMED in Naples Italy. The purpose of his position was to travel with the supply ships of the U.S. Navy's 6th Fleet. As they visited European and North Atlantic ports, he and two assistants developed intelligence within the Mediterranean and the Eastern North Atlantic concerning potential drug and immigrant smuggling operations. The daily secure and encrypted reports filed by LT Lubar provided intelligence sufficient to interdict and prosecute eight major trafficking operations during his three years at COMMSCMED.

Rewarded for his contributions, Vince was promoted to Lieutenant Commander. His next assignment, second in command of the newly commissioned USCC ESCAPE, was the dream job he had hoped for. The vessel and crew made Charleston South Carolina their home port. While assigned to the European command, Vince fulfilled a dream of many service members stationed overseas. He and Denise travelled to the Mercedes Benz factory in Stuttgart. There they took delivery of a brand new 1985 Series 500 Turbo Diesel sedan. Once finished touring around southern Europe, they delivered it to the MSC terminal in Naples Italy. In Charleston, it was waiting for them on the dock. Since arriving, he had been so busy with the details of the ship he had only been able to drive it a couple of times. Denise however thoroughly enjoyed cruising around in one of the nicest imported rides in Charleston. Vince looked forward to the opportunity during this upcoming time at home to go somewhere and enjoy his new toy.

Chapter Four

The fifteen-hundred-ton ship slowly moved past the jetty. The iconic Fort Sumter stood proudly on the port side. They slowed slightly as a tour boat transited from Patriots Point to the south towards the moorings at the fort. It looked like the first group of visitors for the day. Turning right, they proceeded through Charleston Harbor into the Cooper River and made the left turn under the bridge at Drum Island. Vince was organizing his thoughts on all the post patrol reports required by Commander Seventh Coast Guard District in Miami. He would be working closely with LT Phil Sutton, the vessel's Operations and Law Enforcement Officer. They would meet four or five times in the next week to go over all the evidence and narratives of each crewmember involved in the boarding, seizure and arrest of the crew of Sally Mae. They would examine and re-examine every document and photograph while preparing the package for the US Attorney. Usually, a young new attorney took on such cases. The title on the file would be U.S. VS. Crew of S/V Sally Mae. The trial would not even start for ten months and everyone called on to testify must recall exactly, precisely and truthfully what had happened on the day of the arrests and seizure of the vessel.

For the next day and a half though, Vince would return to his home in a subdivision on the west side of the Ashley River. He had not seen his wife and son for over a month. In spite of Vince Lubar's devotion to duty as a Coast Guard Officer, his family was the center of his life. He was also thinking he might finally be able to get his Mercedes out on a highway and see how she felt on American roads.

In two days, he would get back to the ship and all his duties. Denise's parents were coming to visit. They would stay on for a couple weeks after the ship left for the next patrol. They had joined them several times in Europe but Jeffrey was growing so fast they wanted to get to know him better. Vince appreciated their visit, as it would help make the time go by when the ship left again.

Denise and Jeffrey were on the dock as ESCAPE rounded the bend in the murky Cooper River. Slowly they approached the pier at the southernmost end of the Naval Station. Most all of the spouses and children and girlfriends were there too.

In the centuries long history of sailors, whalers and explorers returning home after a long voyage, not much has changed. The lines of worry and stress on the faces of the wives and girlfriends turn into smiles the instant the ship comes into view. In the grand scheme of life, one would think a ship being gone for a month or so would not matter much. Life however goes on. Teeth have been lost, football games have been won, cars have broken down and been repaired, clogged toilets have been unplugged, school plays and piano recitals have come and gone and countless other events of everyday life have happened. The separation experienced by Coast Guard and Navy families is one of the greatest sacrifices made in service to their country. When a sailor has a devoted wife and knows business is taken care of at home, he is likely to perform best while deployed.

Dave Flood, Commanding Officer of ESCAPE was not married. Hence there was no wife of the Skipper to be a liaison for the families left behind when the ship deployed. Denise had taken it upon herself to become the "matron" for the families. Early during the first patrol, she contacted wives and girlfriends of each crewmember and organized a family picnic at Coast Guard Base Charleston. There she chose another officer's wife, one Chief Petty Officer's wife and two other crewmembers' spouses as committee heads. She asked each of these to organize and manage interesting outings for the group half way through each patrol. The families of the crew were all getting along wonderfully. If one of the young wives had any trouble, there was always someone else around to help and support. Most of the spouses of crewmembers were enjoying the camaraderie Denise brought to the group. Of course, a few wives and girlfriends didn't appreciate her actions and would rather be left alone. Such is a dynamic in many groups.

As the ship approached kids started to recognize their fathers and occasional shouts of "Hi Daddy!" sang out along the dock.

Ensign Jack "Buzz" Ladner, the most junior officer onboard brought the ship into her moorings. Coast Guard officers pride themselves in their ability to bring big ships up to the side of a dock without the aid of tugboats. Being Buzz's first opportunity, he had been nervous about the impending task. Lighthearted teasing by his fellow officers in the wardroom at breakfast had not eased his anxiety.

With the Captain sitting in his chair on the port side of the wheelhouse, the XO standing close by and his immediate superior

Ops Boss Phil Sutton one step from his side all the way, the twenty-three-year old performed in first class fashion.

"Nice job Mr. Ladner," Commander Flood said, congratulating the novice.

"Thank you Captain, permission to secure the engineering spaces, double-up the mooring lines and allow visitors onboard sir."

"Very well Mr. Ladner. Make her so." He turned to Vince. "I will be gone for four days, going to see my mom. When I get back, we will go over the file on Sally Mae and make sure everything is right before it ships down to Miami."

"Aye-Aye skipper. Have a nice trip, see you next week."

"Now hear this," Buzz Ladner spoke into the ships public address system. "The Officer of the Deck is shifting the watch to the quarter deck, twelve to sixteen hundred watch on deck. Prepare the ship for visitors, lady guests arriving."

Following old maritime traditions, the Boatswains Mate of the Watch blew with a loud report on a brass Boatswain's pipe, repeating in whistle signals the message Ladner had just conveyed.

As the skipper ambled down the ladder from the bridge, he overheard LT Sutton congratulating the Ensign on his abilities, as well as reminding him of all the paperwork, reports and log entries he needed to make before his job for the morning was finished. Upon entering his cabin, just below the bridge, Flood smiled to himself considering how lucky he was to be commanding such a professional and dedicated crew.

Once the gangway was in place, it is custom for the quartermaster of the watch go ashore and escort the skipper's wife onboard followed by the rest of the wives and children. Since the captain was not married, Denise Lubar was escorted along with little Jeffrey up the gangway to the quarterdeck where she was met by Ensign Ladner who showed her to the Executive officer's stateroom.

Denise knocked then opened the door and her husband turned around and immediately embraced her.

Suddenly, there was a knock on the door. Just as Vince was starting to say "enter", the doorknob turned and the skipper entered.

"Excuse me XO, oh hi Denise. I just want to let you know how much I appreciate everything you do with the families when we are gone. I walk around the ship and ask the married guys how their wives and families are doing, I am told the XO's wife has

11

everyone so busy and having fun they hardly even miss us. We have a great crew here and a lot of it has to do with the men not worrying about their families getting lonesome or bored while we're out there."

"Well Captain, I can tell you this is a special bunch of families and we are all having a good time getting to know one another."

Chapter Five

Commanding Officer Dave Flood had 22 years of service in the Coast Guard under his belt. In the mid 60's, he had enlisted after graduating from the University of Oregon. This act is known as "Noble Draft Dodging". Many joined the Coast Guard to avoid being drafted into the Army, Marines or Navy, believing service in the Coast Guard would keep them out of Vietnam. Flood, a college graduate, while still in boot camp was given the opportunity to attend Officer Candidate School. Within a month he left Boot Camp in Alameda and headed to Yorktown VA for training. Upon completion, he was commissioned an Ensign. His first Coast Guard assignment was to Squadron One, patrolling the Mekong River. Upon arrival, he was assigned as Executive Officer on an 82 ft. patrol boat.

Three weeks after reporting for duty, Dave's Commanding Officer took a fatal Viet Cong sniper's bullet in the chest. With less than a year of service under his belt, Ensign Flood was the Commanding Officer of Coast Guard Cutter POINT COMFORT.

Having abhorred the thought of combat as a student, he quickly realized if he were to survive, he needed to learn how war worked and how to be on the winning side of each battle. He carried out his duties with honor, saved the lives of dozens of marines and navy SEALs, earned four and a half rows of medals on the breast of his uniform and returned home without a scratch.

Arriving in the states after 16 months in Southeast Asia, Dave served in a staff job in the San Francisco District Office. He hated it.

As soon as he could, he found another ship and was assigned as Executive Officer when the incumbent was medically discharged due to some sort of heart problem.

Two attempts at failed marriages convinced him another human could not provide the satisfaction and feeling of accomplishment he had at sea.

He enjoyed the challenges of bringing the old ESCAPE back to life. A strange kinship evolved between the CO and a vessel whose keel had been laid the year he was born. The ship had been in the Coast Guard Shipyard at Baltimore for renovation prior to commissioning. There she shed the dull grey skin of a Navy vessel in exchange for a coat of glistening white Coast Guard paint. While dry-docked, he discovered a huge hold in the lower

13

compartments of the ship. Old salvage gear was previously stowed there. He knew he could get the crew to convert this space into a ball court and weight lifting room. Off-duty recreation for his crews throughout his career had been one of his primary concerns. This crew seemed to be dedicated to making her work. The younger officers were all excited to be beginning their careers. His department heads were experienced and capable officers and the XO! "Man," he thought "How did I get so lucky to get this one?"

Having an Executive Officer of the caliber of Vince Lubar was the ultimate dream of any Commanding Officer. Although the ship was old and needed tons of help he knew, with this crew, she would be successful. His only troubling thoughts at this time in his life were once he left ESCAPE, he would probably go to a staff job somewhere for three or four years before he could get back to sea.

Chapter Six

Brothers Robert and Chester Whittaker excelled in school. Both were successful attorneys. Robert attended Harvard and Chester, the oldest, the Citadel military academy in Charleston. Both were athletic. Chester had been a stocky running back for the Citadel football team. Robert, taller and lanky, took up rowing while in Cambridge. Chester planned on joining the Navy upon graduation in 1975. The plan ended when the Vietnam conflict wound down in his senior year. No commissions were available. He went directly to law school at the University of South Carolina, never serving in the military. In 1979, Chester opened a small personal services law firm in Palm Beach Florida.

Robert worked briefly as a public defender on Staten Island, then he joined the family practice in Manhattan. In 1980, Chester convinced his father it would be a good plan for Robert to open a practice in Atlanta. He started out with a family, business and real estate practice then later entered litigation and criminal law as well.

Trish Dixon met Chester Whittaker in Florida during her honeymoon. Her newlywed husband Rohn Villa was busted for cocaine possession in a Coral Gables cocktail lounge.

Rohn was the service manager at Atlanta's largest Cadillac dealer and Trish had just graduated from the University of Georgia with a degree in accounting. She found The Whittaker Law Firm in the yellow pages sub-listed under the heading DUI and Drug Defense.

Rohn was busted in the men's room at their hotel bar, Trish was not involved. In fact, she had no clue about her new husband's drug habit. One of Chester's associates, Tom Thrasher, was able to get him off with probation. They returned from their honeymoon somewhat less happy newlyweds than when they had left.

While reviewing the case for her husband, Chester had asked Trish what she intended to do as a CPA? She wasn't sure and dreaded the thought of doing taxes and payroll for some firm for the rest of her life. Chester asked if she would be interested in a position in the family office in Atlanta. She could work in the trust department as an internal auditor. She jumped at the chance and soon was buried in reams of peg board spreadsheets, audits and trust agreements. She found the work exciting and was amazed at the amount of money Americans put into tax shelters. The trust fund for the Southeast Schoolteachers Association (SEASTA)

Pension Fund alone contained over one hundred seventy-five million dollars belonging to the teachers, custodians, bus drivers and administrators in six southeastern states.

Her marriage to Rohn ended in little more than a year when he was again busted for cocaine possession. This time in bed with one of the female sales associates from the Cadillac dealer.

Robert Whittaker's family law specialist was able to get her out of the marriage on great terms. She kept the house, the Cadillac, a horse, a $300,000 life insurance policy on Rohn and the timeshare condominium in Cancun. Rohn kept his cocaine habit, the Toyota station wagon, two jet skis and the mortgage on Trish's house. He paid no alimony, as Trish's income was double his. It wouldn't have mattered in any case because eight and a half months after the divorce, Rohn stopped along the Atlanta beltway to fire up a bowl of crack cocaine in a nearly new Coupe de Ville he had borrowed from a customer. A drunk driver rear-ended him and he died. The drunk had great insurance and combined with the $300K from the life insurance policy, Trish was awarded $600,000 more for the vehicular homicide. Rohn had been so busy with his drug problems he had forgotten to change his will after the divorce. There was also a mortgage life insurance rider on the original policy which paid off Trish's home on which Rohn had owed an additional $172,000. She also got the two jet skis. The Toyota station wagon she donated to the local community college auto shop class.

Trish didn't worry about much. She was still young, had her good looks and loved intrigue and adventure. When Chester asked her to come down to Florida to discuss a new business venture, she was excited.

Chapter Seven

It was a gorgeous early fall day in Charleston. Jeffrey had no school because of a teacher's conference. Vince and Denise decided to take her parents to explore Fort Sumter.

Charleston South Carolina as a city is a civil war museum. One can spend months there and still only visit half of the historically significant venues. There are eighteenth century mansions lining Battery Park and old plantations along the Ashley and Cooper rivers. Most dwellings still house descendants of original settlers. Quaint bed and breakfast opportunities abound and boast perfectly manicured gardens with lush fields of azaleas and huge century old oak trees. The old market, which has been in operation for several centuries, is a bargain hunter's paradise. Patriots Point is a floating maritime museum featuring the WWII aircraft carrier YORKTOWN, the WWII diesel submarine USS CLAMAGORE and the Coast Guard Gutter I NGHAM. It is also the embarkation point for the ferry to Fort Sumter.

Vince, Denise, her parents and Jeffrey all boarded the ferry. As the boat began to move, the operator launched a standard welcome aboard and quick civil war history lesson.

Always with the inquisitive eye of an investigator, Vince inventoried the occupants of the launch. Thirty-one were aboard. Most were in groups of three to five people. There were teenagers looking forward to climbing on the ruins. Two middle-aged priests dressed in casual lightweight clothes but still wearing their Roman collars sat near the stern. Several other family groups similar to the Lubar entourage were scattered about. Most carried normal handbags and an occasional picnic basket or backpack. Vince noticed one individual in his mid to late twenties. He categorized him as a well-dressed California beach bum. He wore expensive slacks and shoes, a modern sports jacket and an open shirt. His straight blond hair blew in the breeze. He carried a briefcase. That seemed odd. Vince thought he must be connected to the parks department and had business with the staff.

As the ferry eased up to the floating dock, two line handlers in Confederate uniforms attended to securing the vessel.

"Welcome to the birthplace of the Civil War, or as some refer to it, The War of Northern Aggression," a tall and trim chap greeted the tourists. He immediately went into a well-rehearsed history lesson equally informative as the one delivered by the boat operator. He indicated ways to enjoy what the park had to offer.

The ferry they had ridden over on was the fourth run of the day. There were already a hundred or so people scattered about. Passengers disbursed, some wandering off in independent groups and others queuing up for guided tours. Denise's mother was an explorer and wanted to tour independently, so they picked up a couple of guidebooks went about on their own.

Vince watched the gent with the briefcase shake hands with a rebel captain. They obviously knew each other.

Walking a hundred yards from the dock, an interesting looking short and fat fellow in shorts and a 'happy face' tee shirt approached the group. He had two cameras around his neck and an ammunition belt cinched around his chubby waste. Each loop in the belt held a roll of 35mm Kodak film. "Good day, what a handsome family! My name is Beaufort E. Lee. I have a photography studio at Patriots Point. Are you folks visiting Charleston for the first time? Where did you come from? You need a nice family portrait of the gang standing here with all the glory of a wonderful historic city in the background," he jabbered away not, allowing time for anyone to respond.

The group agreed it would be a good idea.

"Do you guarantee a masterpiece?" asked Denise.

"Ma'am, I'm so convinced you will like my work I guarantee in writing if you are unhappy I will pay your way back out to the fort and do the whole thing over again and buy you a frame for your picture," he replied as he handed Denise a business card with the guarantee written on the back.

"Sounds like we can't lose."

So Beaufort E. Lee lined up three generations of the Lubar /Taggart clan and yammered away as he arranged the group, took several shots, then rearranged again. He provided a nonstop monologue about Charleston, history, the rivers, his childhood, his time in the Navy and a multitude of other disconnected topics. Everyone found him amusing and with each snap, smiles were broader and the subjects more relaxed. The experience was fun.

"Now that should do it. I will have proofs available for ya'll in my studio tomorrow after ten. I keep em' for a month then toss them if you don't show up. Nevertheless, I guarantee ya'll gonna love my work. There is a little map on my card to show ya where the shop is," he continued without taking a breath between sentences.

He briefly asked if anyone had questions without allowing time to answer. Next, he pointed to the dock where another ferry was tying up. "I wish I could stay and get to know ya'll a little better but I've got to get back to work." He shook Vince and Bill's hands and bowed in a genteel southern manner to the women. Then he bent down to shake hands with Jeffrey. Looking for and getting Denise's approval, he offered the boy a tootsie pop.

He stood up and walked away talking to no one in particular. He briefly paused to shake hands and back slap with two park rangers. Next he began another amusing assault on two retired couples at the dock.

All the adults in the group broke into spontaneous laughter.

Chapter Eight

"Mr. Whittaker, Ms. Dixon is here to see you."

"Give me just a minute or so and when I signal, please send her in." He opened the special audio-video processor in his computer allowing him to view and listen to conversations in the reception area. He recalled Trish was cute when he had hired her but had forgotten just how stunning she was. Connie asked if Trish wanted anything to drink. She requested iced tea. While his secretary was fetching refreshments, Chester continued to observe looking for signs of timidity or uneasiness. This woman looks like she could undress you, pick your pocket, steal your stock portfolio and get you to confess your innermost secrets with just her smile. She likewise was observing each detail of her surroundings and committing them to memory. He tapped F6 twice on his keyboard and the screensaver showing a photo of a beautiful yacht replaced the image of the waiting room. At the same instant, there was the sound like that of a canary chirping near Connie's desk. "Mr. Whittaker will see you now Ms. Dixon."

"Trish, you are more beautiful than I remember. Thanks for making the trip down here. I hope the hotel and car are adequate."

Adequate! Shit, she had a two room suite in the Hilton overlooking the ocean and the car waiting for her at the airport was a new Mercedes 500 SL roadster. "Everything is just fine sir," she smiled wondering why she was there.

"So, are you happy in Atlanta?"

"Mr. Whittaker, I never dreamed I would be involved in this type of money management. I have learned so much and am amazed at the securities one small law firm can manage."

"Please Trish, call me Chester or Chet. Keep the Mr. Whittaker for the formal situations."

"Ok Chet," Trish blurted out in kind of a deep poker game type of voice. "I hope I didn't get called down here because there is something wrong."

"No, nothing could be farther from the truth. In fact, I want to talk to you about your trustworthiness."

"My trustworthiness?" She wondered cautiously.

"Let me explain. Where do you see yourself in ten or fifteen years?"

"Well, I don't know. I haven't given it much thought. I don't think I'll ever marry again. I like my work now. The department

20

is growing and I'd like to grow with it. My retirement portfolio is looking good, and I suppose I would like to retire early. I like adventure. The Australian Outback has always fascinated me. You know, eating snakes and lizards."

"Just what other kind of adventures would you like?"

"Oh, I would like to learn to sail and go on long trips all over the world not have to worry about money."

"Have you ever done anything illegal?"

She paused in thought. Where is he going with this? Choose your answer carefully girl.

"I speed, I don't report every dime I make to the IRS, and when I was with my fiancé back in college I smoked a little pot."

"Well, I don't think you would go to prison for that. What about gambling?"

"I love blackjack, been lucky at craps twice but had no idea what I was doing and I like to bet at the track," she said, still cautious.

"Dogs or horses?"

"What?"

"Do you bet on dogs or horses?"

"Oh, I've never been to a dog race. What's that all about?"

"Same as horses except you can lose your money faster," he smiled. "What would you think of high stakes gambling with someone else's money?"

"Where is this going?" Trish asked, a serious tone in her voice.

"I'm going to tell you things in the next half hour. You may be surprised. I will invite you to get involved. If you choose to do so, in ten years, you will be one of the richest accountants in the country and able to do anything you want. If you decide you don't want in, stop me, and you can go back to Atlanta with your $75,000 a year job and continue what you are doing. Of course you will agree to never discuss this meeting with anyone."

Something was going on in her body. She felt excited. Her heart rate picked up and she experienced a slight flushing in her skin. "I'd like to hear what you have to say. If I'm not interested, I'll let you know. Then I will live the rest of my life as though this meeting never happened."

"Great!"

Chester explained the intricate workings of his network to fund and operate drug smuggling operations.

He told her of a secret communications system buried within the basement of Fort Sumter. From there his old classmate from the Citadel, Leon Matthews, could track the location of each Coast Guard Cutter on patrol.

Then he went into the money part.

Trish knew through working on the trust accounts in Atlanta, they managed a lot of money for a pension fund.

Years earlier he developed a mutual fund and offered this investment vehicle to the members of SESTA. The fund performed well and several hundred-thousand school employees invested $100 or more each month into the fund. Clients were pleased with the double digit return on their money. As a worldwide growth fund it held stock in many forms of business. One targeted market was foreign banking.

"Here's where it gets interesting." Chester commented. "Six years ago we established a company called Banco Del Escondido."

Banco Del Escondido is listed in the Canary Islands. The only place the bank actually exists is on paper. Escondido serves as a money transferring mechanism. It funnels cash through a trust company in the Turks and Caicos Islands. The money is available to the planners and logistics technicians helping Chester with his operations. The clever part is, the bank was opened with only $300,000 of funds provided by Chester and a client, a successful "commodities" import broker (Translated - drug smuggler). The current value of this bogus financial institute after years of investment money provided by the unsuspecting school employees was in the neighborhood of 12.6 million dollars. The money held on deposit in Escondido was actually in the Turks Holding and Trust Ltd. in the Caicos Islands.

Trish had seen the name of the bank on many documents she dealt with over the past year. It had never given her any cause for alarm or suspicion.

"Are you still with me?"

"Yeah, this is breathtaking. Hasn't the SEC ever asked anything about this bank?"

"No, that's funny. They check out all kinds of other stocks but they never question anything about the equity of the overseas banks in the portfolio. They must think the countries where the banks are located take care of that."

"What role were you thinking I could play in this?"

"Well, you know Tom Thrasher, he is an associate attorney. He got your ex out of his jam."

"Yeah, a time to forget. I guess we all learn from our mistakes. Isn't Tom kind of a beach boy?"

"Yes, not too many people would pick him out of a lineup and say he is a Cum Laude Cornell attorney."

He continued. "Well Tom has been going around the world handing out funds to those who need them. He likes to play the part of a surfer dude when he travels. In litigation however, many US Attorneys wish he would stay out of the courtroom. He's a great trial lawyer and I bill five hundred bucks and hour for his office time and nine hundred at trial. Tom has several million deposited overseas and asked me if I could find a replacement for him."

"It was Tom's suggestion to ask you. He recalled you were pretty smart and you seemed to understand a lot more about the facts of life than your late husband gave you credit for."

"Back to operations; I work with only a few boat skippers whom I trust implicitly."

"How?"

"These people have made a ton of money working with me. They are the best. They assemble crews, load and unload cargo and deal with the purchase and sale of the boats we use. We rarely use the same boat twice. But we have purchased a little freighter for use in legitimate work between smuggling operations. I help them hide and protect their fortunes and we all respect each other."

"I can work with that."

"If you want to get onboard, we start soon. You will meet our operatives, usually somewhere outside of America. You'll run the show. You set in motion the timelines, distribute cash, fund operations and pay the product brokers in Colombia, Mexico and perhaps Europe. Sometimes payments might be made in the middle of the ocean."

"I'm not going to tell you anything else if you are reluctant to get involved."

"What's in it for me besides jail and loss of my CPA credentials and the opportunity to pal around with criminals?"

"Technically, you are not a criminal until you have been convicted. No one in our operation has ever come close. But it is a good question. Before you tell me you are in, I can only tell you it will be well worth your while. None of my skippers use drugs at all. Nor do I or Tom, and from what I have been able to find out about you, neither do you."

"Hell Chet, why not? You only live once and I do like nice things. I would love to retire in comfort and live the good life before I get old. Where do I sign?"

"There is nothing to sign. The only paper in this trade is currency. In answer to your question about compensation, you will get two percent of the gross payment from the buyers. For instance, a month or so ago, we brought a nice twelve-ton load of pure golden grass from Colombia. This stuff has a street value of $140 per ounce. We get $1750 per kilo for it or about $50 per ounce. So, the load was worth $18.4 million. The day after it arrived in Savannah, Tom's bank account in the Caymans received a wire transfer from Banco Escondido for $368,000. It took him about a week of planning conferences in the Caribbean and two short follow up trips. Then he waited a couple months for payday. You will be getting one and three quarter percent for this first load and Tom will get one quarter of the two percent for training you. To cover expenses, we have an American Express and a Visa card. All the statements go directly to Banco Del Escondido. You can charge all expenses on these cards and draw up to a thousand dollars daily if you need to. If you want to shop for clothes and souvenirs, you're on your own.

Of course you will continue to draw your normal salary and bonuses from the Whittaker Law Firm. We need to start working on an operation next month. There is one change from all of our previous hauls though."

"What's that?"

"This load will be smaller in volume but the value and profit will be tenfold. We will deliver two thousand pounds of pure cocaine."

Trish's stomach knotted up just slightly. She had been comfortable with all of the discussion about marijuana but for some reason this seemed a little more serious. "Do you go to jail any longer for cocaine than for grass or hash?"

"No, it's interesting. The US Code doesn't discriminate. A controlled substance is a controlled substance. If you are packing automatic weapons or hurt someone physically the penalties are stiffer. But we've developed our trade as a courier service with a non-violent operational attitude."

"Well, it seems to me if you are trying to hide something it would be easier to hide something weighting a ton than it would be to hide something weighing eleven tons." The CPA quickly analyzed.

"My, you are figuring things out. I think you will find this work very interesting and rewarding.

"As soon as you return to Atlanta, recruit another accountant to help you there. Pick someone good and of course trustworthy. As far as anyone at the office is concerned, you will be on the road, auditing the books here and in New York. You will also be visiting with the directors of companies in the mutual funds portfolio. And I want to make one last thing clear. No one else in the Whittaker family knows what I'm doing down here. My father is aware I have a great practice and although he thinks some of my clients are a few rungs lower on the social ladder than they should be. He remains an attorney. And you know any good attorney will defend anyone against anything for the right price. A few good settlements and lawsuits for medical malpractice and millionaire divorces keep things going on the legit side. It keeps the family happy.

"Don't forget my little brother in Atlanta is also clueless. It's a good thing he's the son of a rich guy from Long Island and those three associate lawyers in the office are aggressive because with all the pro-bono and public service work he does, I doubt he makes over three hundred a year on his own business."

"He has actually made a few comments about running for a seat on the Atlanta City Council." Trish brought up.

"That's great. He never stops amazing me."

Chapter Nine

Denise and Crystal took Jeffrey to visit plantations west of the Ashley River. The wives told Vince and Bill to go to Lee's studio and pick out the best photos and order prints. The women instructed the men to get the picture business done first. Denise had heard them saying something about playing golf.

The studio was located in a strip of retail stores and small restaurants fifty yards from the ferry landing. It was eleven AM and aromas of southern sausage and bacon permeated the still Carolina morning air.

Lee's shop was a museum of photographs portraying Charleston's history. Photographs of celebrities and important government officials adorned the walls. It looked as though two former vice presidents and more than a dozen senators had shared a few moments with this quirky artist. Also on display were wonderful pictures of Spanish, French and Italian vistas he had taken while in the navy.

When they entered the shop, Lee was visiting with the priests seen two days earlier. He was jabbering away prying out of them the names of their aunts, uncles and siblings. He attempted to convince them that anyone who knew them would feel left out if they did not get photo. In the end, they each purchased some sort of bargain pack containing the usual mix of five by sevens, wallet sized and of course the standard eight by ten in a nice wooden frame, suitable to adorn their mothers' mantle or piano top. As he was shaking both men's hands, patting them on the back and asking them to pray for him, he noticed Vince and Bill.

"I'll be right with ya'll, please take a look around."

"Thanks, no hurry." Vince answered. "This guy is a piece of work," he spoke softly. They roamed around the studio. Vince curiously noticed in portraits hung about it was rare the backgrounds were void of other people. After all, it was a crowded public park. Lee did a good job of waiting until passers-by were at a minimum for the most part. Naturally, there were always one or two individuals in civil war uniform in the photos. What caught his eye however in eight of about fifteen photographs, the fellow from the boat, the one dressed more for business than tourism appeared. He seemed to be roaming around and chatting with the park rangers. Vince thought this peculiar. Of course the span of dates the photos were taken were unknown to Vince. He did notice they were in varying seasons by the difference in the blooms of the plants and trees. It just seemed curious for such a random individual to show up in the eye of Lee's Nikon on more than a few occasions.

"What a delightful day we havin," Beaufort E. Lee blurted out as he approached. "Say, where's the little boy and those beautiful ladies?"

"Oh they went shopping and exploring. We thought we would go over to Sullivan's Island and knock a few balls around," replied Bill.

"Oh, ya know I used to be quite a duffer. Had a six handicap. I was a school bus driver for a while and three days a week I would hook up with a couple of other drivers between the morning and afternoon runs. We went out to the Navy course in North Charleston. We all got pretty good at it cuz we couldn't drink beer on account of havin to drive the youngsters at three o'clock."

Lee reached in a drawer near his cash register and handed each one a couple of golf balls. They had a tiny self-photo imprinted on them on one side and on the opposite side was printed the words Beaufort E. Lee Custom Photographer Charleston SC.

"Here ya go gents. I don't have time to play during the tourist season so you take these out and give em a ride. Just make sure the face is looking down the fairway before you smack it and I'll help you find the green. Ha!"

"Thanks, we will be thinking of you when we're out there," Vince smiled.

"I was looking at your prints this morning. I'm proud of my work and not afraid to give myself a pat on the back once in a while but ooowwee! These are some of the best I've done."

Lee opened a large 17 by 2- inch envelope marked "TAGGART" and spread about thirty-five color photographs proofs on the big lighted white desktop.

"Wow, these are nice," Vince agreed. "You've got a knack for this kind of work Mr. Lee."

"Oh, please don't call me 'Mista' I got over that when I quit driving them buses. Just call me Beaufort."

"Yeah….." Vince started to speak but suddenly noticed in one sequence of pictures the dude was there again; the beach boy. His image appeared in one shot. He carried a briefcase and walked from right to left behind the Liberty Square flag pavilion. In the next shot, he had passed the group and was approaching one of the guards just outside an old gun emplacement. In the third exposure, he shook hands with the guard. It appeared to be the one in the Confederate captain's uniform. The next photo showed both men, with their backs to the camera and looking over towards the Charleston waterfront. Eight shots later he had the fellow retreating back toward the ferry landing. Vince continued focusing on the photographs and took in a deep breath when he realized in the last two photographs, he was not carrying the briefcase! His immediate thought was bureaucrats do not leave briefcases around. Then he glanced casually at some of the photos on the wall depicting the same individual. Some of them showed him with a briefcase. In others he appeared empty handed. Vince almost asked Lee who the hell this guy was. He of all people in Charleston would know something about the guy. Next, he reflected Beaufort E. Lee was probably not someone you would trust to keep too many secrets. His question remained unanswered.

"I just don't know how to do this," Bill exclaimed. They are all exceptional. I like these with Charleston in the background but also the ones looking the other way with the Ocean spread out behind us is interesting too."

"I think we should have an eight by ten of one view with the city in the background and another looking out to sea. Then a couple dozen five by sevens and I think he has a deal for post card sized ones. The girls will think they would be nice for Christmas cards. Maybe get fifty of each to match the big ones," Vince offered his choices. "I wonder if he would let us take the lot with us to show Denise and Crystal for a final decision."

"Oh, I'm sure he would."

The shop owner was jabbering away with a couple about arranging to take wedding photos. It appeared he was trying to avoid the job. He recommended another photographer. Their conversation was ending. As they were leaving, he reminded them to come back after they had a couple of little ones and he would do a nice job for them.

"Weddings," he stated as he returned to the big desktop shaking his head. "Somehow I just don't like to get involved. Too many people have a chance to judge the work and besides, you may notice I like to visit with people a bit, and everyone wants the photographer at these things to keep quiet. Well, that plum doesn't work for me," he chuckled. "What did you decide?"

Bill went over the order with Beaufort and seemed to be enjoying the encounter. Vince, lost in thought, tried to figure out what had gone on out there. He doubted if Lee would let them walk out with the proofs. But if they were ordering enough prints he might. He would love to get the shots to a criminal photo lab. He wanted to get something going today rather than waiting a few days for Lee's processor to get the job done.

Vince's mind returned to the details of the transaction as Bill and Beaufort, who seemed by now to be old best friends, were finishing up.

"Do you mind if I take these along with me? I want to make sure with the ladies we got it right?" Vince asked.

"Sure, I guess you can take them along. I will have to keep the negatives in order to get started on the processing. Just give me a call in the morning and if ya'll got no changes I'll send the order in and you should have them back in ten days. I will ship the ones to you in Oregon and your son-in-law or your beautiful daughter can stop by here and pick up the others."

The shop door opened again and another group of three Vince remembered from Fort Sumter walked in, obviously to grace Mr. Lee with another two or three hundred-dollar order of family portraits.

Vince and Bill departed.

"I have to stop by the Base for a few minutes to check on messages." Vince replied as he stuffed three proofs from the envelope into his shirt pocket.

Vince drove back across the bridge to the Coast Guard Station. He told Bill to enjoy a walk around the base while he went inside for a few minutes.

"May I help you, sir?" Yeoman third class Stephanie Gibson asked.

"Yes, I am the XO on ESCAPE. I have some information I would like to send to LCDR Solomon at CCIC in Texas." He pulled six photographs wrapped in white paper from his pocket.

CCIC is the Corpus Christi Intelligence Center, staffed by officers from several branches of the federal government. Thousands of pieces of information are analyzed each month there in attempts to catch up with organized crime syndicates.

Stephanie looked at the packet and pulled a suitable envelope from a shelf. "Yes sir. I have labels ready for CCIC do you want to include a note to Mr. Solomon?"

"Yeah, do you have a pen, I can just write on this."

"Sure, I will get it in the mail before noon and he should have it by tomorrow."

Vince quickly wrote: 'Gus, please find out who the guy in the background is. I will see you next week in Miami.' V.L." The seventh district commander had called a conference of all law enforcement officers in Florida, South Carolina and Georgia for the following week. He placed his business card in the envelope and handed it back to Gibson.

"Anything else sir?"

"Nope, that's it, thanks a lot. I'm headed for the golf course."

"Yes sir, see you later."

Chapter Ten

Enjoying her first class seat on the return flight Trish felt elated and exhausted. She wondered what she had gotten into. She contemplated what women's prison would be like. Quickly she dismissed these thoughts and got the airline magazine out of the pocket in front of her. She opened it up to the map of the airline's flight routes throughout the eastern half of the United States and the Caribbean. She zeroed in on the exploded view of the Bahamas. Chester told her to find a nice resort down there to meet up with Cory Higgins, the skipper coordinating the transport of $45 million dollars' worth of cocaine to Virginia. Chester told her Higgins would be a little hard to deal with and he would be surprised to see a female replacing Tom.

She visited with the flight attendant. JoAnn had been to the islands often and convinced Trish that for one's first trip to the Bahamas, she should try Abaco if she was looking for privacy.

Josie Ford was Trish Dixon's administrative assistant in the trust department. She was excited for her supervisor when Trish was summoned to West Palm Beach. If you were not screwing up and Mr. Whittaker called you for a visit, it usually meant something good. Josie knew nothing in the department had gone wrong since Ms. Dixon had started.

When Trish returned, she told Josie Mr. Whittaker had expanded her responsibilities and she was going to be on the road a lot, auditing the other two offices and calling on businesses in the mutual fund group.

A head hunting firm found two well qualified candidates and Trish interviewed both of them. She liked a nerdy fella named Jake. The other candidate had family issues with a drinking and gambling husband. She made the decision four days after returning. "Ok Josie, we just hired Jake. Give him a call.

"I have to go back to Florida in two weeks so he will need to get up to speed in a hurry. See if he can meet with me for lunch tomorrow."

"Sure thing Ms. Dixon. Oh, Mr. Whittaker in Florida wants you to call him when you get a chance."

With the door to her office closed tightly, Trish spoke into the phone "Hey Chet, what do you need?"

Chester chuckled to himself, "You need to go to lunch with Tom in the next two days. He will set it up. He has a lots to tell you and you will not be able to take notes. How's the search for your deputy coming?"

"Fine, we're hiring a guy named Jake Iverson today. Josie likes him and I think he will do us fine."

Chapter Eleven

It was just past noon. Cory Higgins had been waiting in the Tropical Bar at the Abaco Inn since 10:45. Tom told him he would be dealing with someone new. The meeting set for 11:15 so they could meet and talk in quiet before all the stuck up tourists showed up for lunch. Now everyone was returning from the beach for fancy drinks, and who knows what else to fill out the rest of their day. The tables were filling up and Higgins was the only unaccompanied soul in the place. That in itself could make one conspicuous and was disconcerting. The place was full of honeymooners and a dozen young wealthy couples from all over the world. He didn't want anyone to notice him.

Tom said this trip would have maximum opportunity for rewards. He also advised him Chester had placed a new agent in charge of meeting and planning missions. He wondered who it might be.

It was already October and to make one of these missions successful required 4 to 6 months of preparation. Cory already had about 4.3 million stashed away in banks in Grand Cayman, Canada and Germany and never used any of his own funds to support a trip. Make the rich bastards like Chester front everything. After all, they weren't taking risks. If a boat is busted, they aren't the ones stuck in a south Florida jail waiting for some sleaze ball in a thousand-dollar suit and a BMW to come get them off the hook. No, they just bitch about the bad luck and don't seem to give a shit about the guys taking all the chances and doing the hard work.

While he lamented the lifestyles of all the players, he hardly noticed the gorgeous brunette in a less than modest bikini covered with a knit white top sit down at the table next to his. She ordered a local rum and bitter lemon and scanned the lunch menu as Higgins noticed her. She looked at him smiled, and averted her eyes back to the menu. He enjoyed his Green Label beer as he checked out the scenery.

"Did you just check in?" She asked.

"Yeah, I flew down yesterday from Maine. What about you?" He liked the encounter.

"Oh, it's funny. I'm actually celebrating the first anniversary of my divorce," she stated as she took the slice of lime from the rim of her glass and seductively sucked on and placed it back in the drink, then she added: "You must be Cory."

He felt his heart jump. "Could this be true?"

The brunette slid her chair back, stood up in a stretch that could qualify for the cover pose on Sports Illustrated Swimsuit Edition, sat down across from him and winked.

"Nice to meet you, I'm Trish Dixon. Chester said you would buy me lunch." She seemed to be admiring his fit body and well-trimmed blond hair.

"I don't usually spend money on management, but I do have Chester's American Express Card." He smiled.

"I've been told your success is based on you sticking to your principles so I don't mind going Dutch if it bothers you. I'm on a generous expense account myself."

"No problem. What's for lunch?"

Cory couldn't believe his fortune as he looked across the table as this beautiful woman. She sensually sucked in a chunk of mango from her Abaco Fruit Sampler, then she extended and curled her tongue and licked a spot of juice from her lip.

"Get your mind back to business," he told himself. He didn't like working with distractions. This distraction however he was enjoying. The new millennium was just around the corner and women are getting into all sorts of new business. "I guess smuggling was no exception," he pondered. "I might as well make the best of it. I'll be retiring soon."

The smell of coconut laced tanning oils permeated the atmosphere in the patio restaurant while they made small talk and ate. Cory dipped deep fried plantain chips into an abalone shell filled with mango chutney. Trish finished a small dish of custard and waited for the server to take everything away.

"So when are we going to discuss details?"

"I thought we should keep it as casual as possible. You never know who these people are so I suggest we check out snorkel gear tomorrow morning. We could take the Albury's Ferry to Man O' War Cay and go underwater sightseeing. We've got a whole week in this place. We should enjoy it as long as Chester is footing the bill."

"Sounds fine to me. What should we do with the rest of the day? I was going to roam around the shops and look for Christmas presents." Trish smiled. "If you don't have another date, we could meet for dinner here at around seven."

"Ah, Ok, I'll see you at seven."

Chapter Twelve

On Monday afternoon the lobby of the Miami Holiday Inn at Hialeah looked like some sort of class reunion was going on. Several dozen guests were gathering and shaking hands like long lost friends from a college class years ago. The casual observer would see a group of mostly men and a few women in their mid-twenties to early thirties. All appeared fit and each, even the women were quaffed with close cut hair. Their attire ranged from tropical shorts and shirts to casual business clothing.

Two officers wore Coast Guard uniforms. They were Commander of the Seventh Coast Guard District staff representatives making sure everyone was happy. The District Commander gathered a representative from each ship and station within his jurisdiction to plan strategies for upcoming drug enforcement operations. Other representatives attended from regional offices of the Drug Enforcement Administration, U.S. Customs and the US Attorney's office and the Corpus Christi Intelligence Center.

The Hialeah Inn held the government contract to house transient federal employees and service members visiting the Miami area.

The conference was scheduled to begin in the morning and last for two and a half days. Adjournment would take place around noon on Thursday allowing each attendee to get back to their respective commands in time to brief their own teams before the weekend.

As Vince checked in, his old friend and classmate Gus Solomon arrived accompanied by a civilian from CCIC.

The two men approached one another extending right hands to greet but instead they embraced in a masculine hug as often done by old comrades in arms. "So how's Texas treating you?"

"Pretty good but it's nice to be back near salt water. How are you doing XO? I bet Charleston is quite a transition from cushy Italy."

"Hey, it was tough duty, I had to ride big ships around the Med and sneak around towns like Monte Carlo and Athens. Somebody has to do it while you guys hang out at home."

"Oh, by the way, I haven't had much of a chance to look at those pictures you sent. They only arrived yesterday but I copied

35

them and the intelligence guys here have them too. I will see what I can find out when I get home."

"We all do what we can," Vince responded.

The two officers joked for a moment then agreed to meet for a beer in the hotel's cocktail lounge in an hour after checking in.

Chapter Thirteen

Only four other Abaco Inn guests, and an aircraft mechanic going to the Treasure Cay airport were waiting for the small ferry. Cory and Trish boarded for the half hour voyage to Man O' War Cay.

Lying just one hundred and twenty miles due East of West Palm Beach Florida, the Abaco's are a tropical jewel. Man O' War Cay has been the center of boat building in the Bahamas for over two hundred years. The beach is one of the best in the world.

"You sure know how to dress for the occasion" Higgins watched Trish, nearly falling out of a string bikini covered by a sleeveless chambray shirt, open at the front with no buttons.

She was bent over and stowing the snorkel gear under the wooden bench seats. The eyes of everyone on the launch watched.

"I got this yesterday on my Christmas shopping trip. You know a girl can't wear the same clothes two days in a row."

Higgins wondered where all of this was leading. At dinner last night, she had come off her aggressive attitude and seemed lost in thought. When he asked if she would like to go down to the lounge where a steel drum band was playing she declined. Claiming fatigue from travel, she just wanted to get some sleep.

He was also tired but slept restlessly. Knowing there was a big operation coming up and he would be the main planner kept his mind spinning. Something told him this was not going to be an ordinary run but something bigger. He wanted to get started. Then Chester sent this beautiful hot babe to help him work out the details. What is the world coming to! It was impossible not to look at her.

As the thirty-five-foot boat backed out of the moorings, Higgins observed the receding shoreline and old buildings. His gaze continually went back to the form sitting in the seat opposite him. "What are you thinking about?" Trish inquired.

"I was just thinking about the last time I got underway from Puerto Bogotá. The weather was hot and still just like this, and my crew was excited about the trip. I was nervous because there was a new hurricane forming out there and I didn't want to get stuck or killed in it. Chester insisted I leave without delay so we left. There were new deadlines and all of a sudden everything was on fast forward. It turned out the hurricane veered off and was of no concern. But, in my mind, the whole hassle could have been avoided if everyone up north had his or her shit together in the first place. We could have left well before the storm season started. I like to travel in March, that's the best." He also thought he would love to get her in the sack and explore every inch of her body for a few hours. "I wonder how someone like you got involved in this kind of work."

"That's a long story, I'm not too sure how it all came about either," she replied.

"Couldn't you make just as much money being a Playboy model or something like that?"

"Thanks for the compliment but that wouldn't work for me. The only mistake I made so far was picking the wrong husband."

"You're married?"

"Not anymore."

"How long were you married?"

"Not very long at all but sometimes it seemed like an eternity."

"Are you sure you want to tell me all of this. I've always found the less I know about the personal lives of my business associates, the better off everyone is."

"Yeah, I've been told you are somewhat of a mystery man."

"Oh yeah? Says who?"

"Oh, friends in Palm Beach, they say you are the best there is but no one knows much about you. It seems like Tom Thrasher is the only one who know how to get in touch with you."

"Makes it pretty simple doesn't it? Time to go swimming."

The ferry approached the floating dock amid the bustle of the forty or so dark skinned Bahamian natives hammering, sawing, lifting, sanding and just standing around idle in the various activities of building and repairing boats. There were boats of every size and shape from six to eighty feet in length. Some were in various stages of repair others were decades old derelicts like many found in boatyards around the world. Higgins, whose love of boats was his life's passion, thought this would be an interesting place to visit some day in retirement.

Now however, it was time to go snorkeling with wonder lady from Atlanta and finally find out what the hell this next job was all about.

"Well, here we are; the bell captain said this was the best beach in the Bahamas. Where is it?" Wondered Trish out loud.

"Da beach be da bes in de islands pretty lady. Jus' follow dat little patway true da dunes. You gonna love it." The mahogany colored operator offered. "I come back bout four clock ok? Get you to hotel in time for nice rum punch Happy Timer. Good day pretty lady. Bye Mista, have fun" he grinned displaying a mouth full of pearl white perfectly aligned teeth. He nodded his head towards Trish and winked at Cory.

The other two couples took off up the beach to the northwest. Cory, carrying the tote bag took Trish's hand and led her on a path down the beach to the right.

"Oh my God," she gasped as the shoreline appeared, "This is the most beautiful beach I have ever seen." As far as they could see only sugar white sand and azure water to the left and dunes palm trees and mangroves to the right.

Offshore, they observed two ships. One, a large white cruise ship heading west towards the Florida coast and a small freighter going the opposite direction. Higgins was curious as to the destination and cargo of the smaller vessel.

The wide strand of white sand between the dunes and the water's edge was inviting. There was hardly a ripple of wind on the water and the hot Caribbean sun baked everything. Beach umbrellas were scattered around for public use. Higgins selected the most distant from the others and headed for it. With the exception of three Bahamian kids playing with a dog several hundred yards to the east, they were alone in paradise.

"Is this enough privacy for you?" Higgins joked.

"I think so."

"Can we talk now? The suspense is killing me."

"Ok, can you smear some of this oil on my back while we talk?"

Higgins had been fantasizing how touching her would feel and found it hard to concentrate on the conversation as he slathered coconut laced Hawaiian Tropic Dark Tanning Oil over Trish's back and legs.

"We want you to bring a ton of cocaine into Norfolk Virginia".

Higgins sat bolt upright "No fucking way! I'll haul all the grass and hash anyplace in the world but I draw the line at the hard stuff."

"Look, everyone knows you want to retire soon. This could be a way to do it with style and double your wealth." She laid face down on a woven straw mat. "Go a little higher on my legs with the oil please, Captain". He had already spread the oil as far up her legs as he had dared. In another few seconds though, he was sensually tracing the edge of her skimpy bikini bottom with his oily fingers. He detected the slightest movement as her legs spread an inch.

She moaned slightly and said "Yeah."

His mind was turning cartwheels. His quick mental calculator told him if he did this job and made it, he would make over a million dollars. It would take at least four or five marijuana runs and as many years to match it. He had seen too many friends destroy their lives with cocaine. Of course, he also knew people who used the stuff recreationally and seemed to have decent lives. Concentrating on keeping his cool, he applied several more tablespoons of oil wherever she requested.

"You will earn nine hundred grand, all expenses and you can keep the legally documented North Sea trawler when everything is done."

"Shit! Over three quarter million and a $600,000 boat," Higgins thought. "Go on."

"The boat is already in Honduras, tied up at Puerto Lempira. We have her registered in the U.S. The legal owner is a mutual fund trust account custodian in Atlanta. We want you to spend the next eight months skippering her around, down there. You should take a month or so to replace the crew with your own people. You can bring up to four others. We will pay each of them $50,000 when the job is done. Bring Rob Byrd along as your number two. We will pay him $300,000. I have all the licenses you will need in addition to your fully legit sixteen hundred ton US Coast Guard Captain papers and a Jamaican Admiralty endorsement. We want you to take at least two runs over to Jamaica. Then you will get a job to move some cargo from Jamaica to St Thomas. That will be your signal to get your people in place. Of course we'll know where the Coast Guard is patrolling when you make these trips. We want you to have them find you. Caribbean Gipsy will become famous for being boarded repeatedly. Everything about this boat is legal. If you are in some Jamaican port and a Coast Guard unit is there on a patrol break, you should try to party with them. There is a fax machine installed in the pilothouse. This time though, we have provided you with a couple dozen fax communications concerning the lumber shipping business. The Coasties will be interested in why you even have it on board. All of your cargo manifests will be impeccably legal. You will be known as a viable merchantman in the tropics. Are you with me so far?"

"Keep going, what's the catch?"

"After you deliver the wood to St Thomas, fuel up, and prepare for a long voyage. Someone, most likely me, will contact you in person and bring you money for the product along with final instructions. Timing, weather and what we know about the positioning of the Coast Guard will determine the actual date of your departure.

"A St Thomas shipping agent will find you and ask if you would be willing to carry a load of furniture to an import broker in Norfolk. You will strike a deal and prepare to leave. The furniture will actually arrive and be loaded while one of the Coast Guard patrol ships is in port on a break.

"There are two hidden compartments on the boat. They look like water and sewage tanks. At first glance each hold a couple hundred gallons. There are hydraulic rams to lift up one end of each tank and the product can fit nicely in back there. Each of these compartments will easily hold fifteen hundred pounds of coke in ten kilo blocks. A valve on the water tank will yield water if opened."

"Where will the 'product' come from?" Higgins asked wondering if he wanted to deal with a new team member. He had everyone he needed.

"You will go east of Antigua about eighty-five miles. The final confirmation and coordinates will come through a weather fax. A French freighter will meet you and make the transfer. You will pay for the cargo after the appropriate field tests insure quality. Head north, east of Bermuda and into Norfolk. Because you are returning from the U.S Virgin Islands, you will be waived by customs and proceed to a small cargo pier in the Port of Hampton Roads. The furniture dealer will be there and sign for the legal cargo. You will want a break, so dismiss most your crew and take off for a couple days. Leave the one you trust the most with the vessel. If he is ever asked where the next port of call is, he should explain that you had just delivered furniture and the Captain is out looking for something to take south. The day after your arrival in Norfolk, the remaining sixty percent of everyone's money including yours, will be transferred to their separate accounts just like we have done in the past. A second similar trip is already being planned for one year later. We hope you will work for us on that one too. When the second run is completed the boss is thinking that we should all retire.

"Can you show me how those snorkeler things work?" asked Trish with a seductive grin and the mouthpiece of the J shaped tube entering her mouth.

"Sure, let's swim."

Cory picked up the fins and handed Trish the two masks. He took her empty hand in his and they walked slowly to the water. Once her feet were wet, she darted off until she was waist deep. She then turned around and fell spread-eagled backward into the warm water. "Catch me if you can." She swam towards the horizon.

Higgins dropped the fins at the water's edge, took two leaping steps through the surf and dove in. When he surfaced on the other side of the wave, Trish was standing in front of him naked.

Without hesitation, Cory decided to do the job.

Chapter Fourteen

Captain Dave Snyder, Chief of Staff of the Seventh Coast Guard District, stood at the podium while the thirty some officers, civilians and agents took their seats. Just as the last two men were finding their place, a door on the side of the conference room opened and Captain Snyder raised his voice and chirped "Attention on Deck!" Everyone in the room stood in respect as the District Commander stepped through the door.

Rear Admiral Roger J. Root entered the room and approached his chief of staff. "As you were ladies and gentlemen." He shook Captain Snyder's hand and quietly said, "Thank you Dave."

Admiral Root was a thirty-two-year veteran of the Coast Guard, a graduate of the Academy. He had served in Vietnam as the Deputy Squadron Commander for the small boat group Commander Flood had been part of in the mid-sixties. He commanded three different cutters including a high endurance cutter and an icebreaker, was Chief of Operations for the District in Seattle and was serving in his second position since selected for flag rank. Five rows of ribbons from all of his various achievements including a Purple Heart and a Legion of Merit award were stacked on the left side of his blue shirt. He also wore the gold insignia of a Cutterman, one who had served onboard Coast Guard cutters for more than five years. He wore his authority well and a stern smile on his face conveyed a noticeable indication of stress and concern.

"Thank you all for making the sacrifice to travel here for this very important event. Over the next two days, the district staff and representatives from the Drug Enforcement Administration and Customs will be addressing you on a few dynamic breakthroughs. Intelligence indicates the bad guys ramping up their efforts to concentrate on an onslaught of shipments and stretch our abilities more than ever."

Vince and Gus Solomon sat next to one another in the second row of tables and Lieutenant Phil Sutton was several rows back next to one of his classmates also serving as Ops Boss on a 210ft cutter stationed in Jacksonville.

"In as much as I would like to stay here and be part of this meeting, my present duties don't allow me to be involved in operational details any more. These days I get to attend Rotary

43

meetings and budget reviews more often than I care to tell you. I will leave you with Captain Snyder and the staff to fill you in on what you are here for. Once again, thanks for coming and I will catch up with you all at a little reception tomorrow night at my quarters."

The Admiral turned towards his Chief of Staff. "Dave."

Captain Snyder once again ordered, "Attention on deck!"

All of the attendees quickly stood erect until the District Commander had cleared the room. As they began to take their seats, to Vince Lubar's surprise, a close up enlarged photograph of Tom Thrasher appeared on the screen. Of course, no one in the room at this time knew the name associated with the picture.

"This photograph was collected by Lieutenant Commander Vince Lubar, XO on board our newest, and oldest cutter in the district fleet." There was a bit of chuckling around the room as many knew the history of the ESCAPE. She certainly was not as sleek looking as the 210's and other fast patrol boats. Captain Snyder smiled with the group. Everyone agreed the addition of the three navy ships to the fleet had been necessary and welcome.

"Back to the photograph, first of all, has anyone in this room seen this person or know who he is?"

There were several quiet conversations taking place amongst the attendees but after a moment, no one could identify the person.

"This photo was sent to CCIC by LCDR Lubar a week ago because he observed the individual engaged in suspicious activity. Can you please tell the group what about this person attracted your suspicion?" He motioned Vince to the podium.

Vince was surprised to see the photo displayed as it was but he also knew Captain Snyder had a reputation of putting people on the spot. Vince also knew that when command selection boards convened district Chiefs of Staff were a key piece of the process. The evening before, Gus had told him he had given a copy of the picture to the district intelligence office.

He approached the microphone and began to relate the tale of the day at Fort Sumter, the boat trip from Patriots Point, the photographer and the series of pictures. His presentation took about ten minutes. Several in the audience asked questions but no determination emerged as to whom this person was. When he finished, Captain Snyder thanked Vince.

"Where ever this ends up and I'm confident we will figure out who this guy is and it will lead us to something interesting. But, the lesson learned is we all, each and every one of us must stay diligent in all we do. We must be on the lookout for things leading us to more successful contraband interdiction missions. I'm counting on you to return to your units and impress on all of your crewmembers the importance of everything we see. These days we are all on duty twenty-four hours a day, seven days a week.

"CCIC will find out who he is before long and there will be a bulletin letting each of you know the answer.

"Over the course of the next two days we will be looking at the intelligence gained from recent busts and new techniques the smugglers are using to hide shipments."

The rest of the morning was filled with reports from various commands and other agencies. Most of the presentations dealt with new things being uncovered and the types of people arrested.

One of Vince Lubar's old colleagues from his work with the European Military Sealift Command, Ike Holder, was third to speak.

"Through a few of the projects Mr. Lubar started in his years with us, we are developing a theory. We believe some of the North African and Eastern European cartels are looking at expanding to compete or join forces with our friends in South America. Whether with or without our western hemisphere friends, they are going to be a force to reckon with.

"In the past five years, they have found there is so much money available in this business it has been more economical to simply bribe officials and I mean people in very high places. Targets of the European traffic operators have been Spanish and French Supreme Court judges, police chiefs and coast guard operators all around the Med. You must all be on the lookout throughout your own commands for crewmembers who are suddenly befriending new people. You have to instill a trust between the wardroom and the crew down to the most junior oiler or mess cook."

Holder paused. "New intel indicates people on the land side of bigger operations know the daily patrol patterns of each Coast Guard Cutter and when air surveillance operations are scheduled."

"Now," Holder continued, "here is the big one. We've gotten some chatter making us believe there will be an open ocean exchange of cocaine and money sometime in the next four to six months in the Atlantic. A small cargo ship or luxury yacht, we don't yet know which, will bring a large shipment to be transferred to another vessel for delivery on the eastern seaboard."

"That's a lot of coast and a big ocean," interjected Gus Solomon.

"It is, sir, and from what we believe, the cargo will be well hidden on both vessels and very difficult to discover."

Captain Snyder stepped back up to the podium and stood beside agent Holder. "Tomorrow morning we will be seeing a slide show on every kind of hidden cargo compartment uncovered over the past three years. Some of you submitted great photographs and the staff appreciates your diligence.

"After lunch, we will break up into groups of four or five and I want you to tell one another sea stories. No beer though." Everyone laughed with the Chief of Staff.

"We have a lot to learn. Each of your experiences is a good place to start."

Chapter Fifteen

It is no easy task to fly around the Caribbean adlib during the late fall and winter months. The routes to and from North America are booked up with holiday travelers escaping the winter weather. There would have been no problem getting to Miami but then flights south were all booked. Cory couldn't connect to Central America without laying over in Florida for up to 6 days. He found a flight from Marsh Harbor to Caracas via Kingston Jamaica. From Caracas, he caught a direct Iberia flight into San Pedro Sula International Airport on the north coast of Honduras. Once there, he planned to rely on the locals to get him the last couple of hundred miles to Puerto Lempira.

At the moment he was on the long flight from Venezuela. The sweet scent and soft touch of Trish Dixon was lingering. Higgins knew his success in his career was not by accident. When he began this crazy business, he figured the only way to stay out of trouble was to be a total loner. No close friends, no girlfriends, don't talk to anyone about anything. Above all, a romantic relationship was out of the question. His association with Trish was causing him to reconsider some principles. He thought if he were to get involved with someone romantically, he would have to live a life based on lies because most potential companions would probably object to being involved with a drug smuggler. Trish being a member of the "team" allowed him to change his thinking. She probably knew more about his future activities than he did!

He looked out the window at the vast sea below. How nice it would be to be down there legitimately just sailing from one island to the other enjoying the company of a beautiful woman. He closed his eyes and visualized the hours their bodies had spent locked together in Abaco.

Cory knew his solitary life was now in the past. At the end of the operation he was about to begin, there would be another encounter with Trish. They were going to meet somewhere and spend a week or two on the eastern Spanish coast.

His intelligent side was warning him there was something strange going on within. He contemplated compromising the very principals that had kept him out of jail over the years. The man inside of him was however working on his subconscious, he realized he was a lonely person and craved companionship. His overriding thought was he was getting too old for this shit.

47

He napped restlessly and woke for good as the Boeing 727 started its descent over the Western Gulf. He saw the silhouette of the hills of Jamaica off to the north. As the plane descended and made a sweeping fifty-mile radius turn to approach Honduras from the north, he spotted the rugged mountains of Belize to the west. The exhilaration his work brought him was returning and he was anxious to get started on this operation. Actually, the way things looked next several months was going to be relaxing and stress free. He was excited about becoming a legitimate merchant for a while. He had often thought it would be a neat way to live once he retired from criminal life. Now he had the opportunity to experience it in a proper boat while he learned the ropes.

It was late in the afternoon. Cory did not want to fly in a small plane in darkness with some pilot he had never met. Prior to departing Caracas, he booked a room for two nights at the Honduras Plaza Hotel. The Iberia Airline representative recommended it. It is the place where most of the flight crews stay when they had layovers. The extra day he would use to catch up on Honduran culture and customs. He had long ago learned if you spent a day or so studying the places you were to visit, the result was by not making a fool out of yourself, you were inconspicuous in your surroundings. If he were going to haul Honduran mahogany in the region, he had better know what the hell he was talking about.

The jet was on final approach. The crew in the flight deck maneuvered their ship through a series of towering thunderheads. As the wheels touched the sweltering tarmac, he inhaled and exhaled deeply and said half out loud to himself: "Well, here we go again."

Chapter Sixteen

The fall weather slightly cooled the evening air in Corpus Christi. Gus Solomon finished his shift as the Senior Watch Officer in Corpus Christi Intelligence Center. He had stepped outside to take in the fresh night air. The armpits on his light blue shirt were soaked with perspiration and his normally well-kept closely cropped brown hair was soaked. The CCIC staff numbers 250. The mission is to pour over every bit of drug trafficking and illegal immigration intelligence collected by all federal, state and local law enforcement groups. It was midnight and he had been in the control room since his day started at noon. One of the DEA watch standers called in sick so he and the other team members were covering a larger load than usual.

When the Coast Guard makes a boarding, or Customs searches a vehicle at border crossings, the names and other information related to the occupants and all of the vital statistics on the vessel, airplane or vehicle are sent to CCIC. Within five minutes, the watch standers will compare the information with that contained in the huge CCIC database. Within fifteen minutes, the personnel at the intelligence center prepare a return message to the on-scene law enforcement team with the details of any past criminal activities in which the occupants of the vehicle or boat have been involved. The data will also include the names of any previous owners of the vessel or vehicle who might have a reason to be included in the National Crime Institute database. More often than not, CCIC has no information on many of the people whose boats are boarded. Several times a month a name will be entered into the system and a new case file will be born. Boats will be seized, laundered money will be located, lawyers will be hired, lives will be changed and prison cells filled. Then the crew of a Coast Guard Cutter will paint another marijuana leaf on the stack.

The CCIC database contains information on every drug or illegal alien arrest made in the United States since the sixties.

Since midday, Solomon had supervised the gathering and dissemination of intelligence surrounding eleven boardings at sea and thirty-five car searches. That said it had been a quiet shift. Two of the car searches were at the US/Canadian border crossing in Blaine Washington. One was in upstate New York. The rest were California and Texas crossings where people from Mexico were closely watched. Everyone entering the states from Mexico was clean and without any interest. Their names were held for ninety days. At the end of that period, they would be dropped from the list unless they were stopped again at a crossing. If they only crossed twice in a three-month period, they would be removed from the list. However, people crossing frequently were subject to more than a cursory look. A week had gone by since he returned from the big conference in Miami. It was time once again to look at those photographs.

Solomon shook the contents of the envelope out on to his already cluttered desktop. The way things fell, the narrative was on the bottom of the pile and a blown up photograph of a beach boy looking thirty-year old male in casual business clothing, carrying a briefcase was on the top. On a closer look, Gus knew in an instant he had seen the person before. He couldn't remember where.

Gus walked over to the photo disseminator and fed several of Beaufort E. Lee's photographs into the document feeder. The photo disseminator would compare features of any picture with the likenesses of several million other photographs of criminals or suspected notorious individuals from many underworld entities in the database of the National Crime Institute. If similarities were encountered, pictures and dossiers would begin spewing out of the printer next to the disseminator. If not, the screen on the computer screen would show the message "NO MATCHES FOUND." Three minutes into the search, a file photograph of Vince Lubar appeared. The short narrative identified the Lieutenant Commander as a CCIC Trusted Agent, assigned to USCG South Florida / Caribbean Task Force. Next, a file photograph of the park ranger appeared the caption read Leon Matthews, Supervisor, U.S. Park Service. This information preceded a list of all the places the ranger had served. He entered the service at Yellowstone, gotten transferred to the Everglades and was currently serving at Fort Sumter. The information listed him as a native of Idaho and a graduate of the Citadel. Gus stared into the face of the park ranger looking out of the monitor. "You've got something to tell us, don't you buddy?" he said out loud as he pushed the control and "P" keys on the computer and the whirling sound of the laser scanner began formatting the document and delivering the pages out the top of the machine. The facial photographs of the character in the casual business attire, Denise

Lubar, and Bill and Crystal Taggart each appeared with a notation that no matches were found.

"Wow," Gus thought to himself. He thought surely that this guy was connected to something illegal. He just couldn't place him. The next prompt on the photo disseminator's screen was "Archive or Delete". Archiving would store the images in perpetuity and they would be included in any other matches requested in the future. Solomon chose to archive. This act would require an additional fifteen minutes of paper work for the already exhausted officer but just looking at the photos, he knew this one was significant. He had seen him somewhere and it was the slick guys in suits who were the hardest to catch in this game. He completed the paperwork and went home.

Chapter Seventeen

Up ahead about eight miles, Higgins saw the unmistakable profile of a Coast Guard Cutter and a sail boat. Caribbean Gipsy was headed west out of Kingston where he and Manuel Salvador unloaded half of their cargo of fine Honduran mahogany. The next stop would be Montego Bay. There they would unload the balance, spend a couple of nights of recreation then head back to Honduras for another load.

Manuel and a cook named Juan Castro de Mayo were the only other crewmembers. Both had the appropriate Honduran seaman papers and licenses and true to Trish's word, the vessel was properly documented for its current employment. Manuel was at the helm and Juan Castro asleep, a part of his job he seemed to enjoy the most.

"Well my friend, it looks like we're going to get a chance to meet some members of the other team."

"Jefe, I don't think we got nothin to hide."

"No companero, if we were any cleaner we would be a hospital ship.

"Let's slow down to about six knots and steer a little north of those guys. They will be at least another half hour on this boarding and then we will be three miles away from them."

"Aye-Aye Jefe." He eased back on the ship's engine controller.

"I'm going to go below and get a beer, do you want anything Manuel?"

"If you're buying I might like some iced tea. Do you think we should wake up Juan so he won't be too scared when the Coasties wake him up?"

"Yeah, I'll give him a shake."

Chapter Eighteen

"New contact bearing one zero five on the horizon." The flying bridge lookout shouted down the voice tube to the bridge. "Very well, I've got him," replied Ensign Ladner as he wheeled around and focused his binoculars on Caribbean Gipsy.

The skipper sat in his tall chair inside the wheelhouse observing the activities with the boarding of the sailboat off the starboard bow.

"What-cha-got Buzz?"

"Looks like a little island freighter."

"Have the radar gang get a plot on her and we'll make her our next customer."

"Gina Aloha here is pretty clean. When Lieutenant Sutton and the guys get back on board we will see what we can do with this one."

"Yes sir"

"Messenger."

"Aye-Aye Captain."

"Go tell the XO I would like to see him, and please and stop by the pantry, see if Cruz has any fresh coffee."

"Aye-Aye Captain. Two sugars?"

"You got it Smitty."

"Enter." responded Vince Lubar to the knock on his stateroom door. He was plowing through a deep pile of performance evaluations.

"Sir, the captain would like to see you up on the bridge."

"Thanks Smitty, what's up?"

"It looks like we got another contact."

"Ok, thanks. I could use a little fresh air."

Lubar quickly arranged all of the papers in order so he could remember where he was when he returned. He locked them in his filing cabinet. When the XO of a Coast Guard Cutter on drug enforcement patrols is summoned to the bridge, it could be a day or two before he returns to his bureaucratic duties.

He used the head, grabbed a cup of coffee and two cookies from the pantry. He climbed eleven steel steps up to the bridge. He passed through the aft portion of the bridge where the quartermasters kept the plot. The ships log was open and a junior watch stander recorded every detail. As Lubar passed through the space, an entry was made in the book. "1324hrs, XO on the bridge."

"What do we have Skipper?" He saluted and reached into a varnished teakwood box inscribed with the brass letters XO to withdraw his binoculars.

Flood returned the salute. "Down there to the southeast, looks like a little freighter headed west. Jake on the fly bridge says he thinks it's an American flag." "If we get a chance to go aboard, I would like you to do the honors. Phil has been over on this one for an hour and a half and there is no sense in any of us getting too worn out. Take Chief Loftus and Ensign Merrymore and a couple of the new kids."

"Thanks, it would be a great diversion from the stack of evaluations I've been straining over for the past three hours. I'll get the team together."

"Mr. Ladner, have the messenger of the watch find Mister Merrymore, Chief Loftus and Petty Officer King from Engineering. Send them to my stateroom in ten minutes."

"Aye-Aye XO."

Lubar turned back to chat with his skipper while the crew was assembled.

"Nice looking ketch." Vince looked towards the sailing vessel Gina Aloha. The Avon rubber hulled boarding boat ESCAPE II was pulling away and the crew of Gina Aloha was waving to the boarding party.

"Nice looking crew!" Flood offered. "From the information sent back, the old man is Grandpa, the thirty-eight something in the green bikini is his second or third wife and the two twenty something's in the blue and orange thongs; one is his granddaughter and the other is her cousin. They just graduated from UC San Luis Obispo. Pops picked them up in San Diego twelve weeks ago and is teaching them to sail before they go hunting husbands in corporate America."

As ESCAPE II pulled alongside, Gina Aloha raised her sails and took off on a starboard tack steering about forty-five degrees off of the afternoon northwesterly wind. Many of ESCAPE's young crewmembers were waving at the crew of the yacht as it moved slowly towards the horizon.

"Stand by to receive ESCAPE II in the starboard davits. Deck Force man your stations," Ensign Ladner announced over the PA system.

The shipboard evolution of bringing a small boat alongside a ship requires no small amount of skill and professionalism. The ship is underway making a couple of knots. The Officer of the Deck will position the ship on a course so any wind is on the opposite side. The coxswain steering the small boat takes a station near the stern of the ship. When directed by the Officer of the Deck, he slowly approaches, increasing speed slightly and steering gradually closer. In the bow of the smaller boat, one of the crew designated as the bow hook, stands by to grab the shackle. Once the bow is safely connected, the coxswain maneuvers the stern of his vessel to the side of the ship. When a similar stern connection is made, he signals the Officer of the Deck who directs the deck force to "heave around" and commence lifting the boat out of the water. Usually the Chief Boatswain Mate or a senior petty officer leads the lifting operation. Once he receives the command from the bridge, he takes over. There is a separate winch to raise each end of the boat. If the bow is not lifted at the same rate as the stern, the boat becomes unstable. The boats are kept one or two decks above the waterline. On some ships, as is the situation with ESCAPE, lifting is paused at the main deck where the boarding party and coxswain disembark.

Whenever practical, military etiquette and respect for rank prevails in all evolutions carried out onboard Coast Guard Cutters. While the smaller boat was underway the coxswain, a third class petty officer, was in charge of the vessel and LT Sutton, third senior officer assigned to ESCAPE was a passenger and subject to the orders of the more junior man. As ESCAPE II made its approach alongside the superior vessel, Sutton in the bow became the "Bow Hook" and was directed by his junior petty officer to "hook the bow." Once the smaller craft is secured out of the water and alongside the Cutter, respect for his rank and privilege is honored. Phil was first to disembark. When safely on board, he thanked each member of the crew and promised the coxswain he would buy them a beer when they were ashore in Montego Bay.

Generally, a boarding team will consist of one commissioned officer trained in the Coast Guard's intensive law enforcement program. A thorough knowledge of laws and treaties is required of all boarding officers. This schooling is often augmented by short extra courses conducted at such prestigious training environments as the Federal Law Enforcement Training Centers in Glynco, Georgia or in Quantico, Virginia.

Many enlisted petty officers also attend law enforcement schools. On smaller vessels, these non-commissioned officers make up the majority of the services' law enforcement cadre. The boarding officers and petty officers carry standard issue side arms. They are backed up by others qualified with small arms such as the M16 machine gun, the twelve-gauge riot shotgun and semi-automatic pistols, either the Colt .45 or the NATO equivalent P-1 9mm.

Each member of the team will also carry a can or two of mace or pepper spray, several additional clips of ammunition for their weapons and a pair of handcuffs around their belt. A Kevlar bulletproof vest topped off with a life jacket complete the ensemble. The total weight of gear worn is about twenty-five pounds. Depending on the circumstances of the boarding, the senior boarding officer may choose to leave one or both of the junior members in the small boat. A properly outfitted Coast Guard boarding party presents a formidable intrusion to the occupants of any vessel. The presence of the cutter itself within twenty yards is also intimidating. This fact is amplified when you consider that the occupants of the boat being boarded will notice that the ship has two fully manned fifty-caliber machine guns on the bow and a 20mm grenade launcher on each side of the flying bridge just aft of the wheel house.

Chapter Nineteen

Leon Matthews joined U.S. Park Service the year he graduated from the Citadel. He enjoyed the outdoors. Camping and backpacking were his favorite recreational activities. The Park Service sent a recruiter to campus during a job fair for graduating seniors. Once hired, Yellowstone was his first assignment. While there, he took charge of the parks communication system. His degree was in mechanical engineering with a minor in communications engineering. As a hobby in his off duty time, he operated a Ham radio station. He spent hours chatting around the world with others in the same hobby.

In two years he was promoted and transferred to the Everglades as Deputy Chief Ranger. As a supervisor of forty-five employees, he encountered his share of problem workers. One day, three of his young assistants were arrested for being involved in a small ring of folks who bought wholesale marijuana and sold it in Miami. Leon was not opposed to smoking a joint but as the superior to the individuals caught, he had to act accordingly. Until this incident, he had never given much thought to the drug trade. He became fascinated by the amount of money his employees made on the side. As the investigation progressed, he discovered each had managed to stash away a six figure savings account. When it came time for their trial, Leon was called by the defense attorney. They needed a character witness. He was surprised when the summons arrived and he was asked to meet with the trial attorneys in the Palm Beach law firm of his old college classmate Chester Whittaker.

After greeting one another as old military academy classmates do with handshakes, back slapping and a masculine embrace, it was time to sit.

Chester pointed to the end of the couch indicating where Leon should sit.

"When they brought in the witness list for this hearing, I couldn't believe the Leon Mathews we subpoenaed would be you!"

"I had the same thoughts when I got called to check in with your firm."

They spent the next half hour reminiscing their days of discipline and valor learned at the expense of thousands of pushups, sit-ups and other torture rendered by their superior classmates. They laughed a lot as they enjoyed a couple of shots of thirty-year-old scotch.

About twenty minutes into the reunion Chester got down to business. "Leon, I have been hired by several gents who worked for you. My firm will represent them in Florida Superior Court concerning accusations they might have been involved in the distribution of marijuana."

"I know."

"Well, let me ask you this old buddy. Were these kids good at the work you assigned them?"

"Actually, if I had to rank all of the apprentice rangers and interns in the Everglades, these three kids would be in the top fifteen."

"And so what good would it do for the rest of the citizens of Florida and the general population of the United States if these gentlemen were incarcerated for a number of months? Say Leon, have you ever taken a puff of marijuana?"

"I'm not sure what it has to do with this case."

"Come on Leon. You know what I'm talking about. Look around you. I didn't come upon these surroundings because my dad has a great law practice in New York. I'm the best at what I do. It is a sad day around here when one of my clients is not acquitted. And I bet you haven't seen a sad face since you got here." He hadn't.

"Do you know, the weed you smoked in your quarters in the swamp two and a half weeks ago was actually sold wholesale to your bartender friend in Boca Raton by Jeremy Coyle, my client and your former protégé? Now, let me tell you what I need from you in court tomorrow."

Chester groomed his old buddy on how to answer the questions he would present. Each and every possible question presented by the prosecuting attorney was also rehearsed. The meeting lasted three hours and at the end of it, the ice water was gone but no more scotch had been consumed.

As the interview was winding down, Chester once again reached for the liquor bottle and offered a shot. Leon asked for a double.

"So how did you get so involved in this shady business?"

"Shady? My work is not shady, I simply provide a constitutional right of defense for people who have been accused of crimes and misdemeanors. But how did I get into it? Well, after I passed the Florida bar exam, I told my father there were so many northeastern folks moving to Florida we should open a practice here to continue to help them out. He agreed.

"I did property, probate, real estate and domestic law for a while until the son of an old friend from Newark got involved in a dealing problem and I was able to get him off the hook. His dad paid me better than any divorce or probate, so I started a new specialty. My father isn't sure this is the kind of law we should be practicing and he still thinks I'm making it on family law. I have two associates who handle all of the easy crap and I work with three other trial lawyers on cases like this. Over the past six years I have been doing better than I thought possible. And the excitement of it gets my juices flowing."

"Jeeze Man, you must meet a lot of interesting people."

"I sure do. We'll do this hearing tomorrow morning and then why don't you check out of your hotel and come spend the weekend at our house on the waterway?'

"Hey, that sounds great. Is it OK with your wife?"

"Gina loves company. She will put on a spread you won't soon forget. Later we can take a little cruise at sunset and recall our old days in the corps." Chester stopped abruptly for a second and then went on. "Oh shit Leon, pardon my rudeness. I never even asked if you were married and if so, did you bring your wife with you? I feel like such a jackass!"

"No, don't worry. I guess I haven't found the right one yet. I keep busy with the parks, then sometimes I am up all night chatting with my ham radio pals. When I find one to put up with that, I guess I will succumb."

"I know. We all have our quirks. Every once in a while I get into an interesting poker game lasting too long and Gina gets annoyed. But, as long as she gets a new BMW and a couple of nice vacations each year, she sticks with me."

"Well, I would love to sit and talk for hours but I have a couple more witnesses to chat with. Connie has a little packet of information we give to all of our witnesses. It would be a good idea if you looked it over tonight and we will see you in court tomorrow. And I'm looking forward to the weekend. It will be fun to let our hair down for a while." Leon stood to leave.

When Chester opened the door there were two other individuals in the room. One was a scruffy beach boy type. The other dressed casually but one could instantly tell the golf shirt and slacks he wore were tailor made.

"Give me just a couple, gents." Chester spoke to both of them.

"Connie, could you give Mr. Mathews a witness guide? And let's give him one of those Surf & Turf deals from Jimmy's.

"Dinner is on the Whitaker Law Firm tonight buddy," he told Leon, shook his hand once more and closed the office door.

"Here you go sir. It is important reading and it should only take you fifteen minutes but it will help a lot. There might even be a couple of things in there that will make you laugh. And here is a certificate for dinner at Jimmy's. I will call and let them know you are coming. Tell the hostess that you would like to sit in Thomas' section. Don't call him Tom and don't try to tip him. That's all taken care of. I'm sure you will enjoy your evening."

Inside of his office, Chester was observing his old roommate on the screen of his computer. "Where in my organization could I use him? He has the talent to scan through radio frequencies and zero in on conversations and messages to help my captains to move their precious cargos undetected?" he asked himself almost out loud.

Chapter Twenty

"Ahoy on the Caribbean Gipsy, this is the United States Coast Guard Cutter on channel sixteen, over." Ladner spoke into the microphone of the short-range bridge to bridge VHF radio in the pilothouse.

"Good afternoon Coast Guard, this is Caribbean Gipsy." Higgins answered after an appropriate wait of about a minute.

"Caribbean Gipsy, this is the Coast Guard. Please switch to channel six eight."

"Roger, switching to six eight." Higgins replied with the confidence of someone who had nothing to hide.

"This is the Caribbean Gipsy. What can I do for you today?" He knew exactly what he could do for them. They wanted to get a look around his boat and take a few photographs. They want to know the names of everyone onboard, and if I am hauling any contraband. They want to bust you and seize your ship and take you to jail and throw your cargo in some incinerator and watch it go up on smoke while you sweated your balls of in some stuffy southern Florida jail waiting for a dirt bag lawyer to get you off the hook. Well boys and girls, you can have a look at the boat and take your pictures and write down all the shit you want to but that's all you're going to get. This boat is squeaky clean and as legal as a brand new Catholic bride.

"Caribbean Gipsy, this is the Coast Guard, we are conducting a routine patrol in the area for maritime safety and enforcement of laws and treaties. Please answer a few routine questions," Ladner advised. Flood was listening to every word spoken by the young officer, pleased with his confidence. The junior quartermaster attending to the ships logbook was recording the radio conversation.

Sounding a little annoyed but cooperative all the way, Higgins replied, "Sure fire away." He was actually enjoying the banter.

The ships yeoman, Petty Officer second class Jensen stood next to Ladner prepared to fill in the blanks on the pre-boarding questionnaire. There were different forms for each kind of vessel and they were designed to be quickly entered into the ship's teletype system.

Ladner went through the check-list. "We understand the name of your vessel to be Caribbean Gipsy and you are of U.S registry."

"That's correct."

"What is the length of the vessel?"

"One hundred and thirteen feet."

"How many persons do you have on board?"

"Three, myself and two crewmembers."

"Thank you, sir, what is your last port of call?"

"Kingston Jamaica."

"Thank you, and where are you headed now?"

"Next port is Montego Bay Jamaica."

"What is the purpose of your voyage?"

"We are hauling mahogany and teakwood logs to a mill in Mo Bay."

"Who is the legal owner of the vessel?"

"It is my employer up in the states. It is some kind of investment group. I have worked for them on a couple of projects like this. She's documented in the name of Trust Custodian for the Southeast Schoolteachers Association of America. I think it is some kind of tax shelter. They buy and sell freighters and have a few guys like me work them while they are trying to sell them. It's a good job for me they pay pretty damn well, and I get to do work I like. I used to run tugs up in the Seattle and Portland area but the winters weren't any fun and the whole union thing got to me."

As Higgins rambled on, Dave Flood looked towards Ensign Ladner and Yeoman Jensen and rolled his eyes. "This guy won't shut up. I think he's starved for American company. Tell him we are coming aboard."

"Aye-Aye Sir"

"Roger Cap, we will be sending a boarding party over to look at your documents and gave you a quick safety inspection."

"Heck, I would enjoy the company. C'mon over. Say, you wouldn't be able to spare a carton of American smokes would you? I would be happy to pay for them. I'm getting a little sick of the Honduran stuff and I can get some in Montego Bay but they are pricy and I think those exports are different than what you get in the states?"

Ladner looked over at his Commanding Officer who was smiling and nodding his head in agreement to the tobacco sale. He motioned to the Messenger of the Watch and asked him to find the storekeeper to open the ship's store and get out a couple cartons of Marlboros.

Ladner continued. "I think we could arrange that. Would a carton or two of Marlboros for fifteen bucks each help out?"

"Hell mate, I would give you fifty." Higgins never smoked in his life. He knew his crew would enjoy the gringo tobacco.

"Captain, with your permission, I will start the boarding evolution," Ensign Ladner requested.

Flood simply nodded his head. Buzz got together with Skip Shout, the Quartermaster of the watch to make sure he was on track to record every move made by the Coast Guardsmen and the occupants of Caribbean Gipsy. The same time, he was giving commands to the helmsman to maneuver the ship closer to Caribbean Gipsy and position ESCAPE with the boat deck to the leeward side of the ship.

Flood was impressed with the way Ladner had taken to his profession and earned the respect of the crew. He had little hope the boarding Gipsy would yield any contraband. She seemed to be a legitimate merchant ship with an expatriate skipper having the time of his life in the tropics. "This will be just another routine boarding for the statistics crunchers at headquarters." He thought to himself.

The Coast Guard boards as many vessels as possible as a means of establishing future budgets. If 35,000 boats are boarded worldwide in a year and at the end of the year have seized two or three hundred vessels in violation of various laws and treaties, then congress and the budget committees can calculate the cost in ship days and manpower it takes to get the job done. If the trend over years shows an ever increasing amount of success with the program, then funds will be provided to continue operations. There is so much paper work involved sometimes Flood would think back to Vietnam and remember how life seemed easier then.

Chapter Twenty-One

"He's a fucking lawyer." Gus Solomon sat bolt upright in bed at three fifteen AM. He had been sleeping for about two hours when he surprised his girlfriend Cindy with the proclamation.

"Who's a lawyer?" she asked. She was used to nocturnal outbursts when Gus had been assigned to ships, but this was the first occurrence since his assignment to CCIC. She embraced him feeling the familiar coldness of perspiration excreted in the dream some ten minutes past.

"Oh it's nothing babe. Vince Lubar sent me some pictures of a guy we suspect to be part of a smuggling operation. I know I have seen him someplace before but I couldn't place him until just now. I think he's' an attorney from a case I was involved in a couple of years ago when I was on COURAGEOUS in Key West."

"You're not going to have to go in on your day off are you?"

"No, the way the bureaucracy works, a day or two doesn't make a difference. I'll just call in and ask the Yeoman to get me a list of all the witnesses from the cases I testified in when we were in Florida. It will take a day or two just to do that. Then I can look it over on my next watch."

"Good, I'll remind you to call in the morning. Now get some sleep, tomorrow you are all mine."

Gus felt a great sense of relief after solving the mystery of the beach boy dude from Fort Sumter.

He turned to Cindy. "Why wait until tomorrow?"

Chapter Twenty-Two

"Caribbean Gipsy, this is the Coast Guard. At this time Captain, please heave to and stand by for a boarding. Have the entire crew and any passengers muster on deck in the forward part of the vessel." Ensign Ladner took control of the boarding as petty officer Jensen recorded the dialogue.

"Sure thing buddy," Came Higgins quick reply. "I've got a little accommodation ladder to hang over the gunwale if that would make it easier for your boys. The crew is on deck, there are no passengers."

This was not Cory's first boarding. He had endured three similar evolutions since leaving Honduras.

Because of the communications network employed by Chester Whittaker, he had advance information as to the whereabouts of the patrol vessels. This gave him an opportunity to either dodge them or prepare for the encounter in a manner to keep him from being tagged as a smuggler.

The inflatable Avon boat with two, two hundred horsepower outboard motors approached the port side of Caribbean Gipsy. Vince sat on the seat just forward of the helm, Ensign Merrymore was taking his turn as bow hook, and Boatswain Chief Loftus was next to the coxswain delivering pearls of wisdom about small boat operation that only a chief petty officer can articulate.

Those in the boat took a quick look at their surroundings. Behind was the two hundred and thirteen foot, sixteen hundred ton looming hulk of the Cutter ESCAPE. On the bow were six fellow crewmen manning the two fifty caliber Browning deck mounted machine guns. Up on the bridge the Commanding Officer, Ensign Ladner and the rest of the watch looked over the rail as though they were tourists observing interesting sea life. On the flying bridge above the wheel house stood a crew with a twenty millimeter grenade launcher at the ready. Everyone in the small boat was wearing either a 9 millimeter P-1 NATO side arm or a Colt .45 semi-automatic pistol loaded and ready for use. The hammers were cocked back, the safety latches engaged and augmented by a thick leather strap on the holster keeping the hammer from striking the firing pin. The second class petty officer boat engineer was holding tightly to his M-16 fully automatic rifle with armor piercing ammunition. The boat coxswain had an M-16 of his own stuffed in a scabbard next to the throttle control. Each of the boat operators also had three spare clips of forty-five rounds of ammunition strapped to their belts. Chief Loftus held tightly on to the sixteen gage riot shotgun with six rounds in the magazine and one chambered and ready to fire. Everyone in the team had two cans of mace strapped to their belts. Each member of the boarding party was expertly trained in the use of their weapons. The way the mace was attached to the belts, upside down with the nozzle pre-positioned, you would only move your hand in an arc, grabbing the mace on the way and spray. Anyone within twenty degrees of either side of the stream would be incapacitated in three quarters of a second.

A person thinking of taking on such a show of force and firepower would have to be nuts.

The water was calm but there was a slight swell causing the boats to heave up and down. The boat coxswain made a smooth approach and Chief Loftus quickly tied the bow line to a cleat near the ladder.

Ensign Merrymore was the first to disembark followed by the XO, then the rest of the party. Once everyone was aboard, the coxswain cast off and made a quick pass completely around the vessel to observe any strange activity. Next he took a position about forty yards off Caribbean Gypsy's starboard bow while Ensign Ladner had maneuvered ESCAPE to a similar but opposite position off the port bow. This positioning of the two vessels allowed complete observation down both sides. If any untoward activity was observed neither of the "friendly" vessels would be in the line of fire from the other.

Chapter Twenty-Three

Leon enjoyed the best seafood dinner ever at Jimmy's Restaurant. His table in a corner overlooked the Intercostal Waterway. As he watched millions of dollars-worth of pleasure craft move by, he contemplated the lifestyle of his old college roommate. "If I could just have a fraction of what Chester has, I would be content," he thought, peering into the contents of a ten-inch-tall crystal wine glass. He happily anticipated getting together with Chester tomorrow.

Returning to his hotel, he spent a restless night trying to sleep. He wasn't looking forward to the hearing, but he hoped Chester would be able to help his old friends. He had gone over all the pretrial information Connie had given him earlier and was nervous about testifying. He finally drifted off to sleep after midnight thinking how strange it was for an employee dealing dope in a national park to have kindled a reunion with his old college roommate.

The next morning, Leon spent two hours sitting on one of those hard oak benches found outside of every court room in the country. He wondered how long it would be until they called him to testify. Then, the door opened and a Deputy District Attorney appeared in a thousand-dollar black suit. He was accompanied by a beautiful assistant complaining about how the cops always screw up and "we just can never get a win up against Whittaker." Next Chester, Jeremy Coyle, the other two former ranger apprentices and the scruffy beach boy type emerged from the court room. Everyone was grinning and shaking hands. The six-foot tall beach boy was now wearing a perfectly tailored dark Armani suit.

"Oh, hi Leon. Looks like there won't be a trial after all. It seems the evidence the cops took from Jeremy got mixed up with some other contraband and they can't find the stuff to bring our friends to trial. The judge tossed the whole thing out."

"Hey Leon, it's great to see you again," Jeremy Coyle spoke offering a strong handshake.

"Likewise" Matthews replied. "I suppose you will want your old jobs back now."

"Nah," replied Jeremy. "We have a little tour boat thing going on over in West Palm Beach now. It's a lot of fun, we make good money, it's all legal and oh my God! You should see the chicks we run into. Thanks for asking though. Hey, it's great to see you again but we got to get going. Take care, Leon. Here's my card if you ever need a tour of the ICW."

"Chester turned to Leon. "Are you all checked out of the hotel?"

"Sure am. I guess you really didn't need me at all. Should I have stayed home?"

"Hell no! You never know how these things go down. It is amazing how often the cops don't have their shit together.

"Besides, we are going to have a great weekend." Chester introduced Leon to the beach boy in the Armani suit. "Leon, please meet my associate Tom Thrasher, one of the best attorneys in the state of Florida."

Leon extended his hand. "Nice to meet you, Tom."

On Chester's recommendation, Leon had turned in his rental car and taken a cab to the courthouse. In the garage beneath the federal courthouse Chester guided Leon to his Mercedes Benz convertible. Chester took the small suitcase from Leon and tossed it in the trunk and said: "Get in, it's party time."

"Man, this guy has it all," Leon thought to himself as he wondered what kind of house he was going to visit.

Chester pulled out of the garage and soon they were on the interstate headed north to Palm Beach. In a short while, they pulled off the freeway and snaked through half a dozen winding roads until they arrived at a snow white gate guarded on each side by a hedge of ten-foot hibiscus. Chester pushed a button in the center of the dashboard and the gates swung inward. Leon could see at the end of a long oyster shell driveway a seven thousand square foot two story home with a four car garage.

Chester wheeled the Mercedes to a spot in the circular driveway and turned the motor off. "Welcome to 'Casa de Whittaker' southern version."

As both men were opening their respective doors, a short, lightweight Latino looking man appeared to assist Leon with his door.

"Good afternoon sir. May I please take your bags? My name is Caesar."

"Why thank you. That would be great."

"Mr. Matthews will use the coral room off of the pool, Caesar.
Please set the bag in there and make sure it is all ready for him."

"Yes sir."

Chester hopped up the three steps to the front door of the house and just as he was reaching for the shiny brass door handle the door swung inward.

"You're a little early." remarked the extremely attractive olive skinned brunette.

"Another win for the team. There were some problems with the evidence and the judge threw the whole thing out." Whittaker gave the abbreviated report to his wife with a shrug of his shoulders and a wink.

"Honey, please meet Leon Matthews, Keeper of the Keys to the Everglades National Park and one of the guiding lights who helped me through college. Leon, this is the love of my life and the world's best Northern Italian culinary artist on the planet."

Gina's smile was genuine. "So wonderful to finally meet you. Chet has often tried to explain your life together at the Citadel and it always seems so unusual. All of those young men living together, it just seems strange. I don't get it. Please come in and make yourself at home."

"Babe, I'm going to get out of this suit. Could you entertain Leon for a few minutes and whip up a pitcher of Bombay Fizzes?"

"I'd be happy to."

Chester met Gina Soriano when he was in law school at the University of South Carolina. She was a graduate nursing student working on a Masters in Hospital Administration. He had been immediately attracted to her strong northern Italian beauty and her casual confidence. They dated informally for a while, attending a few USC sporting events together. Things had gotten more serious after he made arrangements to bring her home to Long Island for a Thanksgiving Holiday in his final year of law school.

Chester's family was immediately captivated by Gina's beauty and confidence. When she joined Mrs. Whittaker and the family cook in the kitchen, a serious courtship began.

Chester and Gina were married the summer after graduate school. It was the kind of a wedding one would expect for the eldest son of a successful Manhattan attorney and a beauty like Miss Soriano. Five hundred elite guests were in attendance and the whole affair was capped off with a luxurious honeymoon in a villa owned by one of Gina's uncles in Tuscany. The marriage was a good partnership, and the West Palm Beach Whitakers were a happy and contented couple. Their jet set lifestyle had thus far precluded them from raising a family. This situation was a continuing source of stress for Gina's second generation Italian-American parents.

"Please get comfortable." she pointed towards the huge sunken living room.

Matthews could not believe his surroundings. The modern mansion was open and airy. The shape of the living room was similar to a small theater. There was a rounded two step drop from the kitchen and dining area into a room adorned with tropical plants and leather upholstered couches and chairs. The floor was of large slabs of quarry slate in varying sizes and oriental and other woven rugs were in various locations throughout. Large pieces of original Italian art adorned the walls and a twenty-five-foot long series of sliding glass doors divided the room from a luxuriously appointed pool and hot tub plaza. The ceiling in the living room was nearly twenty feet above the floor and sky lights illuminated the room. Five life sized Italian marble statues were arranged around the patio as if to provide a Roman Guard to the enclosure.

"Not quite the average digs for a U.S. Park Ranger." he thought as he was taking it all in.

"These Bombay Fizzes are a great way to wind down from a long day in the Florida humidity," Gina announced as she stepped down into the living room. She carried a bamboo tray with a crystal pitcher full of an orange yellowish beverage with streaks of green liquid migrating downward. Floating in the vessel was one large ice cube and five or six pieces of fresh tropical fruit. Three tall glasses stood on the tray with the same liquid already poured into them over a healthy collection of ice cubes. Each had a colorful straw inserted and a slice of orange split and hanging half in and half out of the glass.

"It's a little thing we discovered in Bora Bora a couple of years ago. You start with a bottle of Bombay Gin and mix it with whatever fruit you find in the kitchen then add a half a bottle of 7up. Not hard to remember and it's very refreshing and a little different each time."

Gina leaned over and placed the tray on a glass topped table and as she did, her ample tanned breasts pushed with force on the upper edge of her lightweight cotton blouse. Matthews took notice and was admiring her beauty but quickly averted his eyes as she looked up. Gina smiled, handing him his drink and said "I hope you like them." Somehow he knew she was more than likely talking about her own tits than the drinks on the tray.

"I'm sure I will, they look great to me." Leon suddenly flushed.

The embarrassing moment was quickly interrupted.

"No matter how many times you go to the courthouse the feeling of winning never loses its impact," Chester smiled as he

exited from the long wide hallway. "Those look great!" Chester announced pointing towards the tray as he placed his arms around Gina.

Chapter Twenty-Four

"Good afternoon Captain, I'm Lieutenant Commander Vincent P. Lubar United States Coast Guard. This is Ensign Merrymore, Chief Petty Officer Loftus and Petty Officer Jones.

"I'm going to send Ensign Merrymore and Petty Officer Jones through the vessel for a quick security inspection while we all stay right here, then we can go over some of your safety requirements and the vessel's documents. Do you have any questions?"

"Nah, you guys go right ahead. I'm in no hurry. This isn't my first boarding. I'm just heading up to Mo Bay for a couple of days. Gotta drop off this mahogany and see if my expediter can get me something to take back to Honduras."

"So how did you get involved in this business?" Vince asked. He had good vibes about this guy. His gut feeling said he was legit.

"Oh, I was running tugs in the Northwest to Alaska and back. The weather sucked and I didn't like all the bullshit with the unions. If anything is going to ruin the United States, it will be those assholes. I've never seen an outfit with so many reasons not to do things needing to be done. Down here you can sign on a crew and they all want to work. None of the crap about this trade and that one. I got a chance once to bring a couple of barges down from Portland Oregon to St Thomas through the canal on a sweet contract with the Navy. What a trip! Anyhow, one of the partners who owned that tug set me up with this little group of investors to drive ships around here delivering stuff. This gig just started last month, but this is the coolest boat they have given me. If I had any business sense, I'd try to buy her and run it myself. But they take good care of me and I'm enjoying this ex-pat lifestyle. Besides, they are the ones with all of the business connections."

"Engine room, galley and staterooms all clear." squawked Vince's radio. He knew Merrymore and Jones would spend about ten more minutes looking for any signs that might indicate a violation. They would also look at all the firefighting and lifesaving equipment onboard to be included in their report of the boarding.

"You know, I think this is about the tenth time I've been boarded between the west coast and down here. But this is the only boat I have been on for more than one boarding. I was just trying to think of how many different boats I've been on. I think it's about fourteen."

"Wow, that's a lot. I've only been on four cutters since I started."

"I wouldn't trade life out here for anything. Course I'm single, so there ain't no one waiting for me to get back. How about you Commander?"

"Oh, I have a wife and son. And all this at sea stuff is great but there is nothing like time with your family," Vince replied.

"I'd like to bring them down here and charter a sailboat one of these days. But there just never seems to be enough time."

"Too much paper work eh?" grinned Higgins.

"You got that right."

"Another reason to do it the way I do. I get a phone call from these guys up in Atlanta to go here or there and pick up a load of wood or a couple of cars or some furniture. They fax me a bill of lading and we fill out a few customs documents and a manifest. All of the Latino dudes in their cute uniforms rubberstamp the shit out of everything and we deliver it. It's pretty simple to me."

"How do you get paid if you don't mind me asking?" Vince inquired.

"I get a decent salary in the US as a registered agent for the manager of the fund who controls the purchases and sales of the boats. You see on the documents the boats are owned by the trustees of the SESTA Funds Administrators LLC. They manage some sort of retirement fund for school teachers in Atlanta." Higgins spoke while he was pulling the vessels documentation papers out of a locked drawer located behind the back cushion of the settee astern of the helm. "I pay good old U.S. income tax and social security but heck, for me it's a good investment to have ya'll down here to save my ass if I get in trouble. The companies we ship for pay the guys in Atlanta. I get a cut paid right into my Cayman bank account. It's all legit, one of the bureaucrats in the embassy in Kingston helped me set it all up."

"Sounds like you have it all figured out."

"Well," Higgins added, "There is so much crazy shit going on down here, I decided from the get go to find out how to stay out of trouble."

It was ninety degrees in the hot sun when Ensign Merrymore and Petty Officer Jones emerged from the engine room; they were drenched in perspiration. "This is a very nicely kept boat XO."

"Excuse me for a minute Skipper. I need to talk to the guys for a moment," Lubar turned his back on Higgins and spoke to Ensign Merrymore.

"Well, what's it like down there?"

"It's hotter than hell sir. Nice boat though if there is anything bad down there, we can't find it. There are four slings of mahogany plywood and teak planks and the normal collection of crew clothing and groceries. There are enough life jackets down there for ten people and all of the pyro is current. This is a clean boarding. What do you think Jones?" Merrymore turned to the rookie boarding officer with a smile.

Billy Jones was drenched in sweat. His smile radiated the enthusiasm of a young adult experiencing a real life adventure for the first time and loving it. "I like this ship XO. I didn't see anything out of the ordinary. It would be pretty cool if we could get some of that wood down there and panel our mess deck."

"Whose budget do you think would pay for that?" was Lubar's response. "The engineers are spending every dime we get keeping the old tub running." He was pleased that the young petty officer was energized by the boarding activity.

"When we get back to the ship, I want you to bring me rough drawings of all of the compartments on this vessel and a short paragraph on what you saw down there. I'd like it within an hour after we get back on board."

"Yes sir!"

The XO turned his attention back to Higgins. "Do you and your crew have passports?"

"Sure do." He re-opened the drawer containing the vessel's documents"

Higgins produced his dark blue U.S. Passport issued three years earlier by the State Department office in the Federal Building in Seattle Washington. There were also two greenish covered booklets containing the passports of Manuel Salvador and Juan Castro de Mayo. Working visas were included in the two Honduran documents for work in the British West Indies and Belize.

He handed the passports to Ensign Merrymore who took Jones aside and to instruct him on completing the identity section of the CCIC generated boarding form.

"Rookies?" Higgins grinned to Lubar and nodded towards the two.

Vince smiled and nodded.

Vince turned back to Higgins. "We should be out of your way here in just a few more minutes. The guys on the bridge said you were interested in a carton or two of smokes."

"Yeah, if it is all right. I don't want to break any rules," Higgins laughed. "Actually, I've been trying to quit. My crew on the other hand will work twice as hard to load and unload heavy hardwood if they think they might get a pack or two of Yankee smokes at the end of the day. I brought three cartons down last time I was up in the states but they are all gone and I ain't going back for a while."

"Well, we brought you two cartons of Marlboro's if you are still interested. They're fifteen bucks each. I think that's about a third of what you would pay in Jamaica."

"Sounds like a good deal to me." Cory extracted a small stack of currency out of the drawer where the documents were kept. He handed Vince a ten and a twenty. "Say Commander, where are you headed next?"

"We've got a couple more patrol days left then we will probably take a break around here someplace. Why do you ask?"

"Cause we're going to be in Montego Bay for a while until we get another job and if I ran into you on the beach, I would like to buy you a beer."

Vince was thinking in another setting he and Higgins might have a lot in common. "If we get to Montego Bay and I see your boat there, I will try to find you. Thanks."

Ensign Merrymore and Jones were finishing up the boarding paperwork and preparing an official U.S. Coast Guard Certificate of Boarding attesting to the seaworthiness and safety features of Caribbean Gipsy.

"Here you go XO." Merrymore spoke as he placed the document in front of his superior for his signature.

Vince boldly scribbled his signature across the bottom of the certificate and handed it to Higgins.

"Here you go Captain, with this document and three or four bucks, you should be able to get a rum and coke in any bar in Jamaica."

"Thanks, I will add it to my collection." Higgins extended his right hand with a firm grip on Lubar's. "Have a good patrol and I hope you find what you're looking for."

"Thanks, have a safe voyage and stay away from the stuff we are looking for."

Higgins exchanged handshakes with Ensign Merrymore, Chief Loftus and petty officer Jones.

The coxswain maneuvered the Avon alongside on a hand signal given by Chief Loftus. The boarding party embarked in order of seniority and Petty Officer Jones was the last to leave Caribbean Gipsy. Once everyone was seated, the coxswain gunned the throttles. The propellers on the outboard motors bit harshly into the calm surface of the Caribbean Sea. Within five seconds, they had accelerated to nearly forty miles per hour and for a few moments everyone was refreshed with the cool moist spray of the sea and the wind on their faces.

Cory felt exhilarated. His heart was hammering in his chest and he felt a little euphoric. As he watched the little Coast Guard craft return to the 'Mother Ship', he thought to himself "I bet Trish would have enjoyed that."

Chapter Twenty-Five

"It's the craziest thing, there was this family I took pictures of last month, and they bought all of the pictures, I mean two whole rolls of film. Then he wanted to keep the proofs too," Beaufort E. Lee explained to Leon over a brown bag lunch while sharing a picnic table.

"When was that?"

"Oh, about three weeks ago. I don't know if you recognized them or not. It was one of them typical American families. Attractive athletic wife, handsome kid about eight years old and I think dad's in the Coast Guard. They were here with the wife's folks," Lee volunteered. "They came on the same boat as that Park Service fella who comes to see you once in a while, you know, the suit."

Mathews felt his anus go into an immediate spasm as a little liver bile dripped into his stomach. He was immediately nauseated.

"Were all of the photographs ones you would want to keep?"

"Nah, you know most of them I would have tossed. There were a couple of really nice shots with the flags in the background. Some of them had too many other people involved ya know."

"Wow, that's strange. How often does someone buy all of your photos?"

"Only once before, when the Vice President was down here during the last campaign. And it wasn't the boss who wanted them, it was those secret service guys in the suits and shades needing them."

Mathews interjected "Maybe this guy is a movie star or something." His nausea continuing to build and a headache started to throb.

"Nah, he's just on one of those Coast Guard ships up at the Naval Station. Name's Limbar or Lucas or Lubar, something like that. I didn't really get it because the father-in-law took care of the bill. He's a skipper or XO, a big shot of some kind. I tried to get to know a little more about him.

"Ya'll know that Suzie Steadman over at the newspaper is always asking me about interesting people I meet so she can do stories about them. I guess this guy just checked in to head up that new "used" Navy ship the Coasties got. An old buddy of mine at the communications station told me his last job was over in Italy working with Interpol or some other sleuth operation. I guess he was helping nail some big names in drug trafficking over there.

"Of course ya'll know Suzie, didn't she write a nice story about you when you came up from the Glades?

"Shit, look at that couple ain't she a doll. They look like newlyweds I better get to work. See ya later, Leon."

The little short fat photographer trotted off barely taking a breath after ending his conversation with Leon and beginning his pitch to the young couple over thirty feet away.

"Yeah right, I better get back to my paper work too, see you next time." Matthews mumbled unheard as Lee waddled away. On any other occasion, he would have stood and observed the always comedic and friendly man. Leon returned to his office, went directly to his private bathroom and vomited.

Chapter Twenty-Six

The Coast Guard Cutter ESCAPE hove to a mile and a half outside the channel leading into Montego Bay. It was 0815 in the morning. The skipper was sitting in his chair in the port corner of the bridge with a hot cup of coffee in his hand and the always present pair of Bushnell marine binoculars on a macramé lanyard around his neck. Ensign Merrymore was Officer of the Deck. His gut was tight. He had been scheduled to stand the 0800 to 1200 watch and until he was awakened by the reveille whistle at 0545, he was unaware of the late night message allowing ESCAPE to take a three-day port call in Jamaica. This was only his second opportunity to bring the ship into port. And this was a famous tourist destination. He wondered how many curious onlookers would be on the dock waiting for him to make a mistake.

Vince and Buzz were in the communications center waiting for their clearance and docking assignment to appear out of the teletypewriter. The duty radioman second class Dave West was fantasizing out loud to his superior officers as to all of the hot cruise ship female tourists he was planning to meet in the next seventy-two hours.

Suddenly, a jingle like an old bicycle bell rang and the rhythmic tat a tat a t a tat a tat of the mechanical teletypewriter began to sing out a written message from the Coast Guard Liaison Officer, U.S. Diplomatic Mission, Kingston Jamaica.

TO: COMMANDING OFFICER USCGC ESCAPE WMEC6
FROM: USCG LO US MISSION JAMAICA
INFO: COMMANDER CG DISTRICT 7 MIAMI FL
COMMANDER COAST GUARD GROUP CHARLESTON SC
COAST GUARD COMSTA CHARLESTON SC

CLASSIFIED CONFIDENTAL

SUBJECT – PORT CALL MONTGEO BAY

72 HR PORT OF CALL REQUESTED YOUR MESSAGE OCTOBER 12TH AUTHORIZED.
CO, XO CONTACT COM D7 DUTY OFFICER VIA SECURE LAND LINE WITHIN 4 HOURS OF ARRIVAL

MOOR SLIP 2 CRUISE SHIP TERMINAL WARF. ONE NCL SHIP IN PORT, ETD 1800HRS TOMORROW. NO OTHER VESSELS SKED DURING YOUR PORT CALL.

EMBASSY STAFF ENROUTE MOBAY FOR CREW AND CUSTOMS INDOCTRINATION ETA 1000 HRS LOCAL. NO SHORE LEAVE OR LIBERTY UNTIL INDOCTRINATION COMPLETED. ALL HANDS REQUIRED TO ATTEND IAW LOCAL AGREEMENTS WITH HOST NATION DIPLOMATIC MISSION.

WELCOME TO JAMAICA. ENJOY YOUR VISIT.

BT /

"Well that sucks" was the first words spoken by Petty Officer West after the teletype stopped. "Only one cruise ship here and they leave tomorrow."

"You will find a way to survive, Westy. You know there are a lot of interesting things to do here. Who knows, you might meet someone besides an American tourist if you look around." advised the XO.

While they were joking, Petty Officer West made copies of the dispatch for distribution. He handed the clipboard to Vince who initialed it and passed it on to Ensign Ladner. Ladner turned and opened the secure door and pressed a button signaling the messenger of the watch to come. He would quickly deliver the message to the Commanding Officer and all the other officers indicated on the cover sheet. This passing of the word would take five minutes.

"Wonder what's up in Miami," the XO inquired out loud to Ensign Ladner.

"Don't ask me. You're the one with all the stripes," joked the younger officer. He wondered how many years it would be until there were messages arriving at his own duty station asking him to get involved in some high level discussions on secret plans.

"Let's go topside and watch your buddy bring this old gal into Jamaica."

Chapter Twenty-Seven

"Law Office."

"Good morning Connie. This is Leon Matthews, is Chester available?"

"I believe so, let me check."

"Mr. Whittaker, Leon Matthews is on the line."

"Oh yeah great, I'll take the call. I wonder what he is up to." Chester replied into the office intercom.

"What's up Leon?" Chester picked up the phone and pressed a key on his computer that created a static shield in the office phone system, making it impossible to record the call.

"Hey, I think I need some legal help." There was an obvious shakiness to the voice. "Someone took a photograph of me in an inappropriate situation at the park last month. It could be pretty compromising and some of my best friends from college could be pulled into the mess if I can't take care of it quietly."

Chester knew what Leon was talking about had something to do with the drug operations payoffs or the communication intercept gear.

"What the hell have you done Leon? You weren't screwing one of the interns from the Citadel were you?" Chester asked with a chuckle while small beads of perspiration formed above his upper lip. "Hey, it's Friday. Why don't you come on down to Florida for the weekend? In fact, take a few vacation days and stay through the week. We'll go out in the boat and talk about your problem. It might do you some good to get away for a while. Tell you what. I'll even take care of your ticket down here and Tom will pick you up at the airport."

"That sounds great, I could use a little break from all of this southern hospitality. It would be fun to see Tom again too. We have a lot to catch up on," Matthews answered with a slight quiver in his voice.

"Great, we'll see you tonight." Chester hung up and could see his hand shaking as he cradled the handset.

"Connie, get in touch with Boca Travel. Tell them to get Mr. Leon Matthews on a flight down from Charleston South Carolina this afternoon. Have a first class ticket ready for him at the counter then call him with the details. When that's all set, get in touch with Tom. Have him meet Leon at the airport and bring him to the boat. Tell Tom we are going to have a little reunion on the boat and he should plan to come along."

"Yes sir. Sounds like fun. I will take care of it right away. Is there anything else?" Connie jotted down on a yellow legal pad the instructions dealing with Mr. Matthews and Tom Thrasher and the boat.

"Yes, on another matter, I think it is time for me to get together with Ms. Dixon, the SESTA Fund auditor gal in Robert's office in Atlanta. She is working on a new project for me and we need to hammer out details next week. Could you make the usual arrangements for her to be here Tuesday or Wednesday?"

"Sure thing sir."

"That will do Connie. Thanks and I don't want to take any calls for the rest of the day unless it's Gina."

"Yes, sir."

An hour earlier, Chester Whittaker had been feeling pretty good. He heard from one of the associates in Robert's office that a class action law suit over credit card fraud charges was shaping up to be worth a lot more money than originally thought. Things were going well. Then an associate in his own office reported the State of Florida had dropped the charges on one of his clients. The preliminary investigation showed the Dade County Sheriff's department had botched up the chain of custody on ten pounds of cocaine by leaving it in a restaurant overnight. Apparently the detectives had stopped for a late night snack on the way back to the station house and left the cocaine on the counter in the cafe. The happy client will cheerfully relinquish the twenty-thousand-dollar retainer to the Whittaker Law Firm in exchange for his freedom.

Now, concern over his conversation with Leon was burning a hole in his stomach. He quickly downed four or five antacid tablets and poured a stiff shot of single malt scotch. He consumed it in one gulp.

"What else can screw up the day?" Chester wondered as he pulled up Leon's vessel report on his computer screen.

At the moment, there were three operations underway. The big one was Cory Higgins vessel, Caribbean Gipsy, which was still three or four weeks away from the pickup date and today appeared to be located near the western coast of Jamaica. He had been boarded by the Coast Guard a couple of days ago and as expected, nothing unusual had been discovered. Rob Byrd and Carl Petersen were in a chartered sailboat southbound toward Colombia. They were on their way to pick up two crew members and about four tons of grass and half ton of Lebanese Hashish.

At least for the next couple of days there wouldn't be anything to worry about out on the ocean.

He picked up the telephone and called Gina with the news that Leon would be in town for the weekend. She was delighted at the opportunity to show off her culinary wizardry.

Chapter Twenty-Eight

Approaching the government moorings in Montego Bay, the old Coast Guard Cutter presented a formidable presentation of organization, discipline and professionalism. On the bow, stern, amidships, on the bridge and in the engine room, crewmembers with sound powered telephone headsets were standing by to take orders from Ensign Merrymore.

On the wharf stood three dark skinned men, employees of the port authority. If personnel safety were a concern of the local maritime industry, it was not apparent from this trio. The tallest, a bit older than the other two and obviously the supervisor, wore a pair of cutoff jeans, a rope belt and flip flops. His dark black naked chest and shoulders sparkled in the late morning sun. The shortest of the crew and probably youngest looking about fifteen years old, wore a bright yellow tank top bearing a silkscreen print of Bob Marley holding a large marijuana joint in one hand and an electric guitar in the other. He had close cut hair and wore a very brief bright orange bathing suit and nothing on his feet. By contrast, the third member of the dockside assist team wore a long sleeve chambray shirt with a faded insignia of a second class petty officer in the U.S. Navy on the left sleeve, a nice pair of flowered shorts and almost new American sneakers on his feet. There was no sign of gloves, hard hats or life jackets.

The skipper was sitting comfortably in his chair. The Executive officer stood on the starboard bridge wing with Ensign Merrymore. Ops Boss LT Sutton was standing next to the skipper. All four officers were adorned with a set of binoculars, each stenciled with their shipboard designation CO, XO, OPS, and OOD. As all four officers focused on the dock, Dave Flood chortled "Looks like the chamber of commerce sent their best to greet us."

With butterflies in his gut, Ensign Merrymore issued orders to the helmsman and engine order telegraph operator commencing ESCAPE's approach to the wharf. The XO standing beside him concurred with various commands with a nearly imperceptible nod of his head. Moving the sixteen-hundred-ton ship slowly up to the dock was accomplished perfectly by the young ensign.

As the ship approached the dock, a black GMC suburban with official diplomatic license plates appeared on the dock. All of the windows were tinted to a shade just as black as the exterior of the vehicle. The car stopped about fifteen yards from the edge of the dock. All three of the passenger doors opened simultaneously and three men stepped out. The driver remained inside. All three were dressed in tropical shirts and wearing lightweight trousers. They assembled next to one another just out of the way of mooring lines. The youngest of this trio was carrying an attaché case. In the center, Vince recognized his old classmate Gus Solomon holding a large parchment colored envelope.

As five minutes elapsed and the ship moved closer to the dock, a crowd of curious onlookers grew. Fifteen or twenty had ridden up on bicycles and many just seemed to appear to see the large white Cutter. The supervisor of the "welcome committee" directed the young lad in the orange swim trunks to take over crowd control while he sent his other companion to the stern of the ship to receive the stern lines. The young Jamaican in the swim suit took to his authority like a Texas Ranger and directed a score of onlookers to remain behind an imaginary line on the wharf.

With the unemployment rate in Jamaica around twenty-eight percent, whenever a ship full of American servicemen arrived in a port, an immediate spike in local economic activity ensued.

Once the position of the ship on the dock was determined, several in the group immediately erected small portable kiosks from which they would be marketing all manner of Jamaican goods and souvenirs. Their companions appeared with bags, boxes and carts containing everything from teak carvings to fresh coconuts. Within an hour of the ships arrival, an entire mini street market would be in full operation.

With the bow of the ship eight feet from the wharf, Ensign Merrymore after observing a slight nod from his commanding officer, initiated the mooring process. He then looked at the oldest of the host nation line handlers and gave him a thumbs up signal which was returned in kind. Then he gave the command: "Put over line one!" Immediately, Yeoman Second Class Jensen repeated the command in the mouthpiece of her sound powered phone; "Put over line one!" Second Class Boatswain Mate Smith on the bow of the ship repeated the command loudly and it was again repeated by Seaman Wilson as he wound up like a major league pitcher and let fly the heaving line attached to ESCAPE'S six inch mooring line. The knotted monkey fist on the end of the heaving line landed on the old wooden planks on the dock with a loud thud. The young Texas Ranger Jamaican in the swimming trunks scampered over to the spot and reeled in the heaving line followed by the heavy mooring line and upon a signal from Ensign Merrymore, looped the eye of the line over a large bollard on the wharf. For the first time in three and a half weeks, the ship was once again attached to land. Similar commands and activities were carried out over the next five minutes until all four lines were securely made up to cleats and bollards on the dock.

As the lines were being attached to the dock, Commander Flood spotted a vessel moored across the harbor at the fishing pier. "Hey XO, isn't that the lumber freighter we boarded a couple of days ago?"

Vince picked his binoculars and looked in the same direction as his commanding officer. He spotted the nicely painted dark blue hull of the Caribbean Gipsy. "Sure is. He said he was headed here and it looks like he is doing exactly what he told us he would. That forklift has a good-sized load of mahogany logs in front of the mill."

"Nice way to make a living if you ask me." Flood hopped down from his seat.

"Yes, he said he has a girlfriend up in the states is meeting him here for a few days before he heads back to Honduras."

"I bet she is one hot cookie. Like I said, nice way to make a living."

Once the ship was secured to the dock, a new flurry of activity ensued. The deck force hoisted the gangway over the side to allow shore side access to the ship. Next, the heavy four-hundred-amp shore power lines were lifted to the dock and connected to the Jamaican power grid. Each island in the Caribbean seemed to have a different type of receptacle for connecting to shore power. ESCAPE'S electricians quickly invented yet another adapter for this port and tagged it with a large yellow label inscribed with the word MOBAY. Everyone onboard was anxiously wrapping up their duties anticipating a few days ashore in this historic town. Once the gangway was secured, Ensign Merrymore and the Quartermaster of the Watch made the appropriate announcement about the Officer of the Deck moving his watch from the bridge to the quarterdeck. An announcement was also made; no one was to leave the ship until the Coast Guard representative from the Embassy briefed the crew on local important issues. This would take place in a half an hour and attendance was mandatory.

Vince waited at the quarterdeck when his old friend Lieutenant Commander Gus Solomon bounded up the gangway saluting the American flag then returning the salute rendered by the quartermaster of the watch. Solomon was followed by two other men in their late twenties. One was Lieutenant Steve Pope, the Coast Guard Liaison Officer assigned to the American embassy in Kingston and the other was Jim Mitchell, also a Coast Guard Lieutenant. He was an attorney assigned to the Law Enforcement Division at Seventh Coast Guard District in Miami. Crisp military salutes and handshakes were exchanged between all of the officers even though the three visitors were bedecked in tropical shirts and Bermuda shorts.

Vince directed the quartermaster or the watch to have Ops Boss LT Sutton hailed to the quarterdeck. When he arrived, introductions were made and Phil Sutton took charge of working with LT Pope to organize the briefing for the crew. The trio of Solomon, Lubar and Mitchell worked their way down the passageway to the executive officer's stateroom. Once inside, Vince offered seats. A photo of Vince, Denise and their son Jeff was on display over the desk and a couple official photographs of other ships were hung on the bulkheads. His desk was awash with personnel records and several legal sized pads with notes written everywhere. "This looks familiar." joked Solomon. "The XO's life is a constant paper drill."

"Yeah, you start on your first day aboard and keep going until you are relieved by the next guy and wonder if you ever really got anything done," replied Lubar. The military attorney glanced at the clutter of papers, just shook his head and grinned.

The XO asked Gus, "You must have found something interesting in those photographs."

"Well, yes, no, and maybe. We think you may have stumbled on to something but we aren't too sure what."

"What do you mean?"

"It appears that the guy who brought the briefcase to Fort Sumter is named Tom Thrasher. He's an attorney. He looks a lot like a surfer bum but I found he is a Cum Laude graduate from Cornell Law School. Pretty smart too. He finished high school at sixteen and was in his second year of law school when he turned twenty. He's never been married but from what we have been able to find out, he is not gay. Lots of girlfriends, fast cars and travel seem to be his main hobbies. Coincidentally, he defended a case for a couple of suspects when I was Ops Boss on COURAGEOUS three years ago. He got the case dismissed because the customs guys had a breach in the chain of custody.

The custody issues seem to screw up more cases than ever these days. It took me a few days to figure out where I had seen him before. But then he woke me up in a dream at three am one night after a 48-hour shift at CCIC."

Lieutenant Mitchell added, "He works for a law office in West Palm Beach called the Whittaker Law Firm. It is part of a three office family operation with dad in New York, Chester Whittaker running the firm in Florida and a brother Robert has a practice in Atlanta.

"In New York, the senior Whittaker is basically retired and lives on Long Island Sound while his senior partners run the practice in midtown Manhattan. In Atlanta, Robert is more in to politics than his law practice. His wife is the Lieutenant Governor's daughter and he is making a run for Atlanta City Council in the November election. His big brother in Florida looks after things in Georgia with a couple of the senior partners there. The Atlanta firm also manages investment funds through their securities department.

"When you add up all three offices, there are about sixty lawyers and paralegals and a dozen CPAs and four or five investigators involved. They do everything from family law to criminal trials and pension fund management. From all we have found, they are squeaky clean. No problems or issues with any government agencies whatsoever. The Florida office is the only one having anything to do with the drug smuggling industry. They defend a lot of the people we arrest. And, they are extraordinarily successful at it."

Chapter Twenty-Nine

When the plane touched down in Fort Lauderdale, the jolt woke Leon Matthews from a dream just as a prison guard was slamming the door to a cell in some unknown house of incarceration. His upper lip and forehead were soaked in sweat. He glanced to his left and remembered the seat next to him as been empty when they departed Charleston. He wasn't accustomed to flying first class and hadn't expected to but when Connie from Chester's office made the reservation, it had not occurred to her to make any other sort of arrangement. Leon was startled at first when he picked up his ticket and found he was assigned to row two, seat number four. The stewardess offered him a cocktail within ten seconds after he had taken his seat. He was able to down two mini bottles of 100 proof vodka before the plane backed away from the terminal. The flight had taken an offshore course from North Charleston. As the plane ascended he could see the island housing the historically important monument of Fort Sumter.

It was his to manage, it was his to protect and it was his to show off with pride to his fellow citizens. He was pondering how many visitors had come there through the years and been able to learn about the history of the great civil war. Then his thoughts quickly turned to how he had betrayed the trust of the country and with the help of his old Citadel buddy, had turned the famous island into an important logistical asset of an international drug smuggling operation.

During the incident with his employees from the Everglades Monument, Leon couldn't recall exactly how the topic had come up. But when visiting Chester at home after the courtroom incident he had mentioned his tour of duty in Florida was about over so he was looking forward to being relocated. He also mentioned the possibility that the superintendent job at Fort Sumter might be available. Getting back to South Carolina would be a treat for him. Chester indicated his father was a good friend with the Secretary of the Interior and if he wanted, he would see if dad could put in a good word for him.

Whittaker had also defended the brother of the secretary four years earlier on a charge of possession of large quantities of prescription narcotics. His team of lawyers had gotten the case dismissed and managed to accomplish the task without any press coverage.

Matthews said he didn't want to bother people in such important positions but Chester insisted. Within two weeks, Leon was reassigned to become Superintendent of Fort Sumter National Monument. The position included a twenty-five percent pay increase and housing on the island.

Once situated in the new job, Leon made arrangements to travel back to Palm Beach to treat his old roommate to a fine dinner and a night out. He knew Chester could afford anything he wanted but the attorney accepted the offer and the two old pals enjoyed a great night out on the town in South Beach Miami. The new Superintendent was happy to pick up the tab for most of the evening. Leon was then invited back to Whittaker's home for the remainder of his stay in Florida.

Out on the boat, anchored in a cove along the ICW the following day, Chester began playing Matthews like a carp on lightweight tackle. The conversations began with the attorney inquiring into the old hobby of high frequency single sideband radio communications. Leon was still very involved and the location of his new job on the island provided a perfect intercept point for radio signals. It had something to do with the geographic location of Fort Sumter and some sort of frequency anomaly allowing voice messages to be heard from as far away as China. Something about a good frequency bounce off of the atmosphere and a thermal layer over the Atlantic amplified something. The technical aspects bored Chester within two or three minutes, but he already knew the region around Charleston was a very hot area for the reception of radio communication waves. That was why the U.S Coast Guard had placed their worldwide communication station just eight miles up the Ashley River.

"What kind of stuff do you listen to?"

"Oh, it's all over the chart. There are fishermen talking about catches and who got drunk last night, wives talking to their husbands on big tankers going across the ocean and the Coast Guard talking
about their choppers and boats helping people out," Leon stated. "Sometimes when people are in a little trouble or need to talk to someone on a telephone, I'm able to hook them up through a phone patch and they can talk to each other from halfway around the world."

"That must be interesting." Chester replied, his mind stuck on Leon's mention of being able to overhear Coast Guard communications. "So how big of a pay raise did you get with the transfer and promotion?"

"Well," pondered Leon. "I'm making as much as a bird colonel and it would have taken me twice this long to have this kind of an income if I had gone into the army after college."

"And you wouldn't have been able to smoke a little dope once in a while as an officer in the army either would you?" Chester stated with a wink and a smile as he lit up a fat Cuban cigar. He had offered one to Matthews but he rejected it.

This question had caught Leon a little off guard. He wondered why Chester had brought up the subject of salary. He downed a double swallow of single malt scotch.

"What if you could add the annual salary of a three-star general tax free to your present Park Ranger pay?"

"I'm not sure what you mean." Inquired Leon

"Oh, I was just thinking about something." There was some caution in the attorney's voice but the statement was made to get Matthews to go a little further.

"When you look at the things I have, what do you think?"

"Well, it looks to me like you've done pretty damn well for yourself. I doubt anyone from the Class of '74 has done as well as you."

"And how do you think I make all this money?"

"It's obvious. You are a damn good attorney, you have great people working for you and you get people out of trouble. For your service they pay well."

"Well, that's part of it. But when you carry on a continued relationship with your clients as most attorneys do, often new opportunities come your way."

"Yes."

"I have spent a few years bailing out some of the most successful business and political people I know. Couple that experience with the knowledge I gained at how poorly the law enforcement authorities prepare their cases, I thought there must be place in the industry for an investor like myself."

Leon's brain felt like it was going to burst. "Do you mean .. .?" was all he could muster. He took another gulp of whiskey.

"Do I mean what?" knowing exactly the question his friend wanted to ask but was unsure as to how.

"Are you, I mean, do you, you're not like involved in, you know um."

"Come on man! Say what you want to say." Whittaker enjoyed sparring with his tongue tied friend and poured him another double shot which Leon immediately consumed in one gulp.

"Are you somehow involved in drug smuggling?" Leon was finally able to ask.

"Well old buddy, I can't really answer your question until you answer the one I asked."

"Which question?"

"The one when I asked you if you would like to add tax free three-star general's pay to your income." Chester leaned over the teak table and placed three more chunks of ice into Leon's crystal glass then again filled it with whiskey.

Leon wore a loose it fitting Hawaiian shirt but still felt a lot of moisture in his armpits even as the cool evening marine breeze kept the space comfortable. He picked up the glass of liquor and drank a third of it.

"Well, how does it work?"

"How does what work?"

"You know, the thing with drugs."

"You need to answer the other question first."

"Ok, yes of course who wouldn't want to quadruple their income and not have to pay taxes on it."

"There is some risk though. But isn't there risk in just about anything we do in making our lives more comfortable?

"Tell me Leon, if you could make an extra couple hundred grand a year and have the very remote risk of losing your cushy government job, would you consider doing something just a little bit illegal? Heck, I have seen drunk drivers spend more time in the clink than most of the people involved in this stuff.

"Here's the deal. We can quit this conversation right now and you can go back to Charleston tomorrow and it will be as though we never talked. Or, you can stick around here for another day and I will show you how you can help me with my businesses and I will see to it that you are quite comfortable in your life."

Leon thought you only live once and here was an opportunity to get ahead in life, albeit in an illegal fashion. He didn't know what role Chester had for him. His friend was such a successful attorney, if things did go a little sideways down the stretch he certainly would have a good defense counsel.

"I'll try one of those cigars now. I suppose I should get used to the finer things in life. So what could a park ranger in a confederate uniform do to help your business?"

Over the next two days, the two former cadets acted like college students on a research project. They decided upon his return to Fort Sumter, Leon would prepare a request for the Parks Service to replace the six flagpoles on the pavilion at the monument. They were thirty years old and rotting at their bases. Matthews would report his predecessor he had noticed this flaw and determined it to be a safety issue. The new flagpoles would be made of a fiberglass composite material. Chester knew a manufacturer in South Florida. The owner of that firm also a client of the Whittaker Law Firm. Each of the flagpoles would contain an antenna extending ninety feet above the surface of the island. Each of those antennae would be connected to a receiving device. Leon could monitor the radio frequencies used by the U.S. Coast Guard, the Customs Service and the Drug Enforcement Administration. The receivers would be located in a lower basement of the Fort Sumter garrison. Twice daily he could obtain a report titled the "The Two a Day Report."

The Two a Day is a requirement of every Coast Guard ship and aircraft on patrol. It provides the service with strategic information as to the whereabouts of each unit and their operational intentions over the next twelve hours or beyond. Knowing this, various rescue coordination centers around the world can begin lifesaving search and rescue missions the moment a distress signal is received.

Chester's motivation for obtaining this knowledge was to advise any smuggling vessel in which he had an interest as to the whereabouts and intentions of law enforcement.

An interesting development in the advancing technical world was the wireless facsimile receiver. These were designed so ships at sea could contact service centers and obtain printed weather synopsis data and maps. Such information helped plan passages and avoid storms and low-pressure systems. Chester would purchase a state of the art weather fax machine and had have it installed in the basement of Fort Sumter directly below Leon's office. Leon would request a weather map from NOAA. When it arrived, he would plot the positions and intentions of all Coast Guard vessels in the area.

Obtaining the fax receivers for the boats was not a problem either. They were readily available at most fishing supply outlets.

Whenever a boat Chester controlled was underway with contraband, they would receive from Leon a weather facsimile map of their global location. Coast Guard patrol information was inscribed and diagrammed on the map. The crew of the smuggling vessel would now have real time knowledge of the location and activities of law enforcement units in their vicinity. With this information, they could avoid detection.

After installation, the system worked flawlessly for nearly four years until a little mouthy fatso photographer had fucked it up by taking a few pictures of that son-of-a-bitch from the Coast Guard. Waking from his vodka induced dream state, he was ready to fill Chester in on the details of the photo grab by LCDR Lubar.

The airplane taxied up to the terminal and the flight attendant welcomed the passengers to the Palm Beach International Airport. Leon stood up, got out of the comfortable seat and forced his mind to focus on the problems at hand.

Chapter Thirty

"So what happens next?" Vince asked the attorney.

The three officers looked at one another and agreed the next move was going to be made by someone with a higher pay grade.

"Well, the guys at DEA know what we know and will be coordinating things on their end."

"They plan on placing someone undercover inside Fort Sumter to see what they can find. There will be a classified bulletin advising everyone to be on the lookout for connections to the Whittaker family and I guess we just keep doing our jobs."

Vince told the group: "We need to brief the skipper."

The indoctrination of the crew concerning local customs and courtesies being delivered by Lieutenant Pope was just winding up. Laughter was coming from the fantail where the Skipper was addressing his crew. He cautioned everyone to watch out for one another.

Lubar picked up the sound powered phone and rang the quartermaster of the watch.

"Quarterdeck aye XO!"

"Yes, please send a messenger to tell Mr. Sutton I would like to see him in my stateroom."

"Aye-Aye sir."

"Captain." Vince saw his boss approaching.

"Well XO, are we ready to grab your buddies and go out for a couple of beers and Jamaican food?"

"There's nothing I would like better but we have a little situation I think you need to know about. It's got to do with those photos from Fort Sumter."

"OK, what's up?"

"Yeah, I'm not sure what it is all about but I think you will be as amazed as the rest of us. We could not have written all of this if we were making a movie script. I'd like to get OPS, Gus Solomon and Lt Mitchell, the lawyer from Miami, in your cabin for a short meeting." Vince requested.

"Sure, let's talk. Give me five minutes."

"We'll be there."

Vince walked a few steps to the door of his own stateroom as the skipper closed the cabin door. When he entered his own domain, Gus and Lt Sutton were sitting on the couch and LT

Mitchell was standing looking at a lithograph of an old revenue cutter in a frame on the bulkhead.

"So, what's up?" asked Solomon.

"Give him about five and we will meet in the cabin."

"I've been filling Phil here in on the details."

"What do you think?"

Sutton's voice was interrupted by the captain's on the squawk box near the XO's desk. "Ok, XO." was all he needed to say.

"Let's go." Lubar opened the door and exited, walking four steps to the commanding officer's cabin. The others crowded into the small companionway behind him as he knocked on the door bearing a brass plaque engraved with the solitary word "Captain". Vince knocked three times.

"Enter."

The short parade of Coast Guard Officers followed Vince in order of seniority. The attorney was the last to enter and close the door. Commander Flood was sitting behind his desk neatly arranged with a standard issue desktop blotter with a one-year government calendar displayed. Behind him was his neatly made up bunk, slightly larger than Lubar's and at the foot of the bed there was a two tiered bookshelf containing several dozen novels and documentaries. Most of the titles were of stories concerning life and adventures at sea or historical readings of shipwrecks and storms. Closer to the desk another bookshelf contained all the reference material required to aid an officer through a tour of duty as Commanding Officer. Bolted and welded to the inside bulkhead was a two foot by three-foot iron safe. About the cabin were various photographs of ships. One shot caught the eye of Solomon, a black and white photo of a much younger Dave Flood. He stood on the bow of a grey and camouflaged eighty-two-foot Coast Guard patrol boat. He was holding an M16 automatic rifle, had two bandoliers of ammunition strapped around his chest, a canteen on his belt and several hand grenades clipped to his shirt. He looked dirty and sweaty and his trousers cut off at the knees. He was flanked by six other men. Behind the boat was dense jungle. Typewritten and fading on a strip of paper at the bottom of the picture were the words Mekong Delta Yacht Club Class of '68.

Flood noticed Gus looking and when he turned around he saw him smiling and said "Life was so much simpler back then. Do your job well and you may live. Do a shitty job and you will die. So what brings you gents to my humble abode?"

"Yes Captain" began Vince. "You know about those photographs from Fort Sumter; well Mr. Solomon has been working to find out who the guy is and interesting information is emerging."

Vince, Solomon and LT Mitchell went through the history of the preliminary investigation.

"You gents have been busy. Let's let the system do its job and after this patrol we will be able to hunt for some interesting folks."

Then smiling the Skipper slapped both hands, palms down on his desk blotter and said "OK XO, like I asked a half hour ago, are we ready to go have a few beers and some jerk barbeque? I think it's time to relax and enjoy Montego Bay."

"We have a cab waiting." LT Sutton replied.

The skipper responded. "What say we all meet at the quarter deck in ten minutes."

"Uniform of the day is Hawaiian shirts, sandals and shorts. Oh hey, what about your friend from the embassy, Mr. Pope?" The skipper asked LT Mitchell.

"Oh, he's already set to go ashore with a couple of your junior officers. We'll probably run into them along the way."

Gus indicated he would take Mr. Mitchell for a quick tour to show him what a real working ship was all about and Vince and the Ops Boss went to their respective staterooms to change into "the uniform of the day."

Chapter Thirty-One

"This is Trish."

"Yes Miss Dixon, Connie from the Florida office is calling."

"Ok, thanks. I'll take it."

"Hi Connie. How is everything in your sunshine state?"

"Just fine Miss Dixon. And how is everything in yours."

"It's great here but I would love to dip my toes into the ocean."

"Well dear, a wish just came true. Chester was wondering if you would fly out on Sunday for a day or two to go over a few things."

Trish paused, knowing she had other plans but when Chester called and it had to do with SEASTA, it meant some discussion of an upcoming contraband shipment was in order and everything else in life needed to be cancelled. "Ok, I'll get things tidied up here and be there probably late Sunday or Monday."

"Sounds fine, is there anything you want me to take care of over here for you?"

"No, Jenny here will set it all up. I will get my regular room at the Shorebird. I will give you a call when I'm settled."

"Ok, I will leave a note for Mr. Whittaker. He is getting ready to meet with a couple of old classmates for an afternoon of 'guy time' out on the boat this afternoon."

Knowing that Chester was meeting with old Citadel cronies confirmed the reason for the summons to Florida.

"Thanks Connie. See you soon." Trish hung up the phone and said to herself; "Aw, shit!" She had been reading reams of reports on company profiles and management changes within the corporations listed in the portfolio. She needed a distraction but this was not it. She took off her reading glasses, placed her head in her hands rubbing the back of her neck beneath her hair she massaged her own neck. She was thinking if she were not such a strong woman, she just might cry. In all of the important financial work she did, her life of crime took precedence over everything else.

For two weeks, she had been trading telegrams with Cory. They were planning a rendezvous in Ocho Rios Jamaica the following Wednesday. She knew this would probably be the last time they could get together before the big shipment to Virginia. She had already made the flight arrangements on Cayman Air and had a limo scheduled to drive her across the Island to a bungalow on the north side of the island. She had been looking forward to a little diversion from work stuff, time on the beach and glorious sex. Now it felt like the encounter would be out of the question.

Trish quickly regained her composure and picked up the interoffice phone and called the office travel coordinator Jenny. She asked her to make all of the arrangements for her trip to Florida.

She then pulled a blank Western Union telegram draft from her desk drawer and placed it in her typewriter. In the text line she wrote simply "Duty calls at CW. I will catch you next time." And on the "from" line she simply put in the initials TD.

She folded the document up and placed it in her handbag.

Trish knew of five Western Union locations within a mile of the Whittaker Law Firm. A fax machine was a quick way to communicate with routine matters but when a receipt for important correspondence was needed and time was of essence, a telegram is still the best way to exchange information.

She would stop at one of these and drop the telegram and Cory would get it when he stopped in Montego Bay. She was very disappointed in having to call off the rendezvous. She just hoped he would be as disappointed too.

As she shuffled through endless piles of spreadsheets and financial reports, she thought back to her first meeting with Cory on Abaco. He had been so standoffish upon meeting her but he warmed up to her during that lunch. She reflected on his masculinity, neatly trimmed blond hair and a small tattoo of a whale on the back of his left calf. She grinned and thought how Cory was so different from that jackass Rohn Villa.

"Christ," she thought "He's only been dead a few years and I haven't given him a second thought for months."

How different the two men were. Villa had been a businessman with an unending need for cocaine and an ego that comes with most people in the automobile industry. In his peer group, he had many friends but everyone seemed so phony.

And then there was Cory. Here was a guy who was a criminal business man smuggling contraband and he was the gentlest and kind man she knew. His life though was lonely and she hoped in some way she was bringing him the love and companionship he lacked.

Chapter Thirty-Two

Leon always felt good when he set foot on Florida soil. The smell of the tropical foliage, the ocean and the breezes always refreshed him. After a brief stop at baggage claim, his suitcase was the second piece on the conveyor. He was feeling lucky. He hoped luck would prevail because he was quite worried about his future right now.

As he walked through the automatic doorway leaving the air conditioned terminal, the full force of the warm Florida air engulfed him. At the curb about thirty feet from the doorway, Tom Thrasher stood next to the open driver's side door of a brand new black Porsche convertible. He was talking with two very attractive, well dressed and deeply tanned women. Leon envied Thrasher's confidence around women. His golden blond hair was blowing in the breeze and his smile displayed perfectly aligned snow white teeth. He was wearing a dark tropical shirt and professionally pressed tan cotton trousers. He handed one of his business cards to the taller of the two women and said, "Give me a call next week." He winked at her. Then he turned his attention to Leon with a big smile, handshake and a slap on the back.

"Hey Ranger Rick. How's everything up at the fort?"

"Never better." Leon replied with a quiver in his voice.

Thrasher clicked the key fob in his hand and the Porsche's luggage compartment popped open. He grabbed Leon's bags and stuffed them inside.

"This is a nice one." Leon spoke as he ran his hand along the top of the passenger side door.

"Oh yeah, but it's not exactly mine. An attorney friend of mine is overseas for a couple of months and asked me to take care of it."

"Wow, that's nice babysitting duty. He sure must trust you."

"Yes she does," Tom smiled as he jammed the shifter into first gear and released the clutch, leaving a slight chirp from the rear tires as they pulled away from the curb.

Within seconds, they were speeding down interstate 95 towards West Palm Beach. Tom was enjoying the opportunity to drive this car. As he accelerated through the gears, Leon felt pinned to the back of the grey leather seat. "So what's going on? Chester says you may have someone snooping around."

"Well, it's just a feeling in my gut. You know that little fat fucker Beaufort Lee who is always taking pictures?"

"Yes. He's harmless isn't he?"

"Oh yeah, he ain't really involved but it seems like the last time you came by there was some big wig Coast Guard officer at the park and he took pictures of him."

"So, isn't that how he makes a living?"

"Well, I think you and I were in some of the pictures."

"Shit, you hang out at a park and a photographer takes pictures, there is a chance that you might get your picture taken." Tom still didn't understand the significance.

"Well, the Coast Guard dude came by Lee's studio a couple of days later and walked off with every picture the guy took that day!"

Thrasher eased his foot off the gas and the car slowed down to about seventy miles per hour. "Whoa! You mean this guy came by and snapped up all of the pictures Lee took at the fort last time you and I met there? Did he say why?"

"No, only one other time a customer wanted all of the pictures but it was when the Vice President was there four or five years ago. His security guys wanted them.

"I can understand the VP, but a Coast Guard Officer, why? I wonder if there were any shots of us."

"I'm not sure and I didn't want to say anything to Lee. You know how he talks to anyone who will listen and a lot who don't."

"This might be serious," Thrasher mumbled as he downshifted, merging right into the Palm Beach exit. "Chester is going to be pissed."

"That's what I was thinking but I had to tell him as soon as I found out. What do you think?"

"I don't know but we may have to lay low for a while. I know there is a big operation early next month. It will be the biggest one yet. Everyone will do pretty well on payday."

"A big one? What makes one bigger than another?"

"I'm not sure. It might be the size of the load or the destination. Anyhow we should hear all about it this weekend. I also think Chester wants to introduce you to Trish while you are down here."

"Trish?"

"Yeah, this might be good timing. She is new and is taking my place doing all of the running around."

"A woman?"

"Yes and a pretty hot one. You will be the talk of the park service when this one starts calling on you a couple of times a year. Good luck trying to get into her pants though. She is all business. I have been trying for a couple of months and am getting nowhere."

Tom decelerated as they approached the turn off to the marina where Chester moored his boat. He was enjoying the driving and Leon enjoyed the ride. On two occasions while on the freeway, he noticed very attractive women check the two of them out with sensuous smiles. He imagined hanging out with Tom for a while could be a lot of fun.

"You haven't seen the new boat yet have you?"

"New boat?" The last time Leon had been in Florida Chester he had some kind of fast, open bridge fiberglass boat he operated himself. It seated four adults comfortably.

"Oh, you're gonna like this one." Tom pulled up to the curb next to a huge or eighty-eight-foot yacht with a dark blue hull. Three decks rose above the waterline. "You might like the cabin attendant too." The classic rattle of the Porsche engine became quiet. "What do you think? We'll leave your bags in the car for now. I don't know where he wants you to stay."

They walked to the gangway leading up to the open rear deck area. A young man of Spanish descent dressed in starched white shorts and a knit golf shirt with the boat's logo "Just One More" embroidered over the breast pocket greeted them.

"Welcome gentlemen. Mr. Whittaker is waiting for you in the lounge." He looked at Leon. "My name is Tomas, please follow me."

He walked up the steps, the park ranger followed him and Tom brought up the rear. As they boarded, Leon saw half dozen rattan chairs and a granite topped teak table on the cockpit deck. Tomas turned left and slid a darkly tinted glass door to the left to reveal the salon. Inside, on a large leather couch sat Chester. An attractive young woman was setting a cocktail glass on the table in front of him. He stood to greet his guests.

"Leon, Great to see you. Welcome aboard." He first shook Leon's hand then embraced him in a well applied bear hug. "What do you think of her?" He gestured with his right hand pointing from stern to bow.

Leon had never been on such a boat. "She's incredible. When did you get this?"

"Oh, only a couple of months ago, a client of mine is in the shipping business in Greece and he is having a bigger one built. He offered this one at half of what she's worth. I couldn't pass up the deal.

"Besides, if I plan to entertain dignitaries like national park directors, don't you think I need a proper place to do it?"

Leon laughed and shook his head. "Sometimes you amaze me, but I'm not complaining."

"What kind of refreshment would you like?"

Leon was still in awe of his surroundings. "Oh, something tropical, I guess?"

"Gretchen, could you make Mr. Mathews a rum cooler. Oh hell, excuse me, sorry, Leon, this is Gretchen, she will make sure you are comfortable here. Gretchen, this is my oldest and dearest friend, Leon Mathews. He's the head honcho up at one of those Civil War parks in Charleston. We were roommates in college."

"Very nice to meet you Mr. Mathews," she answered with a very slight foreign accent, one Leon could not identify. She was wearing a lightweight semi-transparent cotton blouse with the two lowest buttons closed and beneath that was what looked like a string bikini top.

"Oh excuse me again, Tom. Do you want a martini or something?" Chester inquired of his associate.

"Sure," was all he needed to say as he winked towards Gretchen. She turned and left the salon as Whittaker pointed to the couch and chairs.

"Let's sit."

Leon took one end of the large leather couch and Tom perched on the edge of a leather ottoman. Whittaker slumped into an overstuffed recliner. There was a table in the center of the room. An image of the yacht was etched in the glass top.

"So, any problems with the flight?"

"Nope, everything went fine. A couple of cocktails before we took off and I slept most of the way."

"What do you think of that little toy Tom gets to take care of while one of his fillies is off searching for the meaning of life?" Chester asked while gesturing towards the Porsche.

"Hey Boss, I don't go looking for it, these things just happen to me."

"Refreshments." Gretchen entered the salon with a round cocktail tray on the palm of her left hand. As she bent down in front of Leon to place his frosted drink in front of him, he thought her tits were going to fall out of her blouse. He suspected the bikini top had been loosened a notch or two. The smile directed at him looked genuine. The scent of her lotions or perfumes blended coconut and citrus. Her ocean blue eyes penetrated him.

"Here is one frosty three rum cooler for Mr. Park Ranger." She turned slightly towards Tom and bent over as if to display her well-proportioned ass to Leon as well. "And a Stoli martini on the rocks for my favorite lawyer, well, second favorite." She glanced over at Chester to see his broad grin. "I'm sorry sir. Would you like another scotch, Mr. Whittaker?"

"Not just yet Gretchen. Thanks. Could you just bring us a big pitcher of ice water and then I want privacy for about half an hour."

"Yes sir. I'll be right back."

"Well, here's to old friends getting together," Chester raised his glass as did his guests and the three crystal drink glasses met with a resounding clink.

Leon tasted a thousand Caribbean spices in his first sip of the frosty drink and smiled. "Wow! What's in this thing?"

"Oh it starts with a little coconut water then there are three special rums I get from Barbados and then she does all the work to put it together. My wife came up with the formula."

"Here we go." Gretchen entered the salon with the ice water and three more glasses on a tray. Her smile directed at each of the men suggested if there was anything she could do for them they only needed to ask. And, she meant anything. She set the tray down and looked towards her employer.

"Thanks sweetheart. That will be all."

She turned and left the space. All three men lustfully watched while she took three steps towards the door. She closed the passageway door. Leon heard a click as she locked it behind her. "Great addition to the crew," Chester stated with a devilish grin. "Believe it or not, she is a law student at the University of Florida. Her undergraduate work was done through the U.S. Embassy in Brazil. Her dad is a career diplomat and her mom is from Argentina. She fills in here when we use the boat. It helps her with college expenses."

"Have you done any interrogatories with her yet?" Chester grinned and glanced in Tom's direction

"I plead the fifth."

"Very well counselor. Now Leon, what in the fuck is all this picture stuff about?"

"It's a little long and complicated, but it just seemed spooky to me. About two months ago, the last time Tom came up to the fort with the funds from the Fanta Seas operation. . ." Leon laid out the history of Vince Lubar visiting the park. Then he explained how Beaufort E. Lee got involved. Then how the Coast Guard officer had taken all of the photo proofs from Lee's studio a few days later.

"Does anyone know where this Coast Guard guy is assigned?" asked Whittaker.

"Yeah, he's on one of the ships tied up at the Naval Station on the Cooper River. There is an old one up there the Coast Guard got from the Navy last year. They converted it to a cutter. I think he's the Executive Officer, you know, the number two guy."

"Oh yeah, I read about them getting three old mothballed ships from the Department of Defense. I guess they are to fill in for a couple of years so all the regular boats worn out in that Cuban fiasco in '81 get fixed."

"Tom, do a little snooping around and see just who this guy is why he would be interested in pictures taken the last time you visited the fort."

"Will do. I could get on it this afternoon if you don't need me here. Then I'll come back later and let you know what I found out."

"Sounds great," Whittaker said as Thrasher downed the last drops of his martini and stood up preparing to leave.

"See you soon."

"Actually, I think I'll visit with Leon for a while and head back to the office in an hour or so. We can get together there and figure out our next move."

As the younger attorney slid the aft door closed, Chester exhaled deeply and Leon bit his lip. Both men seemed worried.

Leon downed the last liquid in his glass. Chester asked if he wanted another.

"Hell yes! I need to numb my brain so I can sleep tonight."

"You should sleep pretty well tonight. There is a great stateroom up forward for you. Gretchen is probably just finishing making it comfortable for you."

The lawyer smiled. He pushed a small grey button on the edge of the end table next to the recliner and within ten seconds, the perky law student appeared in the doorway.

"Yes sir, what can I get for you?"

"Leon would like another rum cooler and I'll take a scotch now. Oh, do we have any little treats up in the galley?"

"Sure, I'll find something. Be right back."

Gretchen once again departed and left the two by themselves. "You look worried," Chester spoke after a minute of silent thought.

"Well, four years ago it seemed so remote we might get caught. Now, with the Fanta Seas payoff I'm in pretty good shape financially. This new stuff is unsettling. What could happen to us?"

"Now Leon, there is a hell of a long ways things have to go before we are in any kind of trouble," Chester lied to his old friend. Inside he was wondering if he would end up in some country club prison in the hills of Georgia or a regular blockhouse with bars on the windows placed so high that prisoners can't see out.

"I think we should see what Tom can come up with on this dude and then find out if there is some way we can distract him from his job for a while so we can look at all of the issues we may have."

"What do you mean?"

"Well, it's obvious the guy has a family. Didn't the photographer say he was there for family pictures?"

"Yes?"

"Well, if something happened to them. . . ."

"What! What do you mean? You are not thinking of harming or... No, I'm not going to be involved in hurting anyone! I can't do that kind of stuff!"

Leon found himself being more assertive than he thought he could. "We're just smuggling marijuana, not even any hard coke or other bad stuff. We are not in the business of hurting people."

Chester had not yet filled his communications expert in on the facts. The next big load Cory Higgins was going to deliver would be over forty million dollars' worth of cocaine.

"No, we are not going to hurt people. I'm thinking of other types of domestic problems. I haven't thought it through completely but there must be something we could facilitate in Charleston so 'daddy' would have to leave his work for a week or so. You know, just distract him for a while. Let's say, the car goes tits up or the house gets infested with bats or termites . . . stuff like that."

At the forward door to the salon, there was a tap tap and Gretchen spoke. "Is this a good time?"

"Sure, come on in." Chester seemed pleased at the intrusion.

As she opened the door, Leon caught the scent of something delicious cooking beyond the door. She entered carrying a silver tray larger than the one she had used to serve the original drinks. The tray was draped with an embroidered linen cover bearing the vessel's name and a carefully stitched likeness of the boat itself on the leading corner. The tray held the two drinks they had requested and several plates with silver service and linen napkins.

Once again the law student hostess bent over exposing her flawlessly tanned cleavage and sharing her distinct scent with the two older men. She had changed her clothes and was now wearing a sleeveless chambray blouse with the top three buttons undone and a pair of tight white hot pants with the same logo as the embroidery on the linen service. She wore nothing beneath the blouse.

"I will be right back with a few snacks," she announced, setting the tray on the etched glass table.

As she stood erect, Leon Mathews felt himself aroused and knew he was blushing brightly.

Gretchen smiled.

As she returned forward to the galley, Chester spoke. "Kind of takes your mind off your problems, right old friend?"

Leon felt his blood returning to where it belonged once again and simply nodded with a smile and said "No shit. How do you concentrate on work when people like that are helping out?"

"I do a few lectures over at the law school, and when I see talent that may in some way help my own endeavors, I find a spot for them on my team. Gretchen will be a great attorney and I'm happy to play a role in her development. Here comes some grub."

"Here we go gentlemen." She returned to the salon carrying another tray with two steaming dishes containing a dozen gigantic ocean shrimp, sea scallops wrapped in thin ham, and chunks of lobster tail each skewered with a toothpick bearing the burgee of the West Palm Beach Yacht Club. On another plate was an assortment of cheeses. There were several smaller dishes of dipping sauce in various red, yellow and white colors and consistencies.

"Is there anything else gentlemen?"

"Yes Gretchen. Is the guest stateroom all ready for Mr. Matthews? I think he will be staying onboard for the next couple of days."

"Yes sir, Tomas delivered his bags and there are clean sheets and towels. If there is anything you need just ring. I will be up in the pilot house most of the evening reading five hundred pages of Florida Supreme Court case history."

"Thanks, honey." Replied Chester

"Yes sir, if you need anything, just push my button." A final smile and a wink in the direction of both men executed as she spun around and in two very seductive steps was out of sight.

Chapter Thirty-Three

In the early eighties, the small town of Montego Bay Jamaica was just coming into its own as a tourist destination. Several "all inclusive" resorts operated where patrons came and stayed within walled compounds utilizing the pools, sports courts, bars, restaurants and the private beach. Clients could leave a stateside or European airport, arrive on the island and go to the resort in a limo. After a week or so, they could take the limo back to the airport and go home telling all of their friends and relatives they had been to Jamaica. In truth, they never had a chance to look at the fascinating place and the culture of the Jamaican citizens. The artwork, food and happiness of the people of this island colony are an adventure to explore.

The officers and crew of the USCGC ESCAPE and many boaters who visit the island, prefer to explore and enjoy what Jamaica has to offer.

The small entourage of Coast Guard officers assembled on the quarterdeck.

Ensign Ladner briefed the watch stander on the events planned on board for the evening. CDR Flood appeared wearing a crisply ironed blue Hawaiian shirt and white shorts. On his feet were leather sandals. He looked like any tourist, as did the rest of the officers. Even though the skipper was in civilian clothes, Ensign Ladner and the petty officer on watch both rendered crisp salutes to their leader. Vince briefed the officer of the deck as to the general locations they would be should they need to be advised of any events of importance or emergencies.

"Your taxi is over there," Ladner pointed to a white minivan near the gangway. "The driver's name is Sam. He is set up to be at your service for the day"

Sam was wearing flowered shorts ending at his knees. His shirt was a sleeveless New York Yankee tank top. His perfectly aligned white teeth sported a broad smile and contrasted with his dark brown skin. As the officers descended the gangway, he tipped his white Chicago White Sox baseball cap in the direction of his customers.

When the Commanding Officer walked down the ramp, the Quartermaster of the Watch announced on the ships PA system "Now ESCAPE departing" and as the skipper's feet were both on the dock the next announcement "Now ESCAPE ashore." With the Captain ashore, the messenger of the watch hoisted the third substitute pennant, a black and white horizontally striped flag alerting observers to the absence of the commanding officer of this vessel. This is an international signal used by all U.S. Navy, Coast Guard and NOAA ships.

Sam had opened all available doors to the van. He greeted the men with an even greater smile and rendered a salute. "Hello Capitan and mista's. My name Sam Bozo. I be at your service for da evening maybe a coupla days if you like. We got lotta really fine spots here in Mo Bay. Any ting dat be yo pleasure I can take cara dat." He ushered the commanding officer into the front passenger seat on the left hand side of the vehicle. As the other officers entered the van, he shook everyone's hand and said "mista – mista – mista." Sam Bozo then hopped into the driver's seat and asked "Whatcha pleasure mista's?"

Vince took the cue and answered. "We would like to get into some of the older parts of Mo Bay you know where the locals go, the food is good, the beer is cold and we can see the true life of Jamaica."

"I know justa right place. I take ya to Sam Sharpe Square." Bozo continued talking as he shifted the vehicle into first gear and began heading south along the industrial harbor. "Dat's where Sam Sharpe got hanged 'bout a hundred fifty or so years ago."

"Sam, he was da man dat started da ball rollin to get alla da slaves set free. Mama said my grandpa was one of dem. I guess we hada big uprising and da British didn't like it when Papa Sam told dem slaves not to work on Christmas back about eighteen thirty somtin. Nobody knew a slave could taka day off but I guess dey all did. And it messed up all a da dinners' dat year. Lotta da rich folk got pissed and dey killa bunch of em. Later dey snatch up old Sam and hang him up here in dis plaza. Coupla years later, everyone starts thinkin about those days and a new King in England and a new Prime Minister down in Kingston Town get together and tell everyone no more slaves."

During this monologue, Sam Bozo had driven the van from the wharf around the bay and along Alice Eldemire Drive. Then turning north on Montego Bay's main thoroughfare, Howard Cooke Highway, he finally turned right and inland several streets to a beautiful cobblestone plaza. Dozens of locals were moving about shopping, visiting and otherwise doing business of the day.

He stopped the vehicle and turned to address his customers as he continued with his lesson.

All five officers were enjoying the event.

"And right there where dat statue is where dey hanged him. He was a preacher man too so we all think he be a saint but no Pope tell us dat yet. We still waiting.

"Ok! Gentlemen, right there where da fence is around dat land is the old civic center but dat burnt down 'bout twelve years ago. Somebody says that dey getting the money so a new one can get build for a museum may be one day." Bozo went on.

"But on dat street behind the fence is where all a da local business folk and people who make this town work, dey go for lunch and talk about everything. If you go into 'The Cage' my cousin DeDe he takes good cara you and tell you all about da place. If you want, I can come back in 'bout an hour or two and take you down to night life bars."

"That sounds great," Flood responded for everyone. "What is your favorite local food?"

"I like jerk goat da best if you get the little tender pieces. DeDe got a cook he makes it da best in town. And of course, da local beer is Red Stripe and any kin a rum if it be from Jamaica is da best in the world."

"Fine, I guess we will take off on our own and see you in a couple of hours." Lubar responded.

Sam Bozo hopped out of the van and scampered around to open the door for the captain. Everyone else opened their own doors and exited. Dave and the three lieutenants walked toward the statue of Sam Sharpe while Vince made arrangements with their driver for two hours into the future.

The men spent ten minutes touring around the plaza taking photographs and reading the bronze plaques describing the history of the Christmas Rebellion. When the commanding officer suggested it was time to go to "The Cage" no one needed a second invitation.

The five officers all ducked a bit to enter the low archway of the two-hundred-year old pub. The pungent sweet smell of decades of tropical heat, Caribbean cigar smoke and humidity on the stones and planks of the building hit them all as they entered the dimly lit establishment. Several dozen dark skinned men in white cotton business attire were scattered about the room. Some were conversing over the business of life, two were engaged in a robust game of dominoes and others were simply visiting and chatting. There were two groups of Caucasian customers as well and they were visiting with the bartender and an attractive black woman. Visiting with the waitress was a lone white man dressed in cutoff jeans and an expensive tropical shirt. Vince immediately recognized him as Cory Higgins the captain of the Caribbean Gipsy.

The bartender looked up from his conversation as the five Americans entered his bar. So did Higgins.

"Good afternoon gentlemen. You must be the American friends of my cousin Sam." The bartender was adorned with gold chains around his neck. Solid gold medallions and other objects hung from the chains. His grin from ear to ear displayed a full mouth of perfectly white teeth contrasting with the shiny black skin on his face. He wore long white cotton trousers and beautifully embroidered silk shirt.

"Not many secrets in this town." Phil commented.

"I guess we are." Flood answered and approached the proprietor and extended his hand as a greeting. "My name is Dave. You must be DeDe."

"Yes sir, DeDe Ramon Bozo at your service."

Chapter Thirty-Four

Chester left the boat and Leon in the care of Gretchen. Tom was ending a phone call when he arrived in his office.

They met in the hallway outside of Whittaker's reception area and walked into the inner office. "Well what did you find out?" Chester inquired and pointed to the large leather couch indicating Thrasher should take a seat there.

"His name is Vince Lubar, been in the service about fourteen years. He enlisted at first but then went to Officer's Candidate School. He's been around the block in law enforcement. A lot of it was up in Alaska doing fish treaty enforcement. That must be fun. He was in Europe for a couple of years on some sort of exchange deal with the Navy and is now the Executive Officer on a former Navy ship in Charleston. From the news stuff, the ship is old and has its share of problems. There was something about the Coasties needing more ships quickly after the Cuban boat lift deal a few years ago."

"We need to get Leon back up to the Fort so we can check the patrol location of the ship."

"What's he doing right now?" Tom asked.

"When I left the boat, he was chatting with our favorite law student. I have a feeling she will get him into the hot tub and he will sleep well tonight. One thing we know, Gretchen loves to do is flirt with nerdy guys and take control of them. We should probably let her finish before we send him home." Chester grinned.

"When she gets done with him he would probably do anything we want if there is another opportunity for a night with Gretchen."

Tom smiled. "She is an interesting one. Between her and Trish, you are opening up a whole new specialty field for smart, good looking women."

"So what should we do about this Lubar guy? I could go up to Charleston tonight, find out a little about the family and create a diversion. Nothing too serious but we could probably pull off something causing the old man to come home for a few days. It might get him to quit thinking about our next shipment on Caribbean Gipsy."

Chester remarked, "Diversion could help us out, don't want to hurt anyone and you should be a step or two away from anything that goes down. Why don't you give Chad Walgren in Myrtle

113

Beach a call? He'll know some punk street dealer in town who will help you do something. Stealing the family car might be just the thing to do it.

"Run the thing a state or two away and abandon it undamaged. Bingo, Daddy will fly home. Some less experienced dude will be in charge of sneaking up on drug boats down south and Cory can get over to Saint Thomas to load furniture, and head north."

"Right, Trish is getting it all set up. She will be here on Monday and we will sort out the details." He finished the scotch in one gulp.

"Yeah, get up there as quick as you can and let me know what's up."

"You got it boss. I will touch base tomorrow."

Thrasher stood up and left. In the parking garage, he hopped into the Porsche, wishing he had the time to drive up Interstate 95 and through the low country to Charleston. He would love to take this car on a road trip. This time though, he just headed for the airport. Tom always kept a small backpack in his car with sufficient supplies to travel for up to three days on a moment's notice. He arrived at the Palm Beach airport where he had picked up Leon Matthews seven hours earlier. He handed the keys to a valet after popping the trunk to grab the backpack. Quickly entering the automatic door leading to the main concourse he scanned the departures listed on the information boards. An Eastern Airlines flight, departing non-stop for Charleston in twenty-five minutes had plenty of seats available. He purchased a first class ticket and made his way to the gate. Before departing he placed a call to Chad Walgren.

Chapter Thirty-Five

Inside The Cage, DeDe Bozo entertained the American officers with stories of the history of Montego Bay, the legends and tales of Sam Sharp and the lineage of the Bozo family going back five generations. The troupe enjoyed the refreshing effect of cold beer after two and a half weeks at sea.

Vince made his way over to the group of locals chatting with Cory Higgins.

The two shook hands and greeted one another.

"Great to see you Skipper. Is this your usual Mo Bay hang out?"

"It's a good place to find cold beer, the food is authentic and the home boys know how to keep you laughing at their jokes and stories. I've got a girlfriend up in the states who is trying to get down here for the weekend. She usually sends me a Western Union telegram and the office is just across the plaza. That's actually how I found this place. I like it because the tourists don't know it is here."

"So how long do you stay in port before you go find more cargo?"

"Oh, it will be three or four days. I just got an opportunity to move a couple of taxis over to St. Thomas late next week. It will be nice to do something different. I've been over to Honduras a dozen times this year and a new harbor and coastline will be a nice change."

"Sounds like a good way to make a living."

"Oh, it's great and until I found a girlfriend, I never thought I would want to do anything else."

"Where did you meet this lady?" inquired Lubar

"Oh, I was taking a break up at Abaco six months ago and we were the only single people in the resort. She's a knock-out, a recent widow and I was a little horny and what I thought would be a therapeutic roll in the sand for both of us turned into the real deal."

"Well, they say you never know when it will hit you but when it does, it's hard to run away. I was stationed in Oregon ten years ago. That's where mine showed up. Her dad owned a bar in the town where my ship tied up and once I met her, my bachelor days were over."

"Got kids?"

"Yeah one son, he's seven and a handful. I miss getting to see them every day but it's the nature of a career like this. My next assignment will probably be skippering a mahogany desk somewhere in Washington DC. I hope not, but I have dodged the bullet for quite a while. At least I would get to see the boy grow up a little before heading out to sea again."

Higgins gestured towards the sea with his left shoulder and said, "I promised you the other day that I would buy you a beer – Hey DeDe how about two more Red Stripes over here?"

"I'm not sure how long I would last at some desk job but I guess if you're ever going to make admiral you need to pay your dues."

"Here you go Captain Higgee." Bozo placed two bottles of lager in front of the men and slid a bowl of peanuts in their direction.

"Thanks De." Higgins winked towards Lubar.

"How long do you guys stay on patrol? You said you were out of South Carolina. That's a haul just to get down here to the hunting grounds?" Higgins seemed genuinely interested in how life in the Guard worked.

"Oh, we schedule for four to six weeks but we are usually a week late getting home."

"That cutter you are on looks older than most. What's the story there?"

Vince was happy to relate the story of the ESCAPE, including his first encounter in Officer Candidate School.

In half an hour, Skipper Dave joined them. Vince introduced him to Cory. The smuggler was playing his cards perfectly and the two senior officers were quickly growing to like him.

Initially a little stressed, Higgins' gut loosened up and his guarded conversation became easier.

Chapter Thirty-Six

The hour and forty-minute flight gave Tom an opportunity to ponder what type of "incident" he could develop and not injure anyone. It needed to be serious enough to cause Lubar to ask to get off of his ship for a week or so, taking the focus off of boarding boats loaded with cocaine heading for America.

Chad Walgren was a local facilitator in the distribution of imported products. He worked with Chester. His territory covered the east coast between Savannah and Virginia Beach. He worked with the bulk buyers and distributed twenty-pound packages of marijuana and two pound blocks of cocaine to the dealers who made the final sales to end users. He was a well-organized and connected businessman and could get just about anything done in the Charleston-Myrtle Beach area.

Walgren owned a cobalt blue Corvette. Tom was looking forward to riding around town in a rig like that. He emerged from the airport concourse inhaling the sweet odor of azaleas and jasmine. He looked across the circular driveway to Charleston Air Force Base as a huge C141 cargo plane taxied to take off. In fifteen seconds, he noticed the corvette convertible approaching. The driver was wearing a sleeveless t-shirt bearing the logo of the University of South Carolina Gamecocks.

"Hey Tom!"

"Hi Chad, Nice ride." He tossed his backpack behind the passenger seat and hopped in.

Walgren shifted the car into first gear and slipped away from the airport drive. They passed the "Welcome to Charleston – The Low Country" sign and were scooting along at seventy miles per hour enjoying the warm southern breeze and the fragrant air.

"Nice to finally meet you Chad. I hear good things."

"Yeah, I've had a few friends in this business go nutzo and it always seems to end them up in trouble. I keep my nose clean, both literally and physically." He chuckled.

"Well, we've got a little issue with one Coast Guard Officer assigned to a cutter called ESCAPE. He is down in the Caribbean right now and has uncovered information about our operation. It's placing him too close for comfort. The boss wonders if there is a way to cause a little distraction up here. We want to get his mind off of his job for a week or so and let us get a load up the Atlantic coast so guys like you can stay in business."

"Yes, Chester called and told me about this dude. His name is Vince Lubar, so I went to the library and looked up whatever press releases had his name. Apparently, he got assigned to this ship about fourteen months ago. He came here from a job with the Navy where he rode around on supply ships in the Mediterranean working on marine safety issues. One article did describe him as an investigator. Probably why he sticks his nose where you don't want it."

"Wow, you do your homework! I'm impressed."

"His wife is a pretty strong runner, taking care of the younger wives of the crew when the ship is away. She seems to be trying to be the perfect Coast Guard officer's wife. I doubt she knows it but I've got three customers in my market married to or shacked up with guys who are out there on the good ship ESCAPE. Funny isn't it?"

Chad maneuvered the convertible with the skill of a NASCAR driver. He weaved between cars skillfully as he talked. Finally, he downshifted and merged onto the interstate highway southbound towards Charleston.

"Wow, what a sweet ride. You ever have to outrun a cop?"

"Nah, I don't get many chances around here to really get into it, but out west through Georgia and Mississippi, there are roads where I really have fun." He steadied out the car's speed at seventy miles per hour.

Thrasher talked business. "What we want to accomplish is to cause a family issue to give daddy a reason to get off of the ship and fly home for an emergency. Got any ideas?"

"Well I talked with one of these gals about this bitch and she thinks the lady, Denise Lubar is just a little bit too gung ho about the whole Coast Guard thing. She drives around in a beautiful new Mercedes Turbo Diesel S500 sedan. I guess her old man scored it in Europe at the factory just before they came back to the states. She gives all the little enlisted wifely women rides in the car to kids' games and such. Guess this is the first 'new' car they have ever had and it's the old man's second favorite toy. Whenever he calls he asks how she and the boy are then 'how is my car?'

She likes to flaunt her 'rank' as the XO's wife throughout the group. Most of em like it, some just put up with it others don't give a damn and frankly a few of them think she is a number one bitch."

"What about the skipper, what does his wife think about all this?" Tom asked, impressed with Chad's investigation.

"Oh yeah, that's Commander Dave Flood, the Captain. Everyone in the crew likes him a lot. He's not married and enjoys going out with the boys and over to crew members' homes for dinners when they are in port. I think he is a Vietnam Vet, career bachelor and would rather be at sea than anywhere else."

"Man, what else do you know about the crew of the good ship ESCAPE?"

"Well, in every demographic there are going to be a few who end up as my customers. About thirteen months ago, all these new Coast Guard families started arriving and I thought what the hell. Then I read in the paper this new ship, an old navy boat was coming to Charleston to help fight the drug war.

"Well, all the wives and kids came here and the dudes went up to Baltimore to the shipyard getting the boat ready to go."

"So you got to know a few of the wives and developed a little new business right?"

"When the cat's away, the mice will play. These are not mice though; they are horny foxes. That's exactly right and most of these wives are nineteen to thirty years old. They are from places not around here and away from home for the first time in their lives. I bet half will be divorced within five years."

"Why do you think that?"

"Because they are young hot bitches. They like to strut their stuff especially when they are out in groups. It's natural for them to want what a guy can give them. They need more than those Coasties can do for them when they are at sea for weeks at a time. And believe me, they find ways."

"So are you screwing any of them?"

"No, not me, but I know a couple of bartenders and one dude up on the Air Force base who are getting into somebody's pants almost every night when the ship is at sea."

"Ok Chad, what do you think we could do to stir up a hornet's nest and get the good Lieutenant Commander to jump ship and come home for a while?"

"Well, I found out the Mercedes is a diesel and there only three places in town where you can buy fuel. That bitch wouldn't go out to the truck stop on the interstate. I've also been found out when she goes to fuel up she usually goes to the Exxon station at about 4th and Meeting Street because she takes her little bratty son in there and buys him an ice cream cone. Then they stay in the little coffee shop part of the place till the kid is finished and get back in the car and go home."

"So why are we supposed to be interested in where she buys fuel for the fancy car and what kind of ice cream a kid likes?"

"Because my little chickadee Coast Guard wife Annie who buys weed from me says she always leaves the car, house, and all other keys on the console next to the driver's seat. I've heard it drives the old man nuts."

"So?"

"So is right. If we are looking for some kind of distraction to get daddy away from his work, why don't we just steal that fucking car and take it far away. Lubar's otherwise superwoman wife will be devastated. He has told her repeatedly this is going to happen. She will break her armor coating and ask for the old man to come home to 'solve the crime'. I think Annie and her close friends might get a good chuckle out of it too."

"Jesus, you have been thinking about this."

As Chad exited Interstate 26 into historic Charleston, he downshifted through 4th, 3rd and finally into 2nd gear allowing the corvette to emit the tones of the well-tuned V8 engine winding down from seventy-five miles per hour to twenty.

"Yes in my game, if you aren't thinking around the next two or three corners, you can end up in a federal prison. And from what I have heard, those joints are no fun at all. I like to be able to sit down once in a while and use a toilet with a seat on it," Tom chuckled.

"Chester said you would be staying at the Charleston Place on Meeting Street, right?"

"That's right, Connie in our office tries to find me places where the chicks might be hot and too stupid to figure me out in less than three days."

"Well, there are plenty of rich bitches in this neighborhood. Most are third or fourth generation S.O. B's"

"What?"

"Oh yeah, Broad Street runs northeast to southwest in down town Charleston and everyone, I mean everyone who comes from South of Broad Street are called S.O.B's. They don't mind the nickname at all. It's kind of like living on Rodeo Drive in Hollywood. Most of them are from families here during the Civil War. All of them are rich and divorces are happening all of the time. So here we are. What do you want to do about our 'mission'?" Walgren inquired.

"I've got a couple of calls to make. I'll think about this car deal and bounce it off the boss. Do you want to catch dinner someplace? It would be on me."

"Thanks but I need a rain check on that one. I have a meeting with a couple of new sales agents tonight around nine. What say we get together in the morning before ten?"

"Sounds great, do you have any leads on a good seafood restaurant?"

"Hell, for a close by place you should go to Hank's. It's been around since World War II and the little bar there is a real meat market stocked with S.O.B's who could screw your eyes out if you're interested.

"If you need a car, I could leave you the 'vette and call a buddy for a ride back to my place. I have another ride there. Not as much fun as this but it's my work car, a Buick station wagon."

"As much as I would love to drive that puppy, I think I will just stay put and use my shoe leather to get around. This looks like an interesting place." He could understand why Chester had liked the town so well when he was attending the Citadel.

"One question. How do you plan on stealing a rare, nearly new Mercedes and getting it out of town before every Charleston Cop is on our ass?"

"Oh, that's simple. I've got a Sea-Land container set up for hauling cars. I can get it on a two-hour notice complete with a driver. We can park it a few blocks from the 'scene of the crime' and have the booty ready for transport within a minute. It's been done before if you know what I mean. The only cost is a full tank of diesel in the tractor and fifteen one hundred dollar bills."

"Is there anything you can't get done around here?" Tom asked, impressed with the thoroughness of his colleague.

"I concentrate on networking. It's the new buzzword for people in the sales and marketing world. Sometimes I go to those 'pump you up' seminars for real estate and insurance people, I figure if that kind of shit works in the legitimate world, the same principles can apply to my kind of work. So I 'network' and just try to get to know all the people in the dark side of town and we become associates and not competitors. It works great."

"Nothing wrong with your methods. It looks like you are doing well. I hope you are putting a little moula aside in case you need a good attorney someday or have to lay low for a while."

"I'm pretty cautious and got money stuffed in eight different banks. Two of them are out of the country. I also have a little bungalow in Hawaii as kind of a safe house if I need it."

"Good for you. I guess I will check in then and see what Charleston has to offer for a night or two."

Walgren was approaching the elegant circle drive of the hotel. It is a perfectly landscaped cobblestone driveway. As the car came to a stop, a tall and slender tuxedoed black man approached and opened the passenger side door to help Thrasher. Another shorter, white twenty something valet parking attendant appeared at the driver side.

"Just dropping him off, thanks."

Tom reached over to shake Chad's hand. "Great to see you, thanks for the lift. I will catch you in the morning."

"Tally Ho! Till tomorrow." A slight screech of rubber chirped from the rear wheels as Chad departed.

The bellman stood a respectful three feet away and waited to assist the newest guest.

"Welcome sir." He said with a gravely southern accent as he extended his left hand to carry the luggage and tipped his top hat with right thumb and a perfectly manicured index finger.

"Thank You"

"My name is Edward; I expect you are Mr. Thrasher. How many days do you plan to stay sir?"

"Nice to meet you Edward. I'm not sure, two or three I believe."

"I will take you to Rebecca at reception."

"Thank you." Tom enjoyed the hospitality.

Chapter Thirty-Seven

Leon finished his pork tenderloins roasted in a Caribbean marinade and deep fried plantain chips topped with a mango and papaya chutney sauce. He watched Gretchen cook in a skimpy bikini bottom and loose fitting chambray. He was very relaxed, not thinking of the guy with the photos up at Fort Sumter. Any thought of being in jail had left his mind. He concentrated wholly on the gorgeous twenty-four-year old beauty wanting nothing more than to make sure he was comfortable.

"Is there anything else I could get for you?" She poured him another glass of French wine.

"Nope, I'm so full and relaxed I can't think of anything else I need." He removed his glasses and rubbed his forehead.

"You seem a lot more relaxed than you were earlier. I've been taking a course in massage and acupressure for my health science course at law school. Would you like me to give you a little shoulder and neck rub?" She asked and began working on his shoulder muscles without waiting for a reply. "I will call it homework," she smiled.

"Hmmm it feels great." Leon moaned, as she found pressure points he was not aware of. "I didn't know you needed a course in massage therapy to become a lawyer."

"It was either that or some class on vitamins or health food. Hey, did you know there is a hot tub up behind the pilothouse? How about we go get in the water for a while. It will help me sleep better and will probably do the same for you."

Leon felt himself stimulated beyond anything he had ever experienced. He could not understand how he had gotten so lucky. He had no idea beyond the money associated with the smuggling, there would be benefits such as he was enjoying right now.

"Sounds like fun. Let me go down to my room and get my bathing suit."

"Oh, that ain't necessary sir, everything we need is already up there. Let me go get things ready." Gretchen said as she was finishing up with a few light squeezes on the base of his neck. The final touch was a caressing motion with her index finger across his upper chest, side of his neck, and resting for a moment on his earlobe. Leon's response engulfed him in goose bumps.

"Sounds fine to me, I'll be up in a few moments." Leon answered welcoming the opportunity for a moment of privacy as he had become totally aroused by the massage.

As he contemplated his situation, he wondered if she was teasing him or if she somehow cared for him as a person. He hoped it was the latter.

He couldn't believe he was here on a multimillion dollar yacht in Florida with a dramatically gorgeous and sensual young woman. And now, he was about to get into a hot tub with her!

His response to stimulation subsided so he stood, picked up his glass of wine and headed up the stairway. It was five steps up from the salon to the bridge and as he took each step, the space above seemed to grow. In the center, a wooden ship's steering wheel and several polished brass and chrome levers to control the engines and other mechanical parts of the boat stood prominent. There were electronic doodads everywhere near the helm and also radios to cover a variety of frequencies at the same time. He saw several fixed leather chairs for passengers to observe where the ship was going, and behind it all was a three quarter sized bed. A variety of stuffed animals, pirates and ornate pillows decorated the edges. He noticed doorways on each side of the pilot house leading to an outside deck where one could watch the world go by. Both doors were open. The scent of a balmy Florida evening full of salt air and jasmine entered his nostrils. He felt exhilarated. The vista from the bridge, three decks above the water, provided Leon with a three hundred degree look at the Palm Beach skyline. Several dozen yachts every bit as ample as Chester's were moored around him.

"Are you going to stand there and stare at the steering wheel all night or get in?" She was in the hot tub leaning over the edge with her arms over the side and her shoulders just above the top of the teakwood frame. In her left hand, she held a half-full wine glass.

"I'll be right there. Where are those swim suits?"

"I'm not sure, I was just told they were up here someplace," she said coyly with a deep Latin accent. As she spoke, she stood up and took a step backwards and sat on the far edge of the spa. Both pieces of her bikini were floating in the bubbles. Leon's chest tightened and, as if he had lost control of his own actions, set his glass down and removed his own shirt and shorts and joined her.

"Now, why don't you tell me all about your adventures as a park ranger?" She embraced him. "Have you ever met Smokey the Bear?"

Chapter Thirty-Eight

"Yes Connie."

"Miss Dixon is here."

"Oh, that's great, give me about two minutes to finish up and show her in when I buzz."

"Yes sir"

Chester switched the computer screen to the waiting room monitor so as to watch Trish as she sat in the waiting room. She was attractively dressed in a light pants suit and even in the black and white image projected on the screen he found himself lusting over her sexy demeanor. He wondered if there was a lucky guy someplace getting into those pants. He also wondered what the future would be for these desktop computers. In the three years since an associate had encouraged him to get one, he was now on his third and buying them for everyone in the office. He pondered what application there could be for computers in the drug smuggling industry. Chester finished a gulp of scotch and filled the glass on his desk with water. He pressed the buzzer and stood to approach the door to his office. As he stood he looked at the portrait of his father on the wall and mumbled "Sorry, dad."

Connie opened the door and escorted Trish in. "Well, how's the smartest CPA in Atlanta doing today?" He extended a hand to Trish. "You get more attractive every time you come here. The Georgia sunshine looks good on you."

"Thank you, sir. I've been playing a lot of tennis and otherwise keeping busy."

"Connie, can you bring us some iced tea please."

"Sure thing sir, I will be right back." She replied as she spun around on one heel, closing the door behind her. She wondered if her boss was screwing around with Trish but quickly dismissed the idea because of the fifteen plus year age difference, and Chester's seemingly happy marriage to his wife and their contented family life.

"So how's my brother doing up there. Any law being practiced or is he just working on his political career?"

"Mostly it is everything in column B, Chet. The associates are all doing well and no one seems to be going broke. There was talk at the staff meeting two days ago about completing the big real estate merger with four car dealers and everyone feels pretty good about that."

"Great, I was wondering when that one was closing. Didn't your late husband work at one of those companies?" Chester inquired as Connie entered.

"Here you go. I didn't know how long you were going to be so there are two glasses of tea and a pitcher if you need more."

"Thanks so much Connie." Both the attorney and the accountant said in unison as she backed away.

Chester went on. "We've got a lot to go over so when four thirty gets here you can just head home. Keep all calls going to the message machine and I will check them before I leave."

"Yes Mr. Whittaker, see you tomorrow. Nice to see you again Trish." Connie spoke as she exited the office once again wondering about the possibility of an affair.

"Yeah, he worked at the Caddy dealer. Seems like two lifetimes ago."

"Well. Are you ready for your first big one?"

"As ready as I will ever be. I just want to get started so it is action and not planning." Trish replied. Her composure was controlled and she might as well have been talking about reviewing someone's tax return and not getting ready to deliver a million-seven hundred thousand bucks in U.S. dollars, Deutsch Marks and British pounds to Cory Higgins.

"I thought we still had a month."

"No." Chester replied, we're moving the buy date up to weekend after next."

Trish felt a tightness in her stomach accompanied by a feeling of excitement in her libido as she instantly realized the game was on, and within a few days, she would be together with Cory after all.

"This is kind of sudden. What happened?"
"The shipment left Europe earlier than expected and the transporter wants to unload it as soon as he can. And, our folks up in Norfolk are chomping at the bit to get the product to market before more competition shows up. Everything seems to be coming together well and we will all be happy sooner rather than later."

Chester was not going to reveal any details about Vince Lubar, ESCAPE or all of the other bullshit occupying his brain. "And when we looked at the long term weather issues, the whole operation has a better chance of success if we do it earlier."

"Ok so what do you want me to do?"

"Well, it looks like you are going to take a little vacation in Jamaica."

"Sounds like fun."

"It's a working vacation. You will actually fly to Grand Turk Island and visit a bank there to pick up the cash. From there you will meet a pilot, Mark Dean, with a twin engine amphibious plane. He will fly you to the north side of the Island of Jamaica and a limo will take you to the all-in-one resort in Montego Bay. Mark will also help you with the details of picking up the funds from the bank in Grand Turk. Mark will have a duplicate passport for you with all the proper entry stamps and visas and anyone who looks at your documents will believe that you flew into the international airport at Kingston."

"Ok. How do you do all of this stuff?"

"Oh, Tom has been working on the details. When this operation is over, he is going to tell you all of his dirty little secrets and next time it will all be up to you.

"Cory Higgins will catch up with you there and you will give him the suitcase with the money in it. Don't forget to take your bikini out of it. I don't think he will need it." Chester smiled.

Trish also smiled knowing that by her second day there she will already made love to Cory half a dozen times and he will probably have already ripped her bikini off more than a few times.

"Then what?" Trish was convinced her boss had absolutely no inkling of an idea she and Captain Higgins were involved romantically.

"Cory will need you to take your rental car and pick up a couple of crewmembers from the Montego Bay airport and bring them to the marina. On day 4 of your vacation, Caribbean Gipsy will depart for St. Thomas. They will be hauling two taxis and unfinished furniture to a paint shop on the island. Then he will pick up finished teak and bamboo chairs and tables for shipment to Norfolk. In this packet is a lot of very official paper work making everything look very legal." Chester reached in a lower desk drawer and extracted a large brown envelope. It looked like it came from some foreign post office. He slid it across the desk towards his new courier.

"And?"

"Cory will leave and you will enjoy the rest of a week in Jamaica. Then you will come back up to the states and fly into Lexington Kentucky."

"What's in Lexington?"

"Oh, more money. As Cory is pulling into the Chesapeake Bay, our stateside buyers will be keeping track of him and dropping off enough money to pay the crewmembers and Cory. The cash will be in a locker at the Kentucky State Fairgrounds near the horse racing track. Here is a map. It will be in locker number 321 and this key will open it. It will be in a very feminine looking suitcase with a handle and wheels. You will not look out of place carrying it around if you are dressed professionally in a state fair kind of way."

"I can pull that off."

"When you land in Kentucky, pick up a rental car. After you pick up the cash, drive to Norfolk to meet the furniture broker. Customs will not be an issue because Cory will have cleared customs entering the U.S. Territory in St. Thomas."

"Is there anything you haven't thought of? You're making all of this too easy."

"Cory, as you remember, is supposed to leave Norfolk for a week and then return to the boat once it is unloaded. I don't think he has made any travel plans so you may want to ask him when you see him in Jamaica where he wants to go. Perhaps you could pick up a ticket and make a reservation someplace if he wants you to. Just see what he needs."

"I think I could handle that," she responded with a steely expression designed not to reveal her true emotions while anticipating a visit with Cory.

The conversation went on for several hours as Chester went over every detail small and large that it would take to successfully move a shipment of cocaine with a street value of forty-five million dollars from the West Indies to the dealers on the Atlantic seaboard. Her task was to settle the accounts needed to pay everyone involved. Her final stop would be a layover in Charleston to drop off a Tupperware container holding eighty-five thousand dollars to Leon Matthews at the national monument of Fort Sumter.

The excitement had her head swimming more than she ever imagined. She would be dressed to the nines, enjoying the tropics with her lover, sneaking around the world with bags of money and paying off criminals for their services. She wanted to get started and could hardly wait to leave for Grand Turk.

The jug of iced tea was gone and the conversation nearly complete when Chester asked if she would like a little drink.

"That would be great. What do you have Chet?"

"Just about anything you want. I prefer scotch, single malt and aged at least twenty years."

She wished she could share the fact she was involved with Cory but was quite sure he would not approve. She wanted to keep both the working situation and her love life as it was, so she held on to her secret.

"A good stiff scotch would be just what the doctor ordered right now but first I need to visit the ladies' room."

"You know where it is. I will fix a little toddy." Chester stood to make his way over to the liquor cabinet near the leather furniture facing the window overlooking the Atlantic. And to himself he said "If I was only ten years younger, man, could I get in trouble with this one."

Trish stood and left the room walking past Connie's long ago vacated desk and went to the lavatory. All she could think of from a physical standpoint was the anticipation of lying next to her man and exploring every inch of each other's bodies once again. "Everything worthwhile is worth waiting for," she told herself.

She walked back in to Chester's office. "I feel much better now, how about that scotch?"

Chapter Thirty-Nine

The sweet heavy Florida morning air drifted into the pilot house. Leon slowly woke from a deep sleep. Before he opened his eyes, he began to recall the past hours. He remembered being involved in a sexual encounter such as he had never before experienced. In fact, Matthews had never really had any kind of intimate relationship since the days of cadet cruises onboard Navy ships as a fourth year cadet at the Citadel. A stop in Barcelona Spain included his loss of virginity to one of the beautiful Putas frequenting the bars around the Rambalas and the waterfront. Urged on by several junior naval officers also indulging in the pleasures of those long ago evenings, Leon was deflowered.

Wondering if it had all been a dream from the moment he ascended to the bridge then gotten into the hot tub with Chester's gorgeous naked assistant from the University of Florida, he realized it was no dream. He began to recall everything. She had prepared exotic cocktails and joined him in the hot tub. As they showered and dried, Leon said he should go below and sleep before Chester and Tom arrived in the morning.

"Nonsense, they won't be here until after lunch. Besides, I think Tom went up to Charleston on some business."

He slowly opened his eyes, still wondering if the whole thing was a dream. Then, the strong smell of fresh brewed Cuban coffee caught his senses. The large seat on the bridge was turned to face aft and in it sat Gretchen, wearing a terrycloth robe and a pair of dark framed reading glasses. She was studying a green leather bound book about Florida Tort Decisions. She set the book aside, noticing Leon moving slightly, she poured him a cup of coffee and set it on a small tray.

"I hope you slept well Mr. Park Ranger, I did. After your initial nerdy appearance yesterday, you turned out to be quite a stud."

"Is that a compliment?"

"Oh Leon." she half whispered and moaned, "In the hot tub at first, I could tell that you didn't spend a lot of time with women, but when I began to show you the things we like, you became an A+ student." She found herself liking him a lot.

They talked of his time at the Citadel and various jobs he had had with the National Park Service. He told her of the time Chester had helped out his park attendants at the Everglades job, and through Chester's influence someplace in Washington DC, he had been selected for the top position at Fort Sumter.

Finally, Gretchen suggested they get up and dressed for the day. There was a shower room adjacent to the hot tub and they both enjoyed it together. Refreshed and exhausted, they dressed and went below where she prepared a gourmet breakfast for her new lover.

Over Swedish pancakes and grilled bacon, she suggested that on her next break from school she might come up to Charleston to visit his fort.

Leon's heart pounded in his chest. He had been hoping this encounter would be more than a one-night stand, but did not have the confidence to suggest they meet again.

"When would that be?" He inquired.

"Oh, it's in about three weeks. Can you wait that long?"

"I've waited thirty-two years for someone like you to show up but after last night, three weeks seems like an eternity. It will be agony but worth the wait."

Gretchen sat next to him at the bar where she served his breakfast. She caressed his neck lightly with her fingernails and sent shivers throughout his body. Leon closed his eyes and savored the taste of the food and the pleasure of her touch. "I don't think we need to let Chester know anything about what happened last night or our plans to meet again," she said quietly.

"I think you are right. Did he say anything to you about a schedule for today? My last recollection is he and Tom had some business to take care of and they would see me later today."

"That's my take too. The boss just said to make sure you were comfortable and he thought you needed to relax a little. I hope I have helped in that department."

Chapter Forty

Denise Lubar had just dropped off Ginger and Tina Tarzano, the wife and daughter of ESCAPE's Engineering Officer. They lived in officers' quarters at the Charleston Air Force Base. She was headed home. They had spent the day touring an old plantation in West Ashley. As always, she wanted to make sure the Mercedes was full of fuel for the week, so she pulled into the Exxon station on Meeting Street.

"Let's get an ice cream cone Jeffrey."

"Thanks mommy, I love you. Can I have rocky road please? When is Daddy coming home?"

"Hello Mrs. Lubar. Fill with diesel again?" Amos asked, already knowing the answer.

"Yes Amos, how are you today? Jeff and I are going to get a cone."

"I'm just fine ma'am. I'll take care of everything."

"Two more weekends and your daddy should be back."

"I want to play golf again. Do you think we can?"

"I'm sure we can."

Denise and her son entered the deli side of the fuel station and were greeted by the owner, Mike and the deli attendant.

"How about a rocky road in a sugar cone and one scoop of French vanilla in a cup and a glass of ice water."

"You got it ma'am." The attendant set about to prepare the order and Denise engaged in a chat with Mike about news and events around the town.

Tom and Chad pulled into the station in the Corvette with the top down and went to the self-service pumps. Chad went to the restroom. Amos was fueling the Mercedes and after a moment turned and saw Thrasher dispensing gas into the beautiful car. He had not seen Walgren.

"That's a nice ride sir."

"Thanks, it's a lot of fun. How are you doing?"

"I's doing all right, sure is humid. If it starts to rain you gonna need a top on dat thing."

"Oh, I'll have it in the garage in half an hour I think the rain can wait that long."

"Yes sir, you have a nice day." Amos competed fueling the Benz and the attorney finished adding six gallons of high test fuel to the Vette. Both operations complete, Tom got into the corvette and Amos wrote down the details of the Lubar transaction and disappeared into the office to prepare the credit card invoice for Denise.

Thrasher started the car, emitting the smooth sound of power only heard from a finely tuned Corvette. He shifted the car into gear and left the station. Two blocks further down Meeting Street he turned right onto Columbus and drove to the next block, turning right on Nassau. He stopped in front of an eighteen wheeler with a Sea Land ocean container attached. The rear door was opened and a metal ramp extended to the pavement. There were no other cars on the street and he saw no one walking around.

Chad, after hearing the starting of the corvette, emerged from the restroom and looked quickly into the station and deli. Amos was talking with his boss and Mrs. Lubar. Jeffrey was sitting at a table eating his ice cream.

Walgren approached the Mercedes and, as predicted the keys, all of Denise Lubar's keys to the car, house, safe deposit box, locker at the country club and her neighbor's house were right there on the center console. The biggest risk ahead was waiting for the glow plug. In this particular car, glow plugs pre heated fuel as it went to the fuel injectors. Research at the library told him this could take between two and ten seconds. He needed two. He wore surgical gloves and in one swift move he opened the car door, placed the key in the ignition and turned it clockwise. Within four seconds the light went on and a buzzer went off indicating the car would start. A quick twist of the key and the engine roared to life in the klakity klakity sound only a Mercedes Benz diesel makes. He didn't like that. The elapsed time from when Chad had sat in to car to the moment it started to move was six seconds. To him it seemed like an hour.

He was half a block down Meeting Street by the time Amos was able to say "MMMMissus Lubar, yoooourrr cccaaaar. Oh my God!"

Inside the Exxon station, panic and disbelief ensued. Denise hyperventilated saying "Oh Vince, Oh Vince, I'm so sorry," knowing exactly what she had done wrong.

She began to cry. Jeffery was crying and hanging on to his mother's leg. Amos ran down the street but did not see the car. The station owner asked Denise what she wanted him to do. The deli attendant picked up the phone and calmly dialed 911.

By the time Amos made it across the station lot, Walgren had already turned onto Columbus then Nassau and was driving the car up the ramp into the container. He secured the car in the trailer and hopped out. Thrasher and Mitch Atkinson, one of Chad's street dealers, removed the ramp and closed the doors. The engine in the eighteen wheeler tractor was already idling and Mitch had the vehicle in gear and swiftly moved around the block. He turned right onto Amherst then left onto Meeting. He drove past the Exxon station, then wove his way through town and headed towards North Charleston. Five blocks down the street three Charleston Police cars with sirens blasting and blue lights flashing passed in the opposite direction,

He crossed the Ashley River Bridge heading up Highway 61 to meet with Thrasher and Walgren for further instructions.

Chapter Forty-One

Sam Bozo had been summoned to pick up the wardroom entourage at The Cage and take them to the Houseboat Restaurant. According to DeDe Bozo, one could experience the best Jamaican food on earth there. He had dissuaded the officers from eating dinner in his own establishment. His delivery of fresh seafood was late. His cook would not be able to produce a spectacular meal. He suggested The Cage be their dinner stop tomorrow evening.

Of course, the Houseboat was owned and operated by yet another Bozo family cousin. As the van arrived, Vince and the other officers were curious to see Radioman Dave West riding next to Sam.

The XO turned to Phil. "I wonder what Sparks is doing here?" As he was talking, West hopped out of the van carrying a sealed metal clip board, the kind used to provide security for its contents. The skipper was still engaged in a conversation with Cory Higgins and didn't immediately notice the extra visitor.

"Excuse me gentlemen but I have an important message Ensign Merrymore thought you should see ASAP."

"What is it Westy?" inquired Sutton as he reached out his hand and took possession of the clipboard. He knew Petty Officer West would not discuss anything on his confidential message board. Phil Sutton opened the board and began to read the message from Commander Seventh Coast Guard District, Miami Florida:

SUBJECT: AMERICAN RED CROSS FAMILY CRISIS NOTIFICATION

THE DISTRICT COMMANDER HAS BEEN ADVISED BY THE ARC: A FAMILY EMERGENCY HAS OCCURRED AT THE HOMEPORT OF USCGC ESCAPE. DENISE LUBAR WIFE OF YOUR EXECUTIVE OFFICER LCDR VINCE LUBAR HAS REPORTED THE FAMILY CAR WAS VIOLENTLY STOLEN WHILE AT A GAS STATION IN CHARLESTON SC.

FAMILY IS SAFE WITHOUT INJURY. LOCAL POLICE BELIEVE THE THEFT WAS NOT A RANDOM CAR THEFT BUT A TARGETED INCIDENT AIMED SPECIFICALLY AT THE LUBAR FAMILY.

IF CURRENT OPERATIONS PERMIT, RECOMMEND LCDR LUBAR RETURN EXPEDICIOUSLY TO AID THE FAMILY AND WORK WITH LOCAL POLICE.

THIS OFFICE CONTACTED THE AMERICAN EMBASSY IN KINGSTON. STAFF WILL ASSIST IN SECURING A QUICK RETURN TO HOME PORT FOR LCDR LUBAR.

ADVISE IF OPERATIONS PERMIT THIS OFFICER'S ABSENCE FROM THE BALANCE OF THE CURRENT PATROL. UPON ARRIVAL IN CHARLESTON SC, LCDR LUBAR TO CONTACT USCG INTELLIGENCE DETACHMENT AT CG GROUP CHARLESTON HQ OFFICE.

"What's up" Vince asked of his Ops Boss.

"There is no way to ease into this so you should just read it yourself," he responded. Flood approached with an inquisitive look on his face.

He joined his two senior officers.

Vince felt a little sick to his stomach and stepped back to lean on Bozo's van. He was imagining scenarios where his wife and child may have been in danger. He finished reading and handed the clipboard to the Skipper.

"Hey Sam, is there a place I can make a call to the states around here?"

"Yes sir Mista, DeDe he don't have a phone but next door is a telegraph place and peoples always be a callin' the states and even London from dat place. I take you right now."

Flood closed the clipboard and handed it back to West. "XO, just do what you need to, Lieutenant Sutton can take care of things until we get home. What do you think Phil, are you up to the job as XO for a while?"

"I just need to call Denise."

"Go ahead. Phil and I will go over things and see what you may need to fill him in on before you leave. We should all head back to the ship for the time being."

"No, don't spoil your evening. You guys go to the Houseboat place and I will head back to the ship and take care of the details." Vince walked back towards The Cage with Sam Bozo.

"Tell you what skipper," interjected Phil. "Why don't you and the guys keep having a good time. I will head back to the ship and get a little relief organized and if there are any further developments I will send Westy back to get you. It's not that big of a town and the guys need a break before we sail again."

"Ok Phil, are you good with this?"

"Of course sir, I hope my next job would be an XO's spot. There's no time like now to get a little baptism by fire. I'm wondering if this has anything to do with that Lubar family photo session at Fort Sumter and the lawyer in the background. Things are starting to smell bad."

"I was thinking along those same lines myself."

Chapter Forty-Two

Mitch maneuvered the big rig until he crossed the river and headed north on Highway 61.

Tom was at the wheel of the corvette with Chad riding shotgun. Both men were smiling but conversation started only when they were a couple miles away from town. "Do you do that often?" Thrasher broke the silence.

"Nope, my first time too. Mitch though, is good at not being caught. He's a utility guy. He can drive from here to LA and never encounter a scale. He never refers to a map. He is a walking geography book."

"A good guy for the team. How long have you known him?"

"Oh, we went to high school together. He did a tour in 'Nam and came back not too interested in any mainstream work. He hauls a lot of my product around and delivers it to the sales staff."

"So where is it we are going to meet him?"

"About thirty miles up the road where sixty-one meets I 95. You can romp on it a bit if you like, there are very few Smokey's on this road and tight curves through the farmland."

"Cool." Tom touched the gas pedal slightly and the car lurched ahead and went from fifty to eighty in three seconds. "This is nice."

Chapter Forty-Three

Chester's Oldsmobile Delta 98 pulled into his parking place. "Looks like it's time to get back to work. I hope you get to stay one more night."

She took a position at the sink washing the breakfast dishes. Leon sat on the long couch thumbing through a coffee table photo book of tropical sea life.

Chester bounced through the door. "So, I hope you slept well and got your mind off that BS up at the Fort."

"I slept like a baby. It is so peaceful onboard. The motion of the boat gave me one of the best nights I've had in months. Thanks, Chet."

"Good morning Mr. Whittaker." Gretchen smiled and handed him a cup of coffee. "I'll give you some privacy."

"Yes, thanks dear. It sure smells good in here."

"Not a problem sir." The door clicked shut.

"She's a great cook." Leon smiled.

"Well, Tom went up to Charleston yesterday and we've stirred up a little diversion. Our dear Coast Guard officer will be leaving his ship in the hands of some subordinate while he flies home to solve a big family problem."

"What happened?"

"It looks like Mr. Coast Guard's pride and joy car got stolen last night and his hysterical wife needs him to come home immediately." Chester filled him in on all the details.

"Let's just say it happened and we're not sure how or why but one of the newest and nicest rides in all of Charleston is gone. At any rate, Lieutenant Commander Lubar has lost his focus on stopping and boarding northbound boats and we have an operation ready to go."

"So I guess I had better get back and crank up the gear."

"Not that fast, Gina would like to have you over for a late lunch today at the house. We wanted to do a big dinner but she has a charity auction tonight and I have to be there too."

"That sounds like fun. Should I leave tonight?"

"Nah, the operation isn't starting for six more days, why don't you come back here and relax another night and head north tomorrow."

"I wouldn't mind spending another night here. I haven't slept so well in ages."

"Run down to your stateroom and put on some shorts and a golf shirt and we can hit the road in fifteen minutes. I have to call a client."

Leon opened the door and headed for the stairway to the lower portion of the yacht. Gretchen, now wearing the same hot pants from the previous afternoon and the chambray shirt with the buttons undone above her navel, was once again reading a green law book. She smiled at Leon and blew him a kiss.

"I'm staying aboard one more night." He smiled back. "But first
I'm going to the Whittaker's for lunch, Chester will bring me back later."

"Oooh, I'm getting tingly already. It works out great because I must finish reading these last ten files. There's a test in two days and the way you distract me I would be flunking if I don't get on it." Leon went below to change.

Chapter Forty-Four

It was a beautiful south Florida morning. On the flight from Miami to JAGS McCartney Airport outside Cockburn on Grand Turk, Trish relaxed. She was in a small twenty-five passenger turboprop operated by Nassau Air Transport. The confidence she felt was beginning to bother her. Heading into a life of crime, she couldn't get over the sensation. She was more excited about the adventure than concerned about the consequences. During the hour and a half flight, Trish appreciated the fact that one could get on a plane in southern Florida and within a matter of two hours be in an entirely different world. It thrilled her to be headed to Turks and Caicos Islands. She realized she was only going to be there for several hours before she was off to Jamaica, another island colony governed by English influence. Some guy named Mark Dean whom she never met would take her there. She studied his photograph, committing his looks to memory so when she saw him they would meet as though they had known each other for years. Chester told her Mark was doing the same with a photograph of her. He was also a Citadel graduate several years ahead of Chester. In Vietnam, he flew forward spotter planes for the Army. Now, he lived in a small village on the south coast of the Dominican Republic. He kept busy as a commercial charter pilot often delivering celebrities and wealthy individuals to hideaways throughout the Caribbean. As Trish stared at the photo, she found him to be handsome. In different circumstances, she might have been attracted to him. Today she focused on two other goals. First of all, she was about to pick up a suitcase full of money for her lover. He would use it to buy a large shipment of cocaine for delivery to the United States. Secondly, she was less than a day away from being in bed with Cory.

The flight descended towards the chain of islands and cays southeast of Grand Bahama towards the Turks and Caicos. From the cruising altitude of only ten thousand feet, Trish observed the dark blue deep ocean water and the contrasting aquamarine shades near the reefs. She saw boats motoring or sailing about. One day, she wanted to be on a boat out there taking in all the grand smells and motions.

The plane descended, then circled Grand Turk. To Trish, the island's north – south orientation with two long peninsulas at the north end looked like the pincer on a snow crab. The small size of the island peaked her curiosity. How could such an insignificant dot on the edge of the Atlantic become a mecca for smart people involved in crime to store huge sums of money?

When the door opened, the triple filtered dry air from the flight absorbed the warmth, aromas and humidity of the tropics.

Chapter Forty-Five

Vince spent several hours with Phil going over recent intelligence on boat departures from Colombia and the description of those vessels. He was confident his Ops Boss would do a great job handling his duties in his absence. He called Denise and calmed her down. She was pleased he was going to make it home. Inside, Vince was shaken up but one could not tell from his demeanor.

He knew in the back of his mind this incident had something to do with the photographs. If it was connected to his job in the Coast Guard, suddenly this had gotten dangerous. He hoped the theft of his beloved Mercedes was a random act by some local car thief and nothing more.

A vehicle from the Embassy took him over the hills and through the villages of inland Jamaica. It was interesting for him as he was able to see the abject poverty of the country. Barely clothed shoeless citizens wandered dirt streets. Most dwellings were run-down shanties with metal and semi-thatched roofs. There was no signs of electricity or other utilities. Oddly though, everyone he saw seemed happy.

The ride took over three hours and he was dropped off at Palisadoes Airport twenty minutes west of downtown Kingston.

The embassy staff booked him on a flight to Miami departing an hour after his arrival. He remained overnight in Miami then caught a morning flight to Charleston, arriving thirty-six hours after his car had been stolen.

Chapter Forty-Six

Tom and Chad met up with Mitch and told him to take the car to Lexington, Kentucky.

Chad instructed: "Simply leave it parked there with Denise Lubar's keys lying right where she had left them."

He would, of course, wear surgical gloves while handling the prize car. When it was discovered by local law enforcement personnel, there would be no trace of anything tying the car to the trio involved in the heist. Tom handed the driver ten thousand dollars in fifties and hundreds. They all shook hands and departed.

Tom enjoyed maneuvering the corvette back towards Charleston, feeling her response around each corner and the power as he passed slower cars already going well over the speed limit. Within three quarters of an hour, they were back in town and pulling in to the circle drive at Charleston Place.

"So, do you want to keep the car tonight?"

"No, thanks, I'm going to have a few drinks at Hank's and try to get an attractive S.O.B into my room. I met a couple last night but they were on their way to a play. It could be promising."

"Well, sounds like time well spent. Good luck. I can pick you up in the morning whenever you need."

"Ten-thirty would be great. I'm booked on a noon flight." He pulled the vehicle over the cobblestones to the door of the hotel. Edward stepped up and opened the driver side door. Chad opened his own and stepped around the car to take command.

"I think we accomplished a lot today, I look forward to future projects," the attorney spoke to the drug dealer.

"Likewise. I will see you in the morning." They shook hands and he lowered himself into the driver's seat, put the car in gear and slowly rolled away, rendering a somewhat respectful salute to both Tom and Edward the bell captain.

"Dat sure is a nice car your friend has. I don't know if I had a car like dat if I would let another friend drive it. You're pretty lucky sir." Edward chatted as he walked towards the ten-foot high double brass framed door.

"Yes Edward, I do feel pretty lucky. Thank you." he responded and placed two neatly folded five-dollar bills in the snow white glove on his left hand as he shook his right one.

"Yes sir, you have a nice evening Mr. Thrasher."

145

Tom walked through the lobby of the luxurious hundred and fifty-year-old hotel, impressed with the art work, architecture and décor of the building. The desk attendant and one of the bellmen recognized him and greeted him by name. He enjoyed the southern hospitality rendered by everyone he met. On previous trips to Charleston to deliver briefcases full of money, he had always returned to Florida the same day he had left. With his new appreciation for the town, he thought he should come back for extended recreational reasons.

Entering his room, he fell backwards on the large bed and stared at the crystal chandelier suspended from the ceiling and said to himself, "I wonder how many other Cornell law graduates have stolen a car." He laughed to himself, got up and showered and prepared for an evening of nightlife with the S.O.Bs.

Chapter Forty-Seven

Trish walked down the concourse. Off to the right she spotted Mark Dean waiting next to a bank of pay phones. He was wearing khaki shorts, sandals and a tropical short-sleeved shirt. Around his waist were a belt and a fanny pack. "How odd," she thought.

"Hey sis." he said as she approached. Trish immediately understood they would appear to others as siblings. She approached him, set down her carry-on bag and provided him with a sibling type embrace and a quick kiss on the cheek. "Hi Mark, how's dad doing?" she joined in the dialogue game. The photo she had studied showed Dean as a pretty fit and handsome man but in person, she found him to be less than perfect, a slight beer belly and pock marked facial skin and signs of dandruff on the collar of his shirt. "No competition for Cory here," she thought.

"Oh, he's doing fine, can't wait to see you. Did you check any luggage?"

"Yes, one turquoise bag. Oh, there it is." she pointed to the small baggage claim stand near the exit. "That was quick."

Mark picked up the suitcase and said "We will get through customs and then take this over to my plane. Then we can head into town for lunch and any business you need to take care of before we head out."

"Sounds fine to me." Trish felt safe with this strange man. There were no overtures of hitting on her and she liked that. He was all business.

The customs desk at JAGS McCarthy airport was rudimentary at best. She and Mark stood in a line for less than three minutes. When it was their turn to approach the official his first remark was: "Hello Mista Dean. You got a new customer?"

"That's right James. This is Miss Dixon from Atlanta. She is stopping here for the day then I will be taking her to Jamaica for a vacation."

"I see," James responded. Trish handed him her passport. "Why do you need to stop here, are there no direct flights from America to Jamaica?"

"Of course there are, but I hadn't seen Mr. Dean for a few years and I thought it would be fun to fly in his plane. It will make more of an adventure. Besides, I have investments in the Turks Trust and Clearing House and have scheduled a meeting with my agent while I'm in the Caribbean. "

"I understand." James responded as though she was telling him she just stopped here for a cup of coffee. "Enjoy your day on Grand Turk." He stamped her documents and handed them back. He then nodded towards Mark. "Next."

"Not much stress at Grand Turk Customs. Is that how it always goes?" she asked her escort.

"Not for people who are traveling with me. James' brother lives on San Juan Island and once or twice a year I give him a ride there or bring his relatives here for a visit. On this island, the customs folks understand most of the foreign visitors are here to visit with financial folks so the questions aren't too difficult."

"I guess when you think about it the major import export commodity in this place is money." Trish grinned.

"That's about the size of it."

He pointed towards a wide corridor leading to the left. Through the window, Trish could see a dozen smaller planes parked on the tarmac adjacent to the building. He gestured towards a white twin engine Grumman Albatross parked about twenty yards from one of the exit doorways. "There she is. Cloud Dancer"

"This looks like a nice toy. I love the smells down here," Trish remarked as they approached the plane.

"It does grow on you and make you forget all the crap happening in the states."

"So how long have you been down here?"

"Ever since I got out of the army in seventy-three, I guess that's about thirteen years. I haven't thought about it for a while. They say that the slow pace of life makes you lose perspective on how much time is going by. I guess whoever 'they' are know what they are talking about." He turned a key in the left side door towards the rear of the aircraft.

Mark picked up Trish's suitcase and placed in on a small rack just inside the door. "Is there anything else you want to leave here before we head downtown?"

Trish was carrying a small purse containing her passport, a credit card or two, a couple hundred dollars in cash and not much else. She also held tightly on to an impressive leather portfolio containing all of the papers Chester had given her. "Nope, I think we are good."

Chapter Forty-Eight

Tom spent an interesting evening in old town Charleston. He showered and changed into a perfectly tailored ensemble of leisure slacks, a sport shirt and five hundred dollar shoes to enjoy an evening with the SOB's. He left the hotel, walked a few blocks to Hank's and took a seat at the bar. It was interesting to discover when spirits were served in South Carolina instead of pouring from a bottle at the bar, the bartender presented him with two small airline bottles of gin and a frosted glass containing an olive and a shaker to make his own martini. Sam the bartender told him, in this state they could only provide the unopened spirits and the set up to drink them. Tom found this awkward yet interesting. It was just another fact making this mysterious place even more intriguing.

He enjoyed two of the martinis. Halfway through the second one, a couple well-dressed southern women in their late twenties took up seats at the bar next to him. Within three minutes, Sam introduced them to Tom. One was the wife of an air force C5 pilot who was currently on a mission to Germany and the other turned out to be single and a business associate of the military wife. Both were employed in the title insurance industry managing a nationwide office on the south side of Broad Street. Apparently the two were frequent patrons of the bar. Tom offered to buy them dinner and explained he was an attorney from Florida visiting the Carolinas in search of a real estate investments for a wealthy client in Miami.

After dinner, they enjoyed a dessert of Charleston Peach Cream Cake from an old cookbook authored by Hank's mother. When a second bottle of ten-year-old Bordeaux was half empty, Sarah the Air Force wife took the initiative and began to leave. She was aware her colleague and the attorney might just need some privacy. She indicated her husband was due back from Frankfurt around noon the next day.

Jenny, the insurance professional, remained with her new attorney friend and they visited and danced to the piano bar music until Tom asked if she would walk around in the evening air and give him a tour of the neighborhood. She obliged and by eleven thirty, they were in his room.

Jenny left around three am taking a cab home. They agreed, somehow either in Florida or back here in Charleston, they would meet again.

Tom woke at seven, showered and enjoyed a leisurely southern breakfast. Peach nectar served in place of orange juice brought back memories of the evening before. "I like this place," he told himself. He had enjoyed himself with martinis, the company of beautiful women and the passionate encounter several hours ago. It took until an hour and a half after he had awakened to remember yesterday, he had become a car thief. The memory of the previous day's events entered his mind while he read the account of the incident in the morning edition of Post and Courier.

The article described the scene of a brazen heist of Mrs. Lubar's Mercedes. The Charleston police were certain they would find the missing car soon because it was easily identified. They had already raided a chop shop finding ten other stolen cars but no vehicles matching the description of the Lubar Benz.

He wondered how soon the Lexington police would find the object of the Charleston police search. A message left at five am on the hotel switchboard from Chad indicated that "everything is finished and I will pick you up at ten."

Walgren arrived precisely at ten and Thrasher was waiting in the lobby. This time, the local Narco Distribution Manager was driving a Dodge ES 600 convertible. At his side a beautiful brunette nestled up to him beyond the middle of the bench seat. "Hop in Tom, this is Debbi, I didn't think you would mind if she came along, I have to take her to Myrtle Beach after I drop you."

Edward held open the door of the Dodge after loading Tom's bag into the back seat of the open car. "Thank you for visiting Charleston Place Mr. Thrasher sir. I hope your stay was enjoyable." The doorman smiled. The story of his guest returning near midnight with the gorgeous Jenny on his arm already had fully spread through the bell staff.

"It is a wonderful spot and I'm sure we will be seeing one another in the future, Edward." He smiled and winked at the tall black figure pressing a fifty-dollar bill into his white gloved hand as he slid in next to Debbi.

"Let's roll. Nice to meet you Debbi." He was admiring her golden tanned legs extending from a pair of pink shorts. Her ample breasts appeared well contained and braless beneath a tight fitting University of South Carolina tee shirt.

"Very pleased to meet you, sir." She replied in a pleasant southern accent. Carolina and Georgia women know they possess the ability to melt men with their talk. "Chad said you like convertibles so I thought we could bring you to the airport in mine. What do you think?"

"This is your car? I'm impressed."

"I like it. It lets me get sun when I drive and I love the breeze on my skin," she remarked, rubbing her hands on her arms and legs.

"So did you have a restful evening, boss?"

"Sure did, everything was perfect. I like this little town Mr. Walgren."

"Great." He knew Tom's response meant he got lucky.

"I met a couple of real estate folks. I believe I will be back soon."

"Next stop CHS." Chad responded as the car headed north. He turned up the music. A McClinton beach shuffle tune was playing and all three were enjoying the atmosphere. The trio remained silent for most of the trip. Tom enjoyed the scenery, music and acrid scent of the Ashley River to their left. He also noticed that Debbi spent most of the trip with her left hand gently rubbing Chad's jeans while her right hand moved about, brushing her windblown hair out of her eyes. She also randomly rested it on the seat next to his left leg where he felt an occasional caress from her baby finger. "What a horny young woman," he thought.

Chad broke the silence as they pulled into the airport. "Here we are."

To his right, Tom could see a huge Air Force C5 transport plane landing and taxiing towards the big hangars at the Air Force Base. He wondered if it was the plane Sarah's husband was commanding. He visualized his seductive wife welcoming him home from his week away. He smiled.

"Well thanks for the help and the introductions." Tom spoke as Chad wheeled the convertible counterclockwise around the driveway.

"Nice to meet you too Debbi." Tom reached across in front of her to shake the drug dealer's hand.

"I'm sure we will meet again someday," she spoke once again in her seductive accent. "Next time ya'll come up we should all go to Myrtle Beach."

"I would like that."

151

As he started to get out of the car, Debbi leaned over and kissed him on the cheek. "Ok, just say when!"

"See you next time, bud." Tom turned and headed into the terminal.

Check in for his Allegheny direct flight to Palm Beach only took a few moments and he found himself with more than an hour to kill before leaving. He walked about the terminal studying local art and historical artifacts. At a newsstand, he picked up a paperback copy of Lords of Discipline. Reviews made it a best-selling popular new novel portraying some dark history of the Citadel cadet corps. The storyline deals with the awkward way the academy dealt with the integration of blacks into their institution. Tom had heard about this book and since he had visited Charleston, he felt he should read this story to get some insight into how Chester had evolved. When he was ready to board the plane, he was a third of the way through the book and thoroughly intrigued.

Chapter Forty-Nine

For the first time in his career in the Coast Guard, Vince left an assignment, trusting his sworn duties to subordinates. In the back of his mind he knew his beloved wife had against all of his harping left the keys to his cherished Mercedes on the center console attracting the attention of some lowlife car thief. Overnight in the Miami Holiday Inn, he met briefly with several officers from the Seventh District Intelligence Command and a DEA Field Agent. He was curious as to what they had been able to uncover about Thrasher.

The surveillance team, only funded for part time work, had seen him present a divorce case in superior court and he had picked up some unknown friend from West Palm Beach airport and delivered him to Chester Whitaker's yacht on the ICW. The guest on the yacht as far as anyone knew, did not leave the boat.

The Eastern Airlines flight from Miami was to land at noon. A generous tailwind set them down fifteen minutes early according to an announcement made by the pilot as they crossed the Savannah River. Denise would be there to pick him up in a rental car provided by their insurance company. He knew from their phone conversation this morning Jeffrey would be in school.

The 727 descended through the clear blue sky and was floating past a row of six C5 Air Force transport planes lined up wing to wing at the Charleston AFB. He noticed a seventh C5 over by a huge hangar unloading what looked like half a dozen armored personnel carriers. He wondered what a career in the Air Force might be like.

His stress returned as the plane pulled up to the terminal next to an Allegheny Airlines jet. Vince wondered how all of these regional airlines survived with so much competition. He worried about dealing with his wife in the middle of this current crisis and was concerned about the mission of his ship. He felt as though he was abandoning his shipboard duties but was confident that Phil would do a great job. And in the back of his mind he was still wondering what that person from the photographs taken months ago at Fort Sumter had to do with anything.

Vince gathered up his briefcase and retrieved his uniform hat from the overhead compartment. As he stepped into the concourse, he spotted Denise waiting for him. The toll the incident had taken on her was evident in her face.

153

"Oh Vince, I'm so sorry. I love you. Please don't hate me for the stupid thing I did." She was sobbing as they embraced, and she clung to him tighter than he could ever remember.

His eyes were closed and he was absorbing every curve of her body and very happy to be in her embrace.

"Don't worry; we've got great insurance. I'm just happy nothing happened to you or Jeff. When they brought me the Red Cross message and said there was an 'incident' with your family I was scared to death. I'm so glad you are safe. We can always get another car."

He opened his eyes and was startled. He was looking directly at Tom Thrasher approximately twenty feet away as he stepped into the jet way to board the Allegheny flight at the next gate. Just as the attendant was looking at his boarding pass, he looked around and for a second his eyes stopped and looked at Vince and Denise. Their eyes locked onto each other. Vince knew exactly who he was looking at. Thrasher was not sure who it was but for a second thought, this person was someone he knew or knew of.

Thrasher entered the hallway racking his brain to remember who the guy with the chick was. Then he figured it out.

"It's that fucking Lubar Guy. He's off the boat, he's upset, he's gotta take care of the bitch wife, mission accomplished." He took his seat in the first row and opened his book to continue reading about the occult history of his boss' alma mater.

Vince felt his stomach in his throat. He did not want Denise to know what had just occurred. Thrasher, probably a criminal of some sort, had just been sitting in the same airport waiting room as his wife.

"Hey baby, I need to get to a pay phone and call down to Miami. They wanted to know when I made it safely home. It will just take a minute, everyone has been so great in helping me get home, I need to report in."

"Ok, I'll go into the restroom and get straightened out."

His call was answered. "Corpus Christi Intelligence Center."

"Yes, is Lieutenant Commander Solomon on duty, this is XO of the Cutter ESCAPE."

"Yes sir Commander, he is right here by the fax machine, I will connect you."

"What's up XO? I heard about your car. That sucks."

"Yeah, well, I just got to the Charleston Airport and Denise was waiting here for me and it is great to get back. But as I got off the plane from Miami here, that son-of-a-bitch we have been looking for was getting on a plane headed for West Palm Beach. Gus, I think he may have had something to do with the theft of my car. I just want you to know about this, we should probably upgrade surveillance on him when he lands and see where he goes."

"Ok, I will set it up with intelligence and someone will be following him the moment he lands. Anything else?"

"No, I got a pretty shook up wife to deal with so I will be out of touch for a few days and dealing with the local law enforcement and my insurance company. Just keep me posted if anything comes up," Vince responded. "Thanks buddy, let's get together soon."

"You take care of business and we will worry about a class reunion later."

Denise emerged from the restroom and looked fully composed and as beautiful as ever. "OK sir, your limo awaits." They walked out to the parking lot and she pointed to a nice looking white four door Chevy Impala. The both broke into laughter.

"Everything is going to be fine," Vince announced as he held the driver side door open for his wife then walked around and got in to the passenger seat. "I love the smell of the air in Charleston. There is just nothing like it."

Denise pulled away and they were on their way home.

Chapter Fifty

Lieutenant Sutton received all of the reports from the Engineering, Deck and Operations department heads and Buzz Ladner now temporarily appointed as acting Operations Officer. The ship was ready to return to sea after two and a half days in Montego Bay.

He approached the Skipper sitting in his chair on the bridge. He rendered a salute and using the same words he had so often heard the XO utter he stated: "All department heads report the ship is ready for sea, all lines are singled up and the main engines are on the line. Ensign Ladner has the conn. Request permission to get underway, sir."

"Very well XO, let's go catch some bad guys." He returned the salute.

"Aye-Aye Sir" Sutton turned to Ladner, "Take this ship to sea Mr. Ladner."

"Aye-Aye Sir."

The same dockside trio who greeted the ship waited on the dock ready to act when the shipboard personnel told them to. Over the past forty-eight hours, they had befriended several crewmembers and departure greetings were exchanged. A flurry of activity ensued as lines were retrieved from the dock and the graceful old lady made her way back out into the azure waters of the Gulf of Mexico.

As the ship moved slowly out of the harbor, the Skipper asked "XO, where the hell are the smugglers?"

"Well sir, the intel reports had six boats loading on the docks in Barranquilla three days ago. We've got photos of them and Lt. Mitchel from the district says there is a belief they might skirt the east coast of Central America towards the Yucatan. There is a lot of seasonal fishing activity over there. They can move in and out of the fleet and try to sneak through that way."

"Sounds great to me, let's head there. Any weather concerns?"

"Nothing Captain. There is a strong stationary high over the whole Gulf and the Caribbean. There was a tropical wave off the coast of Africa three days ago. It might develop into some sort of depression. We will keep an eye on the daily weather faxes. I'd like to conduct fire and man overboard drills along the way."

"Great, let's try to get at least two or three boardings in each day if we can, too. I feel it in my blood, something exciting is headed our way. I would really like to see you get a bust in your first week as XO. How about you?"

"Like Dirty Harry says, 'Go ahead. Make my day.' Yes, sir!"

It was 0945 in the morning. An abundance of hangovers saturated the crew.

"I guess we have steaks for lunch, it looks like a lot of the crew could use a good dose of protein. I will be down in the cabin for a while, call if you need anything." Flood hopped out of his chair.

Sutton knew one of the hangovers the skipper was talking about was actually his own and he was headed to his bunk for a pre-lunch nap.

"Ok Mr. Merrymore," the acting XO said, "Let's find our way to the Campeche Banks."

Chapter Fifty-One

After a brief stop for a fish sandwich lunch at a seaside stand, Mark drove Trish to the trust company. He would wait in the Suburban while she conducted her business. Trish walked through the door of the stucco-faced office building and immediately felt like she had changed worlds. Outside, the streets were clean but showed age and the lack of serious maintenance. Poverty on the streets was apparent and people were very casually dressed. Once inside the office of Turk Trust and Clearing House, she felt a dramatic change.

The floors were polished marble, the walls adorned with artwork in large depictions of sailing ships, tropical seascapes and Scottish castles. She noticed a polished gold inlay in the floor of some sort of family crest. A tall slender man in a perfectly tailored pinstriped suit and bow tie approached. His shined wingtips reflected the light from windows fifteen feet above the floor. A large tropical fan twirled around in the center of the ceiling, giving a strobe light effect to his shoes. It was subtle; the building was comfortably air-conditioned.

"May I be of assistance my dear?" A deep British accent accompanied the question.

"Yes, I'm from Florida law office of Whittaker and Whittaker and. . . ."

"Ah yes, we have been expecting you. You must be Miss. Dixon," he interrupted with grace. He had been studying a photograph of Trish faxed in from Florida earlier in the morning. "Welcome. My name is Harold Jarvis." He extended his hand in a polite shake. "At your service." He led her into a side office where large glass windows rendered the space visible to the lobby. A beautiful antique British hardwood desk and several leather chairs furnished the area. A file cabinet drawer system was built in and made up part of the marble wall. "Please sit. Can I get you any refreshments?"

"A glass of ice water would be wonderful. This is a beautiful old building."

"Yes, we enjoy life here. It was at one time the office of the Colonial Major who served as the first governor."

He opened another door in the side of the office and inside was a small refrigerator containing several beers, a crystal pitcher of water and ice. On the shelf above were several bottles of well-aged scotch and various spirits and wines. He poured a glass of water and placed two ice cubes into it. "Here we go, dear. Now, I trust you have some paper work for me."

"Yes I do." She unzipped the top of the portfolio removing a sealed manila envelope and handed it to Harold.

"Thank you." He placed it squarely in front of him and opened his desk drawer to retrieve a solid gold dagger he used as a letter opener. Extracting the file, he smiled, read over the documents and said: "As always, very well and in proper order. What has become of Mister Thrasher?"

"Oh, his law practice has been keeping him occupied as has his constant search for the perfect woman." Trish smiled.

"A fine catch he would be someday for a beautiful lass but I wager the barrister's wandering eye would be the cause of ulcers for a wife. He once dined with a cousin of mine here and she found him quite charming. Even on a casual first date he is easily distracted if you know what I mean."

"I certainly do." Trish grinned. "I'm happy our relationship is professional. I'm a certified public accountant and I have a difficult time dealing with lines not clearly defined."

"I understand completely. It looks like the documents match our instructions." He stood while Trish took a gulp of water suddenly realizing she was about to walk out the door with more cash than anyone should be able to carry.

It took three separate keys to access the bottom tall drawer of the file cabinet and Harold finally reached in and pulled out a stately, thick black leather suitcase with wheels and a pull handle, the kind airline pilots carry all of their manuals in. He lifted it up next to the gold dagger. Popping the two latches open at the precise same second he spun the case around to face Trish.

"Two million three-hundred thousand dollars in mixed American, British, Canadian and German currencies. We use larger British and German notes to keep the contents in a manageable weight. You are welcome to take time to count it."

She had been instructed by Chester. "No, it won't be necessary. We have never had any discrepancies with Turk Trust and I don't know why we would now."

Her heart was jumping out of her chest at the sight of so much cash but she remained composed beyond what she imagined she was capable of. She snapped the lid shut. "Is there a key?"

"No, you see there is a combination for the latches. Each is different. The one on the left is 8235 and on the right is 5328 – the reverse of the first. I would suggest committing to memory those digits."

"I've already done it," she replied.

She used little tricks to remember series of numbers and this one was simple. Eighty – two: the year she graduated from college and Thirty-Five, the age she wanted to be when she would retire from her life of crime and sail away to some tropical island with her lover.

"If there is nothing else, I guess I should go." Trish smiled at Harold.

"That is all dear. It has been a pleasure and I am certain we will see one another from time to time. Have a wonderful trip."

Trish shook his hand once again and picked up the briefcase, somewhat surprised at the weight. It was heavy. She extended the handle and towed it behind her. She was happy she had been working out and playing tennis.

She exited the comfortable building and entered the heavy tropical air of Grand Turk pulling the case. Mark was standing next to the passenger door of the Suburban and opened it as she approached.

"Everything go OK?"

"Like getting a car loan."

"Are you ready for your Jamaica holiday?"

"Hell yes, let's get going."

In the airplane, Mark gave Trish a packet of documents containing a duplicate passport already stamped with an entry visa to Montego Bay, a MasterCard and an American Express card both endorsed by the United Bank of Jamaica. He took her original passport and told her when she got back to Atlanta it would be on her desk. She had no reason to doubt.

After a thorough check of the inside and outside of his aircraft, Mark joined Trish in the cockpit and went through checkoff processes, ending with the engines firing up. First a chug, then a blast of blue and grey smoke and finally each engine accelerated and roared to life. They taxied along in front of the tower to the end of the runway. Once cleared for their journey, Mark reached above for the throttles, pushing them forward. The flying boat began lumbering down the runway of JAGS MacArthur. Speed increased to about one hundred ten miles per hour, then Mark eased back on the yoke and they were airborne. Clear of the runway with wheels up, he communicated one last time with the tower and headed southwest towards the Windward Passage between Cuba and Haiti.

"Next landing is on the water. She likes that a lot better." Mark finally spoke to Trish through the headphones.

She was fascinated with the old flying machine. She felt confident, secure, safe and powerful in her situation. She could not wait to get into the sack with Cory.

Chapter Fifty-Two

Lunch at Chester and Gina Whittaker's home was over the top. Gina and a kitchen helper named Nadel, from the Dominican Republic, prepared a feast of fresh local produce and seafood. Leon enjoyed every bite. Gina was very interested in Leon's job at Fort Sumter. She minored in history in college and was hoping for a personal tour of the monument next time she and her husband came to Charleston for a Citadel reunion.

Leon promised Gina if she came to Charleston she would get the same tour and treatment the president would get if he were to show up. All during lunch though, Leon's mind was occupied, anticipating getting back to the yacht and spending the evening with Gretchen. Although he felt stuffed from lunch, he was wondering what she had planned for their dinner and how she would be dressed for the event. At one point, he found he was enjoying himself so much all thoughts of problems with the photographs vanished.

After lunch, Leon and Chester walked across the broad lawn between the Whittaker mansion and the Inter-Coastal Waterway. Tied to the dock was a new sleek 26' Sea Ray.

"Want to go for a spin? Hey, why don't we run you back to the big boat in this thing? Let's go tell Gina what we are up to." He spun Leon around by the elbow and they proceeded back across the lawn.

As they walked, Chester reassured Leon that everything would be fine. He told him the little auto theft caper had been a tactical success. LCDR Lubar, released from his ship was busy helping his wife deal with the trauma.

"As soon as you get back to the fort, let's check on the whereabouts of all ships on patrol. In a week our flagship will be picking up a delivery at sea east of St. Thomas then heading to Chesapeake Bay."

"Not a problem, I have the data down to a science and can turn those reports around and fax them out within half an hour. It's fun."

Back in the house, Chester told Gina of the plan to take Leon back to the boat. Gina thought it was a great idea and invited herself along. Perhaps since her husband was taking the rest of the day off, he might spring for a romantic dinner at some waterfront bistro.

162

Chester agreed. Within half an hour, the three were enjoying the cool wind as they navigated the waterway at thirty plus miles per hour.

It was a beautiful windless afternoon and Chester pointed his speedboat south, passing Munyon Island under the bridge at Singer Island. He then turned left at the Palm Beach Shores inlet and darted out into the Atlantic Ocean. The ocean swells were only a couple of feet and he turned north and ran at full throttle, around forty-five- miles per hour, two hundred yards off the beach. Within what seemed like minutes Chester wheeled the boat to the left again and re-entered the ICW at Jupiter inlet.

"Wow! What a ride! I can't believe those homes."

"Yeah, those are the really rich folks. Some are clients and believe it or not, many of those places are empty most of the year. The owners travel the world or work in New York, Geneva or Tokyo. Some have three or four similar homes someplace on earth."

"That's unbelievable."

Gina chimed in. "A lot of them are very shy and don't socialize or mix in much. I think many are lonely and it seems sad. In our situation, I love living here and being social with all of our friends."

"Yeah Leon, during the holidays at our house we have the best client party of any attorney in South Florida. You ought to come down in December. Gina, make sure we get him back for the party. We have about a hundred and fifty over for food and drinks. I'll bring the big boat down here and tie it up in front. Hell, you could stay there again."

"Sounds fine to me, just say when and I will be here," Leon replied, wondering if Gretchen would still live on board then.

Between Jupiter and the wider portion of the ICW beginning in North Palm Beach, Chester reduced speed. As they continued on, Gina picked out a shore side restaurant where she would have her husband treat her to a two-hundred-dollar dinner. She asked if Leon wanted to join them. He said he was tired and needed to rest for the trip back home. He hoped he would leave the yacht in the morning exhausted, relishing in the ten hours of touch, passion and lust he would enjoy with Gretchen. They passed by Peanut Island where they had headed out into the ocean then continued south about one more mile.

"Here we go. Thanks for taking the time to come down, I hope we can put all of those issues behind and move on from here."

"Thanks for all the good counsel. As always, you were able to put me back on the right track. Gina, it was swell to see you again," he said as he gave her a bear hug and kissed her on the cheek. "Any time you want the VIP tour of the Fort, let me know and I will take you places no one has seen since the civil war."

"Sounds mysterious. I can hardly wait. See you soon."

Chester eased the Sea Ray up to a small dock. Leon saw the imposing bow of Just One More looming above. He hopped onto the dock and reaching down grabbed Chester's hand and they shook with equal and firm grips. "To the corps!" both men spoke in unison.

Gina smiled shaking her head.

"Tom should be here around ten to get you to the airport. I would take you but I have deposition in the morning. See you soon, old friend."

"Right, I'll be in touch." Leon relaxed his grip, turned and walked past two one hundred foot yachts then turned right approaching Chester's. He felt rich and of privilege. Looking up to the wheelhouse, his heart leapt when he saw Gretchen sitting on a tall stool on the port bridge wing smiling in his direction. She was wearing the same chambray shirt, a bikini bottom and a broad smile.

She blew him a kiss and lipped out a silent greeting. "Welcome home, stud." His pace quickened as he heard the sound of Chester's fast boat proceeding north. As he ascended the steps, Gretchen appeared in the doorway.

They stepped towards one another and embraced like high school lovers after ditching their parents for a weekend.

Chapter Fifty-Three

On the way home from the airport, Vince and Denise stopped by the Charleston Police Department and met with Detective Captain Sam Gibbs. Gibbs, a senior cop, fourth generation Charlestonian and a twenty-year veteran offered the Lubar's' iced tea and went over the details of the situation.

Charleston had not been plagued much with auto thefts since a chop shop ring had been broken up two years ago.

"It's a perplexing situation." Gibbs shuffled through the papers.

"There are only a handful of cars similar to yours on the peninsula and one of our patrol team would have seen a Mercedes like that hightailing out of town. Once in a while, off-shore criminals will heist a nice hand-picked ride and have it removed from the country."

"You mean they get stolen and exported?" Vince inquired. "I deal in things being smuggled into the country, I hadn't thought criminals would export their stolen stuff. I guess it makes sense."

"We will keep looking. I'm not offering much hope for your car being returned. We have notified all law enforcement agencies from Maine to Florida and west to the Mississippi. We will see if anything shows up." Gibbs continued. "My advice is to get with your insurance company and start shopping for a new car. I wish I could frame it differently but in my experience I believe ya'll have seen the last of that one."

Vince wanted to share his thoughts concerning the possibility of this car heist being connected to the work he and other Coast Guard and DEA officials were doing. He held back though, not wanting Denise to be concerned the incident may have been connected to his work. He made a mental note to get back with the captain in private within the next two days.

"That's not very encouraging. I know how proud you were of that car honey, and I'm so sorry about…"

"Just stop Denise. I'm happy you and Jeffrey are OK and no one got hurt. Well, Captain, I trust you will do all you can. I think we will head home and get some rest."

"That would be my advice. I will call ya'll if anything changes."

Vince and Denise stood to leave and shook hands with Gibbs.

"What's Jeffrey up to?"

"He's in school telling all his friends about the gangsters who stole our car and how daddy is flying in to solve the crime. He has high hopes, dear."

"How much time do we have before he gets home?" Vince asked as he placed his arm around Denise's waist and drew her close to his side.

"Oh, he is going over to the Tarzano's house until I go get him. I'm way ahead of you." She turned and kissed his ear as they walked out of the police station.

Chapter Fifty-Four

The path Mark took from Grand Turk towards Jamaica led southwesterly through the Windward Passage. Haiti was on the left and fifteen or so miles to the northwest was Cuba. Trish was fascinated with the geography of the Caribbean. The sky was a deep blue with a dozen small puffy clouds floating around like spires of cotton candy. The sea below was like an oil painting with golden reefs below the surface of greenish blue water and white surf breaking on an assortment of white sand beaches, scattered rocky formations and sheer cliffs. Spaced every two or three miles along the southern shore of Cuba, Trish saw small streams and rivers joining the sea. It was mesmerizing to see from ten thousand feet. The old Grumman droned along with a rhythm causing her to feel secure.

Mark said the trip would take just over three hours at 175 knots but they were getting a good thirty-knot tail wind and scooting along well.

"Look at those navy ships down there. They are doing helo operations."

Trish saw three long grey ships well over four hundred feet long and a half dozen helicopters droning around like bumblebees.

"Look! Down there ahead of the big ships, there is a submarine under the surface. Now the choppers are all heading for the sub. They must be playing war games."

Mark banked the plane to the right so they could both get a better view. The choppers suddenly headed in the direction of the sub and started dropping things in the water all around the submerged vessel. The three destroyers suddenly disbursed in three directions and within ten minutes they were all pointing their bows in the direction of the sub.

"Those floating things are sonobouys. They track the sub and send the info back to the ships then the ships can move in for a kill. Looks like the guys on the surface are winning this game."

"I pity the poor Russian subs discovered by our guys." Trish commented.

Leaving the Navy behind, Mark took a slight jog left and headed towards a land mass appearing on the horizon. "There is your island."

"Wow, this is the best way to travel. Where is Havana?" she asked looking towards Cuba.

"Oh, it's way the hell up there on the north side of the island. It's just across the straits from Key West. Have you ever been there?"

"Where, Havana or Key West?"

"Key West."

"No, I would love to visit.

"It's a fun town and crazy people live there. Not crazy bad but just crazy fun. You would enjoy it."

"Sounds like fun."

They continued passing cruise ships, sailing yachts and fishing boats tending their nets. They also passed over two white hulled fishing boats about five miles apart headed for the Windward Passage. From their altitude, Mark could see there were no fishing nets onboard the boats. "Look," he pointed at the boats. "There are two boats headed to the states loaded with dope. I would bet this plane on it."

"How can you tell?"

"Well, those big drums that look like an empty spool of thread should have nets wrapped around them. They don't. Plus, the boats are steaming fast towards the passage and will probably be transiting through at night. I bet they never turn their lights on. Wonder if they will make it. The Coast Guard is stretched pretty thin out here. I haven't seen any of their boats since I left the Dominican Republic two days ago."

"It's amazing what you can see from up here." Trish answered.

"Don't the Coasties use airplanes to search too?'

"Well they do when they can afford it. I have read there are some budget problems and patrols have been cut back because of all the dough they had to spend on the Cuban boat lift."

"I suppose that's good news for people in our line of work."

"Yep."

Time went by quickly as they saw more interesting things floating on the beautiful Gulf. Soon, the north coast of Jamaica was several miles off to the left. Mark took her down to about six thousand feet. Trish enjoyed the adventure, as she was now able to see the lush vegetation covering the island. They passed by Rio Bueno and Falmouth and Mark picked up the microphone contacting the harbor authority in Montego Bay. He advised they would be landing near the cruise ship terminal in about ten minutes. The harbormaster asked if any arrangements were necessary. Mark said someone was meeting them and no assistance was needed. He would however need to buy fuel before he departed the island.

"Then welcome to Jamaica my friend, I hope you enjoy your visit. I will be watching for your approach."

"Thank you, I will park at your marina for the evening then head off to the Dominican Republic in the morning."

"That's fine with us, there is a small fee for overnight stays. I will send an attendant down to take care of that little business and schedule you for the gas dock in the morning."

"Thanks again."

Mark banked the plane to the left and began to transit inland over the top of mangroves and palm trees. Trish could see small villages populated with mostly dark people walking around outside and children playing on unpaved streets. Then the outskirts of urban Montego Bay came into view and she saw cars, scooters and bicycles. It was nearing twilight and the sun shone brightly into the airplane. Mark concentrated on his landing evolution. He flew towards the sun for a minute or two, then banked to the right making a one hundred eighty degree turn, leveling at a thousand feet and heading straight for a white cruise ship tied to the dock two miles away. He continued to descend, and about half a mile from the dock the flying boat made its first contact with the sea. In a few seconds, the pontoons on each wing began to rock back and forth, just skimming along the water. The plane slowed to ten knots and Mark steered Cloud Dancer in the direction of the cruise ship.

"There you go baby, nice to get your bum wet again." He patted his hand on the console between the two front seats.

"She does seem to be happier in the water."

"It's what she was made for and when she lands or takes off from the water she just feels happy. Like a fish being tossed back into the sea. Welcome to Montego Bay."

As they floated around the bow of the huge white ship, Trish's heart leapt into her throat. There, standing on the dock in a mesh tank top, cutoff blue jeans and flip-flops, wearing a Miami Dolphins baseball cap and sunglasses, was her handsome six-foot-two Cory. Somehow he always seemed to be about four days past his last shave. His golden hair protruded beneath the cap and moved about in the wash from the big propellers. Trish was exhilarated.

169

"Oh, there's Higgins." Mark announced. "Have you met before?"

"Yes we have."

Chapter Fifty-Five

It was 7pm. For the next twelve hours, Gretchen entertained Leon with food, chocolate, dessert, Chester's finest liquor and exploits in the vessel's hot tub. Sleep came occasionally due to exhaustion. In the early morning twilight, he awoke in bliss. Never in his adult or adolescent life had he been with a woman like her. He wanted it to go on forever.

"Mmmmm. Do you really have to go home today?"

"I'm afraid so but I will be visiting Florida more now since I have a great reason to do so."

Soon they showered together in the elaborate guest stateroom.

Gretchen quickly produced towels from a small locker. She donned a string bikini bottom, wrapped herself in a terry cloth robe and found shaving equipment for Leon. Next she poured herself into a tight fitting plain white tee shirt.

"I better get you some breakfast. C'mon up when you are all done." She kissed him on the back of his neck and vanished.

Soon he inhaled the spicy scent of southern pork sausage and who knew what else cooking in the galley.

She prepared a grand breakfast and they passed the time talking about national parks, law school and life in the south. Leon never discovered if Gretchen knew anything about Chester's life of crime. He remained guarded when she asked what business he had with Chet. He told her that there were employment issues with a couple of assistant rangers from his old days in the Everglades.

Around nine-forty-five, they heard the sound of the exhaust on
Tom's borrowed Porsche approaching.

"Well Mr. Park Ranger, it looks like this is it for a while. I hope you don't forget me when you get back up to all those Carolina girls."

"I doubt I will ever look at another woman while I have the memory of these past few days in my mind. Nothing could top what you are to me. I could fall in love you know."

"I feel the same." she said and kissed him one last time quickly on the lips and backed away as they heard Tom coming up the ramp.

There was a slight knock on the salon door as it slid open. "Did someone call for a taxi?"

"If that's a taxi, I'm an astronaut." Leon reached out his hand. Gretchen had retreated into the galley, washing dishes.

"Ready to head home?"

"I guess so, although I could get used to living here."

"I know what you are saying, Chester loaned it to my family as a hotel when they were down here last year. It keeps my dad talking. Are you ready to shove off?"

"Sure thing, I need to get back and check some weather reports you know."

"Yes I do know."

Leon leaned in the doorway to the galley and said. "Thanks for the hospitality. You are the best cook in the world. Good luck with your exams. See you later Gretchen."

"No problem Mr. Matthews. I hope to see you again someday. It was nice to meet you."

Tom and Leon exited the vessel and Thomas was standing next to the Porsche holding the passenger door open for Leon.

"Thank you, Thomas, see you next time."

"Yes sir, it was my pleasure."

"If he only knew," Leon thought. Then, after a second, he realized Thomas had probably been on board last night and knew of his relationship with Gretchen. He felt himself blushing.

Tom backed the car out of the parking space and soon they were speeding towards the Airport.

"So how were your nights onboard? 'Mr. Park Ranger'?" The attorney asked with a hearty laugh. "I hope you got laid because two days ago, that young student could think of nothing but getting your ass in the hot tub."

Leon was thoroughly embarrassed. "Does it show that much?"

"I've got to hand it to you man, you look like you need a week's rest! I hope she was able to clear a lot of stress off your plate. How are you feeling now?"

"I feel like a new person. Do you think Chester will be concerned about me getting in the sack with his clerk?"

"Hell, I think he would be disappointed if you didn't."

"You sure?"

"Without a doubt. Now, the big run is coming up and we need to be on our toes for the next couple of weeks. The ocean area we will be watching is from two hundred miles east of St. Thomas and a swath a couple hundred miles wide heading north and east of Bermuda and on into the Chesapeake Bay to Norfolk."

172

"That's not a problem. I have been looking the past few months on the Windward Pass and along the Yucatan Peninsula."

"That's what I heard too, the Coasties have made several busts, all west of Cuba. Let's hope they stay there."

"So what have you been up to for the past couple days?" Leon inquired.

"Oh, not much, just visiting your old digs in Charleston, stealing a car and getting it on with a newly divorced insurance chick named Jenny. I guess Chet told you all about the car theft incident. What a rush!"

"I can't even imagine it."

"Yes sir, slicker than an old banana peel. We succeeded in getting our man off his ship for the rest of the patrol. Mission accomplished! I even caught a look at him at the airport as I was getting on my flight."

"Wait! You mean you saw him. Did he see you?"

"He was busy grabbing his wife's ass. He glanced at me just as I was getting on the plane. No big deal."

"You're right, what a rush. Thank God he is not on that ship."

Neither occupant of the Porsche noticed two Jeep Cherokee vehicles, one dark green and the other white following them from the moment they left the marina. Fortunately for the DEA agents driving the two tracking cars, there were also several Florida highway patrol cars on the same road otherwise Thrasher would have poured the throttle to the sports car. Although the beefed up Jeeps were capable of keeping up, the tail would have been obvious to the criminals. The two passed one another occasionally, following and taking a dozen photographs.

When Tom pulled into the circular airport drive, the two DEA vehicles joined in the queue and each dropped off a passenger as did Thrasher. On foot, two agents kept a tail on Leon while one of the Jeeps continued to follow the Porsche.

With no baggage to check, Leon moved quickly to the waiting area. One of the trailing agents took a seat ten feet from Leon while the other moved about the concourse. When Leon boarded his plane for Charleston the two agents left the airport by different doors. One picked up the jeep and drove to the baggage claim area. The other agent joined him there.

After leaving the airport following Thrasher's Porsche, the driver of the green Jeep followed until he arrived at The Whittaker Law Firm on Peruvian Avenue.

Half an hour later, all four agents were huddled together in a dark room at the Rogers Federal Building. Now, there was a new collection of pictures of Tom Thrasher and a new individual who,

would within several hours be identified as Leon Matthews, Ranger in Charge of the U.S. National Monument at Fort Sumter.

Chapter Fifty-Six

Denise and Vince had been home for about three hours. For two and a half of those hours they were in bed. They showered together and Vince dried off, donned a pair of shorts and a tee shirt while his wife continued to fix herself up in the master bathroom.

Out in the den, the phone rang and Vince answered.

"Commander Lubar." The voice on the other end identified himself. "This is Sam Gibbs with the Charleston Police Department."

"Yes."

"There has been an interesting turn of events concerning the theft of your car."

"Oh yeah, what?"

"Well sir, it seems a patrolman in Lexington Kentucky found your vehicle parked in a faculty parking space at an abandoned elementary school there. It appears the car is in excellent condition. The doors unlocked, and the keys to the car along with ten or twelve other keys were found on the console. The fuel tank is full and it seems like it got to Kentucky without being driven."

"This is great news! But the circumstances seem weird."

"I'll say they are. You would think if someone took a joy ride the gas tank would be empty and the way the nights have been lately, there would be dead bugs all over the grill and windshield. It's about five hundred fifty miles from here to there and that would take more than a tank of fuel. Why fill it up and wash it if you just stole it. That just plum doesn't make any sense to me at all." Gibbs remarked.

"I'm a little perplexed myself. What now?"

"Well, I guess if I were you I would clear it with my insurance company and figure out how to get your car back and make sure there is no damage to it. From the Charleston PD standpoint, this case is closed."

Vince could hear Denise's hair dryer blowing in the distance so he decided to fill Gibbs in on a few of his own suspicions. He told him of the photos taken at the fort, the long search to identify Tom
Thrasher, the fact that he saw Thrasher at the airport this morning, and was wondering if all of this is connected.

"Wow, that's a lot of issues and now to have your car heisted but only moved to another state. It all starts to smell funny, and a little sophisticated too. I wonder if this whole thing was simply to draw you away from your own work. It doesn't seem completely out of the realm of possibility."

"Look, Captain, I don't want my wife to be worried about this thing so we will keep this between the two of us for now. I gotta run. She is joining me in a minute. Why don't we get together for a cup of coffee in a few days? I will call you."

"That would be great, tell me when. See ya'll soon, Commander."

The phone line went dead just as Denise entered the den in their home.

"Who was that, babe?"

"You won't believe it, they found our car and it seems to be just fine."

Vince explained the news relayed by Gibbs. A quick call to the insurance company and they were told that if they wanted to go get the car, they could meet with a representative in Kentucky. The insurance company would pay their plane fare to get there.

It didn't take Vince more than a minute to convince Denise they could catch a short regional flight to Lexington, spend a night in a hotel and drive home. He had been waiting for six months to get his car out on the road. They knew Jeffrey would enjoy the adventure too.

Chapter Fifty-Seven

While Mark Dean was in their company, one would have thought Trish and Cory were just recently acquainted business associates meeting to discuss the details of a marketing presentation. After securing the plane, Mark arranged with the harbor employees to watch it overnight. He then bid his passenger safe travels for the balance of her trip.

Mark hailed a cab and was gone within ten minutes. The second the taxi turned a distant corner, they embraced.

"Oh God! I have missed you so much, all I could think on the flight was how this moment would feel."

"It's been a long wait. I missed you too. Where are you staying?"

"A place called Sands, I guess it's about two miles from here."

"I drove by it this morning." Cory continued to hold her tightly.

Higgins walked her towards an older Toyota sedan covered with dust.

"Wow, nice car!" Trish smiled

"In our line of work, you never want to stand out in a crowd."

"So, where is the boat?"

"Oh, it's right over there." Cory pointed to a spot fifty yards ahead of the huge Norwegian Caribbean cruise ship. There was a blue-hulled small freighter tied to the wharf.

"She is tiny next to the cruise ship. Who are the dudes onboard?"

"Oh, the two Latinos are Juan and Manuel. The yank is Carl Pearson."

"Can I see the boat, Captain?"

"Sure, later."

"Kind of like being in high school," she exclaimed as he slid in and she grabbed his right leg.

"You make it tough for a guy to keep his mind on business. Are you my boss, or am I yours?"

"All I know is that I have a lot of money in this case and I intend to make you earn every penny of it. Do you have ten hours, captain?"

"I've got twelve." Cory smiled back and bit her on the left earlobe.

"Oh, but that's all the money I brought, can you put the two extra hours on my account?"

"Let's get out of here." He jammed the car into gear and sped off along the coast road to the north then east towards the resort.

Check-in was a snap. Trish's room was located one hundred yards from the beach. A private hot tub bubbled away steps from her bedroom. Five seconds after the bellman dropped her baggage in the room, he carried her to the bedroom and placed her on the king sized bed.

"Well, I don't know how long I can last just seeing you every month or so."

"I know. It's tough on me too. When this deal is done we'll take a little vacation someplace like the south of France or the coast of Morocco where no one knows us and we don't speak the language."

"I would love that. So what is in store for today?"

"You know, you give me, I go buy dope and I will see you in Virginia. What could be simpler?"

"Don't I get to see your ship?"

"Right after breakfast."

Chapter Fifty-Eight

In the four days Leon had been away, everything had run perfectly. As occasionally happens, one of his deputy rangers had been called to go over to the Olympic National Forest in Washington State to fill in for two months while someone from there recovered from a fall into a river. The park service sent a replacement ranger from Washington DC to fill in the gap. Leon interviewed Emmett Ridgeway, the new ranger, and he seemed savvy enough to step right into the duties.

What Leon didn't know was that Ridgeway was a DEA agent.

When the second boat of the morning arrived with a couple dozen visitors to the park, Jim the boat operator came to Leon's office and knocked on the frame of the open door. "Hey Mr. Matthews, this package was left for you at the ticket booth at Patriots Point. How was your trip to Florida? Meet any hot babes?" Jim was teasing. Everyone knew Leon had a reputation as a nerdy person not usually interested in women.

"Thanks Jim. Actually, I did run into an attractive lady and she may help me come out of my shell a bit. I've talked her into coming up this way next month."

He looked at the brown paper package. It was postmarked Fort Lauderdale Florida. He could smell a hint of perfume as he turned it over in his hands.

"Oh, so now we've got a Casanova here. Gotta get back to the boat sir, see you soon."

"Thanks. Yeah, catch you later." As Jim left he raised the package to his nose and inhaled deeply. The perfume was definitely the scent he had enjoyed onboard Chester's yacht.

He closed the door to his office, sat back in his chair and once again savored the brown package in his hands. With pair of scissors he snipped the string and the tape. He opened it and recognized the contents. Inside were pink lacy panties and a bikini top. He found a sticky note attached to the front of the panties and in purple ink a note:

"Hold on to these for me, I will be up for a fitting in three weeks. Miss you deeply. G."

Leon held the material up to his face and breathed in deeply. "Three weeks. How can I last that long?" Then he realized within five days he was going to be busy sending out position reports to Cory.

After a generous payday perhaps he and Gretchen could go to Atlantic City.

The daydream was broken as the phone rang. The attendant at the dock informed him the Mayor of Charleston was arriving with dignitaries from Canada. It was time to be a professional National Park Director. He picked up the contents of the package, held it close to his face and inhaled one more time then placed the handful into his desk drawer.

"I'm a happy man."

He left his office and walked to the boat dock. He encountered new ranger Emmett who was escorting a group of junior high students around the site. He noticed Ridgeway was fitting in quickly into his duties. He seemed to have a good grasp on the history of the Civil War.

Chapter Fifty-Nine

ESCAPE, within twelve hours after leaving Montego Bay encountered a thirty-six-foot sloop fifteen miles away northbound under power and moving at about six and a half knots. Lieutenant Sutton, on watch advised the CO of the sighting and alerted Ensign Ladner, leader of the boarding party. Flood, Sutton and Ladner assembled on the bridge wing, all looking through their binoculars. Phil directed the movements of ESCAPE to close in on the sailboat.

"There is a brisk wind of eight knots. I wonder why they are not sailing." Ladner offered.

"Could be they don't know how to sail," Flood stated. "I see at least twenty red fuel cans lashed to the deck. These people aren't sailors. It could be interesting."

"They just changed course to the left. I don't think they believe they can run away from us. Do you Skipper?"

"Let's put two more mains on the line and kick this baby up to twelve knots," the captain spoke.

"Aye-Aye sir." Sutton picked up the phone to the engine room. "Ed, Phil on the bridge. Fire up the other two mains and let me know when we can make twelve."

"Sure thing, XO. I'll give you a ring when we are ready. Got a live one?"

"Yup, a sail boat with no sails in a nice wind, took a left when they saw us pop over the horizon."

"Give us five minutes and you will have the whole plant."

Deep within the belly of the old ship, two big Caterpillar diesel main engines hissed as compressed air injected into the cylinder heads awakened the cold iron. Tarzano gave orders to the watch standers. He selected two enginemen to report to the main deck and prepare the auxiliary boats for launch.

Sutton asked the quartermaster of the watch to compute an intercept course to catch up with the target using the current speed of nine knots for four more minutes followed by an increase in the speed to twelve knots. Within ninety seconds, Petty Officer Jones had the answer and Sutton barked out commands to the helmsman to close the distance.

From the flying bridge above the wheelhouse came a message through a polished brass voice tube. "The name of the boat is

181

Misty Dreams. Home port is San Diego. Looks like they are tossing stuff overboard!"

"Very well." Sutton acknowledged.

"Mr. Ladner, get your team together."

Through the voice tube once again: "Looks like they are launching a school of square groupers Mr. Sutton."

"Try to count and mark them down" Sutton responded.

Square grouper is the nickname applied to floating bales of marijuana occasionally found adrift in the sea.

"Captain, I would like to launch both boats and put someone out there to pick up their jetsam."

"Good plan Phil, get everyone ready."

"Yes sir." He walked over and keyed the PA system. "Now Hear This, Now Hear This. We have encountered a northbound sailboat under power. The crew of the boat is throwing cargo over the side. We intend to intercept and board the subject boat and will be launching both small boats. ESCAPE One will deploy the boarding party led by Mr. Ladner and Boarding Team Alpha. Boarding Team Bravo will man the surfboat. Chief Quartermaster Jensen in charge. We will launch the surfboat first to gather the jetsam, then the Zodiac to make the boarding. Chief Jensen report to the bridge. Now set Law Enforcement Condition One!"

Throughout the ship excitement grew.

Buzz Ladner, with kaleidoscope of butterflies in his gut, briefed his team.

The small red arrows on the engine order telegraph moved and bells rang three times, stopped briefly at all ahead full then returned. Sutton looked at the signal just sent from main control in the engine room. The ship was ready to perform at full power. "All ahead full!"

"Aye-Aye, sir. All ahead full," responded the seaman on the controller. He moved both large polished brass handles forward until they were pointed straight ahead and their black arrows pointed to the word FULL on the side of the instrument. "Ring-ring" went the bells once again, and the smaller red arrows controlled from the engine room found themselves pointing at the end of the black ones. "Engines are at all ahead full sir."

"Very well!" Sutton then gave steering commands to the helmsman. Below decks, the sound of all four big diesels was noteworthy. The ship gained speed. Within fifteen minutes, the distance between the two vessels closed to less than a half a mile.

"Go ahead and give him a call. Tell them to get ready for some company." Sutton nodded towards Ensign Merrymore.

"Yes sir!" He picked up the radio mic and hailed. "Sailing Vessel Misty Dream. This is the United States Coast Guard Cutter on channel sixteen." Everyone on the bridge waited in anticipation for a response. Another square grouper went over the side.

Ensign Merrymore repeated his hailing message.

Finally, two people appeared in the cockpit and waved to the ship. Obviously, they realized their quest to make a quick fortune in the smuggling business was quickly ending.

Through the ships loudspeaker, Merrymore commanded: "Ahoy on the Misty Dream. Stop your engines, heave to with your beam to the breeze and standby for a boarding by the United States Coast Guard. And quit tossing things over the side. Contact us on channel 16 VHF"

Onboard the sailboat, one of the crew drew back on the throttle and took the engine out of gear. He took two steps forward and picked up a radio microphone and said "This is Misty Dream what do you want?"

"This is the United States Coast Guard. Stop your engine and prepare for a boarding. I need information about your vessel. Standby!"

"You want to get this Smitty?" Merrymore turned to the ship's yeoman.

"Yes sir!"

Petty Officer Smith began his questioning of the operators. He asked how many were in the crew, where they had been, where they were headed, why were they under power, passport numbers, dates of birth and forty-five other questions.

As the questions were answered, the deck force and boarding parties went through the evolution of launching their boats and teams. Just prior to boarding the Zodiac, Ensign Ladner reported to the bridge to get last minute information on the vessel he was about to approach. He approached Sutton and his Commanding Officer and saluted.

"Ready to proceed sir. What do we have?"

Sutton was looking over the information form. "They say there are three onboard, all U.S. citizens. They have been in Belize and are under power due to a broken jib block and a fouled halyard in the mast. I doubt that is true. They deny throwing anything over the side but the chief and his gang already have three - eighty pound bags of marijuana in the surfboat. They deny any firearms onboard." Everyone was stern faced and serious.

"Looks like you are going to get a bust Mr. Ladner." Flood smiled. "Be safe."

"Aye-Aye Sir! Permission to launch."

"Go for it." Dave returned the salute.

Ensign Merrymore returned to the radio after observing the conversation between Ladner, Sutton and the CO. "Aboard the Misty Dream, skipper please get your crew and passengers and assemble them in the cockpit. The boarding officer will be alongside shortly."

"Roger." Was the only response from a dejected looking thirty something year old. Three people sat side by side in the cockpit. The one who had been on the radio and seemed to be in charge lit up a cigarette, took two puffs and threw it disgustedly over the side. He spoke to his companions. They could not be heard beyond the cockpit.

Ensign Ladner and the rest of the boarding party soon climbed over the rail. The other two members of the team remained in the Zodiac. Ladner introduced himself to the crew and asked a few questions. He then directed the two petty officers to make a security sweep of the vessel. They went below. Within twenty seconds, Petty Officer Danza stood on the ladder poking his head out and said. "Not much to check sir, this thing is loaded top to bottom with burlap wrapped cargo that smells like marijuana. Jones is doing a field test."

"You got anything to say gentlemen?" Ladner asked the crew. The response was silence.

"Positive for THC sir!" Jones announced.

Danza handed Ladner the three passports found below and Buzz began the process of arresting the trio and reading them their rights.

"We are seizing your vessel and arresting you for a violation of Title 14, United States Code for the illegal transportation of contraband. We will move you to that Coast Guard Cutter. You will be in custody until we deliver you and your vessel to the nearest U.S. Marshal's office. A U.S. Magistrate will arraign you within twenty-four hours of arriving on American soil. Looks like your career is over. You have the right to remain silent, anything you say can be used against you in a court of law. You have the right to obtain an attorney. If you cannot afford one, one will be provided. Do you understand these rights?"

All three responded by nodding.

Ladner keyed his hand held VHF radio, "ESCAPE, this vessel is loaded with a THC product in approximately thirty bales of about eighty pounds each. I have arrested the crew, given them their Miranda rights. I'm sending the boat back with Danza and the crew. I found no weapons, the boat is seaworthy and towing should be no problem. Jones and I will get her ready."

Sutton responded. "Nicely done Mr. Ladner. We will rig for towing."

Commander Flood went to the 1MC and informed the crew they had seized the subject boat and would be heading for a U.S. port shortly. He thanked everyone in the crew for professionalism and hard work. There were cheers all around the ship at the announcement. As an added benefit to making a bust, the ship usually remained overnight in the port where the subject boat was delivered. Crewmembers were speculating, they might get to go to New Orleans, Panama City or Galveston. Everyone hoped for the Big Easy.

Ensign Merrymore prepared a situation report to go to Commander Seventh Coast Guard District in Miami informing them of the bust and providing all the details of the evolution.

For the next three hours the crew made all the preparations to take Misty Dream under tow.

Just before sunset, in a message from the operations center at the district office arrived. ESCAPE was directed to deliver the seized vessel and the crew to the Marshals at Corpus Christi Texas. At a towing speed of five knots, the trip would take just over three days. With only eight days left on this scheduled patrol, the ship would probably then move along the south coast of the Gulf of Mexico, around the Florida Keys then northbound towards Charleston.

Chapter Sixty

Jeffrey's classes ended at noon on Friday. Bags were packed and the Lubar family was ready. The flight to Lexington took an hour and they were met at the airport by a local insurance agent. He took them to City Hall where the Mercedes was safely parked in the police impound lot.

The agent had the vehicle serviced at the local Mercedes dealer. Everything checked out perfectly. There was less than one mile on the odometer from when Denise had written down the mileage at the Exxon station on Meeting Street six days ago.

Vince had more questions than answers. He was concerned about the safety of his family.

After signing a release form at the police headquarters, they were on the road.

In three hours, they arrived at a resort south of Mount Vernon near the Daniel Boone Trail. Vince enjoyed the drive.

A half an hour in the pool and dinner in the resort restaurant and soon Jeffrey was sound asleep. Vince took the opportunity to share his concerns with Denise.

He told her the story of the photographs, the attorneys and seeing Thrasher at the airport three days earlier. Denise was fascinated.

"It's like an intriguing novel."

The Lubar family slept soundly through the night and left early for the North Carolina beaches.

In an oceanfront hotel near Nags Head they were getting ready for another good night's sleep. The ten o'clock national news was on and a reporter broke a story that the Coast Guard Cutter ESCAPE from Charleston South Carolina had seized a sailboat loaded with marijuana in the Gulf of Mexico. Additionally, a small airplane in transit from San Juan Puerto Rico to Cozumel had crashed in the Caribbean. All of the other Coast Guard ships and aircraft in the vicinity were searching for survivors.

"I bet you wish you were there."

"If I were there, I would be enjoying the thrill of it all but since I'm not there, I can't think of any place in the world where I would rather be than right here." Vince was no stranger to diplomacy.

Chapter Sixty-One

In a few short hours the encounter would be over. Trish and Cory would part. Higgins planned to be underway by early afternoon. It would take three and a half days to make the eight hundred plus mile trip to Charlotte Amalie. A track through the Windward Passage between Cuba and Hispaniola would provide a push from the Gulf Stream, saving half a day. He was sure to be boarded by the Coast Guard somewhere along the route. A direct easterly transit south of the major islands would be typical for most merchant ships servicing the Caribbean islands. He wanted to arrive early in the day allowing the warehouse manager to load the furniture. Leaving early the next morning provided ample time to rendezvous with the French freighter.

They discussed the final details of their planned reunion. She would pick him up in Virginia Beach. Next stop would be New England for a week of blissful relaxation. The two lovers left the resort and half a mile into the trip to the harbor Trish said "Oh dear, I think we should go back to the room."

"Babe, I'm going to be worn out and I have to get a ship underway for a very long trip."

"It's not that I don't want to jump in bed one more time, believe me I would love nothing more. But I think you would be a little embarrassed to go all that way and meet with Misère French Capitan and have forgotten the briefcase."

"Oh shit!" He slammed on the brake pedal and stopped the car.
"See what you do to me."

They laughed all the way back to the resort.

Chapter Sixty-Two

In Palm Beach, Tom's career in contraband smuggling was over. With the help of Leon, the Geek as he liked to call him, the last few runs had been smooth as silk. He had coordinated two dozen successful missions and one exciting car theft during his criminal career.

Tom had over two million untaxed dollars in three offshore bank accounts.

He enjoyed helping beautiful women get out of marriages to wealthy executives. He would also help wealthy happily married executives legitimately protect their fortunes from the sticky hands of the state and federal governments. All of this he did, charging his happy clients a mere five hundred dollars for each hour of his time at fifty dollars for each six-minute increment.

On the third day of his new career, he was driving from his Fort Lauderdale condominium into the Palm Beach office complex in the red Porsche.

Since he returned from Charleston, it went unnoticed that his every move had been observed by three different federal agents in unmarked cars. He never knew of or discovered the tail.

The people watching him were the best in Florida. For the agents, it was frustrating. They quickly tired of following him around never observing anything remotely illegal. They were jealous of his lifestyle, the beautiful women he dated and the expensive restaurants he frequented. He didn't seem to be living outside of his means or hanging out with disreputable people. They recorded every move he made for four months. Eventually though, the DEA and local U.S. Marshals would report that Mr. Thrasher seemed to be a young fun loving successful attorney. No criminal dealings were noted.

A three-inch thick binder held all the information on Thrasher. CCIC in Corpus Christi, the Seventh Coast Guard District and the West Palm Beach U.S. Marshal / DEA office each owned a copy of it. The record contained details of the photographs taken a year earlier at Fort Sumter and the documentation of his trip to Charleston during the theft of Vince Lubar's Mercedes. Without new information, these files would slowly move their way to the bottom of the pile. Eventually they landed in a row of file cabinets where in each jurisdiction, very thick open case files by the hundreds were stored waiting for some incident or new clue to bring them back   to   life.

Chapter Sixty-Three

At six in the afternoon Leon opened his command center. He removed the dust cover from the teletype machine. Soon it would receive the Two a Day Reports from all Cutters on patrol.
At eight-fifteen, the machine sprang to life with the ring of a small bell, then the familiar tat a tat a tat a tat familiar to anyone connected with large communication systems. Leon began to read.

"Wow," he said to himself. The report indicated the Coast Guard Cutter ESCAPE was towing a seized sailing vessel to Corpus Christi. Every other unit in the Caribbean was headed for a site one hundred miles west of Jamaica to search for survivors of a small airplane missing for three hours.

Feeling relief from this news, he turned on the National Weather Service receiver and put in the geographic coordinates of a position south and east of Jamaica. Within two minutes, the fax produced a wide thermal page displaying a map of the Caribbean and all the islands within five hundred miles of Jamaica. It displayed curved lines and weather symbols indicating winds, temperatures and future predictions. Tearing the map off, he took it to a drafting table and drew in the coordinates from the report concerning ESCAPE and the plane crash site. He made notations on the page with a felt tip pen. Then he wrote, "Taxpayers getting their money's worth today." Next, he drew a circle and placed a happy face in it. He then went back to the fax machine and fed it into a wide slot next to the TX button. He advanced a hand roller half a turn to get a bite on the edge of the document then on a ten key pad, he entered a series of numbers directing the transmitter to send the page to a receiver onboard Caribbean Gipsy.

Chapter Sixty-Four

It was 2030 when a bell rang next to the fax machine. Carl was on watch. Cory and the rest of the crew were playing cards in the galley. The bell also rang in the galley. Cory excused himself and went to the wheelhouse. He entered the dark space as a wide sheet of paper came crawling out of the receiver. Leon had fed his document into the transmitter bottom first so the first thing Higgins and Pearson saw was a happy face. "This must be good news." Carl smiled.

"I hope so."

The whole page finally appeared and Cory tore it off and placed it on the chart table. "So that's why that C-130 and the chopper were heading west."

"Yeah, I was wondering what that was all about. Should be pretty smooth sailing."

"Yep, this is good news for everyone except one poor shithead with a sail boat and ten souls on the plane." Just as he placed the fax document into a shredder he took one more look at the page. "Oh yeah, the weather doesn't look too bad either. I'm going to hit the sack, Cory said. "I have the mid watch so I will see you in the morning."

"Sleep well Skipper." Pearson picked up his binoculars to scan the horizon ahead.

The little blue ship chugged along. Although the land ahead was not yet visible, he could see the distant glow in the sky from the southwestern edge of Cuba.

Chapter Sixty-Five

In the basement of Fort Sumter, Leon Matthews felt quite jolly. Every twelve hours he found more and more ships and aircraft headed to the west coast of Jamaica. The search for additional survivors was extending into the fourth day. His confidence grew. This next shipment should arrive on schedule without Caribbean Gipsy ever being noticed by the water cops. Chester never told him about upping the ante by becoming involved in cocaine trafficking. He said when this next load got through the payment percentages would be bigger than the past several operations. Having received forty-two thousand for the Fanta Seas shipment six months earlier, getting more was something he had never dreamed of.

Matthews was getting to know Emmett Ridgeway, the new replacement park attendant. He really liked this guy and found him very professional and good with the other employees.

Of course he was unaware Ridgeway was already noticing twice a day at precisely five fifty-five in the morning and again in the afternoon, his supervisor seemed to disappear from his desk or anyplace else in the park and would be gone for over half an hour. Emmett found this a bit mysterious and made a note of it.

Ridgeway was fascinated by all of the catacomb cellars and secret passages in the fort. In his explorations he discovered water filled cisterns several floors below the main structure. He found the dreary barracks for the soldiers during the Civil War. A history major in college, he enjoyed the opportunity to refresh his knowledge while sleuthing.

The fort had accommodations for employees in the old Civil War officer's quarters. About twenty percent of the full time park attendants stayed there through their staggered work weeks. Since Emmett was assigned as a temporary replacement for someone else, it was normal for him to reside where he worked.

Matthews also lived at the fort in the old commanding general's home. All the employees knew Leon spent hours on his ham radio in the evenings talking to people in Antarctica, Africa and onboard many merchant ships at sea. It was an interesting hobby and often the boss would include a resident ranger in this activity.

On day five after Leon returned from Florida, the crew was planning an oyster roast at a picnic and barbecue spot at the bottom of a long flight of stairs leading down to the beach. Leon had just finished sending the evening fax to Cory in St Thomas. He was feeling relaxed.

Six or seven of the staff had gone down to the tidal flats and harvested dozens of fresh oysters. Ridgeway had accompanied them into the mucky soil. The muddy troops hiked up the hillside to the barbecue pit. They were joking and laughing and wondering why their boss had been so giddy since his return from down south.

Leon was skipping down the stairs whistling, obviously happy. One asked, "Hey Leon. We've never seen you so frigging happy. What happened? Did some young beach bunny haul your ashes for you down south?"

Everyone laughed.

Leon felt himself blushing. "No, I'm just happy with my life these days."

"Hey, Leon got laid!" Two of the rangers said in unison.

Another asked: "You got a little package from Jim the other day. He said it smelled like perfume?"

Leon blushed deeper.

"OK, I did meet a nice lady. She's younger than me but seems to like me and for three days she took very good care of me. I'm blown away by the whole thing. She's coming up her in a few weeks and I want all of you to behave yourselves when she is here."

"Oh yeah, you can count on us," laughed the senior ranger in the group.

Leon worried about what his friends would do when Gretchen came up. "C'mon, let's get this barbecue fired up." He twisted the cap off of a bottle of beer.

Chapter Sixty-Six

At ten o'clock in the morning three nights into the trip, Cory directed his ship towards the docks in St. Thomas Harbor. Lying between Long Bay and Crum Bay is the industrial wharf. Tied to the wharf, a container ship was offloading trailers delivering goods to the island.

The harbormaster directed Caribbean Gipsy to a spot on the dock a hundred feet astern of the container ship. Charlotte Amalie's topography presents a very hilly environment. High up, overlooking the Atlantic Ocean, Dan Parker, an expatriate from Kentucky, owned a large stucco mansion. In the basement, he operated a first class furniture manufacturing and finishing shop. Parker had attended the Citadel in Charleston several years before Chester and Leon. He graduated the year they had entered. Unlike those who followed, Dan had gone to Vietnam. Eight months into his tour of duty, he was shot in the leg and his femur was shattered. After a year of surgeries and rehabilitation, he was evaluated and determined to be disabled and retired from the army. In his rehabilitation, he painted artistic land and seascape scenes on furniture. In retirement, he developed his art into a successful business venture.

Two winters in the hills of Kentucky, the cold and damp weather bothered his leg to the point where he became addicted to painkillers. In rehabilitation from that disorder he decided to survive the rest of his life, he would move his company to someplace warm. A late night TV documentary attracted him to the U. S. Virgin Islands and before the next winter he sold his Kentucky farmhouse and purchased property in Charlotte Amalie. Wealthy stateside customers for his tropical furniture waited months for his products. He employed five local artisans in the shop and still did the original painting on the chairs and tables himself.

At a Citadel reunion six years earlier, he had encountered Chester and they kindled a fond relationship. Much of the patio furniture at the Whittaker home on the ICW and a few pieces on his yacht were originals from the St. Thomas studio of Dan Parker. At the reunion, the two consorted to engage another classmate located in Norfolk Virginia to become the exclusive importer and shipper of Dan's products. It turned out to be a good business relationship and all of the former cadets were taking good care of each other in a thriving small industry.

Cory saw Dan standing next to a truck loaded with chairs and tables wrapped in bubble wrap. Higgins and Parker greeted one another as old friends.

"Looks like you are stepping up in the world old buddy." Parker spoke admiring the shiny blue ship.

"Yeah, makes it all look pretty legit doesn't it. She's a great working boat. You will probably be seeing it about every twelve months."

Higgins introduced Carl to Parker.

The three Americans left the crew and two of Parker's employees to load and secure the cargo while they went to eat lunch and enjoy a couple of beers.

Two hours later, they returned to find the ship loaded for the seventeen-hundred-mile journey. The five stevedores were all sitting on a pile of pallet boards smoking and drinking beers. Fueling took an hour and a half and by three in the afternoon they were underway with a U.S Customs clearance to deliver forty-one pieces of custom made tropical furniture to Norfolk. There was one more stop to make along the way.

Chapter Sixty-Seven

Seintespirit is a six hundred and fifty-foot French registered mixed cargo freighter. She is privately owned by three investors in Monte Carlo. One owner was a retired attorney from Florida who had made millions in a class action law suit in the late 1970s. The other two were French businessmen engaged in a variety of ventures. Seintespirit routinely hauls cargo in enclosed trailer containers. The most abundant legitimate commodity is petro chemicals manufactured in Venezuela eastbound to Marseilles. Exports hauled to the Americas included French wines, Michelin tires, cheeses, perfumes and Fiat automobiles.

The three owners and the crew were all involved in making sure each voyage carried some sort of high profit contraband. They had transported tons of untaxed cigarettes, young Latino prostitutes to France and similar French women to Venezuela. Gold, guns, currency, stolen cars and of course illegal drugs were included in many un-manifested shipments.

The American lawyer, Jake Simpson, had met up with Chester Whittaker several years earlier when one of his nephews had been involved in a situation. He and several friends had been arrested for selling marijuana in the Fort Lauderdale area. The Whittaker Law Firm worked their magic, and on some technicality the case had been dismissed. One evening a few nights later while onboard Chester's yacht, the two christened a partnership to smuggle cocaine. Future shipments handled by his teams would consist of this much more profitable and concealable commodity.

Seintespirit approached the line where the western boundary of the Atlantic Ocean meets the eastern edge of the Caribbean Sea. Seven days had passed since she departed France. The contraband cargo on board this time was one hundred, twenty pound packages of pure cocaine. The product originated in Bolivia a year earlier when a North African importer purchased seventeen tons of it from the producer for two million dollars. Jake Simpson and his partners in Monte Carlo purchased eight thousand pounds for four million and stored the stuff in the garage of a house in Niece. Chester was buying a ton from Simpson and his partners for two and a quarter million.

Chad Walgren and his group of distributors would pay six million when it was delivered in Norfolk. By the time end users had the stuff, twenty-five to thirty million would be paid for the final product on the street.

Onboard the larger freighter the cocaine rode in the middle of a container full of tires. Anticipating the transfer, several crew members unloaded it and secured it to two strong oak pallets. They then wrapped it in cargo nets for lifting over the side to the smaller ship.

The two ships were scheduled to meet at very specific geographic coordinates at 8:00 pm local Charlotte Amalie time.

The captain of the receiving ship and one crewmember would climb a ladder to the deck of Seintespirit. Once onboard, he would make a small slit in any three random packages of cocaine and perform a drug field test. He would use the very same test performed by a Coast Guard or U.S. Customs officer. A small amount of the substance would be placed in a test tube. The crushing inside of a small glass ampoule would expose the dope to the test media. Cocaine would cause everything to turn blue. These kits are only available from a small chemical company in Connecticut. Federal, state, local and county law enforcement agencies and companies like the Whittaker Law Firm are the lifeblood of this firm.

Once the tests were complete and Cory was satisfied, he would signal Manuel in the boat below to attach the briefcase to a rope tossed down from the freighter. Once the captain of Seintespirit had opened the case and verified the cash was there he would signal his boatswain to attach the big hook from the ships crane to the cargo net and lift them onboard the smaller ship. The entire transaction and transfer should take no more than three quarters of an hour.

Once complete, both captains would steer their ships over separate horizons.

Two days after leaving the fuel dock in Charlotte Amalie, Cory and Carl stood in the wheelhouse. Carl noticed a faint blip to the east on the twenty-mile radar. Sunset was approaching and they had just looked at a weather fax from Fort Sumter. Every Coast Guard unit was still in the Gulf of Mexico and Seintespirit was on schedule for the transfer.

"There she is." Carl peered through the front port light. "I've got a masthead light and green starboard running light off the port bow."

"Ok, I see her."

He slowly turned the wheel to the right, guiding Caribbean Gipsy towards a point to the right of Seintespirit. Within the next hour the two ships would rendezvous.

Above the drone of the diesel engine three decks below, both men could hear and feel their own hearts beating strong and loudly within their chests. The next few hours needed to proceed without interruption or observation from anyone else on the planet.

Higgins broke the silence. "Well buddy, how are you feeling?"

"A little nervous, very excited and scared to death."

"When we get this one done, I'm going to take half a year off. I think about one more run then it will be retirement time for this old boy," Cory spoke after a few seconds.

"I'm not sure my nerves could take it as long as you have my friend. I've still got a successful body and fender shop and the extra I get here helps me take better vacations. I've been doing some stock market investing with my booty from the last two trips. It's exciting."

"I'm not much of a fan of that kind of stuff. I got me an apartment building in Spokane Washington where college students stay. It is always full, someone else manages it for me and I get a nice check at the end of each month."

"Well, someone up in Denver told me these computer things are going to change the world and within a dozen years everyone in the country will own one. So I bought into a couple of startup deals making something called software and another in the microchip business, whatever that is. Hell, I put ten grand in each and within six months I already made forty percent profit. If it keeps going like that it could double in a couple of years."

"Man that sounds interesting. Let's get this cargo loaded and on our way north you can tell me how it works. How about going below and getting the guys ready. I think Manuel has already lifted the tanks. I heard the hydraulic pump go off about twenty minutes ago."

"Sure thing, Skipper."

In the small eating and cooking area just below and aft of the wheelhouse, Manuel Salvador and his two Colombian partners were smoking cigarettes and drinking dark espresso coffee.

"Are we almost there, jefe?" Manny inquired. This was his fourth trip. Cory asked he would find partners to help load, stow and unload neatly wrapped contraband. They were usually fishermen or shipyard workers. Manuel would receive twenty thousand dollars for his team's help. He would pay his recruits, splitting one third with them and keeping the balance for himself. He was a good supervisor; very trustworthy and pleased with his compensation arrangement.

"Si Manny, is everything ready?"

"Si señor, those tank things are the coolest ever. And those piping directions are made by someone funny."

"What do you mean?"

"Well the whole thing looks just like a two big water tanks side by side. And there is water in them but not a lot like you think. Open the valve and water come out every time. But man there is a lever in there with a sign says 'shit kicker – sewage overboard'. Well you turn it to 'on' and sure enough it kicks all that bad stuff overboard from the other tank. But you twist the handle then pull on it and the water tanks lift up like a couple of dump trucks and down there is a place to store a ton of the other kind of shit." Manuel smiled showing half a dozen gold teeth.

"Somebody really was thinking when they build that. I been on this boat for six months since Honduras and never know it work like that until that fax message came two days ago. Some hombre is pretty smart. The fax also shows a little blue handle down by the deck. It is hard to see but easy to kick with your foot. Be careful with it because it opens the sea chest and señor, this baby will start to sink real fast."

"I wonder why they did that?" Carl asked.

"Cause if the shit hits the fan, we can scuttle her before we get busted. Yea, Manny, some hombre is really smart." Cory said. "Let's hope we never have to kick that thing."

"I'll say," Carl answered. He had been asleep from a midnight ~watch when a fax had come in from Fort Sumter giving directions on how to operate the secret tank system. Chester had not wanted any documentation concerning the tanks or other tricks onboard or to have anyone know how to operate them until it was necessary.

"So everything is ready to load it up?"

"Yes sir jefe. If they just lower a pallet down to us, we can lift that hatch and the three of us can have everything put to bed in half an hour. This gonna be the easiest ever!"

Chapter Sixty-Eight

Special Agent Ridgeway was very interested in what the chief ranger was doing when he disappeared every twelve hours. It was going to be difficult to get into the spaces behind Leon's office. The five-foot thick block walls on the exterior did not lend themselves to unnoticed penetration. The staff knew when this girlfriend from Florida came north, Leon would be taking a week off. Emmett planned to find a way into the area then.

Meanwhile, he was trying to fit in to the routine of an employee of the U.S. Parks Service. He enjoyed wearing the uniform of a Confederate Army sergeant. He accompanied other experienced guides twice a day. The rest of his time, he explored the fort and spent three hours a day in a small rangers' lounge reading every history book published about the Fort.

He didn't need to work hard to befriend Beaufort E. Lee. The photographer usually arrived on the second or third boat of the day and stayed into the afternoon.

During his second week, Emmett was able to sit down at the small southern barbeque concession and engage Lee over lunch.

"So how ya likin this place Sergeant Ridgeway?"

"Oh, just call me Em."

"Em?"

"Yes, just like the letter M."

"Ok, I got it Sergeant Em."

"I'm really enjoying this job. I was a history major at UVA and this job is bringing a lot of reality to things I studied. Coming from the northernmost of the southern states, this job is helping me put everything into perspective. What about you?"

"How much time you got? I've been in and outta this town all my life but we're gonna have to have lunch here more than once fer me to tell the whole story."

Lee related the saga of his life and experiences in between bites of his sandwich, hush puppies, a small Styrofoam cup of baked beans and a quart sized Mountain Dew.

He covered his childhood, schooling, the navy, driving school buses and he was just starting to tell Emmett about how his photography hobby had gotten started while he was stationed in Europe. Half an hour of monologue went by until he saw a launch approaching.

"Here comes another load of customers, I better get back to work."

"Yeah, me too, I got a meeting with the boss in half an hour."

"Oh, yeah, Leon, he's quite the guy. I can give you all the scoop on him if you're interested. He's from the Citadel you know." Lee pointed in the general direction of Charleston. "Wanted to go to 'Nam and get nasty with the Viet Cong. Don't seem like the type. We should talk some more in a day or two. Gotta run."

Beaufort put his trash away, picked up his cameras and bag and ambled off. Emmett smiled to himself believing he had just found the source of all the information he may need during his tenure at the fort.

He took care of his own lunch trash and wandered around killing time before his meeting.

He walked over looking at the seaward approach to the fort. He wondered what the Confederate officers must have felt as the Ironclad Union Navy approached in nine heavily armed ships in April of 1863. History has it the General looked through a long glass at the fleet and told his officers they still had time to finish lunch before they went to war.

The defeat of the flotilla by the combined batteries of the region is regarded as one of the worst days in battle ever for the US Navy.

The administrative office of the fort seemed out of place in the civil war era surroundings. Passing through a century old oak doorway, Emmett entered a short hallway with neatly finished sheetrock walls adorned with photographs of the president, Secretary of the Interior and the director of the national parks. The door to Leon's office was opened and it was clear he was on the phone with someone. Emmett listened.

"Sure, she's coming up middle of next week. Right, yeah, it should be done by then.

"Oh yeah, I will show her the campus then I think we will head up to Hatteras for a couple of days. When will Trish be arriving?"

Leon then noticed a shadow near his doorway as Emmett was looking at the portraits and reading information on a bulletin board.

"Right Chet, I've got to go. Someone is here to see me. Ok. Right. Take care."

Leon stood and walked towards the door wondering if he had said anything compromising. Thinking everything was fine, he

stepped into the hallway. "Well, welcome to my humble situation."
He extended a hand to Emmett.

Ridgeway committed two names to his memory: Chet and
Trish. "Nice digs."

"It does the job. This is the best I have had in twelve years
with the department. So, how are you finding the work here?"

"Oh, this is great. I'm not sure if I would want to be here
permanently but for a few months it is great to get away from DC.
That's for sure. I was a history major at UVA and being here sure
helps make sense out of a lot of Civil War lectures we sat
through."

"I agree. I was into communications at the Citadel and it just
fascinates me how the Confederates had such a great system of
flag and sound signals keeping everyone on top of the operations.

"The guys tell me you are catching on quickly. I think by next
week you could take over a couple of tours each day on your own.
What do you think?"

"That would be great. I'm enjoying getting up to speed.
Another few days and I'll be ready."

"Good because as you may have heard, I have this nice lady
coming up from Florida for a week and I'm going to take some
time off." Leon imagined having Gretchen show up and how the
rest of the staff would react.

"Don't worry boss, I will be ready." Emmett glanced around
the room for obvious signs of mischief. There were two doors on
the back wall, one he could tell led to a bathroom. It looked as
though there was another door inside the bathroom. He could
hardly wait for Leon to leave with his babe so he could start
snooping.

Chapter Sixty-Nine

It was ten minutes before eight. The cloudless sky over the western Atlantic flaunted a spectacle of a million stars, planets, moons and constellations. Many legends and tales concerning these heavenly bodies have emerged throughout centuries of seafaring. Cory memorized many of them and was a well-read student of such yarns. He recalled several he would share with the crew over the next five days.

Cory was in control of Caribbean Gipsy, maneuvering towards the starboard side of the French ship. He closed the distance very slowly and when the two ships were about ten yards apart he had Carl prepare the crew to catch the lines.

"Manuel, is every one ready?

"Si, Jefe. Let's rock and roll."

Higgins maneuvered closer. Two long braided lines flew down from Seintespirit. They landed with thunks. Manuel and his partner gathered the slack, and the two vessels joined together gently while big rubber fenders protected the metal sides of each hull.

The deck of the French vessel was eighteen feet above the tallest deck on Caribbean Gipsy. Slowly a rope ladder appeared. When the bottom rung reached the deck, Manuel shouted upward. "Ahora!"

The ladder came to a stop and someone above said in English with a heavy French accent, "Ok Captain, we are ready. Come up please."

Carl had donned a small backpack containing a dozen field test kits. "Ready skipper?"

"Ready as I will ever be. Manuel, come on up to the bridge." He leaned over the rail. Higgins retrieved the briefcase full of money from the safe under a bench in the wheelhouse.

"Si Jefe."

"I want you to stand next to this briefcase and when I call down we will drop a small rope. You gotta tie this thing real good and we will pull it up to make the deal. You got it?"

"Si Señor. Aye-Aye! I think I know what is in there but you can trust me forever. Besides," Manuel smiled and looked at the horizon.

"I don't got too many places to run if I even thought of doing something stupid. Go do your thing Captain and we will get moving the hell out of here."

"Ok, let's get it done." Cory spoke to the whole crew. His heart was pounding like a jackhammer. He nodded to Carl then grabbed a rung on the rope ladder.

Cory and Carl carefully climbed to the gunwale and stepped onboard.

"Welcome aboard my friends, I'm Jules, master of this vessel. I don't want to know anything about you two except your first names. That's my policy." Jules was dressed in a tropical shirt, denim shorts and Nike running shoes. He looked fit, well groomed, with impeccably coiffed thick black hair and a neatly trimmed goatee. He spoke perfect English with a heavy French accent. He stood next to a pallet loaded with neatly packaged bundles looking to weigh about twenty pounds each.

"Fine. I'm Cory and this is Carl. I'm the master of my ship and Carl is my chief mate." Cory extended his hand and the two captains shook cordially.

There were a dozen curious onlookers standing about the deck. A friendly dog came over and sniffed each of the Americans. It didn't appear as though there were any secrets among the crew as to what was going on. It was very clear though; Jules was in control of everything. The dog walked over and sat at attention next to Jules without a command. "May we test the cargo?" Cory inquired with an air of authority. His heartbeat returned to normal.

"I wouldn't want it any other way."

Cory nodded to Carl. He removed the backpack and extracted three vials, a small Swiss Army Knife and a role of duct tape. He set them on top the cargo.

Carl reached to the center of the pallet and lifted one of the packages. He set it on the deck and reached for the bag stacked beneath it. The dog walked over and sniffed the package on the deck then returned to Jules' side.

Jules shouted something in French towards a small group of men. Two of them approached Carl and helped him slide the package out.

"Merci," Carl mumbled to the helpers. They smiled and stood by to offer any further assistance needed.

Carl opened the knife and made a half inch slit in the packaging. He brought out about half a teaspoonful of snow white powder and popped the top off one of the test tubes. He then stuck a glass pipette into the tube and broke a vial of reagent. In less than half a second, the entire content of the tube turned a bright blue.

"You could paint a brand new corvette with this stuff, Captain," Cory said to Jules. Carl smiled, putting a small piece of duct tape over the hole.

"I know my friend Charlie in Toulon says this is the best stuff ever."

Carl, with the help of the two French seamen, repeated the test on two random packages and found each satisfactory. "Everything seems to be in order here Captain Jules," Cory spoke. "Now I will get you what you are waiting for and we can adjourn our meeting."

"The sooner the better is good for me."

Cory stepped over to the gunwale and tossed a lightweight rope downward to Manuel. "Ok, Chico."

Manuel caught the line and ran it through the handle on the briefcase twice and then tied a perfect bowline and tugged on it. At that signal, Cory hoisted the heavy briefcase up to the deck.

Attached to the forward bulkhead of the deck, under a canvas canopy was a big metal desk-like table. Jules motioned towards it and he and Cory marched together without speaking. Cory's heart was beating strongly again. He hoisted the valise onto the neatly organized space and told Jules the combinations to the two latches: "There is a combination on each latch. The one on the left is 8235 and on the right is 5328 – the reverse of the first. I suggest committing those digits to memory."

Jules said in French to one of the men standing close by "Écrire les nombres 8235, 5328 et gauche à droite." The crew member wrote down the numbers. Jules then rolled the combination and popped open the lid.

"Two million three hundred thousand dollars in mixed American, British, Canadian and German currencies." Cory stated.

To the man who had written down the combinations numbers Jules ordered: "Compter les billets britanniques et les projets de loi allemandes dans un tas de cheminée."

The crewman then stacked the German notes in two piles, one stack of one hundred mark notes and the other a five-inch-high stack of five hundred mark bills. He then counted the British, Canadian and U.S. notes. Jules took a small retractable tape measure out of his shirt pocket and with a smile measured the depth of the piles of Deutsch Marks.

"We do our field test too on a portion of your product." The Frenchman said with a laugh.

Cory and Carl and those standing around joined in the laughter. "Ce qui est exactement sur la paperasse." The crewman spoke after counting for about five minutes. The mariners spent the time discussing the types of radars they had on their ships and how nice it would be to get moving through the darkness on such a beautiful starlit night.

"Merci'," Jules responded.

Jules issued several orders in French to his crew. Immediately an engine started and a young Frenchman sitting at the controls of the ship's boom went into action. He lifted the long iron pole, maneuvering it over the cargo. The dog went over near the desk where the money had been counted and lay down. A cable with a large hook dropped slowly down and another man grabbed it and hooked it into the netting holding the cocaine.

Cory leaned over the gunwale and spoke to Manuel who was standing on the after cargo deck with the rest of the crew. "Ahora Chico."

"Si, Capitan."

Cory nodded to Jules. He in turn nodded to the boom operator who in turn nodded to the gentleman who had counted the money and written down the combinations. He was now standing next to the ship's side and was looking down at Manuel. There was an un-signaled sense of agreement, both crews were ready and within ninety seconds, the pallet was lowered to the deck of the smaller ship.

"Well Captain and Mr. Carl, I believe all is in order and we should all be on our merry way to other destinations." The three smugglers shook hands. "Until we meet again." Jules saluted Cory.

First Carl, then Cory climbed down the rope ladder. The second Cory's feet were on the deck the ladder disappeared. Cory went forward and Carl astern to untie the lines belonging to Jules. Manuel and his partners were busy transferring the bundles from the pallet to a makeshift slide, guiding each package directly into the hidden space beneath the water tanks. The pallet was already half empty as Carl entered the wheelhouse. "What about this, Jefe?"

Carl looked at the pallet inscribed in Egyptian naming an Algerian shipping company. He simply tilted his head towards the sea.

"Ok, señor." Manuel picked it up and tossed it like a big square Frisbee.

The two vessels drifted fifty yards apart as Carl joined Cory.

"How about that!" Carl spoke first.

"Man what a cool cucumber Jules is. I wonder how he handles a Coast Guard Boarding."

"Probably quite a bit differently than what we just did. But I bet you he has a program." Cory placed the vessel in gear and pushed a few buttons on the Loran C receiver. He plotted a course to guide the boat northeast of Bermuda before turning towards Norfolk. While they were talking, the bell rang on the fax receiver and the 'wish wosh wish wosh' sound of the heated fax transducer sprinted back and forth across the paper.

The weather map showed a well-defined stationary high pressure system centered over the Carolina coast. A tropical wave was developing east of the Lesser Antilles. It looked like a good week of boating ahead for the crew of the Caribbean Gipsy. Cory and Carl both noticed the fleet was getting back to patrol work after terminating the search for plane crash survivors. Two ships were in port in Montego Bay, one was heading south eastward probably for the Windward Pass, and ESCAPE had just left the port of Corpus Christi and looked to be on the way home, west of the Florida Keys. One new cutter had just left Jacksonville headed south. They would probably patrol the Old Bahama Channel.

"Looks like clear steaming ahead." Cory stated. "I'm feeling pretty good right now, I had no idea how this thing would go down. Man it was right out of the movies. I don't know why people need shit like cocaine to get a buzz when a good adventure gets you to a better place."

"I agree. I would work with Jules any day. I sure wouldn't want to be his enemy though."

Cory steered the ship north, getting lined up with the Loran C tracking directions and bringing the speed to nine knots.

"It's about ten now, I'll take the first six. I couldn't sleep now for anything. Tell the guys to sack out and send one up around midnight and you can relieve me at four am." Cory opened a Pepsi Cola.

"OK. Do you need anything from the galley?" Carl asked.

"Nah, I just want to drive this boat and look at the stars. See you in six hours."

Chapter Seventy

ESCAPE rounded the southernmost point in the United States six miles south of Key West. In the absence of his superior, LT Sutton had perfectly orchestrated the transfer of the sailing vessel Misty Dream, her crew and contraband to Customs and the U.S. Marshals in Corpus Christi. The crew enjoyed a thirty-six-hour unexpected port call while all the paper work was being done. Ensign Ladner, the senior boarding and the arresting officer, had no time to go ashore and enjoy the time there. The paper work and documentation for drug enforcement seizures and arrests must be meticulously attended to while all the events are fresh in the minds of the Coasties. It could be six months to a year before Ladner might have to come to Texas to testify at the trial. Every detail required documentation and each photograph had to be identified correctly. Criminal defense attorneys were notorious for picking holes in the chain of evidence custody and as time passed, memories of exact details erode.

At the end of this patrol, ESCAPE was scheduled into a shipyard to address mechanical issues and to install more modern radar and communication equipment. The yard winning the bid was a local Charleston facility and the crew grew excited about spending the time at home. Since being assigned to ESCAPE many of the officers and crew had worked tirelessly to make her ready for deployments. The big talk about the cutter was how excited they were to be able to spend a little time ashore and explore Charleston.

Two young petty officers would encounter a slight dilemma when they would discover their wives had become associated with Chad Walgren. They were involved in helping the local drug king distribute the very stuff their husbands were working hard to keep out of the United States.

Chapter Seventy-One

Completing her week of touring and tanning, Trish left Montego Bay. She enjoyed traveling first class and could not imagine riding in coach again. The itinerary took her from Montego to Atlanta. She thought about stopping off at the Whittaker Law Firm to see how things were going but chose not to. She didn't want any little detail at the office to cause a delay in her meeting with Cory. She would be back to work in ten days. Robert Whittaker knew she was going to the Caribbean to relax and then meet with several investment officers along the eastern seaboard exploring opportunities for the firm's clients.

On the short flight from Atlanta to Lexington she took out the map Chester had given her. She palmed the key to Fairgrounds locker number 321.

At the Atlanta airport she had changed from tropical attire to a pair of expensive jeans, leather boots, a silk blouse and a lightweight leather jacket. She had consulted several magazines dealing with horse racing and emulated the fashions she found.

A race was just about to start as Trish walked into the grandstand. She picked and empty seat 6 rows back from the rail and enjoyed watching the fans engage in the race as the thoroughbreds thundered down the home stretch. The cheering of successful gamblers and the disappointment of the losers was fascinating. She memorized the names of the first and second place ponies just for the fun of it. They were Axel Grease and Somebody's Girl. The next race would post in half an hour so she went into the clubhouse for a gin and tonic. She contemplated what was to happen next. She took the locker key out of her pocket and tumbled it around. "I wonder how much money is in this brief case and how much of it will belong to my lover tomorrow."

At post time for the fourth race, betters were heading out from the wagering windows.

Trish left enough to cover the cost of her drink and a substantial tip on the bar. She walked past the large betting window auditorium and through a doorway marked "Lockers". There were four banks of lockers and signage directed her to the 300 series. She took the key out of her pocket, inserted it into locker number 321. She opened the door. Inside was an elegant attaché case with a brass engraved name tag on it displaying T.

DIXON. She smiled, picked up the case thinking Chester covers everything. The case sported wheels and an extendable handle.

As she turned to head for the exit she saw two security guards heading her way. Her heart skipped a beat but she kept her composure in check. "Leaving before the daily double?" asked one of the guards, tipping his cap.

"Oh, I just came to see one of my uncle's horses run in the first." Trish spoke with a slight southern accent and an air of confidence.

"How did he do?"

"Actually it is a 'she' Somebody's Girl and she came in second. Now I have to get back to my office and finish work before someone notices how long I have been out to lunch." Trish smiled at the two.

"Ma'am." Both guards tipped their caps once more and strolled along as the fast talking man on the PA was calling the finish of the fourth race.

Trish was happy she chose to wear the leather jacket because her armpits were soaked with perspiration after her encounter with the guards.

She was curious as to just how much money she was packing. This was one-third of Cory's compensation for the trip. He and the crew were to be paid upon delivering the contraband cargo to Norfolk. Of course, Trish also had instructions from Chester if for some reason the cargo never made it to Virginia she was to return the briefcase to locker number 321.

To kill a little time, she drove around Historic Lexington and found a park on the outskirts of town. The theme there was a factory making long bore rifles. The Remington Company had purchased the business in the early fifties and the business owner had donated the land for a park. There were no cars in the parking lot. She drove to a spot where she could observe the entrance/exit and backed the rental car in with an old brick wall behind it. She opened the briefcase. It was unlocked. She stared at the bound up packages of hundred dollar bills. She knew each bundle contained one hundred bills or ten thousand dollars. She also knew Carl would receive one hundred thousand for his part and the Colombians would split twenty-five. She stopped counting when she got to fifty bundles. That was about a third of it.

She took in a deep breath thinking three quarters of a million minus one hundred for Carl and thirty for the crew meant Cory's compensation was somewhere around half a million! Could it be her lover was making one and a half million for this haul and she would get around a third of a million on her own? She liked this business.

Trish buckled the case closed and sat in the car for a few moments reflecting on things. Half an hour later, she was on her way to Virginia.

Chapter Seventy-Two

ESCAPE transited home without incident. The ship encountered two suspicious vessels along the way. Commander Flood decided in each case they should be boarded. He had each vessel heave to and sent the law enforcement teams to check them out. One had been a fishing trawler heading northbound with no apparent fishing gear onboard. A quick check and investigation found the skipper was truthful when he indicated he was heading for a repair facility on the Savannah River. He had left all his gear at his homeport in Daytona Beach. The other was a sailboat transiting northward under power on a perfect sailing day with ten knot winds from the southeast. It turned out this was a vessel in charter and the company was moving it from Key West to Saint Augustine Florida for the fall season.

The cutter continued northbound in perfect early fall weather. Two mornings during the transit they encountered fog and extra watches were deployed to the bow and the speed of advance was slowed to five knots. Five days after leaving the Gulf Coast of Texas they were finally nearing home.

Mooring a two-thousand-ton ship alongside a dock in the Cooper River was no simple task and Commander Flood and Lieutenant Sutton had discussed the evolution. A quick check of tides and currents indicated a high slack water, meaning the tide would be the highest and current almost negligible at twenty past noon on Thursday. So early in the day on Wednesday they adjusted the speed of the ship to arrive at the entrance buoy at just after ten am. The two junior officers, Ladner and Merrymore, flipped a coin after supper the night before and Merrymore won the toss. He would be conning the ship into port. Skipper Dave enjoyed watching the two young men mature into their roles.

Everything went as planned and the early October Thursday morning dawned with a beautiful sunrise. Phil, on the 0400 to 0800 was relieved by Ensign Merrymore.

The young officer performed perfectly and Sutton needed to offer only one or two suggestions on the trip up the river. The Commanding Officer was confident enough of his crew that he spent most of the transit telling jokes and sea stories.

Vince was anxious to get back onboard but allowed the wife of the senior enlisted chief to board ahead of him while the quartermaster of the watch announced: "Now lady guests aboard."

The Senior Chief met his wife at the gangway, briefly embraced her then quickly turned and saluted Vince as he stepped aboard.

"Welcome back XO."

"Sounds like it finished up pretty well. We will get together in a couple of days for a little debrief."

"Sure thing XO." Chief's wife was holding his hand tightly and looked anxious to get him home. It was a school day and with a little luck, they could enjoy some private time at home before his kids got off the bus.

The door to Dave Flood's cabin was open and he was standing a couple of feet inside looking at a clipboard full of messages. He glanced up. "Well, well landlubber, welcome back." Vince could tell the CO was in a good mood as he initialed the final message and sent the messenger on his way.

"So we had a pretty good patrol. Lots of boardings, a decent bust and a day and a half in Corpus Christi. The crew seems pumped. Phil did a great job on the turnover and Buzz Ladner is taking the evidence package very seriously. I saw him double and triple checking everything before he released the prisoners and contraband. If he has to go to trial, he will be ready."

"Sounds like we still have a pretty good crew here. It could be a lot worse. I heard they caught a couple of people on one of the Gulf Coast 210's selling pot. I hope we never have to deal with that."

"You've got that right. So what was the deal with your car?" Vince related the whole story about the theft of his Mercedes. How it had turned up in Kentucky with no more miles on it than it had when stolen. He also related the sighting of attorney Thrasher in the Charleston airport. "I'm not sure what is going on but there is some suspicion I was intentionally distracted from the ship for some reason. The DEA is convinced there is an organized group working coke and heroin between southern Virginia and Savannah."

"That's a big area."

"Yes, the agency figures this region could absorb two to three tons of cocaine a year."

"You're kidding. How much of that stuff can a person use and stay functional?" the skipper wondered.

"I don't know but a local agent told me that up in New York half the stockbrokers on the floor of the exchange are hopped up and working. One was busted a couple of months ago with eight pounds in his flat."

"Eight pounds? That's a Christmas turkey!"

Vince agreed. He also told his skipper of the trip out the Cape Hatteras and Nags Head.

Flood was planning another trip to see his mother in San Diego and returning by mid next week to go over all the specifications for the shipyard. They arranged to have that dinner Denise had invited him to months earlier.

The debrief between the CO and XO went on for half an hour more, covering routine issues until the two were satisfied all the important concerns were addressed.

Vince opened the door to his own stateroom and felt a comforting aura of being back onboard. There were stacks of files and papers to review. The ship's yeoman and Phil had arranged everything in good order. He dug in and was making good headway for about an hour when the Operations Officer knocked on the door.

Another hour passed in discussing the balance of the patrol Phil had taken care of. Vince also went over the details of the car theft with him as well. They agreed, if it wasn't so personal it would be pretty exciting.

Sutton was taking four days off to go to Boston to visit his girlfriend. Vince needed the time to go over the pile of paperwork on his desk.

Chapter Seventy-Three

Two hours after ESCAPE made the left turn into the Ashley
and Cooper River channel, Cory made a westerly course change
and directed Caribbean Gipsy towards the mouth of Chesapeake
Bay. The transit north had been quiet.   The boat cruised along at
nine and a half knots. The early fall weather had been perfect with
starlit nights and calm seas. The only clouds were high puffy ones
offering magically orchestrated sunsets each evening.
They stopped for an hour when a school of Dorado swirled
ahead on the second afternoon of the transit. Manuel and his
helpers quickly boated half a dozen ten pounders and they were set
with fresh fish for the rest of the trip.   Manuel was an
accomplished chef and for the next several days used the fresh
catch on a variety of tasty meals enjoyed by everyone.
The route Cory had chosen was one seldom used by shipping.
Only twice between the West Indies and north of Bermuda did they
encounter any other traffic. These were container ships making
east/west passages between America and either Europe or the
northwest coast of Africa. Now they were heading in a westerly
direction and could expect more traffic.
Cory and Carl had interesting conversations concerning how
to invest their money to realize a healthy and legitimate return.
The days of the late seventies money market funds paying interest
rates in the neighborhood of twelve and thirteen percent were over.
Carl talked about the advent of computers. He heard experts saying
everyone in the country would own one. Software, a critical piece
in each computer makes the gadgets perform word processing,
accounting and even photograph management.
"Can you believe they are putting a whole array of satellites up
in space to eventually replace Loran C? It's called 'global
positioning," Carl said pointing at the black box that received all
the Loran position reports.
"You're kidding, where do you find out about all this stuff? I
can't believe they could do anything better than Loran."
"Some really smart people say one day you will have some
sort of thing in your car and it will actually know where you are
and somehow will give you directions on how to get to where you
want to go. It will even be able to find a certain restaurant for you
if you just talk to it. I saw something about the new age of
computers in National Geographic about a year ago. So I asked

this stock broker who helps me invest to look into it. He thinks it will be a gold mine for investors and got me set up. Do you want to hook up with him after we get this job done?"

"Hell yes, if you have something getting you more than ten percent on your money, I would be all over it."

It was hard for Cory to grasp the concept of such things. The wireless fax machine on which they received the twice-daily position reports about the Coast Guard was magic enough for him.

Another beautiful sunset took shape. The fax machine sprang to life and once again within a few minutes Leon, a thousand miles away, pinpointed the location and destination of all units in the U.S. Coast Guard. There was a buoy tender working aids to navigation around Cape Hatteras and a large 378-foot cutter leaving Portsmouth heading for fisheries patrol near the Newfoundland coast.

"Whoa," Cory stated as he was looking at the fax weather map and comparing it to the large chart on the table displaying the western shoreline of the United States from Savannah Georgia to Cape May New Jersey.

"What?"

"Well it looks like this big guy, the Cutter SHERMAN could get in our way if we are not careful. We've got a three-day window for the delivery so I think we should slow down to seven knots. We will arrive sixteen hours later than we had planned but it will put those guys who travel at sixteen a chance to be a couple hundred miles north when we hit Hampton Rhoads." On the edge of the fax report Cory had been doing some quick arithmetic in the 'distance equals rate times time' formula learned by all tenth grade math students in the world. He inched back on the throttle control reducing the engine RPM's from twenty-two hundred fifty to twenty-one hundred. The monotonous tone of the engine burned into their heads for the last six days changed noticeably.

The two Americans smiled at one another as they heard Manuel running on the metal decks and leaping up the stairs to join them.

"What's a matter Jefe? Is somebody coming?" Genuine worry and a little fear shown in his face.

"Oh, it's nothing, we are a little ahead of schedule so I want to slow down so we are not hanging around a harbor waiting for the right time to go to the dock. Don't worry."

"Oh, holy Mary mother of Jesus I was afraid someone was coming to check us out. I go tell the boys. They got scared when you slow down." Relief showed on the Colombian's face.

"Hey Jefes I been cooking up some choco chip cookies. You want me to bring some up for you?"

Carl responded. "So that's what smells so good. You better get some up here pronto and a little leche' too."

"I come right back. You gonna like these cookies."

Chapter Seventy-Four

The trip up interstate ninety-five was uneventful. Chad and six friends picked up the Kenworth and Sea Land trailer from a truck stop lot forty miles west of Charleston. Rural route U.S. 17 took them eastward to a resort near Virginia Beach. Chad was driving and two others, minor dealers from Savannah and Myrtle Beach named Lenni and Elwood, accompanied him in the cab. Following along in Debbi's Dodge convertible were Debbi and three of her friends; a single twenty-six-year old coed Jennifer from Clemson and Nick and Judy, a mid-twenty-year old couple from Folly Island. All were involved in the end distribution of contraband. Everyone came along to help cut and divide the ton of coke. Chad had collected money and guarantees from fifty local dealers from southern New Jersey to Georgia. When the cargo was delivered and removed from the Caribbean Gipsy, he would transfer six million dollars to Chester Whittaker. A million five-hundred would be personally delivered by a FedEx driver. The balance would be wired from six different banks to the Turks Trust and Clearing House. Chester would see the recording of the transfers on his computer as they occurred.

Chad and his crew would unload the product and take it to a warehouse Chester owned in Virginia Beach. In the trunk of his Dodge convertible were thirty rolls of aluminum foil. In the Sea Land container, he had collected three dozen bread pans, a box of surgical gloves, fifty rolls of saran wrap, two postal scales, three hundred pounds of sucrose, four hundred pounds of talc, three hundred pounds of powdered Novocain and twenty-five rolls of duct tape. There was also a large industrial sized bread dough mixing machine and two huge metal bowls in which to blend the products. Over the next three days the group would cut, mix, weigh, and wrap thirteen hundred and seventy-five two pound packages of the product for local dealers up and down the coast and inland to Atlanta and Lexington. They carried enough materials to cut and prepare most of the next load as well.

The local dealers would pay Chad and his team ten grand for each two-pound package.

At the end of each work day, six of the team would return to the resort enjoying the beach and pool while one remained to guard the shop.

When all the work was done, Chad would keep twenty packages for his own business. These he would extract from the system before the product was fully cut. His supply would be the best available. He could sell his product to end users for up to eight hundred bucks an ounce. In the end, each of the street dealers would make a one hundred percent markup on the product they sold. Some would try to further cut the product but in the end, their customers would be unhappy and their profits would shrink. It was well worth their while to simply repackage the stuff in one ounce bags and sell it as it was. This product would be the best on the east coast. Chad's supply would be the best of the best. Many of his clientele were the most affluent and well respected professionals in the Low Country of Charleston and Myrtle Beach.

Chapter Seventy-Five

The Chrysler Fifth Avenue Trish rented in Lexington was an enjoyable car to drive. The route took her from portal to portal along interstate highway 26. Having left the state fairgrounds in the early afternoon, driving the entire distance in one shot although possible in about ten hours, she chose to stop in a nice riverside hotel in Charleston West Virginia.

She secured the briefcase in the hotel safe and had a wonderful dinner and 2 glasses of French wine. She dressed casually and wore wedding and engagement rings. She carried them to dissuade roving males from trying to pick her up. She always felt if she saw someone interesting she would approach them. In this location, she found no one of interest and retired to her room to watch a movie.

After a quick morning workout, she enjoyed a healthy breakfast of fresh fruit and yogurt. Knowing she would be in the arms of her lover within a few days prompted her to keep fit.

It was Thursday morning. The way things were going she would arrive in Virginia a few days earlier than necessary. She decided to legitimize the journey by calling on the CFO of Newport News Shipbuilding. The company was one of the investments in the SEASTA portfolio.

Chapter Seventy-Six

"What the fuck!" Carl looked through his binoculars at an outbound fishing boat four miles ahead. Caribbean Gipsy was lining up to enter Chesapeake Bay. They were two and a half hours east of the Chesapeake Bay Bridge connecting northern Virginia to the Northampton Peninsula of Maryland.

"What now?" Cory entered the wheelhouse.

"It looks like we've got a boat on fire up ahead."

"You've got to be shitting me. Not here, not now."

Black smoke and bright orange flames erupted from the boat ahead.

Over the VHF radio, they suddenly heard the call. "Mayday, Mayday, Mayday! This is the fishing vessel Zeus. We are on fire twelve miles east of the Bay Bridge. I have a fire on board and one injured crew. Please send help. Mayday, Mayday, Mayday!"

"Vessel calling, this is the United States Coast Guard Portsmouth. I understand you have a fire on board and an injured crewman," the watch stander answered.

"Yes, yes! We are getting the fire under control but running out of fire extinguishers. We need help right now!"

"What the fuck are we supposed to do Cory?"

"Well, if we leave the scene of a maritime emergency, they will track us down and we will be in the deepest of shit imaginable. Shit, shit, shit, why now!"

They continued listening. Inside the wheelhouse the two had just looked at the most recent fax from Leon. It showed the Cutter SHERMAN as expected headed northeast two hundred miles off the coast of New Jersey. A simple afternoon boat ride into the dock near Hampton Roads was turning complicated.

"Roger, Captain. We have a forty-one footer underway to your location. ETA is about thirty minutes. We will hail other boats in your vicinity and try to get you help."

"Here it comes." Cory said. "It looks like they have the fire under control. What is the distance?"

"Three miles."

"Get Manuel up here. He knows a lot about first aid. We will play Good Samaritan and hope for the best. Our hidden compartment is about to earn its money. Let's not panic."

"Hello all stations this is the United States Coast Guard Group Portsmouth with a report of a fishing vessel on fire east of the

Chesapeake Bay Bridge. Any vessel in the vicinity is requested to contact this station on channel sixteen."

"Everyone stay calm. We are going to see what we can do. If we run away from this, there is a thing called Karma. It comes in good and bad. Let's stick with the good. Manuel, they got a guy burned badly over there will you be able to help?"

"Si Jefe. I can play it cool and help. Mary mother of Jesus help us." Manuel made the sign of the cross and kissed the crucifix on a gold chain around his neck. His heart was beating about a hundred twenty but no one would know. "I get first aid kit."

"Great, thanks, every one stay cool." Cory picked up the microphone above his head.

"Coast Guard, this is the freighter Caribbean Gipsy. We are inbound and two miles east of the vessel with the fire. I have him in sight. I will render what assistance I can until you get here."

"Caribbean Gipsy this is Coast Guard Portsmouth. Thank you. I will need some information about your vessel."

"Roger."

"Yes, what is the home port of your vessel?"

"Saint Thomas U.S. Virgin Islands."

"Yes Captain." There was about a thirty second pause in the conversation. "You are a long way from home."

"Roger that, I'm delivering a load of custom made furniture to a company called 'Tidewater Décor' in Hampton Roads."

"Roger, skipper, what is the length of your boat?" The watch stander continued asking questions until all the information necessary for his paper work was provided.

"Coast Guard, we are approaching the vessel Zeus. I have a crewman well trained in first aid. I will send him and one other over to render assistance. It looks like the fire is out. We are taking two additional fire extinguishers. The captain is out on deck and there is a guy there with his left arm and shoulder pretty burned up."

"Thank you skipper. Our boat is still about fifteen minutes away. Will you be able to remain on scene?"

"Roger, Coast Guard. It looks like it was an engine fire and the master is indicating he has no power and will need a tow. I'm lying about forty feet away right now. He is about sixty-five feet long. Will your boat be able to get him in?"

"Shouldn't be a problem. We are dispatching a chopper to pick up the injured crewman. Please stand by."

"What a cluster fuck," Cory stated to Gallo standing on the bridge next to him. He sent Carl to help Manuel on the fishing boat. If he weren't sitting on top of ton of cocaine, he would have enjoyed the adventure. He downed a cup of lukewarm coffee in one swallow. Next he threw three Rolaids into his mouth and handed the cup to Gallo.

"Negro por favor'."

"Si Jefe."

"Coast Guard, this is Caribbean Gipsy"

"Go ahead."

"Roger, my crew onboard Zeus reports the fire is out, they have no power and the vessel was taking on a little water through a broken raw water hose in a heat exchanger. We have the leak under control. The injured guy is burned on his shoulder and arm but should be ok.

My guy has covered the burn with moist sterile dressings. That's the best we can do. He's in a lot of pain but all we have here is aspirin and Rolaids. We've told him a chopper is coming. I hope they can give him something for the pain. He is scared and in shock. I see your boat coming now about a mile out."

"Roger, Captain, thank you for helping. We will coordinate everything else with the 41 footer. One of their crew will come aboard your vessel to collect any further details."

"Roger that, standing by." Cory ate three more Rolaids from a jar next to the chart table and washed them down with fresh coffee just delivered by Gallo.

Over the next hour, the scene got busier. Another forty-one-footer arrived on scene and a helicopter came flying in from someplace south. It took five minutes for the chopper to lower a stretcher and pick up the injured crewman. It was impressive to watch and Cory thought how great it was that the Coast Guard was there for these emergencies. But how fucked up it was if they really searched his ship, he would be in jail for the next ten years. It just didn't seem right. The initial patrol boat crew made up a towing line to take the crippled Zeus to Portsmouth. The second one approached Caribbean Gipsy. Carl and Manuel arrived in the Zodiac.

"Ok, everyone be calm," he said to Gallo but more to himself.

"You OK?"

"Si Jefe, Manny tells us to act cool we do that."

"Great. You know we only haul tables, chairs and nice furniture. Right?"

"Exactamento! Don't you worry Jefe."

The patrol boat stayed twenty feet off the starboard side while Carl and Manuel raised the Zodiac. Once the skiff was secure, the petty officer in charge of the Coast Guard vessel picked up his microphone and said. "Thank you for your help today. Just heave to right here, captain. I'm sending a couple of people over there to finish the paperwork."

"Not a problem." Cory responded and chewed more Rolaids.

Carl and Manuel entered the wheelhouse.

"Our information says you have a crew of five. I only see four in the wheelhouse," the petty officer in charge asked over the radio.

Cory keyed his own microphone. "Yes there is one more in the galley fixing lunch."

"Well, captain, please have your entire crew muster in the bow while we come along side."

"Roger." Cory spoke into the microphone then said to the rest, "Well, here we go. We all know the drill. Manny, go get Sam and Stephen and meet us in the bow."

"Si." The Colombian answered with a demeanor of steel.

Once the crew was mustered well forward on the cargo deck the patrol boat came alongside and dispatched three heavily armed Coastguardsmen.

"Good afternoon. I'm Petty Officer Julian Kankelfritz. Who is the master?"

"I am, Cory Higgins."

"Yes, Captain, glad to meet you." Kankelfritz extended his hand and firmly shook Cory's. "Thank you for the help you rendered today. For our own safety, I'm going to have one of my crewmen make a quick security tour of your vessel."

"I know how it works. I have been boarded a dozen times."

This took the young petty officer by surprise. "You have?"

"Yes, we work in the Caribbean and the West Indies. There are so many of you guys down there if you don't see someone once a month, something is wrong. I have each boarding report in a binder up in the wheelhouse."

"We will check that in a few minutes."

Cory sensed that Kankelfritz was awed at boarding a boat from the Caribbean. He was losing his grip on control of the situation. Cory noticed this and figured he could use it to his own advantage.

"So you have been boarded before?"

"Yeah, eleven or twelve times in the last nine months. I'm all over the Caribbean and the Gulf. About two and a half weeks ago I was having a beer in Jamaica with the XO from one of your ships. ESCAPADE or ESCAPE, something like that."

The young petty officer who was making the 'security sweep' arrived back on the foredeck.

"It's a clean ship here Jules. No one hiding down there, no oil in the bilge, nothing seems to be leaking."

"Sounds good," Kankelfritz answered. "So Captain, why don't you and I take a tour of the boat? Then we will go to the wheelhouse and have a look at your documents and you can be on your way."

"Sounds like a great idea. I'd like to get this stuff in to the dock before midnight. There is a truck waiting for us in three hours and we still have five to get there."

"This is a clean ship, Captain. We see so many boats with oily rags all over the place and leaks everywhere."

"Well, I'm proud of her. Manuel spends all of his off watch time down here making things shine," Cory told the boarding officer in the engine room.

Kankelfritz sat on top of the water tanks aft of the main engine. He was sweating. Cory was confident this boarding would go away quickly and they would be on their way.

"If this son of a bitch knew that he was sitting on top of a ton of cocaine he would shit his pants," Cory thought. The stress abated and he was feeling like karma was working in his favor.

"Let's go take a look at your documents skipper, then we will be on our way."

The pair made their way to the wheelhouse while the rest of the crew of stood on the cargo deck visiting with the armed boarding party.

Inside the bridge, Cory answered questions about various pieces of equipment. "Wow! You have a wireless fax machine? I haven't seen many of them on boats."

"This is a cargo vessel and shippers need to contact us about a pick up or delivery. The fax is the best way to communicate. It is also pretty handy for getting weather synopsis from NOAA," It was obvious to Cory, this young Coastguardsman had never actually been out to sea. "Here are all of the vessel documents and passports for each crewmember." Cory handed over a white three-ringed binder. Each document was inside a waterproof protector.

"You sure are well organized Captain."

226

"Well, when something happens out there," he gestured over his shoulder in the general direction of the Atlantic Ocean, "You have to be ready to act quickly. When everything is in order you can grab what you need and head for the lifeboat. I think you guys have some sort of motto like Semper Paratus. Doesn't that mean always ready?"

Kankelfritz felt mentored by an old salt of the sea. Cory figured he could get this gullible kid to eat shit out of his hand.

"Yup that's our motto."

Cory handed over another three-ringed binder with the label 'Boarding Reports'.

"And here are all the boardings we have been through on this ship. When your report goes in here we will have fifteen I think."

"Wow! Jamaica, Puerto Rico, Grand Cayman, Jamaica again." The young boarding officer was impressed with all of the places Caribbean Gipsy had been. "You get around."

"Well, that's kind of what you have to do if you get paid to haul cargo." Cory was tiring of the BS and wanted to get this dumbass off the boat. "So is there anything else you need? This whole fire thing slowed us down by four hours. A truck is waiting for us and we are still hours from Norfolk. The flood tide we were counting on is over and now we will be bucking the ebb. I'd like to get going as soon as I can."

"Oh, I'm sorry. Here, just let me check a couple more boxes and sign this thing off and we can all be on our way." Kankelfritz answered as he signed the bottom or the form. "Here we go Captain Higgins. I'm a little envious of your job."

"Well, Petty Officer. . ." Cory glanced at the signature on the boarding document. "Klinkerfritz, just learn all you can about ships and boats in your time in the guard and keep your nose clean. Someday you might be doing the same thing." He smiled to himself thinking what a jackass.

"And on behalf of the U.S. Coast Guard, I would like to thank you and your crew for stopping to help today."

"Yeah, I wouldn't have wanted it any other way." In the wheelhouse Carl pressed the start button to bring his diesel engine back to life. This would be a signal to dumbass it was time to get the hell off our boat so we can get back to the job you so obviously covet.

Kankelfritz signaled the forty-one footer to come along side and the boarding party disembarked. Before disembarking he turned to shake hands with Cory but he was already in the wheelhouse waiting impatiently for this whole ordeal to be finished.

.

Chapter Seventy-Seven

Chad and Debbie cruised around the docks at Hampton Roads. There was little activity on the docks. A large container ship had just departed after dropping a couple dozen containers to waiting truckers. Fifteen more units had been loaded and the ship turned around in a matter of four hours. From the information he had gotten from Tom, the shipment should be arriving this afternoon or evening. There were no other ships calling on this dock for the next three days. They found a security guard in a booth at the entrance. Chad asked where the Caribbean Gipsy would be tied up he looked up from a comic book and simply pointed down the dock. Chad told the guy they had been hired to clean up and change the oil in the engine and generators.

"Whatever."

Debbi pointed towards a large delivery truck with the logo of Tidewater Décor on the side. A note along the bottom of the logo indicated they specialized in imported items from the Caribbean.

"That must be the truck."

It looked like they had been waiting a while. Two of the four men hanging around were sitting on a stack of pallet boards playing gin rummy.

Chad's instructions were to wait until the crew unloaded the cargo and get onboard at night to get the cocaine. They were to meet a woman described by Thrasher as a "pretty hot thirty something babe with a Georgia accent." She would be driving a Fifth Avenue. She was to take the captain and crew to the airport.

Debbi sat very close to her man on the bench seat. "Looks like they're running late."

"Yeah, I hope everything is all right." Just then on the car radio, the half past five news reporter announced the Coast Guard had responded to a vessel fire near the entrance to Chesapeake Bay earlier in the day.

"An injured crewman from the fishing vessel Zeus was lifted off the boat by a helicopter and another vessel passing by had stopped to help extinguish the fires." The reporter went on with more details.

"Jesus." Chad spoke out. "I wonder if our guys were involved.

This could be a big problem."

"Yes babe, you would have a lot of upset customers. Wait a minute!" She pointed towards the entrance to the harbor. "Look at that little blue ship. Where is that picture Tom gave you?"

Chad shuffled through a file folder. "Yup yep, that's him."

Having no reason to stay around they pulled away from the wharf.

As they were leaving Chad noticed Trish's Chrysler.

Trish knew from Tom to be looking for a couple of people in their late twenties driving around in a Dodge convertible.

The drivers maneuvered their vehicles to meet facing in opposite directions driver's side to driver's side. Trish hit the electric window control and the glass disappeared into the door. "You must be Chad."

"She really is a hottie," Chad thought as he absorbed her accent. "Yup, that's me. And you must be Ms. Dixon." He already sensed Debbi was showing a little jealousy as she squeezed even closer to his side and dug her fingernails into his thigh.

"And I'm Debbi."

"Nice to meet you both, have you seen any sign of the ship?"

"Yes ma'am. He is pulling up to the dock right now. We are going to go to the beach for a swim and dinner and come back a little later."

"Perfect. I will meet the captain and crew and take care of things on my end."

"Sounds good to me." Chad pulled away.

Trish inched her luxury car forward. She was wondering what kind of life Chad had. He dressed well, was neatly kept and seemed to have a great personality and apparently a decent girlfriend. She had expected to meet some tattoo laden long haired druggie type. He seemed more like a genteel young southern executive. She contemplated the people she had met since beginning her life of crime. Each of them was friendly, good looking and presented a professional demeanor. She couldn't picture any one of them as a felon.

She rounded a long row of shipping container trailers and finally saw Caribbean Gipsy sliding sideways very slowly towards the dock. Then she saw him. There was her captain standing just outside the wheelhouse giving hand signals and voice commands to the crew. She drew in a deep breath. Carl, who Trish had yet to meet, was inside following the commands Cory gave to inch closer to the wharf. Finally, when they were only a few inches away he signaled the crew to throw the lines on to the dock. The crew from the furniture truck caught the ropes and fastened them to cleats.

Satisfied with the position of the vessel, Cory leaned against the rail and began a conversation with one of the crew from the truck. He turned and said something to Carl and then jumped eighteen inches to the dock. It was the first time in ten days his feet had touched land. He shook hands with the truck driver and handed him a clipboard.

"That's a nice looking ship. How long do I have to get everything off?"

"Well, were going to be tied up here for three or four days but tomorrow there are four guys coming down to change the oil and do some work on the generator. I would guess you've got until then if you need it. Some of this stuff is pretty darn neat," Cory commented. "I really like the teak couches and wing chairs. Your customers are going to be thrilled."

"They always are. We should have it all knocked out before midnight so we won't be in the way of your mechanic."

Cory had just noticed Trish sitting inside of her car and acting very businesslike. "Oh, I see my shipping agent's representative over there. We are going to go have a little meeting and then be back probably after dinner."

"Nice looking agent."

"Yeah, all in a day's work." He smiled walking towards Trish.

She saw Cory moving her way and instantly a knot formed in her stomach. She wanted to go back to the hotel and jump in bed with him for the next week. There was business to take care of first. "How are you doing Captain, was it a good trip?"

"Smooth as glass." He extended his hand and shook hers wanting to yank her through the open window and into his arms. They both knew more than a couple sets of eyes were watching. It was hard for anyone not to notice a very attractive woman in a fancy car parked on an industrial wharf.

"So what is happening now?" Trish asked

"Well, the guys are going to spend the next four or five hours unloading the furniture. When that's done, we need to get the crew to the airport for their ride home. Then I'm going to take a few days off and walk around on dry land. Would you care to join me?"

"Well, I have a couple of payday issues."

"That's right so they will be busy for a while. You want to go get something to eat? I'm starving. I can tell you all about our Coast Guard boarding this afternoon."

"What! You're kidding!"

"No, I'm not, there was a boat on fire and we stopped to help out. Otherwise, we would have been here four hours ago. I'll tell you all about it over a great non-seafood dinner. I'll go let Carl know we'll be back later."

Cory walked forty feet to the rear of the truck where a forklift was already lifting the first pallet of furniture into the rig. Carl and the driver were talking about the boarding and boat fire while the crews from Caribbean Gipsy and the Tidewater Décor performed longshoreman duties.

"She's pretty hot," Carl said leaning his head in the direction of the Chrysler. "Is she the one replacing Tom?"

"I guess so. She has offered to spring for dinner on the company American Express card. Will you be OK here?"

"Not a problem skipper. We have a butt ton of stuff to do once the cargo is gone. We'll get her all washed down and ready for the grease monkeys. If we've got a week, I might fly down to Texas for a few days."

"That works. We'll come back in a couple of hours and take care of last minute business then I'll get Ms. Dixon to drop you off at the airport."

"Great."

"Ok, see you later."

A long early fall twilight ensued and the sun fell behind the cranes at the Newport News Shipbuilding Company. Cory pondered how flawlessly this whole operation had gone. He broke into a broad carefree smile as he neared the passenger side of Trish's car.

"Let's get out of here for a while."

Inhaling deeply, Trish moaned slightly. "Yes admiral, I will go any place you want me to."

Chapter Seventy-Eight

While monitoring the Coast Guard radio traffic around Chesapeake Bay, Leon heard of the fire onboard Zeus. He was a nervous wreck when he saw a message saying Caribbean Gipsy had aided with the fire. The report also said a subsequent boarding by Petty Officer Kankelfritz had found the freighter be a "well maintained ship operating in accordance with all applicable U.S. and international laws."

The next shipment would begin in six weeks when Rob Byrd and Carl Petersen would bring a three-ton load of Lebanese blond hashish from Barranquilla to St. Petersburg Florida. He covered the communications gear with the tarp and climbed the stairs confident and smiling.

This evening, Leon began his first vacation away from Fort Sumter. The park was already closed and he prepared take the last launch to Patriots Point at seven pm. This boat brought over a housekeeping crew and the food and drink necessary to prepare the park for the next day's business. Gretchen was flying in. She would arrive in Charleston around eight.

He had booked a room at the Tides on Folly Beach for three nights. He couldn't stop thinking about the blissful time ahead.

Leon had taken quite a ribbing from the staff about his upcoming rendezvous. The assistant chief, Ben Baker, would be filling in as the head ranger while Leon was gone. He and several other resident rangers including Emmett Ridgeway waited at the dock as the boat approached. They wanted to get in their last jabs as the boss departed.

"Make sure you use your aftershave and she takes her birth control pills," Ben interjected as Leon stepped aboard.

"Yeah, yeah, yeah, you guys are just jealous. I will bring her over here for a tour next week and you will see why I've been smiling."

"We can't wait. Don't chicken out on that," Emmett chimed in.

"All right guys, take good care of our fort. I will see you soon." He nodded to the boat operator and the little diesel motor groaned slightly, moving the vessel across the River. The staff wandered off.

Emmett looked towards Leon's office determined to get a look behind door number two this evening. First, everyone was gathering down on the oyster beach for a barbeque and beer.

Leon disembarked the launch and walked to his truck towing a suitcase. He felt great. Approaching his Toyota pickup, he realized he had not driven a vehicle for nearly a month. It had been impossible to think about leaving the park while the Caribbean Gipsy operation was underway.

Chapter Seventy-Nine

"Why can't we just go to my room and then go back to the boat?" Trish begged Cory.

"Nope, we stick with the plan. There has been too much preparation, travel and risk to deviate now." They were leaving the dockside restaurant where they spent two hours consuming a Chateaubriand, garlic mashed potatoes, Caesar salad and a ninety-five-dollar bottle of Spanish wine.

Trish made her obligatory phone call to Chester who in turn informed Leon and anyone else their part of the mission was completed and their payments would be coming around soon.

"Once we get the guys to the airport, we will have a week to catch up on where we left off in Montego Bay."

"Wow, Montego Bay. It has only been two weeks and it seems so long ago."

Cory drove as they headed back to the wharf. Trish spent the short trip with her hand tightly gripping his leg. "Looks like the furniture is all gone."

The Tidewater Décor truck had left and Carl and the crew were all lounging on the cargo deck playing dominos. Their bags were packed and they were ready to get the hell off the boat and be on their way.

Trish and Cory crossed the gangway to the bridge and stepped down the ladder to the deck. "This is Miss Dixon. She is taking over for Tall Tom. She has a little something for each of you." "Gentlemen." She started as she reached in to her leather satchel. "I have an envelope for each of you. Of course our leaders want me to thank you for your great work."

"Si Señorita," Manuel offered for the crew. "We are always happy to do this work with Captain Cory."

"Thank you Mr. Salvador. We may be calling on you again in several months." She handed each of the Latino crewmen an envelope containing the promised fee plus a bonus for each of five thousand more. Chester had been in quite a generous mood when she had talked to him from the restaurant.

There were also airline tickets to get them back to Colombia within the next two days.

"Carl, I have heard great stories about you. I hope you will stick with us for a while."

"Any time," he responded as she handed him an envelope quite a bit thicker than the others had received.

"I didn't know exactly where you are thinking of going but I assume you aren't interested in staying on this boat until Captain Cory gets back. So I just put an American Express card in there for you to use. It expires in a month and we are hoping you will use your discretion."

"That's not a problem," Carl remarked as he patted the envelope. "I'm just going to head down to Texas for a while until I hear from the big dude here." He nodded towards Cory.

"Ok Carl. We will be in touch. Now let's get you gents to the airport so you can enjoy your time off."

Chapter Eighty

Chester felt wonderful. "Connie, I'm going to take the rest of the day off and treat my wife to a romantic dinner." He spoke into the intercom. "What's left on my calendar?"

"Actually Mr. Whittaker, the only thing left for today was a reminder for you to call Tom Thrasher and Miss Dixon in Atlanta. I was just making notes for you."

"That's great, can you just have Tom stop in my office. Is he in the building?"

"Yes he is, I will send him right in."

Within ninety seconds, there was a tap-tap on the door

"Come in."

"What's up boss?"

"Well, I just got word that our little freighter is tied up in Hampton Roads and the new owners of the furniture are loading now."

"That's great, any problems along the way?"

"Could have been but I guess it didn't get serious. They stopped to help with a boat fire someplace up in Chesapeake Bay and ended up getting boarded by the Coast Guard."

"Yikes, you're kidding me."

"No, Trish just called. She was taking Captain Cory out for dinner while the guys unloaded the furniture. I guess after helping put a fire out on some fishing boat, the Coasties came over and did a little inspection. Cory says the fat little boarding officer actually took a break in the hot engine room and sat right on top of the tanks."

"Man, Cory must have been one cool dude while that was happening."

"He is." Chester continued as he walked over to the table near the leather chairs and poured two glasses of the Glenlivet XXV. He handed one to Tom and elevated it in a toast. "To another success."

"Here here."

"So anyhow your buddy Chad and company will be offloading the stuff around midnight. All the money is in the banks and about an hour ago FedEx delivered this little package." Chester slid a box out from beneath his desk. It was about the size of two shoeboxes. Removing the lid, he extracted a handful of neatly stacked currency in various denominations. "Three hundred and fifty in U.S., British and Canadian notes." He handed Tom a small bundle containing about twenty-five grand. "Here is a little stipend for passing on all you know to Trish. Looks like we are in the big time now."

"Well thanks." Tom placed the bills in the inside breast pocket of his perfectly tailored Joseph Banks sport coat. He had learned long ago not to argue with Chester when he was trying to give you a little ill-gotten money. Several years earlier on a similar occasion when the street price of Lebanese hash had skyrocketed overnight and a payment much larger than anticipated arrived he offered Tom a fifteen-thousand-dollar bonus. Tom had said "Oh that's not necessary."

Chester had responded immediately by shrugging his shoulders and pocketing the bills and saying "Have it your way."

"We need to get in touch with that welder in Honduras. He designed the fake tanks. We should slip him and extra ten grand. He's a good one to keep in the rolodex."

"Do you want me to take care of that?" Tom inquired.

"Sure." Chester answered as he walked back over to his desk and reached once again into the FedEx box and extracted two stacks of hundred dollar bills, split one in half and handed his associate fifteen grand. "Give him a call and let him know what's coming. I guess you could just do an overnight express mail."

Chester poured two more shots of scotch and continued. He was in a jovial mood. "I'm taking mama out for dinner tonight over at the Yacht Club. How's your social life doing these days?"

"Oh, the less I'm travelling, the more confusing it gets but I keep juggling encounters. I can't imagine what it will be like if I ever settle down."

"Kind of scares you don't it? When I met Gina I had been an attorney for two years and courting seemed pretty natural. But I wasn't a player like you. I don't know what kind of a woman it will take to break your spirit." He laughed and changed the subject. "So I think Trish was a good choice for your relief. How do you feel about her?"

Tom answered. "I think she was a great selection. She is into all of these logistic challenges and enjoys the travel."

"Speaking of romance, do you know if she has anyone on the hook? She is always so well composed and I don't know how to read her. She would make a good trial lawyer. I can't see some dude putting up with all of the spontaneous travel and secret messages though."

"I have no clue. We could put an investigator on her for a while and see what she does in her spare time," Tom suggested.

"Spare time hell. Do you know what she did up in Virginia when she had an extra day in her schedule before she met the boat?"

"No. What?"

"Well, you know she manages the stock portfolio in Robert's office for all those school employees."

"Yes. Everyone knows that. It's her day job."

"So she left Lexington with a suitcase full of cash to pay the crew. She ended up being a day ahead of schedule. Did she take a day off and go to the beach? Hell no, she got in touch with the CEO of Newport News Shipbuilding, one of the publicly traded firms in the portfolio. She got a tour of the whole fucking shipyard. Then she went to dinner at the guy's oceanfront home in Virginia Beach. And now, he is setting her up with a buddy of his to tour the General Motors plant in Detroit in couple of months."

"You're kidding me. We better keep an eye on her. She may end up running the whole shebang here."

"Nah, I don't think we need to track her. I wonder what she thinks of Captain Cory."

"Now that would make an interesting couple," Tom answered. "We should keep an eye out and see if anything develops there. At least they both know each other's dirty little secrets."

"It would be interesting for sure." Chester finished and downed his third shot. He poured a fourth and then put the bottle back into the lower cabinet. This was Tom's signal. This encounter was coming to an end and the boss wanted to get going.

Tom patted his front trouser pocket where he had placed the hundred bills for the welder and told Chester, "I will take care of this first thing in the morning. I'll be in the courthouse most of the day
tomorrow taking depositions on the medical malpractice case with Fort Lauderdale Treatment Center."

"Oh yeah, how's that going?"

"I hope for an out of court settlement for about three and a half. That should bring us between four and five hundred grand. A good two weeks work."

"Sounds fine to me, keep it up." They both finished the last drops of liquor placing the glasses on the table. "Thanks for all you do Tom. Have a great evening and be careful with the dames."

"Not to worry." They shook hands and Tom opened the door to show himself out.

Chapter Eighty-One

"It's just like making cookies." Debbi said as she watched Chad explaining the recipe for cutting the cocaine. Everyone was holding a respirator, the kind used by people who paint cars.

"Yes, without the eggs and butter." Chad laughed.

"First we will mix all of the cutting ingredients together."

Chad and his crew had gone back to the ship around midnight with a rented box truck. They checked in with the security guard. He let them in without question. They found the precious cargo under the altered water tanks and spent three hours lifting each ten kilo bag carefully up to the cargo deck.

Debbi found frozen, shrimp, Mahi-Mahi, lobsters, sauces and pasta. While the guys were working she prepared delicious seafood lasagna in the galley. At around three in the morning when they had all the cocaine on deck they stopped to eat. Chad directed that no one would drink alcohol while they were working, so water and soda pop were the only beverages consumed.

After their meal, Lenni Baker, a dealer from Savannah who was helping went out to check on the security guard. He found him sound asleep in the cab of his pickup truck with the engine running and the radio on loud.

It took the guys a little over half an hour to quickly transfer the cocaine into the truck using a hydraulic lift gate. With all the cargo inside, they secured the door. Chad kept the key.

They went back onboard for a short while to make sure everything was in order and the fake tanks were back in place. Around four-thirty they left headed to the warehouse two miles away.

The security guard never saw them leave.

Once the cargo was unloaded, Chad told Lenni and one other helper to stay and keep watch over the goods while the rest went back to the hotel to sleep.

The team returned before noon to begin the work of cutting and packaging the product for delivery to local dealers.

The sucrose came in fifty pound bags like sacks of rice. The unscented talc was in four similar looking bags and the pharmaceutical powdered Novocain was in two twenty-five kilo cardboard drums.

"We are going to take one third of the total of all this and put it in each of these big bowls. Todd, put two bags of the sucrose in

241

each, Debbi, you and Julie take three of the bags of talc and put one in each bowl and divide the other one by thirds and put a third in each. The Novocain we will weigh out on the scale."

Everyone got to work and once the Novocain was divided up for each bowl, the first one was attached to the big mixer. For twenty minutes each bowl was stirred by the large wire hoops. When finished, each was about a third full.

Once everything was mixed the three bowls were covered with black plastic wrap and set aside. It was six pm.

"Ok, let's get back to the hotel and hit the pool and hot tub. I need one of you to stay here and watch the stuff."

Lenni who was very thin and alabaster white with acne on his face and neck volunteered. "I'm not too big on pools and hot tubs. I can stay and ya'll go have some fun. I've got a good book."

"Good." Chad responded and reached into a duffel bag. "Here is a CB radio. Just stay on channel eighty-seven and if anyone comes close just call and say: 'Breaker-Breaker this is Johnny Paycheck. My load is slipping can you help.' That's all you will need to say. Repeat it once again in two minutes to make sure we hear it and we will be back here in five minutes."

"Sounds fine to me. I feel safer here than running dime bags out on the streets of Savannah. Don't worry about me."

"Ok gang, we've got a great start. Tomorrow will be more technical. Let's go relax." Chad pointed to the door.

Chapter Eighty-Two

Leon was at the Airport an hour before Gretchen's arrival. He had gone into the men's room four times to make sure his hair was combed, and his clothing looked good. He checked a dozen times to make sure the zipper on his pants was up. He went to the Magnolia Bar inside the terminal and ordered a double vodka martini. Peering out the large panoramic windows he saw the brief cloud of smoke erupting from the landing gears as his lover's plane touched the tarmac.

When he sent Gretchen her ticket, he had splurged and made it first class. He figured, what the hell.

As the plane eased towards the gate his stomach was in his throat. Perspiration formed on his forehead and upper lip. He took a handkerchief from his left back pocket and wiped it away. Finally, the doorway leading down the jet way opened and there she was, the third person to deplane, his lover.

Gretchen was wearing coral colored shorts accenting her beautifully tanned legs and an aqua blue tank top with dainty strings tied in a bow above each shoulder. If she was wearing a bra it was one of those that made you ask yourself if she was wearing a bra. She smiled when she saw him waiting for her. In ten seconds, her lips met with Leon's and they kissed and embraced a little too passionately for the venue.

"Oh God, I have missed you,"

"I missed you more. You don't know how I have worried you might change your mind and not come see this nerdy dude up in the Carolinas."

"Oh baby, after you left Florida, I spent every hour having some thought about you. And, in my sleep, wow! You have dreams to make come true. When can we get started?"

"It's half an hour drive to Folly Beach. Then, I'm all yours." As they walked down the concourse Leon asked. "How many bags did you check?"

She stayed glued to his side. "I didn't check anything. Everything I need I'm wearing, or is in this little bag." She smiled.

They continued out of the airport and into the early evening scented air of the Low Country.

Chapter Eighty-Three

Emmett left the rangers at the oyster beach. They were all telling stories and drinking beer. In his pocket, he had his SouthOrd Jackknife lock picking tool. It had been several years since he had worked in the field. Using these things all came back naturally and within fifteen seconds he was heading for the second door beyond the bathroom. It led to a stairway and a fifteen by thirty-foot room, probably been some sort of powder magazine during the civil war.

On one wall there was about ten feet of something waist high covered by a long black plastic tarp.

"What the hell." He said out loud when he pulled back the cover.

There was an entire communication station before him. The teletype machine was similar to one he had operated as a radioman on destroyers off the Vietnam coast ten years earlier. He saw a vertical Plexiglas panel with rectangular boxes like some sort of tote board you might find at a horse race track. All of the squares were clean but he could make out some partial words like pieces of the names of Coast Guard cutters. He made out Dau...ss, which could be Dauntless. He saw Esca. . . , and Sp_nce. . .. Those seemed to represent Escape and Spencer. He recognized Spencer as a large cutter stationed in Portsmouth. On the other edge of the board he made out the remnants of the words Cari. . .ean Gip...

He found a large shredding machine placed atop a thirty-gallon garbage can. Most interesting was a facsimile machine with a three-foot wide element for producing and receiving large documents. It had an old identity tag riveted to it indicating at one time it had once belonged to the National Weather Service. He noticed a small red light blinking near a button that was tagged "REC". He pushed the button. The roll of paper advanced an inch and began to reel out a weather map of the eastern Caribbean. It took ten minutes to print the whole map showing high and low pressure gradients and many other weather related symbols.

A similar flashing light on the teletype machine blinked every few seconds. He was familiar with that one and when he pushed it the paper in it advanced a couple of inches and then a continuous list of reports from Coast Guard cutters around the Atlantic, the Gulf of Mexico and the Caribbean and even the Mediterranean started pouring in.

The subject line on each message read "Confidential – Twenty-
Hundred Two-a-Day Report" followed by the name of the unit.

He had never seen these reports before but quickly determined they shouldn't be going to Leon Matthews at Fort Sumter.

"Holy shit," he muttered to himself. "This stuff tells you where the whole Coast Guard fleet is and where they are going."

To the left, there was a large drafting table with a dozen pencils, erasers and drawing tools and a black push button telephone. On a typewritten 3 x 5 card taped to the table top were two names followed by phone numbers. The names were Chet and Tom. In ink over the type, Tom was crossed out, and below was printed Trish. Next to each name was a pound sign followed by a two-digit number. "Those are the two names he mentioned when I was standing outside his office." He said half out loud. He photographed the card with then ripped off the weather fax and took it to the table. Then he picked up a couple of the Twenty Hundred reports and looked at all he held.

He walked back over to the fax machine. There were notes written on tablets indicating radio frequencies followed by what looked like boat names. Caribbean Gipsy, Fanta Seas, Lou Anne and a few more. Each vessel had a different frequency assigned. Next he found on a dog tag chain secured to the fax machine a laminated one-page instruction sheet explaining how to enter the frequency number for each boat. It was obvious, the job here was to feed the previously received document back into the device and re-transmit it. He started looking closely at the reports from the various Coast Guard units. The information he was looking at made him gasp.

"So Leon is getting these reports telling him exactly where each ship on patrol is located twice a day," he spoke quietly to himself.

As he observed what was on the large weather fax, he realized he could plot the position and intentions of the cutters at sea and re-send the whole thing back out to other boats.

His next question was how was the chief park ranger receiving and transmitting all this stuff. The only antennae he had seen on the
island were the TV receivers. He looked around the large space. On the left side of this communication center, he found a small doorway. It looked like a closet. There was no lock so he turned the knob and opened it. He found a rack holding several rolls of

paper for the teletype and wide thermal paper for the fax machine. Beyond the rack, he saw another door about two feet wide. To the right of the door was the wall behind the communications equipment. On the left was the two hundred and fifty-year old exterior wall of Fort Sumter. Emmett guessed his geographic location within the park. This wall would be below ground level and to the rear, or west of the flag pavilion.

He opened the small door and viewed a narrow vault like passageway. Stepping inside, he saw to the left four white five-inch diameter plastic tubes sticking out through a concrete wall. The concrete was obviously not part of the original fort but added at some time probably within the past ten years. Marked on the wall above each tube were groups of letters: US, CFS, SC and PARKS. Extending out of each of the conduits were heavy coaxial antenna cables. They ran overhead and down the wall to Emmett's right. On the inside of the wall separating the telecommunication equipment outside were a series of buss bars where the coaxial cables were attached. There were tags on wires leading towards the equipment. The tags were annotated with words and abbreviations indicating teletype antennae and fax machine. Emmett put it all together.

"The antennas are located inside the flag poles. Holy shit!" he spoke softly to himself. He had a small 35mm camera in his pocket and took pictures of everything

Once finished photographing everything inside the wiring vault he turned to leave, making sure there would be no evidence of his visit. Something caught his eye. On a shelf above the doorway he spotted a grey attaché case. Before he moved it, he observed exactly how it was lying so it would look undisturbed once he had explored the contents.

Emmett brought the case out to the drafting table, laid it on top of a large sheet of facsimile paper with the weather report on it. He photographed the case then snapped open the latches and lifted the lid.

"What the hell?"

Inside the case were five bundles of U.S., German and Canadian currency. The denominations were all fifties and hundred dollar bills. The Deutsch Marks were all two hundred and five hundred-mark notes. A quick estimation in his mind, he thought there must be around a hundred thousand bucks.

He snapped another picture. He also saw a green notebook. He opened the record book and started piecing things together.

Apparently, Leon would start one page with the date one of the smuggling boats would load contraband someplace in the southern Caribbean. Then he checked off twice a day for usually twelve to twenty days as some kind of report had been made. Each page had a boat name, and numbers seeming to indicate a weight notation like 32T then another initial either M or H or M/H and the last page had indicated Caribbean Gipsy had a large C with a circle around it and the note 1T. The date of the last entry had been one day ago! At the end of each record was a printed dollar amount. Each one was somewhere between fifteen and thirty-five thousand. This information was missing from the documentation on Caribbean Gipsy. But, he did draw a smiley face and a dollar sign larger than any of the previous entries. He photographed the cash and the pages in the notebook.

He considered the letters M, H and C. "Probably identifying the cargo," He thought. "Marijuana, Heroin or Hashish and Cocaine."

Emmett had seen all he needed and spent the next half hour folding up the fax paper, the teletype messages and slipping them inside his shirt. Checking three times, he made sure there was nothing to indicate he had been here.

Darkness encased the river delta when he emerged on to the flag pavilion. Emmett offered a crisp salute to the flags flying proudly in the illumination of twenty spotlights. He smiled and walked to his quarters. In two days, he would leave the island for an afternoon at the Charleston field office of the DEA.

Chapter Eighty-Four

ESCAPE had been in the shipyard three days and the routine of life at sea seemed like distant history. All of the spaces onboard not being renovated or serviced were lined with thick pieces of cardboard. Air hoses and thick black electrical wires strung through every door and many porthole openings in the old ship. She was high and dry on the floating dock and the port propeller was removed and the shaft taken out for servicing. The two hundred and thirteen-foot ship looked broken and violated. The crew had settled into the routine of noise and dust. It was going to be a long two months.

Vince was in his stateroom when a messenger from the quarterdeck knocked.

"Enter."

The messenger stepped inside and closed the door behind him to lessen the noise. "Yes sir. XO, there is some guy with a badge on the quarterdeck. He would like to talk to you about something in Charleston. I wonder if he found out anything about your car."

The tale of the executive officer's stolen car and the peculiar manner and where it had been found was well known throughout the ship.

"Hmm, I wonder what it is all about. Please get him and show him in."

"Aye-Aye XO."

Vince closed the personnel folders he had been reviewing and buzzed the wardroom pantry telling the mess cook to bring in a pitcher of iced tea and a couple of glasses.

Tap, tap, tap on the door and Vince once again shouted over the noise. "Enter."

The door opened. "Yes sir. This is US Special Agent Kippy Gibbs." Vince stood and shook the visitor's hand and dismissed the messenger. The mess cook arrived with a tray holding iced tea and glasses. "Thanks Willy."

"So what's up? Gibbs, that's a common name around here isn't it? Are you related to Sam Gibbs over at the Charleston PD?"

"Yeah, we are cousins. You should see our family gatherings. We can field a couple of teams for any sport you want." Gibbs accepted the glass of tea and pulled a manila folder from his briefcase and got right down to business. "Over at Fort Sumter where you had your family portrait taken something very strange is going on."

Kippy started laying out the photographs Agent Ridgeway had taken in the bunker below Leon's office.

"What the...." Vince began. "A teletype a weather fax, a briefcase full of money. What's going on there?"

"As close as we can figure, it looks like the head ranger is receiving the Coast Guard's Two a Day reports then plotting the information on the weather faxes and sending it out to boats at sea."

"So some dude in a boat with a fax receiver can know where every ship on patrol is and avoid encounters with them. This is crazy."

"We bet the briefcase full of money might be the one you found missing from the photographs taken by Beaufort Lee."

"All right, so what happens now?"

"Well, Emmett Ridgeway, the agent assigned undercover at the Fort, will spend another week keeping an eye on Matthews. He just took a week off and is due back tomorrow. In nine days, Ridgeway will have a weekend off and come in to our Charleston office. We will get together with the South Florida Caribbean Task Force from your Miami district office."

"We had a big meeting there before our last patrol. That's where we identified Tom Thrasher from the original photograph."

"Right, well they will send a couple of officers up and we will hash over everything."

"Sounds good to me, I'm not going anywhere. You can see it is kind of hectic around here."

"Yes, this is interesting. I have never seen a ship in a dry dock. Looks like a lot going on."

"Yeah, we came in three days ago with thirty-five projects to complete in two months. Now that she is out of the water there are at least fifteen new things we need to fix."

"Sounds like the budget folks won't like you."

"Oh, this old ship has a good heart and she didn't cost the Coast Guard a dime. It was a gift from the Navy. So, the guys in Miami are willing to put a few bucks into her. It's an interesting project.

Vince gave Kippy a brief history of the ship. Beginning with his first sighting anchored in the York River thirteen years ago to the present.

"I didn't realize what an impact the Cuban Boat Lift had on the Coast Guard," Kippy interjected.

Vince escorted his guest up the ladder to the bridge while telling the story.

From the bridge wing, while the ship was in dry dock, everything seemed much bigger, longer and taller. He pointed out a few of the major projects.

Kippy needed to get back to the office. "Someone thinks there is a new shipment of cocaine being distributed from Virginia Beach to Savannah."

"Hmm, I wonder where that came from. I bet it has something to do with this Fort Sumter issue."

"There is a good chance it's connected. If it is, we have a big project ahead to catch as many of these folks as we can all at the same time.

"There was a recent bust up in Seattle. They picked up fifteen dealers, tons of contraband, a couple of legit business people funding things, some bad felons and a couple million in cash. It took nine months of planning to coordinate."

"I hope we are back in the water and on patrol when this deal goes down. I would like to be part of an operation like that."

"We will just have to see what happens when the time comes. Gotta run along Commander. We will see you next week."

The two shook hands both thinking perhaps they might become friends both professionally and privately as the case progressed. Vince found himself excited and anxious to get work done so when the time came for action, ESCAPE would be up to the task.

Chapter Eighty-Five

Trish and Cory drove to New Haven Connecticut and spent three days in bed at a waterfront guest house. Their top floor suite overlooked the marina and they enjoyed making love with the curtains open as the sunrise brightened the environment each morning. Their reunion was interrupted once every six or ten hours by getting dressed and going to eat or to relax in the spa. On the third day, they were walking along the seawall. Cory suggested: "Let's go and get Caribbean Gipsy underway and put out to sea for a while. We could go to Bermuda for a few days and I could bring you back to Charleston. You can get together with Leon and fly back to Atlanta from there."

"You're kidding! We can just get on the boat and go like that?"

"Of course, I'm the captain and I can take you anyplace." He held her hand tightly.

"What are we waiting for?" They reached the end of the boardwalk. She turned and embraced him and they sensually kissed.

"Let's go back to bed then pack and get the hell out of here." She whispered in his ear as she nibbled on its edge. "You know I do have to get back to work within two weeks."

"We can make that work." Cory spoke as he pressed himself even tighter to her body.

They checked out of the inn and drove to Virginia Beach, stopping in Pennsylvania at a freeway hotel for six hours of sleep. They arranged for Hertz to have someone pick up the Chrysler at the dock. By five pm two days after leaving Connecticut, they cuddled in the wheelhouse watching the sunset. They would leave at first light and be in Hamilton Harbour in two and a half days.

From the Hotel in Pennsylvania Trish called Chester. She felt it was time to reveal to him how close to Captain Higgins she was.

"I haven't been a trial attorney for so many years without learning how to read people." Chester chuckled on the phone. "Every time I mentioned you would be meeting the boat your face would blush slightly. I started to figure it out when you got back from Abaco."

"Oh, now I'm really blushing."

"You two just stay focused on what we do and one day we will all retire in style. I will find something for Cory to haul back to the islands when you get to Charleston. Give me a call when you get to Bermuda." With the cocaine shipment from the south now in the hands of Chad Walgren and his local dealers and everyone paid off with the exception of Leon, everyone in the Whittaker Law Firm's extracurricular activity department relaxed.

"Tell Cory I'm setting up a similar trip for about ten to twelve months from now. I don't think the Gipsy should be used for anything but standard cargo for a while. Carl and Rob can be our go to captains in the meantime. Have a great trip. There will be lots for you to do in Atlanta when you get home."

"Yes sir, Chet. Thanks for the vote of confidence."

"Not at all, I think you two are a pretty good match. I have an appointment now so keep in touch and we will get together next month."

"Right, boss."

She turned to Cory, getting out of the shower. He had a large white towel wrapped around his waist. "He knew all along! He suspected something when I got back from Abaco."

"Well, he didn't get to where he is by being stupid did he?"

Chapter Eighty-Six

The glow on Leon's face was apparent as he stepped off the launch. Gretchen was holding tightly to his arm as they walked up the steps towards the massive granite walls. She looked like a rock star with her long hair, tight fitting tank top and a short pink skirt ending at mid-thigh clinging to her body in the light breeze.

"Welcome home, boss." Emmett was heading for the dock to greet the tourists. He was the first ranger to see Leon's lady. He smiled at both of them.

"Thanks Emmett. This is my friend Gretchen. Emmett is our newest ranger here and really catching on fast."

"Nice to meet you, sir."

"The pleasure is mine. Are you going on the grand tour?"

"So I have been told." She smiled leaning tighter towards Leon as they continued towards the administrative offices.

"He's a great guy. He actually works in DC but came down here six weeks ago when another ranger got an emergency transfer to the west coast."

Leon spent the next two hours showing his fort to Gretchen and showing Gretchen to his colleagues. He had never felt so masculine.

When they finished and Leon had administered his Civil War history lesson they arrived in his office.

"I just want to stay here with you forever." She walked over to the door leading to the hallway outside and locked it. She turned around facing her lover and removed her tank top and bra. She pressed herself against him and waltzed towards the couch.

"What are you doing?"

She unbuttoned his shirt.

Fifteen minutes later Gretchen went into the bathroom to freshen up. Leon sat on the leather couch smiling. He hadn't given the contraband business a second thought in the past four days. Suddenly he was wondering when Trish from Chester's office would show up. He hoped it would not be within the next hour.

"I bet this hasn't happened here since the war." She joined him on the couch. They kissed once again. "When can we see each other again?"

"I have lots of vacation time and it looks like this place runs fine without me. I will see if I can come down and spend a few days on Chester's boat when it gets cold."

"If you can, I will love it."

"I will make it work."

"I like this Charleston place. Maybe when I finish school I will move up here and clerk in a big law firm and study for the bar exam. How would you like that?" She was leaning back on the arm of the couch and caressing Leon's lower abdomen with her heel while he tenderly rubbed her toes.

"Do you have to ask? It would be my dream. I think I'm falling in love." It was the first time in their relationship he had dared to utter the word.

"You said it! I have wanted to tell you I love you since the second day on the boat. Oh Leon." She embraced and kissed him.

When she was done, he said. "I think we better get going. God I wish you could stay here forever right now."

Leaving the island, Leon felt the eyes of each one of his staff watching.

Chapter Eighty-Seven

Commander Jessie Warburton, Deputy Chief of Military Readiness in the Seventh Coast Guard District in Miami called the meeting at the U.S. Customs House in Charleston. Special Agent Gibbs arranged for a conference room opening into the first floor courtyard. The iconic granite structure, commissioned in 1853, is a looming edifice on the shore of the Cooper River. Each of the conference attendees felt drawn into a special piece of history as they ascended the broad steps leading to the portico. Passing through the thirty-foot tall Corinthian columns Vince remarked to Phil. "What a place. I've seen it from the ship, but wow!"

"I was reading up on it yesterday. It was built to replace the customs office in the old Exchange Building. In 1840, this was the busiest seaport in America," Phil offered. "After the revolution, most of the original Coast Guard cutters were positioned here and in Philadelphia."

"It is an amazing building, look at all the marble. Can you imagine the poor slaves who did all the work on things like this?"

"It sure was a different time. Now the town has a Negro mayor and the Citadel has black basketball champions," Phil continued then pointed to a gathering in the southwest corner of the grand checkerboard plaza. "Looks like our spot."

About fifteen men aged from mid-twenties to nearly forty, some in uniform and the others in casual business attire, were assembled. They gathered around a long table bearing a starched white linen cloth. Laid out for everyone's pleasure were coffee and teacups of fine antique china, doughnuts, maple bars, butter horns and other assorted pastries. The spread was attended to by two short older ladies in pastel dresses and aprons. Several small groups of two to three men assembled as colleagues from around the region were reunited.

Vince and Phil approached Commander Warburton accompanied by the only female present, Lieutenant Junior Grade Susan Rico. All four officers had met previously. Salutes and handshakes followed and the Commander motioned towards the buffet. "You gotta love this Southern Hospitality." He bit into a richly glazed chocolate doughnut and muttered "Mmmmm."

"This is so different from Miami," Susan added. "Everyone is overboard on being nice and no one is in a hurry. I think I know where I'm going to ask to go when transfer time comes around."

"It's a great place. I thought I wouldn't care for it but it just grows on you and pretty soon you feel like you never want to leave," Phil responded.

"Well, good to see you again Mr. Lubar." Kippy Gibbs approached the group.

Vince introduced the special agent to his colleagues.

By now, there were thirty people gathered. Commander Warburton asked Kippy to get everyone into the conference room.

As they entered the room, Vince noticed a large portrait of Alexander Hamilton placed above the mantle on a fireplace. Hamilton was America's first Secretary of the Treasury and is considered the father of the Coast Guard.

Within minutes, everyone was seated. Most had a cup of coffee and a small plate with pastry on it. The two ladies brought in additional silver pots of coffee placing them around the table. They quietly left and closed the doors.

Commander Warburton stood and nodded to LTJG Rico who pushed a remote control button on the slide projector. On the alabaster wall a photograph of Tom Thrasher appeared. It was one taken while he still had the briefcase in his left hand. Warburton nodded again and the next photo appeared. Thrasher was leaving the guard post at the fort without the satchel. "Here is where the story started. Lieutenant Commander Lubar," he gestured towards Vince, "noticed in a proof sheet of family photographs, something was amiss."

Most were familiar with some details of this investigation but few had heard the whole story.

"It is a lesson for all of us to keep our eyes open to things in our everyday world. You never know where the next lead will come from.

"Agent Gibbs has compiled the dossier on this project and from now on it will be called The Charleston Mystery 1986 or 'TCM86'. Whenever any of you have correspondence dealing with this case, you should insert simply TCM86 in the subject line. Of course all correspondence involved in TCM86 is classified 'Secret'. We have reasons to believe we are on to a major syndicate of contraband smuggling. Each of our agencies must coordinate our efforts. When we act, we do it as a task force. We don't want any participants going rogue to make a bust for the sake of a bust when if we all work together there is a potential for an enhanced result

Agent Gibbs will now go over the history of TCM86."

"Thank you Commander. Many of you know a lot about this project and some may only know a little. We are here today to bring you up to speed and plan our approach."

Kippy spent the next hour going through every detail of evidence gathering from the last three months. From the Fort Sumter photos to their analysis at CCIC in Corpus Christi then the theft of Vince's car and the encounter at Charleston Airport where Vince saw Thrasher. The West Palm Beach field office agent gave a brief report on how their investigation of Thrasher had only found an active playboy and successful trial attorney at the Whittaker Law Firm.

Next, Emmett Ridgeway joined Kippy in bringing everyone up to speed on his discovery in the old magazine beneath Leon's office.

For four hours in the secured room, the best drug intelligence minds on the east coast brainstormed.

In a question and answer period, Vince offered, "On the Plexiglas board in the basement of fort, there were some partially erased words, boat names I believe. Right?"

"Yes sir," Emmett responded. "Susan, can you get back to that slide." It was obvious a few special agents and others in the room had found LTJG Rico attractive. Flirtatious overtures were not masked.

"Yes sir." She blushed slightly and clicked the remote half a dozen times nodding her blond head with each click.

On the right side on what looked like some sort of status board you could make out in red grease pencil: C.. ri. . .ean Gip...

"Now this Matthews character at the fort is a Citadel Alum so he has some military training. In combat information and tactical air control situations, we place the name of a ship or aircraft on top of a column and beneath we keep track of where it is and what he does. I suspect this is the name of a boat."

Across the table, Phil worked on a piece of paper with the group of letters. "When we fill in letters it starts to look like something named 'Caribbean'. Wait a second. Didn't we board a boat called Caribbean Gipsy on our last patrol?"

"Yes, a little blue freighter. He hauls wood around for furniture plants in the West Indies. We boarded him near Montego Bay about six weeks ago. I wonder how many other Caribbean Gipsy's are around." Vince commented.

Commander Warburton spoke up. "At the break I will call the vessel identification office and get a list of all boats and ships registered with any combination of those words."

"What about those phone numbers on the 3 x 5 card?" Sutton asked.

"We checked with the phone company. Only six to ten calls a year go out from that phone and any information on the numbers gets deleted ninety days after calls are made. Next time, an alert will be sent to our east coast communications division. We will know the time and receiving phone number within an hour."

"I assume Tom is this Thrasher guy but what about Chet and Trish?" Vince asked.

Gibbs responded. "Well, Chet might be Chester Whittaker, the principle at the Whittaker Law Firm and Trish has us all baffled."

Emmett spoke up. "I overheard Matthews on the phone. He referred to Chet as the guy on the other end and asked about scheduling for Trish."

"Wow! Interesting, this is complex." Jessie thought out loud.

The conference continued late into the afternoon. Around three pm, Jessie was handed a note from Kippy's office assistant.

"There are at least four vessels registered with the name Caribbean Gipsy. One was the little freighter, two are sailboats registered in south Florida and the other is a salmon trawler currently fishing in Alaska."

An interesting note concerning the little freighter; she was recently boarded in Chesapeake Bay after rendering assistance in a fishing boat fire. The boarding report was faxed to Kippy's assistant.

It looked to everyone as though the ship was genuinely engaged in legitimate commerce.

The task force continued to discuss the communication tools at Fort Sumter. All agreed, one more agent should be assigned to help Emmett get deeper into the happenings there.

Meanwhile, Commander Warburton would assign a Coast Guard investigator to find the two Caribbean Gipsy sail boats in Florida. He would have his counterpart in Virginia check into the activities of the little cargo ship.

Chapter Eighty-Eight

Trish had never spent more than a day on a boat and found the trip to Bermuda fascinating. A low-pressure system moved over the western Atlantic while they were in New England but when they left Hampton Roads, clear skies and calm winds were predicted for a week. Early fall is a great time to head south.

"I didn't know you could use an automatic pilot and just chug away without steering?" she asked Cory as they traveled from Norfolk to the rocky mid Atlantic colony. The radar alerted them with a beeping alarm any time it found another vessel approaching closer than five miles. Only twice in the seven-hundred-mile journey did that happen. Trish prepared meals in the galley and brought them up to the wheelhouse. The ship stayed on course making ten knots. In three days they arrived in St. George's Harbour.

"I could live here the rest of my life." Trish commented as they enjoyed a fresh seafood lunch at a pub boasting a fifty-year collection of business cards and graffiti on the walls and ceiling.

"I'm not sure this would be the place for me. You know, about seventy percent of all Atlantic hurricanes pay a call here before they peter out."

"Oh, I wasn't aware. Maybe someday this could be our non-hurricane season getaway. The people are so nice and I think they like my southern accent as much as I enjoy their lilt."

Caribbean Gipsy was anchored in the harbor at Grotto Bay. They rented two Vespa's to get around. The skiff served them well as ferry a between the anchorage and dock. They easily covered all of the islands from Hog Bay to Tuckers Town.

"Why do we have to leave?" Trish asked. Cory reminded her there was still work to be done.

They were lying in the day bunk enjoying a plate of local fruit. Trish fed Cory and vice versa. "Look love, I really like it here but you still have a stop or two to make and I need to get back to the islands before someone else takes my place and my legitimacy vanishes." He shoved the plate aside and gently caressed her. She rolled over on top of him.

"Ok my Captain."

Twenty or so minutes later Cory spoke up. "So, we will leave in the morning and head down to Albuoy's Point for fuel. We can

259

spend one night there and go out to dinner at the Royal Bermuda Yacht Club."

"Wow! Dinner at the Yacht Club. How romantic. I don't know what to wear."

"Oh, you will do fine. I was there a couple of years ago and in spite of a lot of pomp and circumstance, they are quite casual."

"How long will it take us to get there? Will we have a little 'auto pilot' time?"

"Nope, it's only eight miles and we need to pay close attention to the reefs and rocks."

"Aye-Aye Captain. I will stand a tight lookout." She kissed him softly. The couple drifted off to sleep and woke just before sunrise.

Cory controlled the weighing of the anchor and showed Trish how to rinse the sand and seaweed off the chain with the fire hose. She was evolving into an avid mariner quickly. "This is fun. Will he have to anchor again at the Yacht club?"

"Nope, we will tie up at the fuel pier. I just spoke with the dock master on the radio, we can fuel and spend the night there but have to be underway by eight in the morning. It's a three-day run to Charleston. We will be back to redneck civilization by Thursday morning."

"I know I have to get back to work. I just don't want this to end." Trish was back in the wheelhouse now and they were moving along the south shore of St. George's Island then through the narrow channel north of Coney Island. Once clear of the rocks Cory turned left heading towards the dredged channel into Hog Bay and the capital city of Hamilton.

Fuel in Bermuda was duty free so Cory purchased as much as he could carry. Chester's platinum American Express Card covered the three-thousand-dollar transaction without question.

Sunday evening dinners at the Royal Bermuda Yacht Club are an informal festive affair to say the least. Many visiting yachtsmen from clubs with shared privileges gather there. After securing Caribbean Gipsy the couple dressed for dinner. Cory wore a pair of bleached white cotton trousers and a tropical shirt and Trish was seductively dressed in a short coral pink skirt and a turquoise top.

"Isn't that the same outfit you wore when we went to dinner in Abaco last year?"

"You are very observant Captain. It seems so long ago."

"You know I was counting the days in my head last night and from Abaco to Jamaica then Virginia and New England and now this little cruise we have only been together for about a month and a half."

"I feel like I have been in love with you forever." She was holding tightly on to Cory's right arm as they approached the gate. The two story coral pink building with its white tile roof stands proudly over the boat basin. They entered and were taken back two centuries into the history of British admiralty and yachting. There were a dozen highly detailed models of sailing yachts from bygone eras displayed in glass cases. The walls were adorned with oil paintings of boats and regattas from past years, and trophy cases and engraved bronze plaques completed the décor of every corner and wall.

A tall gent in a white tuxedo with gold buttons approached. "Welcome to the Royal Bermuda Yacht Club. Do you have credentials Mister . . . . . . ?" He spoke with a crisp British accent and sincere congeniality.

"It's Higgins, Cory Higgins. Yes, I'm a member of the Montego Bay Yacht Club." Cory extracted the brown leather checkbook sized wallet from his pocket and presented his boldly embossed yacht club membership card.

"My name is Chester Wentworth. I'm at your service Mr. Higgins." He extended his white gloved hand to Cory and bowed slightly to Trish. "I see you have a dinner reservation, Captain. Would you like to be seated now or enjoy a cocktail in the lounge first?"

Trish leaned her head in the direction of the bar and Chester responded. "As you wish." He led them into the bar overlooking the youth sailing basin. He brought them to a small round table near the bar and offered a dark blue leather upholstered chair to Trish then alerted a waiter.

The yacht club evening was just what the couple needed to redirect their thoughts. In the bar, they met two couples sailing a fifty-foot ketch from Boston to Trinidad with plans of spending the winter in the eastern Caribbean. When dinner time came, all six dined together and stories of business, sailing and cruising occupied the evening.

The Bostonians were intrigued with Cory's occupation as a merchant in the southern latitudes. Trish hit it off with the wives and went into deep conversations about shopping in The Turks and Caicos Islands, Jamaica and Abaco.

They ate, drank wine and chatted until about ten when Cory indicated the need to sleep in order to get underway early.

Everyone parted as good new friends and agreed to look for one another on future adventures.

Trish was up early and made breakfast and by 0700 they slipped their lines bound for Charleston.

A freight-forwarding broker with a connection to the Whittaker Law Firm had secured a load of American made plumbing fixtures warehoused in Charleston for delivery to three ports in the Caribbean.

Chapter Eighty-Nine

The second launch of the day arrived full of excited visitors. Emmett stood on the float and took the bow line. "Welcome to the birthplace of the Great Civil War. 'The War of Northern Aggression'" Emmett spoke with a deep southern accent. He offered his hand to many of the ladies tipping his hat repeatedly saying "Welcome to Fort Sumter."

When the launch was nearly empty, the last person to disembark was a very attractive dark haired woman in a well-tailored casual business suit. Emmett offered a hand and she gripped it tightly as she transitioned to dry land. The sweet scent of her perfume enhanced her beauty.

The part time ranger was curious as to why someone would come to the park unaccompanied. "Thank you, I'm Patricia Wilson from the Department of the Interior." She handed him an official looking business card. "I have an appointment with Superintendent Matthews."

"Well, welcome to the fort, I will have an escort come and show you to his office." He was reaching for the phone when he noticed Leon walking down the steps.

"Well, you must be Ms. Wilson." Leon approached extending a firm handshake.

"Very nice to finally meet you. Thanks for making the trip. Why don't we head up to my office then I will give you the grand tour?"

"Sounds wonderful."

The two hiked up to the entrance to the fort. It was obvious this was the first time the two had met. To himself Emmett muttered "I bet blondie from Florida would jump in his shit if she could see the smile on the head ranger's face right now." Then he turned professional and made notes to himself about this strange visitor.

Inside Leon's office, Trish took a seat and Leon handed her a cup of coffee. He brought two cups on an antique Civil War era tray. Creamers and sugar were on the tray as well.

"Here we go Ms. Dixon. How are you?" He couldn't hide the eagerness in his voice.

"Oh I'm fine, I know this is about a week late but I got called away on a special job for Chester."

"Oh, not a problem. A week ago I was on vacation so timing is just fine."

"Well, I guess this was the biggest project ever." She opened the briefcase, "Here is your piece of the pie. It is forty-five thousand dollars. All of it has been in circulation." She handed him a rectangular plastic box with a lid on it, the kind of container in which you would take a cake to a party.

Leon did all he could to hide his excitement. "Wow, this is about ten more than I was expecting."

"Chester feels pretty good about the success and wants everyone to know he appreciates us.

Now for your planning: We are cutting back from the regular every other month shipments with Carl, Rob and the others to one big one like this about every nine to twelve months. Then there will be two or three marijuana and hash hauls each year just like we have been doing."

"It all sounds fine to me."

"Would you like to show me your little operation?"

"Sure, it will only take a few minutes. Come on into my chambers." He stood up, finishing the coffee from his cup. Then he went to make sure the door to his office was locked and the DND or "do not disturb" button was pressed on his phone. He picked up the box Trish had just given him.

Leon then took a small key and opened a locked drawer in his desk. He lifted a small locked coin box, the kind vendors might have at flea markets. Unlocking that box, he took out the removable tray. In the bottom was a six-inch long harmonica box containing two keys on a ring.

"Let's go." He pushed the desk drawer closed and locked it.

She followed him through the lavatory. He unlocked the door, flipped a light switch and started down the stairs.

"Wow! This is a big space."

"It's where the Rebels kept the gunpowder for the cannons." He marched proudly over to the tarp. "And, Ms. Dixon, it is the brainchild of Chester Whittaker and the system that's making our project successful." He pulled back the fabric like a matador baiting a bull.

"So what is it?"

Leon explained how he could intercept all of the position reports from the Coast Guard units and learn what their intentions were. He could also get cool tidbits such as boats being seized and how such action would effectively remove a patrol boat from action for a couple of days. Next, he activated the weather fax machine and showed her the maps provided by NOAA. He told her how to transfer the information on the patrol ships to the map and then send it out to boats like Caribbean Gipsy.

Trish was fascinated.

"This is unbelievable. Who came up with the idea?"

"You see; Chester has his fingers into just about everyone's business. We did a little research on the communications used by the Coast Guard and when a friend told him about the upcoming head ranger vacancy here he used his influence to have me considered for the job."

"Where did all of this come from?"

"Well when I got here, in my first budget I determined all those flagpoles out in the courtyard were rotted, dangerous to the public and needed to be replaced."

Leon picked up the box of money and walked over to the door leading to the vault behind the communications gear and he opened this door. "With the help of a contractor friend of Chester's we installed new flagpoles. But, inside of these poles are the antennas." He pointed out the leads from the back of the communications suite to the conduit leading to the flagpoles. During the construction project, all of this stuff was delivered."

"What a genius."

"He couldn't do it all if he wasn't so well connected to so many people in government."

"How does he make all those connections?"

"Oh it's easy. These days just about everyone who has visions of a higher government office has a brother, kid or cousin who has past indiscretions or current bad habits. Chester finds out who they are and figures a way to make sure problems with relatives don't surface to destroy a political career."

"Wow, I knew he was crafty, but jeeze."

"Yep, there is hardly an agency in the government where someone doesn't owe Chester a favor."

Leon placed the plastic box with the money on the shelf above the doorway.

"That's a good hiding place." She watched him place the box next to the briefcase Emmett Ridgeway had photographed six days earlier. Leon closed the door and locked it. Then he replaced the tarp over all of the communications equipment.

He pointed towards the stairway. "Are you ready for your tour of Fort Sumter?"

"Sure, let's do it. This is my last task on this project and time for me get back to Atlanta."

Leon squired her around the park answering dozens of questions any administrator from Washington DC would ask. Many other rangers whispered to one another about how their nerdy boss seemed have developed an air of composure with beautiful women.

An hour later, they were at the mooring.

"Well Superintendent Matthews, thanks for the tour and the great report. We will work on getting an updated film for the tourism bureau."

"Oh, there is nothing like bringing a production crew over here to create new activity. Thanks Patricia. I expect you will be back occasionally?"

"I will. I have twelve operations to oversee. I'm going to try to get around to each at least twice a year."

"Ok. Here comes Captain Jethro."

Emmett once again caught the lines. He helped all arriving tourists disembark then turned towards Leon and his visitor. "Ma'am." He tipped his hat and offered his hand, smiling once again as her scent reached his nostrils.

"Thank you."

Half a dozen other passengers embarked and soon the launch headed towards the mainland.

"What a nice looking bureaucrat," Emmett offered once the vessel was out of earshot.

Leon smiled. "If I didn't have this little thing going with my friend from Florida, I would be asking for a transfer to headquarters."

"I don't think you would like DC."

"You're right. I like things here just the way they are." Leon was thinking about the plastic box she had just given him. He smiled happily, "See you later Emmett." He strolled away towards his office.

MID PATROL BREAK

Interlude

The winter holidays arrived on the eastern seaboard. The crew of ESCAPE was happy to be home. The shipyard closed down for the last ten days of December. The generator replacement ran into problems with old worn out wiring and the work was extended for a month. Many additional projects were added along the way to make the ship more efficient. In February EACAPE was refloated.

Early in 1986, the president declared an overall war on drug smuggling. He signed legislation providing an additional $1.7 billion to support enforcement efforts.

As the new War on Drugs ramped up, further legislation was passed allowing U.S. Naval ships to deploy with Coast Guard law enforcement detachments. Now, if in the course of normal operations, a navy ship encountered a suspicious vessel the captain would raise the Coast Guard flag in the rigging of his ship. Then, the embarked Coast Guard team would take control of the ship and in some ways it became a cutter. This new tactic surprised many contraband smugglers and within several months, seizures of marijuana and hashish in the Gulf of Mexico and the Caribbean increased dramatically.

To keep track of the whereabouts of Coast Guard teams deployed on Navy ships, position and intentions reports went out to the Coast Guard communications center in Charleston twice daily.

Over the winter and into early spring the crew of ESCAPE participated in underway training with the U.S. Navy in Norfolk Virginia. They performed gunfire exercises, towing training and tactical maneuvers. The training went well and the ship returned to Charleston for two weeks of provisioning before deploying south once again.

Meanwhile, in Palm Beach, the clandestine branch of the Whittaker Law Firm was not idle. Shortly after New Year's Chester entertained Jake Simpson from Monte Carlo and a French-German

267

associate named Andre' Jürgen. They are two of the three owners of the container ship Seintespirit. They enjoyed all of the hospitality
Chester was capable of offering. The two men shared a suite on the tenth floor of the Palm Beach Four Seasons Hotel on South Ocean Boulevard.

On a balmy Saturday morning, Chester took Tom and Cory out for a two-day cruise to Nassau on Just One More.

Gretchen was not onboard. She was in her final semester in law school. Chester's professional Captain Jim McCurdie managed the operation of the vessel.

This cruise was a business trip. Cory hadn't seen Tom for over a year and they caught up on things. By now, it was common knowledge Cory and Trish were an item. This was Cory's first visit to Chester's yacht and he was impressed. He spent a lot of time visiting with Captain Jim on the expansive flying bridge. The hot tub was empty but he could imagine himself someday sharing an experience there with Trish.

Thirty miles off shore, the group planned Caribbean Gipsy's next rendezvous' with Seintespirit. This time the cargo would be nearly four thousand pounds of cocaine. The scheduling of the move would be around the end of the upcoming hurricane season in October. On the maiden trip, Cory evaluated the hidden compartment. He was satisfied there was ample space to double the load.

As the year progressed, Cory continued to operate Caribbean Gipsy as a legitimate merchant.

Once, he was surprised when a team of Coast Guardsmen visited him from a navy destroyer. The secret compartment beneath his water and sewage tanks was never an issue and more than once, a young boarding officer sat on top of it while completing paperwork.

In late March, Carl and Rob met with Trish on a dock in Corpus Christi. She handed them the keys and all necessary paperwork to take delivery of a gulf long liner fishing boat in a repair yard in Costa Rica.

Once the boat was delivered, they made their way to Puerto Lempira Honduras where Cory put them onboard the fully documented and equipped shrimp boat Billy Jean with a home port of Gulfport Mississippi. They visited Bogotá and took on five tons of Lebanese hash and powerful marijuana from Thailand known as Thai Stick. This cargo went into a newly constructed secret space near the anchor chain locker in the bow. Once loaded, Billy Jean cruised up the east coast of Central America and engaged in the robust shrimp fishery off the Campeche Banks. There, they were boarded by the Coast Guard and once legitimacy was determined, they were left alone for the remainder of the voyage. When sixteen tons of shrimp had been caught they headed to Mississippi. There they delivered the fresh seafood to a local buyer who also took possession of the contraband. The twice-daily weather fax documents originated at Fort Sumter kept them informed of enhanced Coast Guard patrols and naval units. It seemed as though there were twice as many ships on patrol as there were a year earlier.

When Carl and Rob were finished with this project, Chester had a new assignment for them. Trish met them for their payoff and gave them first class tickets to Juneau Alaska where they were to go and pick up a ninety-five-foot steel freighter similar to Caribbean Gipsy. They could enjoy a month and a half of life at sea without worry. Once through the Panama Canal, they transited up the east coast of Central America. They delivered the ship to the same little Honduran repair facility where hydraulically activated water tanks were installed in Gipsy. This new vessel named Polly Anna would move into a legitimate business of hauling cargo between Venezuela, the Lesser Antilles. Carl was to become the permanent master of Chester's newest freighter.

Other than dealing with the logistics of the Billy Jean operation, Trish kept busy with her job analyzing balance sheets and financial reports. She did make a visit to the General Motors Company in February and had a dinner meeting with the Vice President of Marketing. On the way home she dropped off fifteen thousand dollars for Leon as his proceeds from the Billy Jean project.

In late April, she was able to squeeze in a quick six-day vacation in Montego Bay to tune up her love life.

After the holidays, a second federal agent, Dutch Swanson, joined Emmett at Fort Sumter. Their observations of Leon did not reveal anything suspicious. In fact, Leon's primary focus appeared to be his new love affair with the law student from Florida. Three times between Thanksgiving and Easter he took vacation days to either travel to southern Florida or meet her in Charleston. Then suddenly in April, for about two weeks he was on a rigid schedule and routinely disappeared every twelve hours.

On the second day of this behavior, Emmett took the first launch back to Charleston for a trumped up dental appointment and went directly to special agent Gibbs' office to report the activity.

By the time the Coast Guard and DEA agents had a chance to get together at an attempt to analyze what was going on, Leon's activity stopped.

Emmett did notice however about two weeks after Leon's behavior returned to normal the very attractive woman from headquarters once again paid a visit to the fort.

In April, ESCAPE and her crew left on their first operational patrol of the year. By this time, many of the cutters involved in the Mariel Boatlift were returning to their drug interdiction patrols. Coupled with these new and enhanced operations funded by the president's $1.7 billion financial transfusion, the Coasties and other agencies were seizing a new prize ship nearly every other day.

PART TWO

Chapter One

With six patrol cutters underway and three navy ships cruising around the Gulf of Mexico, Coast Guard Law Enforcement Detachments embarked and the operations staff in the Miami headquarters were very busy. They also worked with the law enforcement officers on each ship to insure evidence chain of custody issues did not cause court cases to fail.

Chief of Staff Captain Dave Snyder and the Director of Military Readiness Jessie Warburton often discussed the status of major intelligence projects.

"So Jess, what's up with ESCAPE'S XO, the Fort Sumter photo connection and those Palm Beach Lawyers?"

"Well sir, DEA, Customs and local agencies have been building a file. They are finally shining some light on the issue."

"Go on."

"Yes sir. There is this suspect vessel named Caribbean Gipsy. The name has appeared on a few pieces of paper found in the basement of the Fort where we believe a communications compromise is taking place."

"There are actually three boats with the name. Two are Florida registered sailboats and the other one is a small U.S. flag freighter operating in the Caribbean and the Gulf of Mexico."

"Oh yeah, what's that all about?"

"Well, he hauls raw woods like teak and mahogany from Central America, mostly Honduras to furniture, millwork shops and factories from Grand Cayman to St. Thomas. We've boarded this guy a dozen times and he is always doing exactly what he says he is doing. His paper work is in order and the ship is in great condition. Some of our wardrooms and crews have encountered the skipper at a bar in Montego Bay. They all agree he is a standup guy. Most who meet him are envious of his job."

"I think I might be too." The captain smiled. "What about the sailboats?"

"Very interesting because one of them is on the hard down in Abaco. He has been getting a total refit for two years. But the other one, a sixty-five-foot ketch out of Stuart Beach Florida left for a circumnavigation two years ago but was recently boarded by the cutter RELIANCE a hundred miles south of Jamaica."

"That's probably the one we should be watching." Snyder offered. "Tell you what; are there seven cutters on patrol down right now?"

"Actually six and one more on the way from Boston."

"Next week, let's get two or three of them in to Fort Lauderdale and fly down a couple DEA agents from Charleston. You can put your heads together for a day or two and see if anyone has stories that might not seem important to them but when connected with others might change everything."

"Ok sir, what about funding?"

"Hell, the President just gave someone over one and a half billion for the war on drugs. Have the Comptroller call around find some of it?"

"Yes sir! We will get on it."

"Also, get in touch with your DEA buddies, see if there is some way to track international money transfers."

"What do you mean sir?"

"Well, I was reading in the Wall Street Journal, the Treasury Department has a new system requiring banks to report when large sums of money are transferred internationally. It used to be a monthly paper report filed with the agency but now with these babies coming on line," the Chief of Staff tapped the side of his computer, "they require banks to make real time reports of transfers in and out of America of large sums of money."

"Really? I will check with Gibbs. I have a classmate running the Intel desk at Headquarters. I will see if he knows anyone at Treasury. I expect you are thinking we should keep an eye on those Palm Beach lawyers."

"How astute of you, Commander. I will make sure to note your skills in your next fitness report."

"I will get right on this. These computers are changing our world. I was reading an article in a flight magazine a couple weeks ago. This guy said within a few years, computers will become so affordable people will actually have them in their homes."

As Jessie gathered his papers and stood to leave, Captain Snyder added, "It's crazy, I have been thinking of investing in these outfits." He tapped the side of his computer again. "If it all takes off like people are predicting, it might be a chance to make some real money."

Chapter Two

The phone rang in Leon's office.

"Matthews."

"I graduated!" Gretchen's excitement was overwhelming.

"Wow! Great news, what's next?"

"I want to come up to Charleston and start looking for a job. I need to relax for a while first. Will you be available next weekend?"

"Sure."

"I'll be up in three days."

"That will be great! Things are quiet here and I shouldn't have any problem taking a week off."

"OK, I have a lot to do. I'm moving off campus. Chester is letting me stay on the yacht until I figure out where I will be working. Tomas has a couple of friends who will help me move. I will call you when I get my ticket. I can't wait to see you." She lowered her voice to a husky whisper. "I'm getting horny just thinking about it."

The phone went dead. Leon smiled and picked up a picture from his desk and stared at it.

The workday was over. Leon went downstairs to check on what the Coast Guard was up to. He removed the tarp. A flip of one red switch had the teletype machine tapping away and spewing out a roll of yellow paper.

One message caught his attention:

CONFIDENTIAL
FROM: COMMANDER SEVENTH COAST GUARD DISTRICT
TO: USCGC CONFIDENCE
USCGC ESCAPE
USCGC LIPAN
COAST GUARD GROUP CHARLESTON
COAST GUARD GROUP SAVANNAH
USDEA FIELD OFFICE CHARLESTON SC
SUBJ: STRATEGY CONFERENCE TCM86

ESCAPE AND CONFIDENCE PROCEED TO CG BASE MIAMI FOR TWO-DAY CREW BREAK.

LIPAN PROCEED TO CG STA FORT LAUDERDALE FOR TWO DAY CREW BREAK

DEA CHRLESTON DISPATCH APPROPRIATE PERSONNEL TO MIAMI FOR CONFIDENTIAL CONFERENCE WITH ADDRESSED VESSELS AND CREW. PURPOSE OF CONFERENCE: TO STRAGEGIZE NEXT SIX MONTH OPS AND INTEL GATHERING SUBSEQUENT TO THE FALL TCM86 CONFERENCE IN CHARLESTON.

FUNDING FOR NON-SHIP TRAVEL PROVIDED BY SPECIAL OPS FUNDS FROM DEA ACCOUNT.

EXPECT CONFERENCE TO RUN TUESDAY 1000 TO 1400HRS AND WEDNESDAY 0900 TO 1200.

ALL UNITS RETURN TO PATROL ON THURSDAY MAY 14TH.

MIAMI STAFF CONTROL POINT IS CDR J. WARBURTON /

LT SUSAN RICO

BT

CONFIDENTIAL

"What's this all about?" Leon wondered.

He looked at other messages and none seemed very important. He tore the message announcing the strategy conference out of the long roll of paper. He folded it up and placed it in his pocket. He shut down the system and replaced the plastic tarp, locked the room and climbed the stairs. "Chester needs to know about this," he mumbled as he locked the door.

Chapter Three

"Yes Connie."

"Yes sir, Mr. Walgren is here to see you."

"OK, show him in and could you please get Tom to join us."

"Yes sir."

The door opened and Connie showed Chad in to Chester's domain.

Six-foot-two Chad was dressed in white slacks and a tropical shirt. His bushy blondish brown hair had him looking like someone in a rock and roll band.

"Welcome." Chester reached for Chads hand and they firmly shook.

"This is a nice spot." Chad looked past Chester's huge mahogany desk out the fourth story Peruvian Avenue window towards the Atlantic.

"Is this your first trip to Palm Beach?"

"Yes it is. It's an upgrade from Myrtle Beach." He laughed. "I didn't see any roller coaster."

"Not likely around here."

There was a knock on the door as it opened and Tom entered. "How you doing, stud?" He extended his hand to Chad.

"Just fine, how about you. Are you still chasing every skirt in Florida?"

"I try to keep him busy but he always seems to have time to play with the ladies," Chester interjected. He motioned for the two to sit on the large leather couch. "I hear you steered him to a nice meat market in Charleston."

All three men shared a laugh recalling the night of the car theft. Chester began. "I guess our last little journey to Virginia worked out well. Cory had a few scrapes with the Coast Guard but overcame all of it and got the cargo in. Chad, how is the supply keeping up with the demand?"

"Well, you know the president threw a lot of money at enforcement this year and detective squads are growing. I have a few cops bringing me information too. So far, a few users are getting busted but no more than before. My dealers are all clean guys and gals and are working with white-collar professionals and business people. It's a good niche."

"It sure is." Chester said. "Who gets the stuff to the street addicts and people down the food chain?"

275

"There is a Hispanic gang centered in Baltimore. They are growing larger with new members from Puerto Rico. I'm not sure where they get their stuff but it is cut intensely and sells just a little cheaper than our product."

"So, what's up, boss?" Tom asked.

"Well, you know we've got about four months before our next project and I want to get the details ironed out. Trish can't make it today, but I will brief her as the time gets closer."

"So, when are we talking about?" asked Chad.

"Let's shoot for mid-October. The hurricane season will be winding down and a new load of furniture will be ready in St. Thomas."

Tom interjected, "That's the best cover you ever came up with Chester."

"Yeah, I'm proud of it. You know Cory is making a pretty decent income just in the wood and furniture shipping business. In fact, I'm bringing another little freighter down from Alaska this summer and Carl Pearson from Texas will be doing the same thing. He will be working between Venezuela and Trinidad.

"Hell, when all is said and done, we can abandon all this contraband stuff and become a legitimate shipping company," Chester half laughed. "So Chad, the reason I asked you to come down is I'm thinking of increasing the next load by a hundred percent."

"Ok."

"Can you handle it, and will there be enough market?"

"Oh, we can always find more customers. The market is untapped. About handling it, I don't see a problem. The warehouse in the Hamptons is perfect and my team is top notch. I may have to work a little harder to get the front money but let's see, two months? Heck yes I can do that. I have a guy in Nags Head. I can bring him in to manage more distribution. He is a disabled retired North Carolina Highway patrolman."

Chester raised his eyebrows. "Where do you find all of these people?"

"Well, when I finished high school my dad wanted me to go into real estate with him. He sent me to this four-day class with some guy named Hoskins or Hopkins, something like that. It was all about networking. You know working everyone you know for all they know. Then dad and my stepmom moved to California and I stayed here. I've got a little two agent real estate office in

Myrtle Beach to make myself look legit but it was a networking class that got me thinking about marketing stuff with much bigger margins."

Chester got on his feet and opened the liquor cabinet. "Anyone want a little scotch?"

"Sure." Tom spoke first.

"No thanks, I don't drink." Replied Chad.

"Wow, that's a surprise. I would have just figured. . .." Chester noted.

"No, I never drink when I'm involved in a project. If I travel and am on a vacation, then I will have a few cocktails or a beer."

"And how old are you?" Chester asked.

"Twenty-seven. Why?"

"You just seem to have your shit together."

"When you do the work I do, if you don't have your shit together you end up dead or in jail. Simply not my plan."

"I admire you. I'm glad you are part of our team." Chester spoke as he poured a double shot of scotch for himself and Tom. For Chad, he poured a glass of ice water. "I think all of us should seek an endgame in the next several years. You know get out while the getting is good."

Chapter Four

Commander Warburton stood in front of two dozen officers and federal agents seated around a long oval shaped table covered with green felt.

"Welcome to Miami, thanks for joining us. As you all know, about a year ago, photographs of a person at Fort Sumter opened up an interesting trail of inquiry. This event may lead to upsetting a sophisticated smuggling operation. Agent Ridgeway has been undercover at the fort for four months. Please share with the group what you have found."

"Thank your sir." He smiled at newly promoted LT Susan Rico operating a slide projector. "The superintendent of this national park is involved in something quite shady."

More slides of the park, the flagpoles, and teletype and fax machines appeared. Then, she projected photographs of the Two a Day reports submitted by various ships, some of whose operations and executive officers were in the room. A murmur ran through the attendees. Next, copies of the weather fax documents. Caribbean Gipsy was a vessel name known to all the Coast Guard officers in the room. There was a file photograph of a boarding report done by the cutter DILLIGENCE a year earlier. Nearly every one attending had conducted a boarding on the freighter. Warburton commented on other vessels with the same name out there as well. Susan showed pictures of the Plexiglas status boards next to the communication equipment and finally a shot of Matthews himself.

He went on to tell the group of Mathews' activity, going down to the communications center was sporadic but when he did go he would do it twice daily usually for a week or so.

"I have a feeling the times corresponding to his extra-curricular work are the periods a particular vessel is underway smuggling contraband."

"So that's the briefcase missing from pictures taken a year ago?" Vince spoke up.

"Yes it is. Our Charleston office confirms it from the photos. There is a scratch on the side just below the handle and we identified it by that."

Gus Solomon, now the Executive Officer on USCGC CONFIDENCE asked, "So what do we know about the lawyer in those pictures?"

Warburton cleared his throat. "He is Tom Thrasher and over the past year he has dropped off of the radar. He did make one appearance in Charleston. LCDR Lubar spotted him coincidentally at the airport when he came home last fall to deal with a stolen car incident. The DEA put two agents on him for months and all they found him doing was defending people in court and chasing hot women all over Florida. He seems pretty clean and has never been seen again at the fort or in Charleston."

Agent Gibbs raised his hand. "The boosting of Lieutenant Commander Lubar's car is still a confusing issue. Some of you may not be aware, but out of the blue his Mercedes was stolen from a Charleston Exxon station and dropped off in Lexington Kentucky. What is interesting is, the trip happened without any new miles on the odometer. Everyone has run into dead ends trying to figure it out."

Gibbs went on. "We have investigated the whole Whittaker Law Firm conglomerate ever since Mr. Thrasher was made. There are three offices, one in New York, the one in Palm Beach and another in Atlanta. The New York place belongs to the senior Whittaker, active for over fifty years. The Palm Beach guy is the older brother Chester and the Atlanta one is Robert. He is currently running for city council there."

"What are their specialties?" Solomon asked

"Well, in New York it is all old family and estate management, the Florida operation does it all too but one niche they work very well is defending folks caught up in the drug trade. I'm afraid to say it, when an associate from the Whittaker firm in Florida defends a case, we don't have the best record of convictions. They have a propensity for poking holes in cases.

"Up in Georgia it is mostly family and corporate law. They are also a registered securities exchange office and manage a large pension fund for the school employees in the southern states."

Warburton started. "So we are all here today and tomorrow morning to chat and brainstorm. I want you to talk it up and see if any unusual circumstances will help find another piece of this big puzzle."

The conference broke into three smaller groups each with seven or eight members and a cross section of agencies. There was one district staff officer in each group to assist with administrative tasks.

Vince found himself with his old friend Gus and Special Agent Ridgeway along with Susan, the Operations Officer from the cutter LIPAN and Gibbs.

Emmett led the discussion and those who had never been to Fort Sumter got a history lesson.

"Now you have been there for a few months, have there been any similar type of visitors? You know, ones looking just a little out of place?"

"You know, there is this woman, a pretty one who has come twice to visit. She says she is from the U.S. Park Service in DC."

"Do you know her name?" LT Rico asked.

"Let me see." Emmett thumbed through a little notebook. "Here it is, yes, Wilson, Patricia Wilson. She's from the Department of the Interior."

"Let me check up on her." Susan stood up.

"Yes, she has been there twice. The first time he gave her a tour of the whole place and the second time, about a month ago she went with him to his office but left within an hour. They talked about concrete repair on the back side of the fort where old stones are loose."

In five minutes Susan returned smiling. "There is no person named Patricia Wilson working anyplace within the Department of the Interior."

"We will check her out." Gibbs interjected. "I wonder if she works for the Whittaker Law Firm."

"That's where I would start." Gus suggested.

"One more thing on this person," Vince nodded towards Emmett. "Take a look at that notebook of yours and let's get the timing of her visits compared to the periods when Leon goes to the basement."

"Let me see." Emmett again searched through the dog-eared pages. "OK, I first noticed him disappearing in October, twice daily for ten days."

"And she shows up fifteen days after he returned to normal operations."

"Ok, we might be getting somewhere." Gibbs spoke and drew a time line on a blank piece of paper.

"Yeah, yeah, here he goes again. In early April Leon starts to disappear like clockwork each morning and evening."

Commander Warburton wandered over. The conversation about Patricia Wilson was robust and excited.

"What's happening over here?"

Vince spoke for the group. "We think we have something."

"How's that?"

"There is a woman posing as a Department of the Interior executive calling on Matthews about two weeks after he quits his clandestine communications work. We think when he goes into the basement, a smuggling operation is underway. A couple of weeks later this Wilson woman comes around and makes the payoffs to people who helped."

"Just the kind of breakthrough I was hoping for."

The group broke for the evening and everyone made plans to go out for dinner and a little evening relaxation in South Florida. The shipboard officers all returned to their respective vessels to report to their Commanding Officers and made plans to meet later at a Fort Lauderdale nightspot.

Chapter Five

Trish convinced Chester and Cory to let her ride aboard on the next mission. She would join her lover in Montego Bay, cruise to St. Thomas and then up to the Chesapeake Bay. On the trip south, she would make a stop in the Turks and Caicos Islands to meet once again with Harold Jarvis.

Rob Byrd and Manuel recruited two additional Colombians to board in St. Thomas. It would be a crowded sailing. Rob was skeptical about a woman onboard. He knew though this would be his last trip as second in command. The new freighter in Honduras would be ready for business in ten weeks. He would begin legitimate trade with Venezuelan merchants similar to what Cory did in Honduras.

Chester and Gina flew to the South of France for an early summer holiday. While there, he met up with Jake Simpson and finalized arrangements for the September shipment of thirty-nine hundred pounds of cocaine. It was the last of the inventory in France and the investors enjoyed substantial tax-free profit on wholesale distribution. An associate was shopping the world for another large score.

Gretchen got a job at a South of Broad law firm of Friend and Fair. The two partners George Friend and Nicholas Fair were both Citadel graduates and associates of Chester. She was clerking and kept busy doing research on several complicated criminal cases for Nick. She lived in a small one-bedroom apartment off Calhoun on Elizabeth Street. Leon left the Fort often now. She never tired of his love for her. He bought her flowers and took her out to dinners at the best restaurants in the low country from Savannah to Colombia. He never knew if she had any clue about Chester's little project. When he told her there soon would come a period he needed to stay at the Fort continuously she was not at all concerned. Her work sometimes kept her at the office well into the evenings.

"Well, when you get done maybe we could go up to North Carolina for a few days."

Leon agreed.

Chapter Six

Vince, Emmett, Gus and Skipper Dave Flood assembled in the second floor bar at the Bent Elbow on Beach Boulevard in Fort Lauderdale. They occupied a table near the rail looking out at the wrinkled horizon of the ocean. North and southbound freighters and tankers passed by slowly and larger yachts made their way to Port Everglades Inlet just to the south. They were waiting for Jessie and Gibbs. The plan was to have a couple cocktails then head out to dinner a few blocks away at Café d' Mar. The evening was warm and the sun was setting. The federal officers enjoyed wearing lightweight civilian clothing.

"So there is some chick involved where Thrasher used to be," Gus began. "And he has gone on to be a model citizen."

"I'm not a gumshoe but it all seems intriguing," Flood interjected.

"If we can figure out who this Wilson woman is we will be getting close," Vince added.

"Still, that little freighter Caribbean Gipsy is an interesting story. Lieutenant Rico did a little research and found out last October she was up near Newport News. Just like the skipper tells us, he was delivering a load of tropical furniture to a distributor. Turns out, they had stopped to help with a fishing boat fire. The crew might have saved a life or two. Then they came through a quick boarding just fine. Everything is up to date and as we all know, she's a pretty clean ship."

"What about those other two boats with the same name?" Emmett wondered.

"Oh we will know all about them by morning," Gus promised.

"Well, well, here they are, trying to protect America by drinking Mai Tai's and checking out bikinis on the boulevard." Jessie approached. His aide LTJG Mitch Swanson was a few steps behind, flirting with the barely clad cocktail server. He ordered a beer for his boss and a club soda for himself. Swanson was the driver for group.

With the exception of Emmett, whose hair covered half of his ears, all of the Coast Guard officers wore closely cropped hair. Gus was the only one sporting a beard.

To a casual observer, the group in their casual civilian clothing would look like a group of sales representatives on a convention trip

"I've got some interesting information. Just as Mitch and I got back to the office, the sailing ketch Caribbean Gipsy was boarded by a law enforcement detail from the Navy destroyer McCLEAN. She was loaded with four tons of Mary Jane, a thousand pounds of hashish and a suitcase full of cash."

"You're kidding!" Vince responded.

"Nope, RELIANCE is headed for a rendezvous and will bring the boat, crew and cargo into Brownsville in about three days. They caught them on the Campeche Banks sneaking through the fishing fleet."

Emmett spoke up. "I wonder if Dutch observed anything suspicious over the past few days. Not much was going on when I left."

"That will be interesting." Vince added

The buxom cocktail server arrived with Jessie and Swanson's drinks and took orders from the others for refills. The conversation concerning the bust ceased and all eyes were on the young lady. She enjoyed the flirting.

"Just what are you gentlemen doing in Fort Lauderdale?"

"Insurance." Jessie answered quickly. "We sell boat insurance."

"Oh, how fun! My boyfriend sells insurance but it is just for cars. So does everyone want the same thing again?"

"Why not." Emmett spoke for the group.

"Ok gentlemen." she spoke with a hint of a southern accent as if she was from Georgia or Mississippi. "Would ya'll want to take a peek at the dinner menu?"

A reservation was set for the men to go down the boulevard to Café del Mar so Vince spoke up. "We would love to stay but our boss here already made a reservation for us over at the D' Mar." He pointed towards Jessie.

"Oh, you should ask for Susan when you get there. She is my roommate and I know she will take great care of you."

"We will do that." Jessie responded.

"I'll be right back gentlemen."

Each of the men admired her backside as she strutted away. Everyone smiled and she knew it.

"Did ya'll hear the news?" Agent Gibbs approached the group carrying a beer.

"Hey, I was wondering if you were going to show." Jessie greeted his DEA buddy.

"Yeah, I got a little tied up in the office. But, it looks like the watch shift has everything under control until they get the Gipsy to Texas. I'm going to head out that way tomorrow. Tonight, let's celebrate." He lifted his beer in a toast to comrades around the table.

Warburton cleared his throat. "So Mitch here is going to go and meet with the law enforcement folks in the eighth district. Emmett, a couple of your people from Charleston will be heading west also. We will figure out just how this Caribbean Gipsy and the Fort Sumter operation are connected."

"I wish we were still in the yard. I would like to go down there too," Vince added.

"I'm so glad we are done with that crap," Flood offered. "I would rather be out here at sea than living in that noisy, dusty yard. Let's wait and see what they figure out. Mitch, you can keep us all up to date can't you?" He was actually looking towards Jessie who was nodding.

"Of course sir."

"Yeah, you are right Skipper. It would be interesting to be involved in breaking these guys down. I bet we can get this house of cards to tumble when they start spilling their guts in trade for a little leniency."

Emmett spoke up. "Keep in mind gents, there is more than one vessel name on that status board. We could be on the verge of breaking down a major operation. We must keep this quiet. It shouldn't be openly discussed onboard your ships or anyplace else. There is a lot of time and resources invested. We must suspect within our own operations there are people who either by plan to or by accident can deliver information to the bad guys. Let's stop here and enjoy the evening. We will continue tomorrow morning at the conference table."

"You're absolutely right," Jessie announced. "Good call Emmett."

The last day of the conference got started at 0800 the next morning. Warburton opened the conversation. "Everyone looks pretty bright eyed and bushytailed this morning!"

Many attendees showed signs of varying degrees of hangovers. "It was a great and necessary break for us all," Vince commented. "I do believe sir, we are all ready to tackle the project."

"So, does anyone have any bright ideas?" Jessie threw out the question.

Gus raised his hand.

"Yes XO, what are you thinking."

"Well sir, when you're in CCIC, you start to analyze stuff with a different set of eyes. I was thinking about just what the hell kind of things Matthews is using to communicate with his target vessels."

"Go on."

"I bet with the precision and precise timing of his visits he is dealing with receipt of our traditional Two a Day Reports."

For a few seconds, Coasties related to their civilian colleagues what he was talking about.

Emmett spoke up. "Do you mean every twelve hours you guys are transmitting your location and then disclosing where you are headed before your next report?"

"That's correct." Warburton answered, his face beginning to flush.

"For many reasons, I can see the value, but for law enforcement it exposes you to a strange situation. The bad guys can quickly plot a way around you."

Vince responded. "We have this statutory duty of saving lives at sea and the folks at the Atlantic Area rescue coordination center need to know quickly where all the assets are in case a plane goes down or there is a collision at sea."

"We all get that," Gibbs interjected. "But you're giving out dynamic information. It's too easy for others to keep track of you."

"And in this case they do." Emmett stated.

"This is embarrassing and it is staring right at us. Anyone got any ideas about how to address it?" Warburton asked. LTJG Swanson raised a hand.

"Yes Mitch."

"Well sir, when we do search and rescue operations, we divide the ocean up into grids for ships and aircraft to cover."

"Yes."

"Well, what if we did the same for Two a Day reports? What if we divided the patrol areas into grids and make them like Grid A, 1-50 for the Atlantic and Grid C, 50-100 for the Caribbean and then take Grid G, 100-150 for the Gulf of Mexico. Then, ships report they will be in a specific grid or two for the next twenty-four hours."

Jaws dropped around the table, senior officers were smiling and civilian law enforcement agents were all nodding their heads.

"This is why we recruit the brightest students from around the country to sign up for the Coast Guard." Warburton looked at his young assistant. He put both thumbs in the air and everyone around the table applauded.

"He's not a bad designated driver either." Gibbs added and everyone laughed.

"Next week, we make our quarterly visit to Commander Atlantic Area in New York. Mitch, I would like you to prepare a report and come along with me and the Chief of Operations to present it."

"Yes Sir! I will get it together." The young officer was grinning from ear to ear.

"Well, let's wrap this up, get the cutters back on patrol and bust some bad guys. Mitch and I have a new project."

The meeting adjourned. Handshaking went on for another half hour while everyone made sure their contact information was up to date.

As the room emptied, LTJG Swanson was gathering his papers and his boss approached him followed by Captain Snyder.

"I hear you had a great idea this morning Mr. Swanson."

The junior officer stood at attention as his senior officer spoke.

"I guess so Captain. I just suggested a different way to keep track of ships and maybe confuse people who are trying to figure us out."

"It was a great suggestion, and from what Commander Warburton says, you presented it so well we are going to get you up to New York to do it again for the three-star Admiral. Are you up to it?"

"I would be honored, sir."

Chapter Seven

Summer in Charleston flew by for the Lubar family and the crew of ESCAPE. Once out of the shipyard and underway training was finished, ESCAPE was scheduled for three six week long patrols with a month break in between each one. In late August, the crew prepared the cutter for the third trip in the series. Five busts for boats hauling contraband to the states were now in the record books. Along with successes like this comes the executive task of managing the crew of the ship. Various boarding and arresting officers are called to testify at trials, most of which were done in Miami. One seized boat, Misty Dream, had gone to the U.S. Marshals and Customs officials in Corpus Christi. A patrol break there would allow Buzz Ladner to testify. Phil had been involved in another bust early in June on the second patrol. He would be in Miami when ESCAPE left Charleston.

Vince was hoping for a mid-patrol break in Corpus Christi. The timing coincided precisely with a pre-trial hearing for the crew of the ketch Caribbean Gipsy. As hard as every law enforcement interviewer had tried, no one could get any of the smugglers to tell them about the connection between their boat and Fort Sumter. Additionally, while Gibbs had been interrogating them, he brought up the use of weather fax machines. None of the arrestees knew anything. Witnesses onboard the destroyer USS MCCLAIN observed the crew jettisoning a suitcase sized box overboard as the boarding party approached. The crew swore the box contained firearms not a fax machine. Another twist seemed too strange not to ponder. Bruce Claycomb, the attorney leading the defense for the crew, had been an associate in the Florida office of The Whittaker Law Firm several years before moving to Texas. Even more intriguing was the fact he had graduated from Cornell law school with Tom Thrasher.

Chapter Eight

Dutch and Emmett continued on at Fort Sumter. Daily observations yielded no strange activity. They did notice the boss was romantically involved with a young attorney in Charleston. Leon often left on a late afternoon launch and did not return until the first boat in the morning.

In a conversation with Dutch during a staff picnic, Gretchen mentioned how busy she was at work and often had little time to spend with Leon except late at night.

"It will be better after the two-week inspection you guys are having in September. When that's over we are planning a trip to Nags Head before we get too far into fall," she explained. "I'm excited to go. Charleston is the northernmost place I have ever been."

Dutch knew of no such inspection. Something might be going down in September. "Yes, sounds like a lot of fun. I have been there a couple of times and it is a great place unless a hurricane is heading for you."

"Oh I grew up in Florida, those storms are in my blood."

Dutch absorbed the new intelligence and wandered over to Emmett, chatting with the wife and kids of another ranger.

"Hi buddy!" Emmett spoke as Dutch approached him.

"Got a minute? I was wondering if you wanted to go into town with me tomorrow for a couple of beers. I've noticed we are both scheduled for the early shift and then a day off."

Emmett knew when his undercover partner wanted to leave the island it meant he had information not to be discussed at the fort. "Sure, I hear there is a new country-western bar up near the Naval Station. It would be fun to hear some shit kicking music and watch cowgirls dance."

"OK."

"Fine with me," Emmett responded, wondering what new information his partner had uncovered.

From a phone booth near the tourist center Emmett called Agent Gibbs in Charleston. "You up for some country music buddy?"

"Sure man, I could use a break. Where and when?"

"Let's meet at the Horse Barn."

"Sounds great to me, about five pm for happy hour?

"Ok, see you then."

Emmett turned and walked down toward the boat dock to fill Dutch in on the details of tomorrow's event. He stopped and looked towards the shipping lanes. He watched the Coast Guard Cutter ESCAPE heading out to sea. "Be safe Vince," he whispered to himself. "Maybe tomorrow we will be sending you something interesting."

He approached Dutch and joined him in silence watching the cutter move quietly south.

Chapter Nine

"Mr. Thrasher is here."

"Send him in. Thanks Connie. Please hold all calls for about half an hour."

Tom knocked and entered. "How you doing Boss?"

"Just fine Tom. What's up?"

"I just wanted to get an update on things. I miss being in the middle of all the action. I've done five divorces, two family estate projects, got an encroachment lawsuit in court this week and I'm taking depositions on a hostile corporate takeover this week." Tom gave his work schedule to Chester. "Then there is Senator Hilling's grandson getting nailed with five ounces of hash last month."

"How's that one going?"

"Just fine, I will know by Monday. It looks like the chain of custody between the Charleston County Sheriff and our local DEA office has a two-day gap in custody of the evidence. That's a new little discovery I will bring in to surprise everyone."

"Well, it sounds like you are earning your keep."

"Oh yeah, we are making a living but I thought I would stop in and get all the poop on the fun stuff."

Chester filled him in on Leon's continued affair with Gretchen and the news on Trish working on her seamanship skills. "Cory is moving from Honduras to Montego Bay and Trish is heading for the Turks and Caicos. They will have a romantic cruise to Saint Thomas. Then it is time to go to work."

"How's my friend Chad doing on his end?"

"Oh that kid is on the ball. The shipment will be in Hampton Rhodes by the tenth of October and he will have the stuff cut, repackaged and delivered to the community a week before Halloween."

"Yeah, he does understand the business world. When I was in Charleston I got to know him. That dude has his head on straight."

"This is going to be a great mission and every one will enjoy the holidays. A ski trip to the Alps sounds fun to me."

291

Chapter Ten

ESCAPE and her crew were once again adjusting to the routine of life underway. They covered the Straits of Florida between Miami and Nassau. In the first three days, they boarded nearly a dozen ships and boats. Every vessel boarded was generally in compliance with all maritime rules and regulations with the exception of a few with expired flares or other minor safety infractions. Each crew encountered was more interested in doing the hard work of an ocean going industry or enjoying the pleasure of recreational sailing. Shortly after leaving the yard in Charleston, Ensign Chuck Sweeney reported aboard. Sweeny was a graduate of the Coast Guard Academy and excited to be part of the crew. LTJG Ladner received orders to go work in the operations center at District Seven in Miami and would be leaving at the end of the current patrol.

During the 4 to 8 evening watch, two messages arrived in ESCAPE's communications center. One indicated Operations Officer Phil Sutton was finished testifying and would be ready to embark at Miami Station at 0600. The other, classified 'Secret' detailed all the information about the timing of a possible upcoming interagency smuggling interdiction operation. ESCAPE was directed to proceed and patrol in a zone one hundred miles south of Corpus Christi Texas then take a three-day break in the coastal town before departing for the Eastern Caribbean.

Vince's heart was pounding loudly within his chest as he accompanied Smitty, the radio room messenger, to the bridge where Skipper Dave Flood was seated in his elevated chair on the port side of the bridge.

The messenger saluted and spoke. "Good afternoon Captain, here are a few messages for you."

Flood returned the salute and opened the top cover. The first page was highlighted with two immediately obvious bright red rubberstamped notations. SECRET and PRIORITY OPERATIONAL TASKING. He closed the top of the clipboard and handed it back to Smitty. "Let's go down to the cabin." He glanced and nodded towards Vince and the trio departed the bridge. In twenty seconds, they were in the Commanding Officer's quarters.

The skipper reopened the aluminum clipboard. He read the first communication concerning Phil Sutton and quickly initialed it. Next, he studied the content of the three-page operational tasking message. He jotted a few notes on the blotter on his desk and handed the board back to the messenger.

"Thanks Smitty."

"Yes sir," Smitty took the board in his left hand and rendered a quick and respectful salute to his commanding officer. He spun around and exited the space.

"He's a good kid," Flood spoke to Vince, searching for something to say about the message traffic.

"He sure is skipper. We've got a damn good crew on this old tub. It is a lot more fun than it was a year ago."

"You're right. Last fall when we were breaking down two or three times a week, we probably wouldn't even have been included on that Ops stuff. So what do you think Vince? I guess we go in at first light and pick up Phil and head to the gulf. We've got enough fuel to last until the mid-patrol break but check with Ed and have him come up and chat with me."

"Yes sir."

"Your little photo session at Fort Sumter is finally turning into something. You must feel pretty good."

"Yeah, it's been interesting. A little screw-up here and there is all it takes to change everything."

"Has anyone tried to figure out who the big boss might be?"

"There is a lot of suspicion on a Palm Beach law firm. We will just have to see how it plays out."

"Anything else?

"No sir, things are running smoothly, we have a few drills to do on this patrol and I hope to get them in before the break. I would like to have OPS back on board before we do though."

"Yeah, Phil will need to hone up on things. The Lieutenant Commander board should be finished in a couple of days and I'm sure he will make the cut. I expect him get an XO spot on some medium endurance cutter down here."

"He has earned it."

"OK, I think I will go up to the bridge and see how Mr. Sweeney does on the celestial navigation exercise at sunset."

"Right, see you in the wardroom at twenty hundred for the movie?"

"Yes sir. Right after the Two a Day report."

Chapter Eleven

The flight from Atlanta to Miami was smooth and uneventful but after the two-hour layover and transfer to a smaller jet, Trish was feeling woozy. Huge thunderclouds loomed high over the western Antilles. The plane dropped hundreds of feet every two or three minutes as it sliced eastward through the storm.

"Shit," She said once when the bump felt like they had hit a log.

"Double shit," said the woman in the seat across the aisle. Both women had been trying to divert themselves from the impact of the storm on the plane by reading books but at the 'Shit - Double Shit' remark they both began to laugh and were able to enjoy the rest of the trip making small talk along the way shouting over the loud drone of the engines.

Mark Dean was waiting at the same bank of pay phones in JAGS McCartney Airport as he had eleven months ago. Trish could swear he was also wearing the very same shirt, shorts and sandals. "Odd," she thought to herself.

"Hello Trish, welcome back to paradise."

"Thanks Mark, it is great to be back. We had quite a storm. I didn't enjoy the flight. It is great to be standing on solid ground."

"I heard there were boomers to the north. They shouldn't bother us. The system passed north of here about two hours ago."

"Good."

They cleared customs quickly. James, the same agent who cleared her last time, welcomed her back to Grand Turk. He passed her through with a smile, a rubber stamp and no questions. Mark's suburban was waiting in the two-hour parking lot outside the departure gates. They stopped for a brief lunch and tea in a small waterfront bistro in Cockburn Town. It was the last chance to eat before the flight. Finished, he drove to Turk Trust. Harold Jarvis was waiting with a smile and a polite handshake when Trish entered the lobby.

The stop was as cordial as the previous one and both were more relaxed. They finished in fifteen minutes and Trish left the building
pulling the very same briefcase with the same combinations on each latch as before.

Harold had said with a sly grin, "Here it is. You might recognize it. And the combinations are just as you left them."

"Can you refresh my memory please?"

"Yes but of course, the one on the left is 8235 and on the right is 5328 – the reverse of the first."

"Oh yes, now I remember I recall them as a combination of dates in my past and future. Thanks."

As she approached Mark who was leaning against the suburban, she wondered how this briefcase had made it from the Caribbean Gipsy to the Venezuelan bound Seintespirit then back to the Turk Trust Company. She recalled Chester had visited his colleagues in France last spring and he had probably brought it back for delivery to Harold.

"Interesting" she thought with a slight grin.

"What's so funny?" Mark held the passenger door open for her.

"I will tell you on the plane. Let's head west."

The drive back to JAGS McCartney took five minutes. Trish wheeled the briefcase and Mark had both of her suitcases in tow.

"You didn't pack as light as last time."

Trish didn't know how much Mark knew about everything. So she thought, "What the hell." "Yes, I'm going on a cruise. From
Montego to St Thomas on board the good ship Caribbean Gipsy."

"Wow! I never saw that coming."

"Yeah, Cory and I have been dating for most of the past year and we thought what could it hurt."

"Well, it sounds exciting. I know you will have fun. It's a great trip."

Mark was doing his preflight checks and just before he turned the switch to start the starboard motor, Trish spoke. "That is exactly the same briefcase I picked up last year. I can't imagine the route it took to get back here."

"Oh that's Chester!" Mark exclaimed as he pushed half a dozen buttons and switches. "He is always gambling with millions while pinching pennies." The roar of the engines firing up drowned out the simultaneous laughter.

Chapter Twelve

Once Phil was on board, recently promoted Lieutenant Junior Grade Ladner orchestrated procedures to get underway and guide the ship out of Fort Lauderdale. Ensign Dave Beal, who reported aboard two months earlier after graduating from the OCS, brought course recommendations to the OOD suggesting they maintain close to shore, within two miles of the beach southbound to avoid the strong northerly Gulf Stream currents. Buzz shared the recommendation with Phil and his Commanding Officer. ESCAPE and her crew commenced the two-and-a-half-day transit to the western edge of the Gulf of Mexico.

They followed a course taking the ship past the Florida Keys and turning south twenty miles west of San Antonio Reef, the westernmost point of Cuba.

Twice a year, each Coast Guard Cutter crew is required to demonstrate proficiency in naval gunnery. ESCAPE was outfitted with two 50 Caliber fully automatic machine guns and two 40MM grenade launchers. Half way between San Antonio Reef and Montego Bay on Saturday afternoon, Vince asked the skipper if they could stop for a few hours to shoot up old empty fifty-five gallon barrels. Flood, who enjoyed watching his crew trying to outperform one another with the guns, agreed. Notices to mariners and aviators kept the area clear and the fun began. The deck watch officers carried out evasive and offensive maneuvers on the 'enemy' barrels. Well riddled with holes, they were sent to Davy Jones' Locker with dispatch. Two more targets appeared and junior and newer crewmembers were included in the fun. Lifetime memories emerge from such events. The afternoon went by quickly and once all the spent brass was cleaned up it was learned the ships cooks had been fishing. Saturday supper was prepared on ESCAPE's huge fantail barbeque. All hands enjoyed a dinner of freshly caught and perfectly grilled Dorado and Sea Bass.

Overnight, the bridge crew guided the ship further south and west of Jamaica.

Sutton, the senior deck watch officer, liked to take at least one watch each day and his favorite was the 0400 to 0800 watch. He enjoyed the experience of total darkness turning to twilight followed by a glorious tropical sunrise. This morning did not disappoint. Phil and the quartermaster of the watch were setting up to take sextant sightings of the early morning stars. Both men collected their readings and were in the chart room calculating their position the same way Christopher Columbus had done five hundred years earlier.

"Contact on the horizon off the port bow!" The lookout on the flying bridge shouted down through the voice tube into the wheelhouse.

The messenger of the watch repeated the same statement into the chartroom. Phil and the quartermaster postponed their celestial calculations. This morning's positions for the report at 0800 would be calculated using the trusted Loran C system.

The messenger handed a pair of binoculars labeled "Ops" to Sutton and pointed to the horizon where the tiniest of white lights was barely visible. Knowing that the height of eye on the bridge provided a view of the horizon at fourteen miles, he directed the helmsman to "Come left forty degrees."

The ship heeled slightly to port as she turned towards the light.

The quartermaster studied the radar and found the contact northeasterly bound at a speed of nine knots. An intercept course was calculated and it was determined the two vessels would be within half a mile of each other in just over an hour.

As Phil reached for the phone to call the skipper and executive officer, he heard the messenger announce "Captain on the bridge!" Flood approached the port side of the big ships wheel as the messenger handed him the binoculars labeled 'CO'.

"What have you got?"

Phil gave him a brief rundown on the sighting and course change to intercept.

"I was sleeping pretty light and when she heeled over I thought something must be up."

Three minutes later, Vince appeared and everyone stepped out onto the port bridge wing. The aurora of the sun was beginning to affect the eastern horizon. A thin layer of cirrus clouds to the east promised a spectacular sunrise. All three men were leaning on the railing and peering through binoculars.

"What do you think Phil?" The skipper asked.

"Looks like a darker hull, maybe blue or black. I think it might be some kind of freighter."

The two vessels were closing the distance by about a mile every five or six minutes. Vince drew in a deep breath. "You know I think we have seen this ship before. I bet it will be the

Caribbean Gipsy. We should board this one. What do you think Captain?"

The three officers maintained their confidence and did not mention the intelligence connected with this vessel. No one else on the bridge was aware of what had gone down at the conference in Miami earlier.

"I agree. Get everyone up and ready to go."

The time was 0540 and the bright orange glow of the sun was just beginning to poke through the horizon.

Lubar turned to the messenger of the watch. "Go make sure everyone in Law Enforcement Team Bravo is up and about. Let the cooks know we will need seven early breakfasts. Let Mr. Ladner sleep. He just got off of the mid-watch."

"Aye-Aye XO." The messenger took off down the outside ladder to the decks below. A second later, the wardroom mess cook appeared with cups of coffee for the skipper and second in command. For Phil he brought a cup of tea.

"What do you guys think?" Phil spoke first. "If this is the Gipsy, I bet he is clean as a whistle. According to the briefs from Miami, there is no activity at the fort. I think it only happens when they are hauling. And who knows, this might not even be the ship we are searching for."

"Yeah but the poor son of a bitch is gonna get boarded again very soon," Vince commented. "Phil, I think you should take this one. Take Mr. Beal with you. It will be a great ship for him to cut his teeth on."

"No problem".

"I will take the OOD watch for you until the eight to twelve comes up." Then he turned to the skipper, saluted and said. "Permission to relieve the Officer of the Deck."

Dave returned the salute. "Permission granted."

Vince turned to Phil. "Sir, I relieve you."

Phil returned the salute and said. "I stand relieved." Then to everyone on the bridge he announced. "XO Has the Conn."

This procedure is a steadfast tradition on all military vessels so there is no question on the bridge as to who is in control of the watch. Next, the quartermaster of the watch picked up the sound powered phone and notified the watch in the engine room. He advised them the XO had the Conn. Appropriate entries in logbooks both on the bridge and in the engine room recorded the change.

"We need to take a look at his fax machine up in the wheelhouse. When I boarded him last year I didn't give it a second thought. It had six or seven cargo manifests in a box next to it. See if you can find any evidence of other uses."

"Got it." Phil responded. "I will go down to the mess deck and brief the boarding party. Think I should tell them this is some kind of suspect boat?"

The skipper chimed in. "These guys are in the business of looking for dope. We should share with them that there is a suspect vessel out here named Caribbean Gipsy but also tell them about several vessels of the same name roaming around here. I agree with the LT Sutton. Even if this is the guy everyone is looking for, he is not northbound and is probably just hauling another load of lumber and raw wood."

"We do have a report on him up in Chesapeake Bay area ten months ago. We might get a hint of his personality if we mention it and thank him for coming to the rescue of the fishing boat he helped save," Vince offered.

"That's a great thought. Let's see if we can find out when he plans to travel north again," Flood suggested.

"Six miles and closing. Estimated time of intercept is thirty minutes," the quartermaster of the watch announced to everyone on the bridge.

The Skipper stepped out to the port bridge wing where the messenger of the watch handed him his binoculars. "Thanks Jake." He brought the glasses up and leaned on the rail. "Yup. We've seen this picture before. Hey Vince. Let's make sure all but one or two in the boarding party and standby crew were not involved in the previous boarding. I want him to think it is a random and not a targeted visit."

"Sure thing Captain."

"Messenger."

Aye-Aye XO."

"Jake, please drop down to the mess deck and ask Mr. Sutton to come up for a quick chat."

"Aye-Aye sir." He spun around and departed the bridge.

Chapter Thirteen

With Cuba in the distance to the north, Mark guided Cloud Dancer through the clear sky over the Caribbean. They were flying nine thousand feet above the sea. Both were wearing headphones and microphones so that they could carry on a conversation over the drone of the two 1450 horsepower rotary engines.

"Looks like someone's day just got messed up." Mark pointed ahead to a large Coast Guard cutter, two smaller boats and a Coast Guard helicopter maneuvering around a rather ragged looking sailing ketch. "Doesn't look like there are any sails on that boat. What a dumbass."

"What do you mean?"

"Well if you are moving about the Caribbean or Gulf of Mexico in a boat that doesn't have the stuff that should be on the boat, you are begging to get stopped by the Coast Guard. Like if you have a fishing boat but no fishing gear, busted. Or a freighter with no freight or next port of call on a manifest, busted. And if you are down here with a sailboat and don't have any sails hanging off the boom or up the mast, you are dead meat."

"OK I get it. So that's why Cory hauls all of that wood stuff around."

"Yep, Caribbean Gipsy has probably been boarded by every cutter down this way but once they check him out, they usually leave him alone. I have heard he has a three ring binder full of his boarding reports. Every one of them determines he is clean as a whistle."

"I will have to ask him to show me."

"I bet this poor slob down below us wished he had a book of clean boarding reports. Wonder if he will try it again once he gets out of jail."

"Do you think he would?" Trish asked and wondered to herself if she ever got caught if she would.

"Depends on a lot. If he has been successful before and has to spend a year or two in the calaboose, he might take another stab at a cool million. If this is his first go around, he would probably find a new way to make quick cashola like robbing a bank."

"Actually, in my business, we say the best way to rob a bank is to own one," Trish joked.

Mark's laughter was so loud she had to remove her headphones.

"I wonder if we will get boarded on this trip."

Mark answered quickly. "If you do, let Cory do all of the talking. He's the expert."

He turned the yoke on the plane very slightly and Cloud Dancer banked southward. The course correction would bring them to the north tip of the west end of Jamaica.

"How much longer?" Trish asked.

"Oh about ninety minutes."

"Do you mind if I take a little nap? It's been a long day."

"Go ahead. I will turn off your headset and put steel drum music into mine."

"Thanks Mark." Trish picked up a pillow from a compartment on her right and leaned on it as the loud humming of the engine just outside quickly lulled her into a deep sleep.

Chapter Fourteen

In preparation for the delivery arriving in Norfolk in late October, Chad collected down payments from his dealers up and down the coast. The quality of the product brought in last fall by Caribbean Gipsy was the talk of the industry. Every dealer wanted to get in on the shipment. At ten grand per kilo package, he collected at least three thousand dollars per kilo up front each from dozens of dealers. Chad did not work with rag bag street vendors. Each of his customers was involved in another legitimate trade or profession. They all knew the cost of doing business was to maintain ready cash. It was all circulated money. Many of his clients flew to Myrtle Beach and used the trip as an excuse to enjoy the festive theme there.

As the summer was waning, Chad amassed quite a pile of money. It was nearing the two million mark when he decided to get in his corvette and head for Palm Beach. He and Debbi would go visit Chester to drop about one and a half million then go spend a couple of days on the beach in Ft. Lauderdale. Chad's business plan included always keeping at least ten percent of any contingency funds in order to have ready cash on hand should a situation such as a botched or seized delivery occur. He owned a small vacation rental duplex on the island of Kauai in Hawaii. He planned to head there if anything ever went sideways.

The anxiety was growing and he was excited about being busy again. Dreams of a great future and early comfortable retirement filled his mind every day.

Chapter Fifteen

Manuel in the wheelhouse saw the Coast Guard cutter heading for an intercept about five miles ahead. He spoke into the intercom to Cory in the galley where he had gone to make a fried egg and bacon sandwich. "Hey Jefe! Looks like we gonna get another boarding. A ship from last spring is headed our way and it looks like they mean business."

"Shit, I will be up in five minutes."

"Well," he thought to himself, "This is a good time to let the son's-of-a-bitches have a look around. We are loaded to the gills with teak and mahogany. We have paperwork to back everything up and a request to go to the U.S. Virgin Islands to pick up furniture.... Let them come."

Cory stepped into the wheelhouse. After nearly two years of operating, he was really enjoying his little ship.

"Over on the starboard side, captain." Manuel pointed off to the south.

"Yup, that's the same guy. I think I had a beer with the officers up at The Cave. They probably have new officers to train. OK Manny, let's just stop here and wait for them."

"Si, Jefe." Manuel reached for the throttle and pulled it back. The drone of the engine wound down. The ship slowed and within a minute was drifting calmly in the middle of the perfectly flat Gulf.

"We might as well act like model citizens and show them what good guys we are. Why don't you go down and wake up Hector and let him know what is happening?"

"Ok boss. Be back in quarto minutes."

"No problem, we have been through this before." Cory spoke as he took a big bite of his sandwich. He reached for his three ring binder marked USCG Boarding Reports. Next, he laid a teakwood paper storage box next to the fax machine and made sure that all of the pickup and delivery orders were arranged with date newest on top. He had not received any reports from Leon in months and he made sure the NOAA frequency, not the 2643 megahertz frequency connecting him to transmitter at Fort Sumter, was programmed into his receiver.

He picked up the microphone for his VHF radio and called out.

"Coast Guard cutter of my starboard beam, this is the Caribbean Gipsy."

On the bridge of ESCAPE Vince responded. "This is the Coast Guard, over."

"Yes sir. Looks like you are heading my way. I thought I would save you a little gas and heave to here."

"Thank you Captain. We are on a routine patrol of the area. We would like to gather information on your vessel. I see you are flying the U.S flag. Are you a documented U.S vessel?" Of course Vince already knew because he was looking at the previous boarding report.

"Yes sir. I should be in your files somewhere. I have been boarded a dozen times in the past two and a half years. I think your ship paid a call on me about a year ago."

"I know Captain. We have a few questions we ask everyone." He began as the quartermaster filled in a standard contact sheet use on all encounters at sea whether boarded or not.

"What do you think, Captain?"

"Tell him we are going to board him. I suspect he already knows."

"Aye-Aye Skipper."

"Caribbean Gipsy This is the Coast Guard. We intend to board your vessel. Please muster your crewmembers near the bow of the ship and we will be coming along your starboard side in ten minutes."

"You got it boss. I know the drill."

Manuel was back in the wheelhouse. "Hector will be up soon. He is getting a bowl of cheerios."

"I like it when we are all eating in front of them. I will save this until they get here." Cory placed a napkin on top of his sandwich.

"I'm a little hungry too. I go get a couple pieces of fried chicken."

"It will be a dandy little early morning picnic. See you up near the bow in a few minutes." Cory picked up a hand held VHF radio and went down the steps to the deck below. As he walked past the cargo opening in the gunwale on the starboard side of the ship, the dropped a rope ladder over the edge. He took his sandwich and a cup of coffee and sat on top of the anchor windlass.

Chapter Sixteen

Interstate ninety-five along the east coast is the fastest moving highway in America. A one-day drive from New Jersey to Daytona or Orlando is commonplace where such a journey in any other part of the nation would usually be broken up into two days. Most cars travel at least twenty miles over the speed limit and the Georgia and Florida state patrol generally ignore cars doing less than eighty-five miles per hour.

Chad chose the middle of the week just after the Labor Day weekend to make the trip to Palm Beach. He had turned in the corvette into Palmetto Auto Sports for a routine tune up and service before the trip. While there he had Jake, the owner and one of his busiest cocaine dealers, install a new set of Michelin high performance tires. He and Debbi traveled southward down the coast on route 17 through the low country. Knowing there were very few patrol cars there, each time he observed a cop ticketing an unlucky traveler, he downshifted, punched the gas and for a few seconds exceeded a hundred miles per hour. With the top down and the warm late summer sun shining on them they cruised towards the interstate. When they reached the interstate, they were moving at one hundred fifteen miles per hour. Within two minutes, a silver-grey turbo Porsche passed them and for a second, Chad thought that the race would be on. But in ten seconds, the beep and light on his radar detector activated and he slowed to seventy-five. The Porsche disappeared ahead. Within five minutes, they passed the poor bastard as two of South Carolina's finest were shaking him down up against his car.

"Look at the poor dude." Debbi shouted over the loud music. "I wonder if he was carrying any of your product or a gun."

"Too bad, he should be more careful." Chad accelerated to about ninety.

They pressed on, covering the six hundred miles in eight hours. They stopped near Stuart Florida for a quick burger and a beer. Debbi had taken care of lodging through another dealer friend in South Carolina. Jenny, who owned a travel agency, booked them for a two day stay in the iconic old and traditional Breakers of Palm Beach. They ate dinner, swam, and enjoyed the hot tub. Once back in the room for the night, Chad dumped the contents of his backpack on the bed. The couple spent the next two hours watching the season finale of the hit show Dallas and sorting out a million four hundred twenty thousand bucks in cash. They secured each bundle of bills with heavy rubber bands and wrapped them in saran wrap.

Exhausted from the day, they fell asleep holding hands on two lounge chairs on the balcony.

Debbi would stay at the Breakers while Chad went to meet with Chester. He was looking forward to finishing up this part of the job and spending a couple more days in sunny Florida before heading north to get the gang ready for the trip to Norfolk and work on the big load.

Chapter Seventeen

Robert Whitaker continued to be so deeply involved in his campaign for city council that he let his law firm run on autopilot. A never-ending stream of guests stayed at the little bungalow in Buckhead. The polls showed him leading his opponent by fifteen points. All of his friends and associates were confident a victory was six short weeks away. His partners and associates were billing up a storm and a new young buck named Jimmy Schmidt, just out of the University of Florida law school, had joined the team. He was the son of German immigrants and a native of Charleston. He had graduated from the Citadel and held a commission as a Lieutenant in the U.S. Coast Guard Reserve. During his breaks from law school, he served onboard a couple of cutters deployed in drug interdiction.

The federal court system often hired contract attorneys to help with heavy caseloads. Once hired by the Whittaker firm, and with the blessings of his boss, he joined the pool of Contract Federal Prosecutors in the Atlanta district. While waiting to be called by the Feds, he helped with the campaign.

Downstairs at the Atlanta Whittaker Law firm, Trish and her team kept the mutual fund portfolio in the fifteen to twenty percent return neighborhood. The phony bank, Escondido Bank, had turned in a nice twelve percent growth over the past year and recently had transferred two point five million dollars to the Turks Trust and Clearing House. Trish's assistant Jake was so involved in auditing the other businesses listed in the fund that he never noticed when she made the transfer.

But, in a small office located at the investigative branch of the United States Treasury in Washington DC, a data processer named Sally Flint noticed.

Sally was working on a prototype study the DEA had jointly funded with War on Drugs money from the president. The program was to link up with the data processing of several test banks. The wire transfer services monitored out of country transfers of sums of money exceeding one million dollars. When a transfer initiated by the Whittaker Law Firm doing business as the Trustee of the SEASTA pension fund was completed, her monitor emitted a barely audible 'ding, ding, ding, ding.' Sally in a few key strokes had the details of the transfer on her screen.

In a stack of yellow sticky notes, she remembered details concerning a suspect called Whittaker Law. Her pulse was racing as she picked up the interoffice phone. "Bob, I think you need to see something."

Chapter Eighteen

Chad left Debbi next to the pool and drove a mile and a half to Chester's Peruvian Avenue office. He had handled the money so often, he wasn't too concerned with the fact that his backpack held nearly a million and a half in cash.

The four-story building was an iconic Palm Beach sample of the local, heavily coded design standards. He approached the large brass framed doorway. The one on the right opened.

A suited door attendant appeared. "Good morning sir, can I help you find someone?"

"I have an appointment with Mr. Whittaker."

"Yes sir." He stood a little more erect knowing this casually dressed young man toting a large backpack had an appointment with the big guy, his boss and landlord of the building. "Take the elevator to the fourth floor sir, Connie will take care of you from there."

"Thanks buddy."

The elevator opened into the foyer. Behind her custom teak desk, Connie greeted him.

"Yes sir. How are you Mr. Walgren, Mr. Whittaker is expecting you." She pressed two buttons on her phone one connecting her to the boss and the other to Tom Thrasher. "Gentlemen, Mr. Walgren is here."

"Send him right in."

Chad picked up his heavy backpack by the loop on the top and followed Connie to the huge double door. She opened it and allowed him past her.

"Well, well Chad, how's the real estate up in Citadel country?"

"Great sir. How have you been?"

There was a brief knock on the door and ten seconds after it had closed, it opened and Tom walked in.

Chester motioned them to the couch.

Tom and Chad sat down and Chester went to his large leather chair. "So how is our marketing department doing?"

"Pretty good, I have a lot of fifty percent down payments." He patted the side of the backpack. "And the market is great. My team is ready and we should be able to get this product to the retailers within two weeks after it arrives."

"I'm impressed with your organizational control." Tom spoke up. "How do you convince the street guys to give you so much cash up front?"

"Well they know what is coming, when it is coming and they are not 'street' guys. Most of my sales go to white-collar guys like you. They know they can count on me and the stuff will get there. There are some Hispanic dudes coming into the market and they deal with the blue jean, beach and street customers. There are disagreements in that society and many broken promises. Plus, their product is cut so deeply sometimes you would be better off powdering a baby's butt with the stuff, it is mostly talc."

"That's funny." Chester responded as he rubbed his hands together. "So let's see what you've got."

The two suited men leaned forward a bit and Chad unzipped the backpack weighing over a hundred pounds. One million four hundred and twenty thousand dollars was laid on the crystal glass coffee table. Each five-inch high stack of one hundred thousand was carefully secure with a rubber band and plastic wrap.

"It's interesting to see it all at once." Tom spoke up.

"Yeah, when you get a settlement check on a big case it all appears on one piece of paper," Chester commented. "Money is interesting stuff."

"So what are your plans now?" Chester looked at Chad.

"We are checking out before lunch and heading to Fort Lauderdale to cool off for a while."

"You driving the 'vette?" Tom asked

"Of course. I wouldn't come down here any other way. I left the top in Myrtle Beach. Now that I have unloaded all of this," he patted the stack of currency, "I can push it a little harder. Should be flying home along I-95 in three or four days. Then, it's time to get to work. It's going to be a busy autumn for my crew."

"Sounds like a fine program to me, we won't hold you up here any longer. Thanks for the hard work," Chester interjected as everyone stood up. "Tom says you found a great hotel for him in the SOB district. Maybe my wife and I will come up for a visit."

"That works for me. Just let me know when."

They all shook hands once again and Chad left the room.

Chester stood considering the pile of cash. "You want to split one of those bad boys so we each have a little walking around cash?"

"That's up to you. It's always nice to have a wad in your pocket. I won't turn you down. Hell I'm an attorney, it is unethical for me not to accept money." Both men laughed.

Chester went to the bar and poured each of them a stiff glass of scotch. "Hell, I have to figure out how to get this in the door of my brother's firm in Atlanta. A smaller pile would be easier to work with for sure. Why don't you open one and we can split it up now?"

An hour and half a bottle of whiskey later the two well-dressed attorneys rode the elevator to the basement. Each had fifty grand in various pockets and smiles on their faces.

"It would be a bad night for this old building to burn down." Chester joked as he slid into the grey leather seat of his Deville. Tom shook his head and just grinned as he dropped into the Porsche.

"See you tomorrow Boss."

Chapter Nineteen

While ESCAPE remained hove to about eighty meters away, the Bravo Boarding Party lead by LT Sutton spent well over an hour and a half going through Caribbean Gipsy. As anticipated, Cory had been hauling a full load of teak and mahogany in rough sawn logs. All of the paper work found onboard appeared well done and included three destinations for delivery of stuff to a milling company in Montego Bay, a souvenir carving business in Georgetown Grand Cayman and the final stop would be in Saint Thomas where the bulk of the shipment was to be delivered to a custom Caribbean furniture dealer. Ensign Beal accompanied Cory and Phil as the team made its way through each compartment. In the engine room Cory sat on top of the water and sewage tanks in front of a stack of six-inch diameter teak logs each about a foot shorter than the beam of the ship. Phil chatted with him about voyages and got a first-hand accounting of the incident months earlier in Chesapeake Bay. Beal and two petty officers took it all in as they shone flashlight beams throughout the space finding nothing amiss.

Next stop was the wheelhouse where Phil casually went through the papers near the fax machine while Dave filled in all of the blanks on the boarding report form. There was nothing on this ship to lend any suspicion as to the purpose of the current voyage.

Phil and Cory were making small talk as the team was wrapping up. "Do you plan a stop in Mo Bay? I'm always good for a Red Stripe up at The Cave if you guys showed up next week."

"Not likely this trip, we're out here for a couple more weeks at least," Phil answered. "Maybe next time."

"Here you go Skipper." Mr. Beal separated the self-duplicating report. "Everything is in order and here is your copy of the report."

"Thanks, I will add it to my collection." Cory pulled out a three-hole punch machine, stuck the long edge of the paper into the device and crunched down on the handle to make the holes. Then he pulled the binder out and placed the report on top of twenty-three similar files. He clicked it shut and placed it back on the bookshelf above the fax machine. "If there is nothing else, I need to get going so that I can make port by sunset tomorrow. I am scheduled for off-loading the next morning at six."

"Ok." Dave spoke into the microphone clipped to his uniform collar. "ESCAPE ONE, approach, we are finished here."

A simple "click – click" was heard on everyone else's receivers and the zodiac milling around halfway between the two ships jumped ahead and approached. Phil gathered the boarding team, shook hands with Cory and was the first down the ladder. He was convinced this boat was not the one everyone was looking for.

As the tender carrying the law enforcement boarding party sped away towards its own mother ship, Cory and Manuel climbed the two flights of stairs and met in the wheelhouse. "Montego, Jefe?"

"Si mi amigo. I wonder what they are talking about," Cory remarked. Manuel engaged the transmission and slowly brought the diesel three floors below up to cruising speed. A few turns of the wheel and they steadied up on an easterly course.

"They probably say 'what a nice ship, it is always so clean.' No one looks at those shit kicker tanks and says nothing."

"I know. I was sitting on top of them the whole time we were in the engine room. If they only knew."

Chapter Twenty

Jules was preparing Seintespirit to get underway from the Port of Sete in southern France. The ship was loaded with two dozen Fiats, five hundred Michelin tires, five containers of French wines, furniture, thirty-nine hundred pounds of pure cocaine, ropes and chains made in France and Germany, two carloads of artwork for South American markets, five tons of cheese and fifteen pretty young French women. The loading had been done at an old wharf at the eastern end of Rue de Richelieu just west of the main harbor entrance. The export examiner Jaime' from the government spent about half an hour in Jules' lavish stateroom enjoying delicious Argentine coffee laced with the best French brandy. All of the paperwork was stamped without looking at anything except a padlock on a container holding wine. "Enjoy your trip to South America my friend." Jaime' shook Jules' hand and they hugged as he began to step onto the ladder leading down to the dock. "I will bring you back some nice beef steaks."

"Oui my friend that would be merveilleux." Jaime' climbed down the stairway to the dock.

Jules began shouting out commands. Engines and generators came to life, shore side electrical disconnected, five-inch thick hemp lines were brought aboard and soon the old ship was ready to sail.

When the last mooring line was aboard, the chief mate on the bridge took control, directing the helmsman on steering and the engine room through the engine order telegraph. Slowly, the vessel began to move. A local tug operator nudged the bow out into the shipping lane to the east. Within fifteen minutes, Seintespirit was moving under her own power south westerly towards the mouth of the harbor and into the Mediterranean.

In twenty-four hours, they would be at the cargo wharf in Puerto de Palma on the Spanish island of Mallorca. There they would load olive oil, Spanish wine, more artwork, custom made clothing and ten thousand cartons of black market American cigarettes.

Once that load was secured, Seintespirit would proceed southwestward through the Strait of Gibraltar then take a northerly course to Povoaco on the southern shore of the Portuguese Azores where Jules would pick up another couple of tons of cheese and one refrigerated container of sweet cream butter from the world famous dairies on the island. He would also deliver three thousand cartons of cigarettes to a local dealer in exchange for a wad of cash. The underworld trade of American smoking supplies often rivaled the smuggling of drugs and marijuana in the Mediterranean and western European coastal towns.

Once finished in Povoaco, Jules would turn the ship southwestward and head for the rendezvous with Caribbean Gipsy. The transit would take nearly a week and transferring the cocaine was scheduled for around 2300 hours on October third.

On the evening of the second day of the southern transit, Jules invited three of the most attractive French hookers to his cabin to enjoy a dinner of fresh Azorean sea bass and Spanish wine.

Chapter Twenty-One

Leon was back to his routine at the fort. Gretchen returned to the office of Friend and Fair. The firm had been hired by the defendants in a complaint over a complicated issue of state and federal tax evasion. A group of physicians owning a dozen medical buildings, two auto dealerships and four pharmacies were the defendants.

For the next several months, she would be busy for sixty hours a week working on complex discovery investigations.

Dutch and Emmett noticed Leon disappear periodically for an hour or so at a time. The timing of these absences did not seem routine or structured around a specific time of day.

"He's probably checking to make sure the gear is working." Dutch spoke as the two agents enjoyed a mid-week lunch. They were sitting alone at a table overlooking the dock.

"I'd like to get a look down there. Soon would be best." Emmett spoke.

"We are having another barbeque tomorrow afternoon. I will get him into a conversation about starting my own Ham Radio station. You could get in and out, take a picture or two and never be missed."

"Let's do it."

While downtown Charleston remained hot and humid in the waning days of the summer, tourists journeyed to the ships floating at Patriots Point or Fort Sumter to seek refreshing breezes from the Atlantic. The fort enjoyed record numbers of visitors and the national parks leadership noticed. Superiors routinely sent messages to Leon congratulating him and his staff for a job well done. The head ranger eagerly shared these accolades with everyone. He had a special announcement to make at the barbeque.

The White House had been working on Presidential travel for the next year and scheduled a visit to Fort Sumter in April to commemorate 127 years since the first shot of the Civil War.

Leon was excited about the news and asked Dutch to gather everyone around while the coals in the oyster pit heated up.

"You gentlemen have been running the best and most visited venue in the whole National Park System." Leon announced and everyone quit chatting to await his next words. "This afternoon I opened a letter from the Director. We have exciting news."

They grew even quieter and drew in towards their boss. Leon's ego was on overload. He didn't notice Ridgeway was not in the group. "Dear Superintendent Matthews," he began. "This morning I had a meeting with the Secretary to firm up planning for the upcoming year. He informed me that this coming April, he and the President will be visiting Fort Sumter to commemorate the anniversary of the beginning of the Civil War."

The rangers now began to chat amongst one another with smiles and excitement.

Leon read on but never again had full control of the staff.

"We will be spending most of the winter preparing for the visit so plan to do a little painting and planting around here." He went on and then finished. "So let's pop the keg and have a party."

Emmett had heard the beginning of the announcement and figured that he would have three quarters of an hour to do what he needed.

Within twenty seconds of unlatching Leon's door, entering the office and relocking the knob, he headed down the stairs.

"Holy shit, Batman."

Leon had been busy. The tarp had been removed from the equipment and was folded in a corner. There were three rolls of fax paper lying on a cart next to the machine. The status board had several lines filled in with a couple of ship names. A few dates in the near future that really caught his attention. He instantly began snapping photographs.

Listed across starting in the upper left corner of the status board was "Gipsy" the next space the words "shipment to STVI (Wood)" appeared. Then "Trish onboard with Cory" and the next space said "Rob + 2."

"This is great stuff," he mumbled to himself.

In the next line, the first box said "Furniture - 9/30". Adjacent to that entry was "Frenchie - 10/3". And in the last box on the second line "NOVA - 10/12-14" The final entry.

There were five or six grease pencils in a tray by the status board. Emmett put one in his pocket. Next he opened the door to the vault behind the communications equipment just to take a look around. Nothing looked out of place but when he looked at the shelf above the door, he noticed that the briefcase was gone. He photographed the empty shelf.

Within eleven minutes he was finished; nothing had been disturbed. He made his way around the edge of the fort walking towards the group of men enjoying the evening activities. To himself he muttered, "Not a lot of time. Things are going to start happening around the end of September and it's already the twelfth." He lit a small cigar and mixed in with his friends. Dutch approached.

"Looks like the President is coming here in April."

"We'll see." Emmett winked.

Leon was approaching the pair carrying a beer for Dutch. "So you will need a pretty high antenna if you want to blast across the ocean. I have good sources for transceivers but the book is in my apartment in town. I will bring it back next week."

"He's not picking your brain about Ham Radio stuff is he?" Emmett blew a blue cloud of smoke towards Dutch. "I told him you would be the one to ask."

"It's been my hobby since I was eight years old. So what do you think of the President's visit?" he asked both men.

"Sounds like a lot of fun to me." Emmett spoke up thinking the head ranger standing in front of him would probably be in jail in April.

The three sat down at a picnic table with a plate full of roasted oysters and corn on the cob waiting for them. "What a great day!" Emmett proclaimed.

"You got that one right." Leon responded.

'Oh Boss, I have a dentist appointment tomorrow afternoon so I will need to catch the first launch over. Is that OK?"

"No problem at all. I think we are a little overstaffed now anyhow."

Leon excused himself and went to bend the ears of other staff and Emmett quietly briefed his partner on what he had found.

Before heading to his room for the evening, Emmett went the pay phone near the visitor center by the boat dock. He put a quarter in the slot and dialed a memorized number.

"Gibbs."

"Coffee tomorrow at Denny's, eleven thirty."

"Roger."

Both agents separated only by a mile by the confluence of the Ashley and Cooper rivers hung up their phones.

Chapter Twenty-Two

Caribbean Gipsy chugged along towards Charlotte Amalie.
Trish had joined Cory on the dock upon her arrival in Jamaica and
immediately moved onboard. With the exception of an hour or
two of passionate lovemaking, Cory was all business. Tide was
ebbing at 8 pm and he wanted to get underway.

The course Cory took brought them along the southern shores
of Jamaica then across miles of open sea through the Windward
Pass separating Cuba and Haiti. The total journey would take three
and a half days. Early fall in this part of the world provided
beautiful vistas, amazing sunrises, sunset opportunities and
peaceful cruising. Trish settled in with half a dozen books to read
and skin to tan.

At one point, they were approached by the Coast Guard Cutter
CONFIDENCE, a 210 footer out of Corpus Christi Texas. After a
short discussion, Cory was able to avoid yet another boarding after
reminding the crew of a boarding he endured five days earlier. The
crew onboard CONFIDENCE quickly verified the information and
allowed him to proceed.

Since St Thomas is a U.S. territory seaport, there would be no
further need to deal with American customs or Immigration. Rob
would be joining them there and the real mission would begin.
The plan was to depart the harbor with the legal cargo at sunrise on
October first.

Chapter Twenty-Three

Carlos Ortiz was arrested by Phil Sutton when Sally Mae was seized on ESCAPE's third patrol nearly a year earlier. He was undergoing pretrial depositions with his public defender Jason Stedman. The deputy US Attorney on the case in Miami was Gary Jones. Ortiz had been in jail for ten months.

"You know you are looking at two to five years in jail don't you?" Jones asked. "Can you think of any way you might help us slow down the big loads of dope coming to America? If you did, I might be able to get you less time in the slammer here."

Ortiz contemplated the situation. He looked for advice from Steadman. He did not want to go home a rat. He wouldn't last a week on the streets of Bogota. "I won't turn any of my friends, it would dishonor me and they would kill me back home señor."

"What about boat names or other shippers?"

Jason told his client: "If you give them something, I can work with the judge and you might just get your time served and be sent home right after the trial. But if you take another boat north with dope on it you are looking at fifteen years. Period."

Carlos thought over what he heard. "There is one thing I might be able to help you with."

"Yes! Go ahead."

"You know I am a good welder but there is no work at home so I went to Honduras in a little pueblo called Puerto Lempira. A shipyard there needs someone to weld stainless steel."

"What are you getting at?"

"Well there was this freighter, about thirty-five meters, a blue hull. They had us build some fake tanks in that boat to look just like water or shit tanks."

Jones perked up thinking: "Now we are getting somewhere."

"We made a cool deal with some hydraulic cylinders they lift these babies up. I bet you could hide a ton of anything back there. It's bigger than this room." He looked around the space. "A lower ceiling though."

"Where is it on this ship?"

It is down behind the engine and near the post for the rudder."

"How long ago?"

"Just about a year and a half, maybe two."

"Do you know if the boat had a name?"

"They were touching up paint all over the place but I remember one day they were painting some word like 'Gipsy" on her but there was another word too like an ocean name."

Jones was getting excited and knew he was on to something. "Was it Atlantic, Caribbean, Pacific or Mediterranean?"

"That's it! Caribbean! Yes, Caribbean Gipsy! It's a nice clean ship, looks like she is made to haul lumber or pipes and other long stuff."

The two attorneys looked at each other and grinned. Steadman knew he would be getting his client a free trip home and Jones could not wait to talk to someone about this great intelligence. He just didn't know who to talk to.

It was 6:30pm on Friday afternoon when the attorneys completed their deposition. An officer took Ortiz back to the Dade County lockup. Gary Jones had a date with a law student he had met at a party a couple weeks earlier. He took the elevator up ten floors in the Federal Building and went in to his cluttered cubical, a ten by ten space devoid of windows. Furnishings consisted of a desk and two chairs and a file cabinet. He quickly scribbled a note to himself. Monday he needed to find out who he could tell about the information obtained from Ortiz. He turned off the light, locked his door and departed looking forward and anticipating a blissful weekend at the beach with a beautiful young woman.

Chapter Twenty-Four

It was time for the 1800 to 2400 watch to start at the Coast Guard Operations Center on the fifteenth floor of the Federal Building in Miami. The place was never quiet. Phones were constantly ringing, large status boards similar to those listing arrivals and departures in airports were lit up with hundreds of bits of information. Lieutenant Grover Holland was relieving Susan Rico as senior watch stander.

A boarding south of Jamaica by the Cutter DILIGENCE was underway. It was a Panamanian flag vessel and a team was working on the diplomatic details to permit a boarding and seize the vessel if it was carrying contraband. It shouldn't be a problem because the crew of the vessel, Santa Maria was casting burlap wrapped bags overboard and the ship's small boat was picking them up. Once the details were clear, DILIGENCE would tow Santa Maria north to New Orleans for processing. During the trip, the crew would be painting the twenty seventh marijuana leaf on the stack.

Susan chatted with Grover about a missing boat off Fort Lauderdale and a fishing boat with tangled nets in her propellers near Nassau.

"Excuse me ma'am." One of the duty petty officers brought a cordless phone and handed it Susan. "There is a special agent Gibbs with the DEA on the line trying to find Commander Warburton."

"Thanks."

"Lieutenant Rico. May I help you?"

On the other end, "Hello Lieutenant, it's Kippy Gibbs up in Charleston. It is important that I speak with Commander Warburton ASAP."

"Yes sir! Is this in relation to the project TCM86?"

"It is, Lieutenant."

"I will patch you through to the Commander right away."

Suddenly there was a third voice in the conversation. "Warburton."

"Do you want me to disconnect sir?"

"No Susan, stay on. Let's hear what's up."

"Well Jessie, I just got a call from Emmett at the fort. We are meeting at eleven-thirty am at the Denny's on Ashley Phosphate Road."

"Eleven-thirty tomorrow? That's kind of short notice. I will try to get someone up there to join you. Anything else?"

"No sir, we will talk tomorrow afternoon."

"Got it! Thanks for the call."

Kippy hung up and Susan stayed on the phone.

"Well Lieutenant, are you up for a little TDY?"

"No problem Commander. I think there is a 0730 flight to Charleston, I could be on it but I would ask you to find someone to cover my watch tomorrow night."

"Not a problem, I am still up in my office, why don't you finish up your relief and come see me."

"Aye-Aye Commander."

The grin on Susan Rico's face couldn't be held back and Grover Holland joined her in her enthusiasm. "Sounds like a good gig. I would have done the same thing."

"I can't pass this one up. After the conference last month, I would love to be part of the big takedown."

"So, anything else happening?"

"Not out of the ordinary." She glanced across the room and noticed three junior officers high fiving each other. "Looks like DILIGENCE got the OK to board and bust."

"Great then, Lieutenant Rico, I relieve you."

The two LT's saluted one another and Susan announced for all to hear: "Lieutenant Holland has the watch."

All in the room in unison responded with a course of "Aye-Aye
Lieutenant Holland has the watch."

Susan was very fit, running marathons when she had the opportunity. She quickly bounded up three flights of stairs. She tapped lightly on the door to the office of the Chief of Military Readiness.

"Enter."

"Yes sir Commander."

"Oh great. Hi Susan."

"Yes sir, what's happening now?"

"Well you know we have two DEA agents planted at Fort Sumter."

"Yes sir, Ridgeway and Swanson."

"Well Ridgeway has scheduled a hurry up meeting with his boss Kippy tomorrow morning and he thought we should get one of us to attend. Are you up for it?"

"Couldn't think of a more interesting way to spend a couple of days."

"Well, just be at the Miami airport around 0600 and your ticket will be waiting at the Eastern Airlines desk. I have finance working on it now. I wish we could let you spend a couple days up there but we will need to get you back down here by tomorrow afternoon to brief the Chief of Ops and maybe the Admiral."

"No problem sir, I will give your secretary a call when I know what time I land. Then I will come right back here."

"Sounds like a plan, see you tomorrow Lieutenant. Oh one more thing, everything is in place for us to pull the trigger on the substitution of new alpha-numeric grid sectors for the Two a Day reports. All of the cutters patrolling now are in the loop and it will begin operation with Monday morning's reporting. Gibbs should probably know that."

"Ok sir, this could get exciting."

"Let's hope so."

Susan left the Federal Building at 1840 hours. In the elevator, she encountered Assistant US Attorney Gary Jones. They exchanged greetings.

"Working a little late for a Friday sir?"

"Well yes, we are getting ready for a trial next week and I have to get prepared. But, right now, I am running late for a date. How about you Lieutenant?"

"Oh, I just got told to be up in Charleston in the morning so it will be a working weekend for me."

"Wow, Charleston sounds like fun, I wouldn't mind being 'sent' there for a weekend."

"I wish. I have a meeting there and need to get back here tomorrow afternoon to brief my boss."

"Wow that is a quick turnaround." The elevator reached the top parking level where watch standers were privileged to park and the door opened and Susan said goodbye and started to exit. "Hey Lieutenant, I have a couple questions about my case, would you be able to steer me in the right direction if I came up to chat next week?"

"Sure, no problem, I have a little office just outside the operations center on the twelfth floor. 1216."

"I will see you on Monday."

As Susan hurried to her car, she wondered if he was serious or merely flirting.

Chapter Twenty-Five

Life was different onboard Caribbean Gipsy for this trip. Cory knew Manuel and Hector enjoyed observing the beautiful woman riding along. He knew they would never embarrass themselves by doing anything stupid. After all, they were making a hundred times more money than they could in Colombia.

When Cory was on watch, she was right beside him on the bridge, wanting to learn everything about running the ship. He enjoyed the company and her antics when she knew the other crewmembers were sound asleep. She provided her lover with some very erotic entertainment during a couple of their late night passages. As much as he enjoyed all of the attention, in the back of his mind, there was a nagging thought that with the seriousness of the job that they were doing, perhaps bringing her along might have been a mistake. He had remembered reading once in a Horace Beck book on folklore and the sea. An old superstition existed on how bringing a woman along on a sea voyage would generally lead to disaster. Putting those thoughts aside came quite easily for him when Trish was near.

Sunrise occurred just after six am and Caribbean Gipsy was eight hours from the entrance to St. Thomas Harbor. The day went by quickly as Cory, Manuel and Hector prepared for whatever the customs officials had in store for them. Once they cleared the breakwater Cory checked in on the VHF radio. The dispatcher directed him to proceed to the customs dock. This was not unusual. He had done the drill several times in the past couple of years. What did get his attention and raise his blood pressure a notch of two was the four Coast Guard personnel and one fellow wearing civilian clothes waiting on the dock alongside the customs agent.

Chapter Twenty-Six

"Mr. Whitaker, your brother is on the phone."

"I've got it Connie"

"Hey Bob what's up, how's the race going?"

"Fine Chet, but the auditors are here and we need Miss. Dixon. Someone down there says she is out on her boyfriend's yacht in the Caribbean!"

"What are the auditors saying? Ask for a thirty-day extension."

"These ain't tax guys, big brother. They're from the fraud department!"

Chester felt his gut tighten and an instant pouring out of perspiration from his armpits. "Well, isn't Vance there? He's been in that department for ten years. He should be able to help them find what they need."

"It has something to do with a wire transfer to one of the overseas banks in the trust fund for SEASTA. You know I hardly ever even go down stairs to talk to those people. I will go find Vance and have him give you a call. I have a rally with the Lieutenant Governor in an hour. Chet, I don't need any bad press right now, make this go away."

"Ok, I will make a few calls."

"Thanks."

The two brothers hung up their phones six hundred miles apart. "Shit!" Chester yelled quietly to himself. He opened his left desk drawer and under a liner on the bottom of the drawer he picked up a key. Next, he opened the larger bottom drawer on the right side. He stuck the key in a horizontal tray and slid it back. On top of a large binder was a Smith and Wesson .357 Magnum revolver. He picked it up, opened the magazine to insure it was loaded then snapped it closed and placed it in his center top desk drawer. Next, he extracted the notebook. He noticed his hands were shaking slightly. He laid it on top of the desk and opened it. The index tabs along the left edge listed each department in the federal government. He opened to the page for Treasury. Listed on the page were six names each one referred to a case where the executive had been or had a child who had been involved in some sort of indiscretion. Of the six, two were marked with red ink and the word 'convicted' appeared. The other four were marked 'acquitted or dismissed'. The second name down was Under Secretary for International Banking, Barry Schultz. His daughter Becky, arrested while attending Clemson University, was caught with three pounds of marijuana and a couple ounces of hashish. Obviously, she was dealing and it could have ended up more seriously if Chester had not defended the son of the mayor of Colombia SC for a similar infraction a year earlier. Soon, the local police made a statement indicating they had arrested 'the wrong person' and Becky was released to her angry father.

He became forever grateful to the Whittaker Law Firm.

Chester took a few seconds to make sure his composure had returned and dialed a ten-digit number. "Yes, is Under Secretary Schultz available? This is Chester Whittaker from Florida. . . Thank you."

"Chester my friend, what prompted you to call?" Schultz was already worried and knew the only reason Chester would call him was if he needed a favor. He knew he was about to violate his oath of office.

"Well Barry, you know my brother is running for a coveted city council seat in Atlanta."

Schultz felt somewhat relieved thinking Chester was calling for a contribution or endorsement. "Yes, I had heard that. We need another good Republican in Atlanta. They are starting to lean too liberal there. What can I do to help?"

"Well this morning a couple of guys from your department showed up to audit a trust account there and the gal who takes care of that department is on an extended working vacation."

"Yes, do you know the purpose of the audit?"

"Bob said it has to do with transferring some money to a foreign bank. You see they manage a portfolio of stocks for a pension fund and I know a small part of the money is invested in overseas banks for a little better return." Chester impressed himself as he was shooting from the hip.

"Yes sir, we have a new computer system tracking larger transfers and this might have popped up on someone's screen. I take it you would like to get the audit postponed until the manager returns and the election is over."

"That would be perfect. I am sure everything is on the up and up but timing is just wrong."

"Tell you what, I will have those agents reassigned this afternoon and we will get back to this one in a month or so.

That's the least I can do after what you did for our family two years ago."

"Well thanks Barry, I appreciate it. This will take some worry off Bob so he can concentrate on the job at hand. By the way, how is Becky doing?"

"Oh she graduated 'cum laude' and just started medical school way out on the west coast at Stanford. She wouldn't be there without your help. All of that other stuff is behind her."

"Yes sir, it's my pleasure. Give her my regards when you talk to her. I guess you are going to have to change your afflation from the Big 10 to the Pac 10."

Both men laughed.

"I suppose. So is there anything else I can do for you?" Schultz asked somewhat relieved that the favor was going to be an easy one to carry out.

"No thanks Barry. I will let Bob know."

"OK then, keep in touch Chester. I will talk to you later." Under Secretary Schultz hung up and noticed he was sweating profusely. He hoped he would never hear from Chester Whittaker again as long as he lived.

Next, he dialed the office number of his Supervisor of International Transactions Monitoring and had him reassign the two agents in Atlanta. "Have them go to Dallas to check another suspicious incident from some newly formed Energy Company called ENRON."

Chapter Twenty-Seven

Cory liked checking in to customs late on Friday afternoons and planned the arrival in St. Thomas for about 4pm. Once secured to the dock, the customs agent advised him that the Coast Guard was doing random inspections of vessels arriving on the island.

"I was just boarded five days ago near Jamaica," he pleaded.

"I am aware of that," Petty Officer Dixon stated. "We have the report right here." He held up a metal clipboard. "We won't detain you long and if everything is in order, you will be on your way."

"Whatever works for you," he responded in a frustrated tone. "I was hoping to get unloaded this evening so I might have a chance to relax a while before heading out."

"Yes, and where is your next port?"

"Norfolk. I have an order, bill of lading and I am supposed to be there in ten days. He pointed to a warehouse and wharf across the bay about half a mile away. "That's where I am dropping this wood and loading."

"I see." Dixon remarked, "So let's get started."

Like so many times before, Cory escorted Coast Guard petty officers around the decks and through all the spaces on his ship. It seemed like they were giving her an extra special going over this time but as always, no one even glanced twice at the shiny stainless steel water and sewage tanks aft of the engine.

After an hour and forty-five minutes, they cleared him to proceed across the bay. Dan Parker was waiting when they arrived.

"Long time at customs today, I been watching for an hour."

"Yes." Cory responded as he jumped onto the dock and turned around to help Trish ashore. "Good to see you again Dan." The two old friends shook hands and embraced.

"And who is this I have the pleasure of knowing?

"She is my new best friend, Patricia."

"Very nice to meet you. I know Cory is probably in a big hurry so I will get the guys to work."

"We will be heading into town for dinner at Bella Blu and probably back by ten or eleven."

Dan responded. "Oh my wife loves that place. It is the best French joint on the city. It is a great place for dinner before a long boat ride. You will love it."

"I am sure we will," Trish responded. "He hasn't been wrong yet." She took Cory's hand and beamed a beautiful smile.

"Everything should be done when you get back."

"Oh, Rob will be arriving in about an hour. He will be joining us for the trip north."

"I will make sure he gets aboard and knows you are leaving early. Have a nice dinner."

Chapter Twenty-Eight

A guy named Merkin penned a novel, 'South Florida Book of the Dead' in 1982. A dog-eared copy stayed in the operations center for months. Many watch standers had read the story of the demise of a marijuana smuggling operation in South Florida. Susan picked it up to read on her trip. She enjoyed the story. It made the hundred- minute flight go by quickly.

Once in Charleston, she had two hours before the meeting with Agent Gibbs. She took a morning drive around town, South of Broad and the Battery. She stopped at the end of Murray Boulevard and gazed out towards Fort Sumter wondering just what kind of shenanigans were going on out there.

She headed to Ashley Phosphate road and pulled into the Denny's parking lot. She found Kippy and Emmett sitting in the back booth looking at photographs.

"Hello."

Emmett and Kippy looked up remembering the attractive young woman. Out of uniform, she was wearing jeans and a light white sweater. "Lieutenant Rico." Gibbs stood and extended a hand.

Emmett remained seated. "Hello Susan."

"Nice to see you again." Susan slid into the booth next to Gibbs.

Emmett began. "You know we are watching things at Fort Sumter."

"Yes sir, I remember it all from the Fort Lauderdale conference."

"Yes," Kippy responded. "But last evening, Emmett snuck into the communication center and found this stuff on the status board." He handed her a stack of about thirty photographs.

Emmett chimed in. "It looks like they are getting ready."

The waitress brought Susan a cup of coffee then left them alone. She seemed to know Kippy was doing business.

All three leaned over the enlarged photograph of Leon's Plexiglas status board.

"Looks like October is a busy month. Caribbean Gipsy is definitely a player. And it is not that sailboat busted in New Orleans'" Kippy offered.

Susan added. "Now, I know NOVA in this case means Norfolk

Virginia. Not some Chevy you had in high school."

The two men laughed.

She continued. "I am puzzled by STVI and Frenchie."

Emmett spoke. "I would bet on St Thomas Virgin Islands. And I don't know, there might be a French crewman coming onboard."

"Well, let's see, today is 9/30 but what's this furniture reference?" Kippy questioned. "Wait, wait, wait." He reached over picked a file from his briefcase. "Here is a copy of that boarding report from Chesapeake Bay nearly a year ago." He flipped through, the pages his excitement growing. "Yep, yes oh yes. The Coast Guard boarded Caribbean Gipsy, a U.S. flagged small freighter a year ago. Guess what he was hauling."

"Furniture?"

"Exactly! He helped put out a fire on a fishing boat and had a cursory boarding afterwards. Here's a picture taken by the boarding team." He had handed the report to Susan.

"And the furniture on his manifest had been loaded in St. Thomas! Hey, I have been aboard that boat."

"What?" Emmett asked.

"Yeah, about two years ago, patrolling the western Caribbean if I remember right. He was clean as a whistle. The skipper was a nice American dude from the Midwest or Seattle. He hauled lumber and teak from central America to Jamaica and other islands for of all things, furniture manufacturers."

Kippy shuffled through another file. It was a monthly report compiled by the DEA. The report title was 'Statistical Inventory of Street drugs by Region and Type.' He pulled out two pages of the report from November and December a year earlier. "The Tidewater Area of Virginia and the coastal Carolinas showed a substantial increase in cocaine available in the last two months of the year and into the spring."

"Looks like Caribbean Gipsy carries more than furniture." Susan completed his thoughts.

"Yup, it's pretty compelling. You folks need to concentrate your effort between The Virgin Islands and Norfolk for the next couple of weeks." Kippy stood up.

"Yes sir," Susan answered. "I better get back to Miami and brief my boss and the admiral. What can I take with me?"

"You can have it all, we have copies."

"By the way, Commander Warburton wanted me to tell you the program to change our Two a Day Reports from the coordinate the grid system starts Monday morning."

"That's great news," Emmett added. "I would love to be in Leon's hideaway when those things start to come in."

"That would be fun." Susan stood and gathered up what photos she wanted. "I would love to stay and be on one of the boats headed to the fort but I have more work to do. There is a flight in an hour and a half. I could be back in the office by three. Nice to see you gentlemen." She stood, shook hands and left the restaurant.

The two agent's eyes followed her out then they looked at one another smiling. "She will be an admiral one day. I would bet a month's pay on it," Kippy remarked.

Chapter Twenty-Nine

Cory and Trish enjoyed a perfect French dinner at Bella Blu then took a taxi tour around town before returning to the dock. Rob had arrived and made himself comfortable in his stateroom. He brought two young men from Colombia, Caesar and Sammie, to help with the heavy lifting and watch standing. When Cory arrived, he and Manuel were sitting on the fantail with the new crewmembers enjoying a beer in the warm Greater Antilles evening air.

After all the introductions, Cory explained how things would go down over the next week or so.

"I know it is a day early but I want to get underway tomorrow morning around 0900. We will go to the fuel dock, top off all of the tanks and head north before noon. Everyone thinks we will be leaving on Monday but a day early will give us a chance to do a little evasive steering. If we get boarded one more time with just this load of tables and chairs, it could be a good thing. We will head northwesterly straight towards Virginia for the first twenty-four hours then take a sharp turn southeastward for our rendezvous Tuesday evening."

"Is Leon at the fort all ready for us to make the trip?" Rob asked.

"I chatted with the boss a couple of hours ago and everything is a go."

"I think we are all set," Rob responded looking at the other crewmen.

"Si Jefe, we all want to get out to sea as soon as we can." Manuel spoke for the others who nodded in concurrence.

"Ok. We're going to call it a night. See you all at around seven-thirty." Cory looked at Trish who was smiling with a twinkle in her eye and nudged her towards his stateroom.

"I'm impressed with my captain. This is exciting."

Chapter Thirty

Susan finished reading South Florida Book of the Dead on the return flight to Miami and found herself contemplating how helpless people in the drug smuggling business must feel when their well- planned operations begin to fall apart. "They all seem to plan for success without consideration for a contingency," she thought to herself. "Wonder why they don't think it through."

Within forty minutes of landing, she pulled into the basement of the Federal Building. Commander Warburton's secretary had taken her call from Charleston and arranged the meeting. Warburton, Captain Bruce Smith, the newly assigned Chief of Operations and Jessie's immediate boss and Admiral Root were all drinking coffee around a green felt draped table in a large conference room next to the Admiral's office when Susan entered.

Being Saturday afternoon, Susan found it a little strange, no one was wearing a uniform. "Admiral, Captain Smith, Commander; good afternoon."

"Please have a seat." Admiral Root was pouring himself a cup of coffee. "Want a cup?"

"Ah, ok sir, thanks." She thought it a bit peculiar that the senior officer in the district would be offering to serve her a cup of coffee. "So how was your whirlwind trip?" Jessie asked.

"That's a beautiful town Commander. It will definitely be on my next relocation assignment wish list."

Admiral Root handed her a cup of coffee. "I was XO on the buoy tender PAPAW there a long time ago. It is a wonderful town. So what's up?"

"Well, Admiral, gentlemen, Agents Gibbs and Ridgeway have been busy." She began handing around copies of the photographs. "From what is on the status board it appears that the freighter Caribbean Gipsy is a busy little ship."

Each of the senior officers made various expressions when looking at the pictures.

"It's like a combat information center." Admiral Root exclaimed with a soft whistle.

"So this ship is in San Juan right now if I am reading this status board correctly," the Chief of Operations interjected. "Jessie, call up to the Ops Center, let's see if someone there can get a look at him." Commander Warburton went to the end of the room and picked up a phone.

"That's quite a setup there. There must be a lot of money and influence someplace along the line to have a blind eye turned while all that was being installed," the Admiral wondered.

"Sir, I have studied everything on this case since LCDR Lubar first produced the photographs over a year ago." Susan began to speak her mind. "I think a key player and perhaps the top dog in this whole syndicate is that Whittaker Law Firm in Palm Beach. Tom Thrasher, the attorney from the firm was the guy in the first pictures. He was seen at Charleston Airport the day after Mrs. Lubar's car was stolen. This Matthews character at Fort Sumter was a Citadel classmate of Chester Whittaker, and that dude is the most successful defender of drug related defendants in the nation. I can't imagine how many celebrities and top drawer officials he has gotten off with reduced or dismissed charges."

"Can we look into the records of who he has defended and how those cases ended?" Admiral Root inquired of the group. "Bruce, can you check it out?"

"Yes sir, I will start an inquiry first thing on Monday. Our legal eagles will love it."

Jessie hung up the phone and returned to the group with an unhappy look on his face. "Caribbean Gipsy cleared customs into St. Thomas yesterday at seventeen hundred hours."

"You're kidding me." The admiral asked. "Can we send a boarding party over to take a look at her?"

"A team actually boarded the vessel at the customs dock last evening and found nothing wrong."

"Well, let's get a cutter on scene to tail him over the horizon after he leaves."

"Too late sir, apparently they went across the bay to load furniture right after leaving the customs dock. Then early this morning they moved over to the fuel dock and departed San Juan Harbor heading northwest before noon."

"Well, let's get someone down there to find this son of a bitch."

"I just started the ball rolling sir. I told the ops center to get ready to move assets around so we can find him. Yesterday morning, I moved ESCAPE from a western Gulf to a Western Atlantic patrol area." Jesse continued. "We do have one surprise in store for them at 0800 tomorrow morning."

"What's that?" Captain Smith seemed caught off guard.

"On a suggestion by a young officer at a strategy meeting last month we decided to alter the Two a Day Reports by changing from a latitude and longitude coordinated to a regional grid system."

"Oh yeah, I was looking at something from the Area Commander last week. It sounds interesting. So what you are saying is that this guy up at Fort Sumter who has been getting position and patrol reports twice a day will get hit with numbered grid locations without a clue as to where they are?" The Chief of Operations and District Commander were both smiling.

"Yes sir. I would love to be a fly in the wall when those messages start coming in. He might have a hard time holding down his breakfast."

Chapter Thirty-One

Dave Flood was reading 'Finnegan's Wake' by Irish writer James Joyce. It was Sunday evening and an encrypted directive had been received from Commander Seventh Coast Guard District to "Proceed at best speed" and spend the last week of the deployment patrolling new sectors Alpha one through Alpha thirty. At the mid patrol break two weeks earlier in Ocho Rios, the Liaison Officer from Kingston delivered the new patrol area design replacing the information on the Two a Day reports. The area was broken into three sectors Alpha for Atlantic Ocean, Charlie for the Caribbean and Golf for the Gulf of Mexico. The design was simple. Each sector was a fifteen nautical mile square with the southwestern most of each sector beginning with the number one. The sectors went from bottom to top until southern coast of the U.S. was reached, or an eastern line drawn south from Bermuda. A similar sector arrangement ran from the eastern edge of Cuba to the north coast of Colombia to delineate the eastern boundaries of the three areas.

It was an uneventful transit anticipated to take until midday on Monday. The off-watch crew were relaxing, watching movies, writing letters or sunning themselves on ESCAPE's fantail. The Skipper was finding the book interesting but hard to follow. He had studied a lot of Irish literature in graduate school and had always wanted to tackle this one.

Vince took advantage of the time by finishing fitness reports on all of the officers assigned. He kept a notebook on each one and made entries nearly every day. Now he had to decipher it all and make sensible reports out of his notes. Once he finished all the reports, he would be reviewing his evaluations with the subjects of each report. Finally, he would visit with and show his reports to the Skipper before the final documents were sent to headquarters. He was not having a difficult time writing positive things about his staff. In fact, it was tough to find much wrong with anyone of them.

Chapter Thirty-Two

Twenty hours after leaving St Thomas, Cory turned to a course heading a little south of due east. The Gulf Stream currents had pushed him further north than he had wanted. Having desired to travel at nine knots, they made a speed of over twelve and were about sixty miles north of where he wanted to be. He was annoyed with himself because of so much time with Trish in his stateroom, he had lost focus on the mission. There was still plenty of time to make up the difference and meet Jules in thirty hours. Trish knew he was on edge.

"What's wrong?" she inquired.

"Oh just a few things. I should have had Rob do a better job of navigation. We went too far north. I wanted to turn right miles ago. It's no big deal though. I can't expect him to know everything I know about this ship. We have plenty of time to make the rendezvous. I am also a little concerned, Leon has not given us a patrol report yet."

"Well, we did leave nearly a day earlier than he thought we would."

"You're right, let's hope he's on target for tomorrow morning. It would sure be nice to know if anyone is patrolling four hundred miles north of St. Croix. I'm also concerned because the weather is getting sloppy. I would like to be tied up in Virginia when the shit hits the fan."

A tropical storm had been the farthest thing from her mind when she left Atlanta three weeks ago.

Trish could sense Cory's stress. She wondered if it might be because she was onboard. "I tell you what my love, it looks like there are things you need to concentrate on. I have a good book to read. I think I will go down to our room and do just that." She hugged him and kissed him lightly on the cheek.

Without agreeing with her that she was being a distraction, he returned the embrace. "Thank you, yes I need to sort out a few things. Have a good read. There is plenty of time for us after next week." He returned the kiss.

Chapter Thirty-Three

Leon arrived on the first launch of the day around six forty-five. The other five passengers were all fort employees. He had had a great weekend with Gretchen and both were ready for a couple of weeks apart.

Dutch and Emmett watched him arrive. They were restocking the tourist brochures at the boat landing. "Morning Boss." Dutch said.

"Hi Guys, how was the weekend?"

"Great, we were packed. This nice fall weather sure brings them out." Emmett responded.

"That's wonderful. Well, it's the first of the month and the end of a quarter. I have to get cracking on the reports everyone wants."

"Better you than me." Dutch joked.

"You guys just keep everyone happy. I will be locked in my office for most of the week."

"OK Boss."

After he was well on his way and out of earshot, Emmett remarked: "I wonder where he will be locked up by the end of the week."

"It's going to be an interesting couple of days. He should be getting his first set of Two a Day reports with the new format in about an hour."

"I would love to be down there when he sees the first one. What do you think he will do?"

Dutch scratched his chin. "He's either going to crap his pants, puke or pass out. At any rate it won't be pretty."

Leon entered the looming complex of the fort. He unlocked his office door, turned on the lights and made a pot of coffee. He played the voice mail messages on his answering machine. Only one significant operational call about a sick launch operator was of note.

There was an hour old call from Gretchen. "I miss you already my love. This is going to be a long two weeks. I can't wait to be in your arms once again."

Leon smiled to himself, happy to have gotten into such a relationship. He thought he might ask her to marry him over the holidays. A week earlier he had taken the briefcase full of money and stored it in Gretchen's apartment.

Making sure his office door was double locked, he went into the head and opened the doorway leading down to the communications suite.

He experienced an odd feeling someone had been there but dismissed it as anxiety.

Leon turned on the power to the NOAA weather fax receiver and set the device to receive the current synopsis from the west coast of Africa to Bermuda. Next, he powered up the teletype machine and set it to receive on 2152 MHz; the Coast Guard operational channel. Immediately, the keys started their tap, tap, tap, ding, tap, tap, ding sounds.

He looked at the two-foot wide piece of paper coming out to the fax machine. "Oh, oh," he said half out loud. This could get nasty. He noticed the gradient markings of the big low pressure system developing east of Trinidad. "I hope we're all done by the time that thing gets going."

Next, he stood in front of the teletype receiver. "What the fuck!" He moaned. He started to see narratives from various ships:

USCGC DILIGENCE CURRENTLY IN PATROL SECTOR GOLF 26 AND MOVING TO CHARLIE 11 OVER NEXT TWELVE HOURS.

USCGC LIPAN ON PATROL IN SECTOR CHARLIE 17 OPERATING ON STATION BETWEEN CHARLIE 17 AND 23 NEXT TWENTY-FOUR HOURS.

USCGC ESCAPE IN TRANSIT FROM GOLF 21 TO PATROL ALPHA 10 THROUGH ALPHA 22 NEXT TWELVE HOURS. USCGC SHERMAN UNDERWAY FROM MIAMI STATION ENROUTE PATROL SECTOR ALPHA 81 FOR NATO GUNNERY EXERCISES.

Leon felt his stomach sour instantly and he spit a mouthful of coffee on the floor. He sat in on a stool in front to the teletype with his sweating forehead in his cupped hands. More and more reports arrived disclosing some sort of new patrol sector plan for the ships at sea. Even two navy destroyers deployed with Coast Guard law enforcement detachments reported with the same type of information. One was patrolling sector GOLF 7 TO 15 and the other was in ALPHA 31 to ALPHA 40.

He picked up the phone and dialed #44 to reach Chester.

In Palm Beach, Chester saw the right end light flash on his desk phone. He knew the only phone to make that light flash was Leon's at Fort Sumter. "What's up?"

"Shit Chester, something weird is happening. All of the positions identifiers are changed. They got some kind of fucking grid system. It looks like Alpha, Charlie and Golf are the new major patrol zones and they have a bunch of numbers and I don't know where the hell anyone is. I don't know what to tell Cory. Boss, I am scared!"

"Now calm down Leon, we will figure this out. You say Alpha, Charlie and Golf??"

"Right."

"Well, I would bet a god bottle of scotch they mean Atlantic, Caribbean and Gulf of Mexico."

"OK, I get that. So we know what body of water they are in. I will assume you're correct." Leon was studying other reports. "That does make sense, there are some ships that I know are on the west coast and they are reporting zones like Papa, Golf/Alfa and Bravo. I bet that means Pacific, Gulf of Alaska and Bering Sea."

"Ok let's run with that. Now all we need to figure out is how the grid sectors are organized.

"Tell you what, you get a weather fax out to Cory and let him know what is happening. Just write it on the map. Tell him we will try to get better stuff by tonight. Give me the numbers and grids from cutters you know are in the area and we will try to make something out of if."

Leon gave Chester all the alphanumeric information he had. They agreed to get back in touch by 7pm.

The ripping sound of the two-foot wide document Leon tore off the fax machine sounded amplified and he imagined the sound to be ripping out his gut. He took the weather map showing a building low pressure system now identified as a Tropical Wave over to the drafting table. With a black felt pen, he circled the storm system and wrote on the paper, "one more thing to worry about."

Then he went to a blank space on the top of the page and wrote:

"Dude, they have changed everything. No more Lat. and Long info. There is some kind of grid system. It just popped up this morning. I am worried. Looks like 3 sections of sea, Alpha (Atlantic), Charlie (Caribbean) and Golf (Gulf of Mex.) For your use, there is one USN and two USCG ships either in or heading for the Atlantic. That's the best for now. Working with Chet for solutions. Back in twelve or sooner."

His hands shook and his stomach tightened as he fed the edge of the weather fax into the machine to transmit. He twisted a large black knob until the pointer stopped at the predetermined frequency channel to send the document to Cory. He pressed TX and a warble tone emitted from a speaker near the floor. Once the tone smoothed out, the paper began sliding slowly through the feed mechanism. Within forty-five seconds the document was sent. Next, a green light appeared on the keyboard indicating the information received at the destination.

"He won't like this."

He stuck the folded up weather fax with the notations on it into the document shredder. The machine turned on automatically as soon as a sensor detected paper. He was ready to shove the position reports into it as well when he thought he might want to study them more. Looking at his watch, he realized he had been down there for nearly three hours. He folded the ones with the Alpha sector listed on them and put them in his hip pocket. He thought he could look at them at his desk and try to figure out some rhyme or reason to the new system. The others he shredded.

In case someone was looking for him, he wanted to get back up to his office. Turning out the lights in the old magazine, he stepped into the stairwell and headed up.

Chapter Thirty-Four

In commercial real estate, agents and brokers come and go in offices around the country. Virginia Beach Industrial Properties Management Inc. was no different. The VBIPM worked for Chester Whittaker managing leases and maintenance on eight warehouses owned by an investment group he represented. A variety of businesses occupied seven buildings. They ranged from small machine shops, auto repair, shipyard support services and office products repair and resale. The warehouse Chad Walgren used for his mixing and packaging operations had not been looked at for four years.

Jenny Wilson began her career with VBIPM in August. She was trying hard to learn the inventory. She had visited all the tenants in seven of the holdings and thought it would be appropriate for her to check out number eight.

She arrived at the site on Monday morning and was curious to find there was no one there, no signage, no vehicles and no sign if life. She felt a little funny but wanted to check it out. At a payphone across the street, she called her husband Nick who was a Virginia Beach police officer. She told him she was going to have a look inside this property and wondered if he was close by.

"What's it like?"

"Just a building, no cars, no people, one light on inside, no sign outside."

"Tell you what Babe, I am about five minutes away and I would rather you wait until I get there. Take a break, I will be right there."

"Thanks."

In her car, Jenny looked at a huge ring with about forty keys on it. She found one with the address of the warehouse written on a small tag. As she did this, Nick rolled up in his patrol car. She also noticed another police car stop in front of a building a block away."

"Not taking any chances?" she nodded towards the other car.

"Nope. What is this place?"

"It's on our list of management properties and I wanted to come by and introduce myself but it looks abandoned."

"Sure does."

"Yes, but there is a light on."

"You got a key?"

"Yep."

"Let's go."

First, they walked completely around the building; it was about thirty by sixty feet. At the far end, they found a wide garage door for loading or deliveries. The key did not fit the lock. Completing the exterior inspection, they opened the smaller door at the other end."

"Hello!" Nick shouted. "Anyone here?" His right hand was resting on the grip of his pistol and the strap securing it to his holster was unsnapped.

A slight echo occurred but no response. Next to the door, they found a line of four light switches. Jenny turned all of them on and the room brightened slowly as old and long idle florescent lights came to life. The end of the building they were in was cluttered with old and obviously used furniture and file cabinets. Everything was dusty. They started towards the other end separated by floor to ceiling translucent plastic and encountered four rows of tables lined up parallel to the outside walls; two rows, an open space and two more rows.

"What's that?" Jenny asked. "It looks like a huge dough mixing machine."

"That's exactly what it is. But look at this."

They found large bags of something on a couple of the tables on one side of the mixer and on the other side were several stacks of bread pans, a dozen rolls of saran wrap, another dozen rolls of tin foil and a box of duct tape.

Nick examined the labels on the bags. "Holy shit, Jen. This is a cocaine or heroin mixing plant. Look at these bags; talc, lidocaine and lactose. That's what they cut the stuff with."

"Really?

"Come join us and call a Narco guy and the DEA," Nick spoke into the microphone clipped near the top of his jacket.

Within twenty minutes, the warehouse was crawling with local police and Federal agents. Jenny's managing broker Tom Cleveland was also on the scene taking notes and photographs. It was apparent
to him what had been happening in the warehouse was all wrong. He decided to go back to his office and call Chester to let him know what was going on inside his property. He would stop for

lunch and drop off the film at a one-hour processor so he could fax the images to his client while he explained things.

Chapter Thirty-Five

Chad and Debbi were in the Corvette and Lenni, Elwood and two girlfriends were following in a van loaded with ten forty pound bags of talc, lactose and lidocaine. Leaving home on Friday, they drove to Lexington to attend a rock and roll concert on Saturday night. Early Monday they got underway headed to Virginia Beach to prepare for the big load of cocaine arriving the following weekend. The further north they got, the cooler the temperatures were and they noticed a little color coming out in the leaves on the trees along the freeways. In both vehicles, loud music was blaring away and everyone was in a grand mood. Eleven months earlier, they finished the job in a week and enjoyed very fruitful year. Cocaine sales were booming in the white collar community served by Chad's team and they were looking forward to another year of five and six-digit tax free income.

Tooling down the interstate, they exited on Lynnhaven Parkway northbound and in a mile made the exit to the west down Dean Drive to the small warehouse district on the north side of the boulevard. Chad turned left into the complex and the van followed close behind. A block behind the van was a sedan driven by Bill Saint, the detective in charge of the Narcotics Division of the Virginia Beach Police Department.

"What the hell!" The tires on the 'vette screeched as he pressed hard on the brake pedal. Ahead at the far end of the warehouse there were at least ten cars, half of them marked police patrol units. Red and blue lights flashed everywhere. Elwood nearly rear ended Chad but also screeched to a stop. Bill Saint cautiously slowed down and passed by watching the whole scene.

The screeching tires alerted several of the officers and agents and they looked towards the entrance to the industrial park. Chad quickly spun his vehicle around exited the parking area heading west on Dean. He motioned to Elwood to go east.

Saint radioed his communications center. "Code Fifty-Four! Two suspicious vehicles, a dark blue Corvette and a white Ford van, one east and one west on Dean Drive east of Lynnhaven."

Five of the cars near the warehouse were soon underway in pursuit along with Saint. For some reason four of the cars went after the van and only two went after Chad. Within a minute, he was on Lynnhaven, then south to Interstate 264 and eastbound to the Virginia Beach Airport. One car in pursuit went east on the interstate and the other west. The westbound one driven by Saint was travelling at over a hundred miles an hour when it left the road. The eastbound patrol car abandoned the chase, exited and went to investigate the crash of Saint's car.

Chad asked Debbi, "How would you like to go to Hawaii?"

She was obviously shaken by the events of the past minute but said, "I think it would be better than hanging around here to see what happens."

Chad was cool as a cucumber. "We will leave on the next westbound flight for the coast and be in California or Washington by sunset." They parked the car behind a dumpster at a Denny's restaurant near the airport. With a couple of Armor All wipes, they cleaned the steering wheel, door handles and dashboard. They got two bags out of the back and hailed a cab. They were at the Delta Airlines desk within fifteen minutes of leaving the warehouse district.

The other chase ended quickly. The authorities had the van pinned down and all four occupants surrendered. Handcuffed, they returned to the warehouse for questioning.

Local TV stations had choppers in the air a minute after the original radio transmission and reporters were gathering at the Dean Drive warehouse location to document this breaking news for the noon news programs.

Chapter Thirty-Six

Chester studied a National Geographic map of the West Indies covering all of the navigable waters from eastern Mexico to Trinidad and Bermuda south to Colombia. With some tracing paper he was playing around with pages of squares. The pages were marked in pencil G, C and A.

"It can't be that difficult and they can't be much smarter."

His intercom buzzed. "Mr. Thrasher would like a visit."

"Send him in Connie."

The door opened and closed quickly. "Turn on your TV boss. We've got problems. Put CNN on."

"What's up?"

"Just watch."

The footage from a helicopter showed a dozen law enforcement vehicles with lights flashing. The reporter was relating a local cop had uncovered what appeared to be a very large cocaine mixing laboratory inside an unused warehouse north of Dean Drive in Virginia Beach. She was also saying the police had apprehended four persons caught fleeing the area in a van but were still in search of a corvette also suspected to have something to do with the warehouse.

"We should have all retired after the last load," Chester began. "Look at this shit."

Tom walked over to the table with the West Indies map on it. "What's that?"

"Well, the sons-of-a-bitches in the Coast Guard just this morning decided to change the way they do the Two a Day reports! They've come up with some kind of a grid system." Beads of sweat were forming along his hairline and his hands were shaking. He poured two glasses of scotch and handed one to Tom.

Tom pointed towards the television. "So far it looks like Chad might have ditched them. I don't know how much his team knows about us. I doubt it is much."

His intercom buzzed again. "Yes sir, there is a Tom Cleveland on the phone from Virginia Beach Industrial Properties. He says it is very important."

"Tell him I am out on my boat for a couple of days. You will try to find me and will have me call him by Friday."

"Yes sir." For the first time ever, Connie felt her boss was in some kind of trouble. The last few days he had seemed on edge. She wondered to herself: "Do I need to worry?"

"Leon called me two hours ago from the fort. He about crapped his drawers when this shit came in. I had him send a fax out to Cory telling him things are changing and to be on the lookout for trouble."

"Wow, what else has been going on?"

"Well, last Friday Robert called me and said that there were a couple of goons from the U.S. Treasury wanting to look at the books of the pension fund in Trish's office. It seems that a transfer to the trust account in the Turks rang a bell on someone's computer in DC. I called in a favor from an old client at treasury and got it postponed until after Bob's election."

"Wonder what that's all about."

"It's these new goddamned computers." Chester pointed at his Apple II C. "I am afraid they will be able to track everything everyone does and put an end to anyone who is trying to make an extra dime on the side. There are companies out west saying people will be walking around with computers in their hands within twenty years. We are just at the start of a revolution."

"I hadn't really paid that much attention."

"Tell you what Tom. Go get a briefcase or maybe even two of them. Come back and take some of this out of here." Chester opened a hinged top on the large ottoman in front of the couch. Inside it was full to the top with money. There were hundred dollar bills, fifties, large Canadian bills, German marks and British pounds. "If the shit hits the fan, there is no reason all of this needs to get found. I moved some down to the boat last weekend."

Tom stood back. "You're kidding me. I had no idea you kept so much here! You just want me to take it?"

"If this all goes sideways, it ain't going to do me any good. You have kept clean for the past year. You might think about relocating. If nothing happens, we will just start to fill it back up again." Chester pointed to the ottoman. "There is more around here too." He made an arc with his hand covering half of his massive office.

"Ok I will be right back."

Chapter Thirty-Seven

Early Monday afternoon ESCAPE was transiting northwestward up the Old Bahama Channel on the north shore of Cuba. At sunset, a right turn into the Florida Straits would put them on a course to pass north of the Bahamas. Phil had filed his first Two a Day report using the new system and was wondering what the people on the other side were making of it.

The weekend transit had been uneventful and relaxing. The crew now knew there was a major suspicious operation underway. Lookouts doubled up and all of the ships guns were cleaned and readied. The general attitude onboard was one of excitement.

Meanwhile onboard Caribbean Gipsy, Cory and Rob were scratching their heads trying to deal with the weather fax Leon had sent earlier in the day.

"I guess we should go ahead with the pick-up and see what Leon and Chester can figure out." Cory commented.

"Yeah skipper, there ain't much we would be able to do if we missed the exchange and then they figured everything out."

"Why don't you go get some sleep. I have a lot to think about and we have a busy night watch tonight." Cory picked up his binoculars and scanned the sea ahead.

"Ok Boss, I will see you at sunset."

Chapter Thirty-Eight

Susan Rico arrived in her little cubicle next to the door to the operations center at 06:45 on Monday. She looked over the reports of activity from the weekend and began writing a memo to herself with the details of the meeting in Charleston and the meeting later on Saturday with her bosses. She enjoyed becoming part of a critical investigation. "I love this damn job!" she said half out-loud at the same instant Assistant US Attorney Gary Jones, accompanied by another young man in a suit, startled her by a knock on her door.

"I love my job too."

"You startled me. So what's up?"

"This is Jason Steadman. He is a public defender and last Friday we were deposing a Colombian kid arrested about nine or ten months ago. Jason was trying to find out if this Ortiz guy could give up any information that might help him go home instead of hanging out in jail for the next five years."

"Go on."

Jason began to speak. "Well, he is a welder. He told us about a small freighter he worked on in Honduras over a year and a half ago. Apparently, there is a small shipyard specializing in installing false fuel and water tanks in freighters. He told us about a boat called Caribbean Gipsy."

Susan sat bolt upright in her chair. "Did you say Caribbean Gipsy?"

"Yes ma'am, a small freighter with a blue hull."

"I know. I know. We are looking all over hell for that ship right now!"

"He said in the engine room, behind the motor is a big tank for water and sewage. Well it's not a tank at all, it just looks like one. There is a hydraulic system that lifts the things up to expose ten by twelve-foot space for storing secret stuff."

"You knew this on Friday in the elevator didn't you?" She spoke with authority and a bit of annoyance.

"Yes. However, it was the end of the week and you needed to get to some kind of meeting. So I didn't want to bother you with it."

"Well, the meeting in Charleston was all about Caribbean Gipsy. Where is this guy?"

"Who?"

"Ortiz, damn it."

"He is over at Dade County Jail."

"Well, you get him back here within the hour. Find a room upstairs and I will get a couple of people who will want to listen to his story. If it pans out, he might be home in a week or two. This is huge! She's been boarded two dozen times and no one has found those tanks! Get going quick, she is underway in the Atlantic Ocean right now and headed for the states. I bet those tanks are packed. I have to meet with my boss and his boss right now. Give me a call when you are set up."

Chapter Thirty-Nine

The low-pressure system was moving northward. Cory wanted to pick up the cocaine and move on quickly. It was just before midnight on Tuesday when the two ships met.

Jules was also concerned about the weather. All of the testing and money counting was expedited. Cory and Rob were on deck of Seintespirit. Both vessels were banging together against half a dozen fenders.

The seas had grown from flat calm to nearly four feet high in the past two hours. Trish spent the evolution sitting on a high stool inside the wheelhouse and out of sight. Manuel and his crew were waiting for the cargo on the after deck.

"What would I do if something happened just now?" she found herself whispering to herself. She had no answer.

Onboard Seintespirit very little talking was done. Jules was all business. Cory noticed a number of very attractive women sitting around on the deck. When he looked their way Jules with a sly smile only said "Working Girls for Venezuela. I haul every kind of cargo you can imagine."

Cory smiled back and nodded.

Carl and an English-speaking crewmember took care of the testing and counting. After about fifteen minutes, the Frenchman stepped towards Jules telling him everything was just fine.

At the same moment, Rob nodded his agreement towards Cory.

Jules snapped his fingers, pointed skyward and twirled his index finger. Blue smoke belched and the crane operator went to work transferring the two pallets of cargo over the side to the deck below. Manuel already had the aft hatch open and with Hector's help quickly transferred the load below to Caesar and Sammie. The whole operation took less than twenty minutes.

"It was good to see you again my friend." Jules motioned to one of the women to come closer. Cory was surprised.

"I would offer you some cognac and we could enjoy a cigar to celebrate our transaction but forecast has me worried."

"Oui, mon Capitan." The young woman smiled and handed him a shopping bag from a Parisian market. Jules handed the package to Cory.

"A little refreshment for your journey. My brother operates a small restaurant near Pigalle in Central Paris. If you are visiting someday, you should stop for dinner. His name is Louis and there is a card in here with the address."

"Why thank you Captain. This is very kind of you. I am thinking of a trip to Europe soon and will include your brother's place on my itinerary."

Cory shook Jules hand and Jules offered a brief embrace. This caught him off guard. "It is very good to see you again and I think you are a good person. We will probably meet next year in this same place. Now however, we must part and outrun the storm. Sail safely."

"I wish you the same."

Rob had already made it to the top step of the ladder. Cory handed him the bag, he descended two steps and handed it to Manuel. Within minutes, the ropes connecting the two ships and the fenders keeping them from scratching one another were returned to their respective owners. Both ships were underway in opposite directions.

Chapter Forty

Tom knocked on Chester's door. Connie was at lunch. He was carrying two dark grey attaché cases. One was a match for the one he had left at Fort Sumter so many months ago.

"Come on in." Chester was still trying to figure out the Coast Guard's grid system. "It looks like ESCAPE is in transit from G to A and we can assume that 10 is a westernmost square and 22 must be further East. If this is at the bottom of the grid system, hopefully Cory is already north of that. It would be nice to know how large each sector is. There is also a Navy ship in Alpha and this SHERMAN is probably headed way north. The best I could tell Leon to pass on to Cory is to watch out."

"Wow, you have been studying this shit."

"One thing in our favor is those tanks. After a dozen boardings, no one has found them. I hope they don't have cocaine sniffing dogs at sea."

"Were you serious about what you said earlier?"

"What's that?"

"About the money." Tom had one of the cases opened on the seat of a leather armchair.

"Hell yes! I have a bad feeling about this week. I suggest you take as much as you can scoop up and get it out of the building. I will be doing the same thing tonight."

'It's your call boss." He was picking handfuls of large bills out of the ottoman. One rubber band secured pile was three hundred British Sterling notes of one-hundred pounds each. Tom whistled under his breath realizing just one stack was worth close to $50,000. Another similar stack of fifteen-hundred Deutsch Marks notes was next to it. There was plenty of room for neatly wrapped $10,000 packages of hundred-dollar bills to lay on edge as though they were mere packaging protection for the foreign notes. A dozen and a half packages went into the case before he closed it and started loading the second.

"How long has this stuff been lying around here?"

"Oh, I started collecting it about three years ago. It's been fun to see people sitting around the office never knowing that they were this close to a couple million dollars in cash."

"I never knew."

"It was fun for me. I actually would go for weeks or months sometimes without thinking about it. Then when I wanted to show off with a big wad in my pocket, I would grab a stack. Trips to Europe and Canada have always been fun because I never needed traveler's checks."

"So what are you going to tell Leon?"

"I'm going to tell him to keep looking over his shoulders and advise Cory there are at least three ships patrolling the Atlantic right now but we have no idea where they are. My biggest concern it what happened this morning in Virginia Beach."

"Yeah, it's kind of shitty. Where is Cory going to deliver the load?" Tom questioned

"From the looks of things, Chad got away. They found his Corvette parked behind a restaurant about half a mile from the airport. I bet he's headed far away. All those local dealers who provided thirty percent down payments are gonna be pissed off."

"Do you think they can trace anything to here? People get angry and violent over much less than what these guys are invested in."

"Chad has kept us insulated. I doubt they would find us. I don't know where the hell to have it delivered. I can't reach Chad, they are waiting on the furniture in Virginia, our warehouse is toast, the Treasury wants to audit the accounts in Trish's office, she's on the boat with Cory and we're sitting here with our thumbs up our asses."

"That's a lot of challenges. I have a 2PM hearing on a child custody issue between two investment banker millionaires. She wants them in Texas and he wants them in Florida. I see two kids spending a lot of time in Lear Jets until they are eighteen."

"Well, why don't you take those," Chester pointed at the two attachés "over to your condo and then go make a few bucks for the firm. Check back with me this evening and we will see where we can go then."

Chester picked up his phone and called Leon.

Chapter Forty-One

Susan rounded up Jesse Warburton, one of the staff investigators from the Coast Guard Intelligence Unit and Jim Simpson, the on-duty DEA agent in the building. In the elevator, she briefed them on Jason Steadman and Gary Jones' revelation about the hidden compartment onboard Caribbean Gipsy fabricated by Carlos Ortiz a couple years earlier. They arrived on the seventh floor of the Federal Building. A student intern was waiting when the door opened.

"Are you Lieutenant Rico?"

"Yes, is Mr. Jones here?"

"Yes Ma'am. He and Mr. Steadman are waiting for you. Please follow me."

They walked through a maze of small cubicles each populated by a young attorney seemingly glued to a telephone receiver, all carrying on dozens of conversations. At the end of the hallway was a glass-enclosed room with three people in it. Susan recognized Jones and Steadman and saw a dark skinned Latin looking man in an orange prison uniform drinking a root beer and smiling.

Gary glanced up as the trio approached. He opened the door. "Here we are."

Jessie, who towered over everyone in the room by at least half a foot spoke sternly and directly to Carlos. "So young man, what do you know about hidden compartments on a blue freighter named Caribbean Gipsy?"

Ortiz went on for nearly forty minutes. Susan brought along some photos taken during various boarding operations in the past year. He showed where the hatch directly above made loading the compartment swift and efficient. He explained how the hydraulic rams operate by turning what looked like a valve. He was very forthcoming and smiling throughout.

"Señor, do you think this helps enough for me to get outta here?"

"Well, is there anything else you want tell us that might help us in our work?" Simpson asked.

"Like what? Isn't this a good fact for you?"

"We will check out those tanks next time someone looks at that ship. If you are right, then we will talk to a judge and see if we can get you a ticket home." Jessie promised. "You got anything else?"

"I just gave you a lot more than you had an hour ago! How about if I tell you where that shipyard is and who the Jefe is that runs it?"

Everyone leaned a few inches closer to Ortiz. "Go ahead," Susan started.

Carlos went on to describe Puerto Lempira Honduras. He also told of two ships waiting for new tank work when he left to take a ride on the Sallie Mae. "One is a big fishing boat from Alaska. I think the name is Smoking Tuna. The other was a little tanker for hauling oil. I never saw a name on that one. I should have stayed there as a welder but I was looking for the big payday and now I sit here in jail for almost a year and all I got to show for it is these new shoes." He grinned and pointed proudly to the Nike tennis shoes on his feet. "I just want to go home and work with my brother in his car repair shop. Is not this enough stuff from one man? Please talk to the judge."

"I think we are done here. Anyone have any more questions for Mr. Ortiz?" Jessie asked the trio.

"Thank you very much Mr. Ortiz. I will talk to the judge and see what we can do for you. Ok, we have work to do. Mr. Jones, please take him back."

Susan leaned towards Carlos. "You know if you go home now and we catch you hauling drugs again, you are going to jail for hard time. It will be at least six years maybe fifteen."

"Si, Señora."

"Just so you understand," she smiled and shook his hand.

The law enforcement team left Steadman and Jones to transport the prisoner. The duty Coast Guard Intelligence agent got a message to return to his boss and the trio of Jessie, Susan and Jim Simpson walked towards the elevators.

"He seems like a good kid who learned his lesson. I hope he gets back and makes a life for himself." Jim remarked. "I better get back to my foxhole. Thanks for including me." Jim stayed on the elevator as Jessie and Susan headed for the Ops Center.

As they walked, Warburton brought up something new. "So Susan, the guys in Intelligence have been going over all the boarding reports ever issued for this Caribbean Gipsy. It looks like Cory Higgins and his deck hand Manuel Salvador have consistently been on board every time. And once in a while, most notably when they are out of the southern patrol areas, there is usually one or two other crewmen from a Latin country and one of two other guys, Robert Byrd or Carl Peterson."

"Yes Sir, they probably increase the crew size for extra lookouts and cargo handling if there is contraband to deal with."

"That's what I think too. On the most recent one, there is a woman onboard. Her name is Patricia Dixon."

"Wow, that is interesting. Not that I don't think women can do diverse jobs." Susan smiled.

"Well, they checked into her a bit and found an interesting history."

"What is that sir?"

"It seems like about four years ago she was a newlywed and on a trip to Florida, her husband got arrested for using cocaine."

"Interesting."

"It gets even better. He hired the Whittaker Law Firm in Palm Beach to handle his situation. They got him off with a little slap on the wrist. Then he gets killed on the Atlanta Beltway while doing more coke half a year later. She had already filed for divorce when he bought the farm. Apparently she knew nothing about his addiction before the wedding."

"I can tell you have more."

"Oh yes Lieutenant, it gets better and better. Let's go get a cup of coffee." Jessie pointed towards the break room. "She's working for the Whittaker Law Firm in Atlanta."

"You're kidding! Is she an attorney?"

"Nope, a CPA. She handles a trust account for the firm. It is a huge retirement fund for all of the school employees in six southeastern states."

"That must be a lot of money."

"Millions, I've been told, and it could be as much as three hundred million. However, here is the kicker. Last month the U.S. Treasury got a hit on a suspicious transfer of money from there to a Trust and Holding company in the Caicos Islands. A couple of investigators were dispatched to check into it but because Ms. Dixon was out of town, they went on to Texas to look at something else for a while."

"Wow! And the little trip she is on just happens to be onboard our favorite, lumber hauling ship with secret compartments welded together by our new best friend Carlos Ortiz."

"Exactly, but we are still not done."

"I beg your pardon, what else could there be?"

"We haven't verified it yet but the photo from her passport copied in Saint Thomas two days ago looks a lot like a picture Dutch took of a lady who came to see the head ranger at Fort Sumter last summer. She identified herself as Patricia Wilson, an inspector from the National Parks Service."

"She's the one we found out doesn't really work for Parks! This is getting crazy. Do you think she is the new money person? We were imagining she might be at the conference a couple weeks ago but never researched more. We've been busy around here."

"Kippy thinks she replaced Thrasher. Then we have this big mixing room uncovered in Virginia Beach. It's been all over the news. We know a year ago Caribbean Gipsy with Cory Higgins, Carl Peterson and Manuel Salvador all on board were in Virginia Beach. And one other tidbit; the warehouse is managed by a guy named Cleveland. He sends the rental money to an attorney representing a real estate trust. Can you guess who that attorney is?"

"I would bet the last name would be Whittaker."

"Yep."

"It is starting to come together isn't it Commander?"

"Yes it is and the plan is to pay a visit to each of the Whittaker Law Firms and Fort Sumter early in the morning either Wednesday or Thursday depending when all of the assets can be assembled. Treasury, U.S. Marshalls and DEA will do the law firms and Coast Guard, Marshalls, and DEA and Charleston Police will visit the fort. And our cutters will continue hunting down Caribbean Gipsy."

"Sounds interesting, I wish I could be there."

"That's why we are having this talk." He smiled and handed her a cup of freshly brewed coffee. "I would like you to head up to Charleston this afternoon and get with the Group Commander to coordinate all of the interagency participation and deal with the press once the shit hits the fan."

Susan felt a knot in her stomach and euphoria in her head. "Thank you Commander! This is the best assignment I could ever hope for." They sat down to go over the details on how the rest of the week would play out.

Chapter Forty-Two

Leon was beside himself and Emmett and Dutch observed him walking around the fort and were enjoying seeing him talking to himself, returning to his office, reappearing within minutes half a dozen times between ten o'clock and two. Around noon, they were on the dock preparing to assist the next launch load of guests.

"I bet he isn't walking around worrying about how to spruce this place up for the President." Dutch suggested.

Emmett, keeping his voice low and just above a whisper added, "We can expect an early morning raid from Kippy and the gang either tomorrow or Thursday before the park opens."

"Is that what happened at your meeting Saturday?"

"Yeah, I called on the payphone last night. Apparently the boat is underway and the new position reporting system should have them so confused they won't know what to do."

"Who do you think will come?"

"I would expect a flotilla of half a dozen boats from the Coast Guard, US Marshal and maybe even a couple of our guys on a local police boat. I think Kippy wants to be in charge of the bust and the Guard will be here for support and a show of strength. There was a young Lieutenant from Miami at the meeting. I wouldn't mind seeing here again. She's hot."

"Oh yeah, she is interesting. Here they come. I wonder if we will close things down on the day of the bust."

"It is bound to be interesting. I imagine the Marshals will close it for at least a day."

Dutch raised his voice and kicked in an authentic southern accent.

"Welcome ladies and gentlemen to the location of the first shot fired in anger to start the Civil War."

Leading the group of tourists up the dock, Dutch noticed Leon standing near the flagpoles just staring out across the channel entrance. He felt good inside knowing the job he and Emmett were doing here was about to bear fruit.

Chapter Forty-Three

Just after sunrise on Wednesday morning, Cory and Rob were in the wheelhouse looking over the weather fax just delivered from Fort Sumter. "What do you think of all this shit?" Rob asked.

"Well it means we are going to stay out of shipping lanes, run without lights at night and stay off of the radio. We should probably leave the radars off too. I have heard some of those bigger ships have receivers telling them if someone is out there using radar."

"Maybe it's time for us to think about investing in the firms making the technical stuff."

"I have been thinking a lot about that in the past couple of days. I'll take the next couple of hours to think things through. Why don't you go get some breakfast and a little sleep? You can come up and relieve me at fourteen hundred."

"OK Skipper."

Cory picked up his binoculars and scanned the horizon ahead. "Not a thing." He said to himself. "Let's keep it that way." He was trying to design a way to tell Trish that things were not as rosy as they had hoped. He decided if things didn't improve tomorrow morning, he would execute an escape plan.

Chapter Forty-Four

The Virginia Beach Police were not getting much information out of Lenni and Elwood. Elwood was more acquainted with Chad than Lenni was but even after a night of sleep deprivation and constant questioning, neither seemed to know much about the leadership of the operation.

The cops quickly understood the girls accompanying them were clueless and had no record. They were charged with misdemeanor aiding in a felony. A night judge on duty arraigned them and dismissed both of them with a year of probation. They caught a bus back to South Carolina.

A local DEA team arrived to have a look at the mixing room. Field samples confirmed the cocaine last mixed here was identical to confiscated products from a few white-collar users up and down the east coast. A notification went out on the DEA alert network and to CCIC in Corpus Christi. Within two hours, a secure conference call, initiated by Kippy Gibbs began. Jessie Warburton, Susan Rico, the duty Coast Guard Officer at CCIC and several other interested parties were all on the phone together. Jessie began. "Well folks, it looks like we are getting someplace. This could be an exciting week."

Kippy spoke next. "I think it is just about time to put the hurts on this whole TCM86 operation. If they are communicating with the boat, and I bet they are, he will probably be headed someplace other than Virginia."

Jessie added. "We are moving two more cutters from patrols in the Gulf and Southern Caribbean to the Atlantic between San Juan and Chesapeake Bay. If I were Higgins, I would head for Charleston or Savannah. There are many places to hide in plain sight amongst all of the smaller freighters in those ports. If he is out there we will find him."

"Everyone knows about the Treasury Department's alert on the funds transfer last month over in the Atlanta Whittaker Law Firm," the CCIC Duty officer added.

A series of half a dozen yeses provided acknowledgement. "Well, the investigators will be there tomorrow morning to audit and raid the trust department. A few hours later, a crew from the Miami DEA office and the U.S. Marshals team be paying a call on the Whittaker firm in Palm Beach.

Jessie spoke again. "I am sending Lieutenant Rico up to Charleston to coordinate with you Kippy, the Group Commander and US Marshals for an early visit Thursday morning to Mr. Matthews at the Fort. We will be publishing an Operations Order in a couple of hours. All, including the cutters on patrol, will be receiving it. We are also including a sketch of the ship showing the hidden compartments. It will go out encrypted. They won't be able to read it at Fort Sumter."

Kippy took the initiative to end the call. "Well ladies and gentlemen, I think we all have work to do. My advice to everyone is to pay attention to how your documents are completed. Remember, we are dealing with a law firm famous for finding breaches in chains of custody. My final hope is, when the ship is found, it is the cutter ESCAPE with Vince Lubar onboard. That would be a fitting end to this case. Ok folks, let's get started."

Chapter Forty-Five

"Hi Betty, this is Chester down in Florida. Is my brother around?" He was contacting Robert to make sure the Feds from Treasury had been successfully diverted. It was Tuesday afternoon.

"Yes he is sir, one moment please."

"Hey big brother, what's up?"

"I was just calling to see how things worked out with the Treasury dudes."

"Oh man, whatever you did worked. A call came in for one of them and they told my receptionist they had a pressing issue in Texas and had no idea if or when they would return."

"That's great news. How's the political life going?"

"Just fine, it's a lot more work than I thought. Today is the last day before the election where I have nothing scheduled for the whole day. I think I will practice a little law then take Elizabeth out for dinner. It will be our last night alone for the next month."

"So what are the polls telling you?"

"Well, if you believe this stuff I am about a fifteen-point favorite. It still depends on lots of things. If we get a good voter turnout and nothing bad pops up it should all be great for us."

Chester's stomach tightened. He was wondering if things happening within his smuggling operation could possibly derail his brother's election chances. "Well, let's hope for the best. Why don't you two try to come down after it is all over? We can go out in the boat for a couple of days. I am sure you will both want a little down time whichever way it goes."

"That would be great. I will talk to Elizabeth tonight and get back to you next week."

"It will be fun we can go over what our practices have been doing and see who is ahead in the billing competition."

"Ok big brother, I actually have a client coming in to talk about legal issues in a few minutes. I better take a look at this file on my desk."

"All right, I will let you go. We will talk more next week."

"Ok, good bye and thanks again for whatever you did with those treasury guys. I will be happy when Trish gets back."

Chapter Forty-Six

Cory and Trish were embracing one another in the bed in the captain's stateroom after a blissful session of mid-afternoon love making while the ship continued on a northern course.

"You seem distracted." Trish noticed Cory seemed on edge. He was staring at the ceiling above the bed. "Oh, there is some shit going on with the reports Leon works on. It seems the Coast Guard chose this week to try out a new system for tracking the location of the cutters on patrol."

Trish sat up and braced her back with a pillow. "What do you mean?"

"They used to report latitude and longitude of the ship's position and where they were headed. Now they just started some sort of coded grid system. The best we can tell now is whether a ship is in the Gulf of Mexico, the Atlantic or the Caribbean."

"What are you going to do about that?" She seemed more than a little concerned.

"Chester is trying to decipher it. We assume there are three cutters patrolling between here, the coast of Florida and Virginia right now. We just don't know where but they will probably be closer to the coast than way out here."

"This is disconcerting." She placed her arms around his torso. "Do you think we might get caught?"

"Well love, we have a couple of things going for us at this point. We are going to go around Bermuda. That is not a normal shipping lane for cargo. Then, we have those nifty little hidden compartments down in the engine room. The Coast Guard has searched this boat two dozen times. No one has a clue. Even on the last trip north, when we stopped to help with a boat fire one of the dummies sat right on top of them within inches of a ton of coke to fill out his report."

"Wow, you hadn't told me that part."

"Well, when you picked me up in Virginia, we had other things on our mind." He rolled over facing her and placed his arm across her naked midsection.

"Leon and Chester are working on a plan and we should be getting something from the fort this evening."

Chapter Forty-Seven

Leon picked up the phone with the direct line to Chester.
"What's up?"

"I am starting to get the evening reports and nothing has changed. There is a lot of chatter on the encrypted networks but you know I can't do anything about that. I do know there is an exercise going on with the Navy over in the Eastern Atlantic. It could account for most of it."

"Here's what I am thinking," Chester began. "I am pretty sure that the A, C and G are what we think they are. So concentrate on watching the ones in sector Alpha. Cory should be a day or two away from Bermuda and well east of the patrol areas. We know from past events they tend to be within three hundred miles of the coast. The big problem I have is we can't take the stuff into Virginia."

"Yeah, I saw the shit on the news about the warehouse. I doubt Cory knows about it. We can't let him go into the bay."

"Here's an idea. Let's have him stop in Bermuda for a couple of days. He can clear customs there with the load of furniture and hang out until this damn hurricane goes by. Tell him to give me a call on a landline. This will give me time to find a buyer for the load. We won't make as much but I just want this one to be over with. The whole operation just feels shitty."

"It sure does. What about Savannah?"

"I will make some calls. Just get a fax out to Cory and let him know the shit has hit the fan in Virginia and we need to find another port. I will call the furniture guy and tell him something. I will blame it on the storm."

"Sure thing, I will go send him an alert."

"Ok Leon, don't get too uptight. I think if we have him lay low for a few days, the ships will all change positions, some will finish their patrols and new ones will come back out. I doubt anyone knows anything about what goes on at the fort."

"I hope that's true. I haven't seen any unusual activity here."

"That's good. The storm will keep the Coast Guard busy doing other things. Call me about eleven in the morning."

"OK Chet."

Leon tore off a two-foot long piece of blank paper and laid it on the drafting table. He began to write in magic marker.

"CORY! BAD SHIT HAPPENING HERE, MIXING SHOP IN VA RAIDED. NEW GRID SYSTEM UNPREDICTABLE, CHESTER WORKING ON SECONDARY DROP SITE. FEDS LOOKING INTO TRISH'S BOOKS IN GA. WITHOUT POSIT REPORTS, WE ONLY KNOW ABOUT 3 SHPS IN WESTERN ATLANTIC. RECOMMEND HEAVE TO IN THE ISLAND TO YOUR NORTH AND CALL ON LAND LINE. BE SAFE MY FRIEND."

Sweat beaded up on Leon's forehead. "At least we are safe here, I hope. I haven't seen anyone poking around down here." He spoke to himself.

He re-read what he had written and stepped over to the fax machine, powered it on and verified he was on the correct frequency. He placed the page flush with the feed roller then pressed the TX button.

Within two minutes, whirring and warbling sound of the machine stopped.

Chapter Forty-Eight

Susan was packed and ready for an extended stay in Charleston. She stopped by Jessie's office.

"Well Boss, this should be an interesting end to the week."

"I hope so Lieutenant. A lot of people are counting on us."

"I know sir. It has been a fascinating year. It will be fun to take down an entire syndicate. Congress might begin to think we are worth the money. I thank you for letting me have spot on this team."

"It's all in a day's work around here." He swept his left arm in an arc around his office pointing at various notes on white boards and piles of messages. "If it isn't drug interdiction, we've got plenty of other stuff going on. We have ship inspections, Merchant Marine credentials and people lost out there." He pointed out the window towards the Straits of Florida. "Then we have two ships down in GITMO and one 378 over in the Eastern Atlantic on a NATO exercise."

"I guess we really are a multi-mission service."

"You've got that right, lieutenant. Have a good trip and keep in touch. Give me a call when everything is ready to go in the morning."

"Yes sir. Thanks again for this opportunity."

"No problem, you have earned it."

Chapter Forty-Nine

Cory and Trish were on watch. They were both startled when the receive bell rang. The familiar warble of the fax machine began and a sheet of paper began to emerge from the roller.

Cory looked at his watch. "It isn't time yet for any kind of message from Leon. I wonder what this is all about."

"Well, let's see." Trish placed her arm around his waist while they watched the paper begin its journey. Trish took in a deep breath and held him tighter when she saw 'CORY, BAD SHIT HAPPENING HERE.'

When the words 'FEDS LOOKING INTO TRISH'S BOOKS IN GA' she gasped and ran her free hand through her hair. "Oh my God! Why are they looking at the books in my office?"

"Isn't it where all the money for this stuff comes from?"

When the whole document was complete, Cory ripped it off and laid it on the chart table. "This doesn't look good." He read the note twice, his brain racing through a dozen scenarios. Turning face to face with Trish, he calmly stated, "Looks like it is time to retire."

"What do you mean?"

"Well, we can't go to Virginia, the Coast Guard will be all over the place and it looks like you won't want to go back to Georgia."

"What do you think we should do?"

"Retire."

"What?"

"Yep, I am done. Let's pull in to Bermuda and get on a plane. We can stop in France for the wine grape harvest season and decide where we want to live for the next ten years."

"Do we just disappear?"

"If we went to jail, we just disappear. I would rather do it freely. I have been thinking a lot about South America lately."

"South America, What's that all about?"

"There are great beaches and money goes a long way. I don't think we will need to look for jobs but we could buy a little apartment building and live off of the rental income for quite a while."

"I don't want to go to jail either so I guess what you are saying is, we will just vanish from all of this?"

"That's right."

"What about this?" She pointed to the deck.

"I am ready to give it to Rob and Manuel. They know what the risk is and they will figure it out. I just do not care anymore. We won't even tell Chester or Leon what we are up to."

"Really?"

"Yes, the fewer people who know where we are, the better our chances are for a successful relocation.

"I guess that's true. When will we get to Bermuda?"

"We will be rounding the top of the island and pulling in to St. George Harbour just after sunrise tomorrow."

"When are you going to talk with Rob and Manuel?"

"I think now. I suppose there is no time like the present." He picked up the phone and pushed the switch to call the galley. In a few seconds he spoke. "Si, Manuel, can you find Señor Rob and both come up?"

There was a pause and Cory spoke once more. "Si, Si." He then hung up the phone. "He's going to wake Rob up." Next, he put his arm around Trish's waist and drew her towards him. "It looks like the next chapter of our life is about to begin."

Chapter Fifty

ESCAPE was eighty miles north of the Turks and Caicos Islands. On the Wednesday morning mid watch, LTJG Ladner was the Officer of the Deck. The trip was going smoothly and with the exception of two cruise ships, no contacts were found in the vicinity. Earlier, at eighteen hundred hours, a northbound sailboat named Whiskers was stopped and boarded. Two retired couples were on their way home to Delaware and trying to beat the storm to the south. Finding nothing amiss onboard, LT Sutton advised them to turn around and spend another couple of days in the West Indies. The storm track showed it making landfall around Daytona Beach. The coast out to two or three hundred miles would be extremely dangerous for the next few days.

The crew of Whiskers heeded the advice and sailed south as soon as the boarding was completed.

Just before 0200 Radioman Smitty appeared in the wheelhouse as Buzz was scanning the horizon with his binoculars. "Excuse me Mr. Ladner, I have message traffic."

The officer of the Deck turned around, returned the salute rendered by Smitty and opened the aluminum clipboard containing five messages.

The top one had a blank page covering it. The word SECRET appeared in red diagonally across the cover.

Ladner turned the page over and read closely. The district commander was changing patrol assignments for most of the ships deployed. ESCAPE would move north and cover the area between Savannah and Bermuda. Other ships were going from the Gulf of Mexico to the Florida Straits

Ensign Ladner handed the clipboard back to Smitty. "Hold on for a minute." Then he picked up a sound powered phone handset and called the Commanding Officer.

"Yes Captain, the District Seven folks want us to head north and patrol between Bermuda and Savannah."

"OK Buzz, make the course change and I will be on the bridge in about an hour."

"Aye-Aye Captain, see you soon."

Buzz turned back to Smitty and thumbed through the other messages. Three were extremely significant. After reading a situation report on a rescue happening in the Gulf of Mexico, he turned the page and saw a message from Chief of Personnel, Coast Guard Headquarters. It was the result of the selection board for captains. The fourth name on the list caught his immediate attention, CDR David Flood, his skipper, made the list. He whistled, initialed the message and smiled at Smitty. The two would keep the information confidential until the CO wanted it released. Two messages deeper into the pile he saw the Commanding Officer selection announcement. Here, Lieutenant Commander Vince Lubar, already selected for promotion to Commander was listed to take command of the 210-foot cutter STEADFAST in Astoria Oregon.

The message in between the two personnel action notices was from NOAA. It seemed the tropical storm was petering out and had been downgraded to a tropical depression.

"Quite a morning for the wardroom and good news on the weather, Smitty."

"Yes sir. This will make a happy end to the patrol."

"No kidding. Take these down to the skipper and XO then tell the wardroom mess cooks both of them will probably be up soon and needing fresh coffee."

"Aye-Aye sir." Smitty saluted and stepped down the ladder to Officer's Country.

Chapter Fifty-One

Commander Warburton consulted with Kippy in Charleston and the officers in charge of the U.S. Marshal's stations in both Atlanta and Miami. Rather than rush things, everyone agreed on simultaneous raids at 10 am on Thursday morning. At 8 am the local police would place signs at Patriots Point indicating the park on Fort Sumter was closed for emergency maintenance until 1 o'clock in the afternoon.

The Marshals, DEA Agents, Susan and a team of Coast Guard law enforcement personnel would board two 41foot patrol boats and the 95foot Cutter CAPE KNOX at the Charleston Coast Guard Station south of Broad Street at 0800. They planned to arrive at the moorings on the island by 0900.

Gibbs would do final notifications to each local officer in charge at 0700 Thursday morning.

Susan made herself at home in the stately Francis Marion Hotel on King Street. Once learning about the delay on the raids, she spent the evening touring the area.

She visited the Coast Guard Base and paid a call on the Commanding Officer, Captain Jim Sweeney. He knew she was excited to be there and advised her of two jobs opening in the upcoming assignment season. One was the Deputy Group Commander and the other was the Department Head in the Law Enforcement Division.

"I am sure Commander Warburton will hate to lose you but that's the way things are in this life. I spoke with him yesterday and he will recommend you for any assignment you care to apply for."

"Really? My boss said that?"

"He sure did and once this little thing is taken care of tomorrow, you just might be in the crosshairs of more than one district commander."

Susan blushed. "I am just doing my job."

"I will tell you one thing Lieutenant. I was originally not too keen on the whole women in the service idea. But, after working with a few graduates from your class and the two before. It won't be long before a few of you are walking around with stars on your collars and commanding large ships. I know a couple Loran stations have already had women commanding officers. Nothing but good reports have come from it. It is 'The New Guard' and many think it is great."

"I sure do." She smiled

"The thing I like the best about it is the Coast Guard is years ahead of all the other services in this transition and believe me, we are getting lots of attention."

They chatted for a few more minutes until there was a knock on the CO's door.

"Enter." Jim stated with a firm voice.

"Yes Captain, the mayor and his friends are at the gate and will be here in a couple of minutes." Yeoman Second Class Rita Isnor announced.

"Very well, I will be in the lobby in a jiffy."

"I will see you in the morning." He extended his hand to Susan.

"Yes sir! I am sure I will have a few butterflies in my gut by then."

"It all comes naturally, take care Lieutenant. Enjoy the town."

Chapter Fifty-Two

Rob and Manuel were in the wheelhouse with Cory and Trish. Cory began. "It looks like things are going south in a hurry." He went over the fax from Leon and the recommendations coming from Florida. "I am not sure what you two want to do but we think it is time for us to retire. Trish and I will leave the boat when we get secured in St. George Harbour. You will be able to do whatever you want to do. There are people in Bermuda who might buy the load or you might want to hook up with the folks in Savannah. Just don't go to Virginia. Everything there is broken."

"Yikes!" Rob began. "What do you think our chances are of getting caught on the Savannah idea?"

"I think if you wait for a while here," he pointed north towards Bermuda looming on the horizon, "the heat might die down and Chester and Leon will be able to find a new buyer. I will give you all of the contact information. You will be on your own. I am not even telling Chester where I end up."

"Really, why not?"

"Well, the fewer who know about anything, the less the chance will be we get caught. We will be on the first available flight out of here and will probably move around for months before settling someplace."

"You have been thinking about this for quite a while haven't you?"

"Yeah, quite a while. Like since noon." He put his arm around Trish and smiled.

"I wish you good luck, Amigo. For some reason I knew this would happen someday. Thank you for making me part of the game for the last four years. I can make it ok. I will tell the guys what's up. We will figure things out."

Manuel shook Cory's hand. "Wherever you and Señorita Trish end, I know you will be happy."

Three hours later Caribbean Gipsy rested at a long wharf in St. George Harbour. Customs was a snap and all papers completed stamped and notarized in formal British fashion.

Cory and Trish bid adieu to their shipmates and former business partners. Chester's American Express card with an unlimited credit line became Rob's. Cory did not want anyone following him through spending receipts. "I would fill her up with all the fuel she will hold very soon if I were you." Cory said. "Don't be afraid to have a nice dinner with this too."

They all hugged one another and Manuel and Rob stood on the deck as the couple walked to a waiting cab. Trish was carrying the little shopping bag Jules had given them and a briefcase. Cory was carrying two duffel bags.

"Get the guys up here. Let's have a beer."

"Si, Capitan." Manuel smiled nervously and went to find the rest of the crew.

Chapter Fifty-Three

Leon couldn't sleep. He had been up all night working on a report concerning the upcoming presidential visit. At around 8:15 am, with a cup of fresh coffee in his hand, he was standing on the portico of his office looking northeasterly towards the Battery on the Charleston waterfront. He considered the blissful weekend soon when he would leave and be together with Gretchen once again.

As the early fall twilight turned to daytime, he noticed flashing blue lights up near the Coast Guard base.

"Either someone is in trouble or they are having an early morning drill" he mumbled to himself. "Their jackass commanding officer probably decided to break into their breakfast with some kind of nonsense."

He sat in a chair to watch. In about twenty minutes, four vessels left the dock together.

Dutch walked by on the lawn below the porch.

"Good morning Boss. What's up?" Of course, Dutch knew, within a couple of hours 'Boss' would be cooling his heels in a holding cell.

"Oh, it looks like something is going on up at the Coast Guard Base. I have never seen so many blue lights. Come on up."

Dutch climbed the five steps to the portico and sat in a chair offered by Leon." "Must be some kind of drill I guess." Leon spoke and sipped on his cup of coffee.

"I have never really paid much attention to that place. I suppose they need to practice things all the time."

"Look. They are all underway now heading towards the channel." Leon commented.

"Here comes a helicopter too." Dutch noticed.

Leon suddenly felt a sour knot in his stomach. He sighted two Charleston police boats, with blue lights flashing departing Patriots Point moving westward towards the Fort. "I think I will go in and make a call or two to see what is up."

"OK, do you mind if I sit here and watch for a little while? This could be interesting. Emmett joined him on the hill with a cup of coffee in his hand and was smiling.

Without answering, Leon disappeared into his office and went directly down to his communications center. He called Chester.

"What's up?"

"I don't fucking know but there is a helicopter coming up from Savannah, four boats are coming in from the Coast Guard station and two police boats are headed this way from across the channel."

"This sounds serious. Can you get in a boat and leave?"

"Shit no, I don't have boats here. I am going down, Chester! How did they find out about our thing here?"

"Don't panic, it might just be a drill."

"I don't fucking think so Chet, I hear the chopper landing in the front of our flag poles right now and no one called and told me about some goddamned drill!" His voice was quaking.

"If you have time, get a fax off to Cory. Looks like he will be on his own damn it. Give me a call later if you can."

"OK Chet, I am pretty scared up here."

"I know I hope you have your money in a safe place."

"I do." Leon answered, wondering if the $400,000 he had in cash at Gretchen's apartment would still be there if he were to go to jail for a few years.

He quickly went to the big roll of paper for fax reports and tore off about a foot. With a thick felt tipped pen he wrote: "Cory - Game over this is my last message. Fort being raided - GOOD LUCK!"

He fed the leading edge of the paper into the machine, pushed the green TX button. Without waiting for the message to be sent, he left the room, turned off the light and slowly walked up the stairs to his office.

Chapter Fifty-Four

Susan was in the wheelhouse of the cutter CAPE KNOX. The Officer-in-Charge, Master Chief Bryce Scoggins a veteran with twenty-six-years in the Coast Guard was directing boat movements. On many of the smaller cutters in the Coast Guard, senior petty officers are assigned in command of the vessel.

"Are you nervous Lieutenant?"

"More excited than nervous. I have been working on this project for nine months."

"Then this must be exciting. I only heard about it a couple of days ago. I knew something was in the air but not sure what. Ya'll kept a pretty tight lid on all of it."

"I only wish the XO from ESCAPE could be here for this one. He's the guy who saw something strange at the fort a year ago and followed up on it."

"What was that?"

"Yeah, in the background of photographs taken of him and his family by some photo dude he saw what looked like a money transfer. We have had two DEA agents under cover here since June. It looks like the head ranger here is going down. Apparently, he has a special communications set up in the basement where he compromises all of the position reports on our cutters at sea. Then he sends out a weather fax with all the information on it."

"That's pretty imaginative."

"Yeah, the investigation has led to the discovery of hidden compartments onboard a little freighter and an elaborate money laundering and cocaine trafficking scheme run by an attorney in Florida."

Once the cutter was secured, Susan said "If we get a chance after all this is done, I will fill you in on the rest. Thanks for the ride Master Chief."

"My pleasure Lieutenant." The skipper saluted his guest as she departed. To himself he said, "The new guard has arrived."

Emmett and Dutch were waiting on the dock. Gibbs came in the helicopter from Savannah and delivered Kevlar vests, badges and side arms to his two undercover agents.

Emmett spoke first. "I think he is in his office. He said he had to make a few calls to figure out what was going on."

Susan nodded to everyone, pointed towards the office and said. "It is about time we all get to know Mr. Matthews."

Chapter Fifty-Five

After speaking to Leon, Chester buzzed Connie. "Is Tom in yet?"

"Yes sir, he just got out of the elevator. Do you want to see him?"

"Yes please, send him in right away."

Within five seconds, there was a tap on the door and Thrasher entered. "What's up Boss?"

"I just got a call from Leon. It looks like a raid is going on at the Fort."

"What! Why? I thought it was our tightest secret."

"I have a gut feeling it all goes back to those fucking pictures your friend, what's his name, Bob Lee gave to that son-of-a-bitch from the Coast Guard last year."

"Beaufort Lee." Tom corrected.

"Whatever. Anyhow, there are half a dozen Coast Guard and police boats heading for Fort Sumter right now and a helicopters just landed in front of my flag poles!"

"Probably time to turn on CNN, it won't be long before they are all over it too."

Just then, Connie buzzed on the intercom. "Mr. Whittaker, your brother Robert is on the phone. He does not sound happy." Chester looked at Tom. "Now what! Why in the hell is he calling? If I were you Tom, I would take the day off and go screw one of your girlfriends."

"Ok Boss, you sure you don't need me around here?"

"Nope, whatever happens is gonna happen. I will see you later." His heart was pounding in his chest.

Chester picked up the phone as Tom exited and the TV screen with CNN show opened with aerial video of no less than seven law enforcement boats tied up at Fort Sumter. He muted the sound.

"Hi Bob, How's life in politics?"

"Well, it kind of sucks right now. Where the hell is that woman who is supposed to run your trust department down stairs?!"

"I think she is on vacation, some kind of Caribbean cruise. If you need her, I will see what I can do."

"You are fucking right I need her. There are eight federal agents here with a search warrant for the whole law firm. I am under suspicion of money laundering and conspiracy to smuggle drugs. What the hell is happening Chet?"

"Jeeze Bob, I don't know what she has been doing down there." Chester lied. "Last time I looked at the balance sheets and income statements everything was fine."

"Well, you don't have a carload of reporters wanting a statement. The Jake person she hired does not have a clue. I am going to tell them this is an operation under control of you from Florida and I know nothing about it."

"Ok, I will take the heat." Chester was sweating profusely. Being chewed out by his younger brother and watching report of a raid on the fort was more than he could handle.

"I will fly up there as soon as I can. Set up a press conference for around three pm."

"Yeah, I will do that but this is screwing up any hope I have had of winning this election. I have spent two years of my life on this and I feel like you have just pulled the floor out from under me. My father-in-law is going to be asking questions. I have no answers and I don't know what Dad will have to say about all this shit. Find that bitch and tell her to get her ass back here immediately and then when this is all over, fire her!"

"I understand Bob. See if the Feds will wait until this afternoon to start."

"Too late Chet. They are already hauling boxes of files and all the computers out of here and Jake and Josie are useless. They are sitting in the back seat of cop cars!"

Chester swallowed hard. He stood up from his desk with the wireless phone receiver in his hand. "I will get up there as soon as I can. Let me see if I can get someone in the government to back off. Hang in there."

Chester looked towards the Atlantic from the eastern window of his office. He glanced down to the street and noticed four black Chevy Suburban SUVs pull in to the reception drive. He swallowed hard as he saw between eight and ten men get out of them. Each man wore a black suit with the exception of one uniformed Coast Guard Officer. A few wore baseball caps adorned with either DEA or FBI on them. One bore the logo of the US Marshals. The Coast Guard officer had three gold stripes on his shoulder boards. "Now what the fuck am I supposed to do?" he shouted to himself. His white shirt and suspenders were soaked in sweat. He put his suit coat on to cover the perspiration and sat down in the chair behind his large teakwood desk. He pulled out his notebook listing high-ranking officials who owed him favors. Nervously he began thumbing through it not really knowing what he was looking for.

Connie buzzed. "Mr. Whittaker, there is a group of very official looking people here to see you."

"Ok Connie, please show them in." Calmly he opened his top desk drawer. He gripped the Smith and Wesson. For a split second, he thought of shooting the first person through the door which would likely result in suicide by cop.

As Connie opened the door, Jessie was the first to enter. "Mr. Whittaker we have a warrant . . . - No!"

Chester raised the pistol up to his jaw, simply smiled and said "Hi there!" Then he pulled the trigger and for a nanosecond thought. "That didn't hurt so bad." The white-hot bullet entered his larynx, seared through the back of his tongue, tumbled around in his brain and out the top of his skull. It finally stopped, embedded in an oak beam on the ceiling. Chester's head slumped forward and crashed on a pile of papers, a map of the Atlantic and Caribbean and his notebook. Blood and brain tissue spewed about the area behind the chair and on the window.

"Shit!" In twenty-six years in the Coast Guard, he had seen his share of dead and dying people. Jessie would relive what he had just witnessed every day for the rest of his life.

Connie fainted. One of the DEA agents revived her and sat her on the couch. The ottoman was open and there was still several hundred thousand dollars lying on the bottom.

Chapter Fifty-Six

Dutch and Emmett lead the group to Leon's office. Without knocking, Emmett opened the door. The head ranger was on the phone with Gretchen. "I think I am in a lot of trouble babe. You take care of my things and I will be in touch." He hung up.

"Surprise!" Dutch smiled.

"What the hell," Leon mumbled as he looked at his two rangers now dressed in bullet proof vests, wearing side arms and DEA baseball hats.

"Yes Mr. Matthews, for four months, you have been under surveillance for conspiracy to commit a number of felonies. Our technical folks are going down stairs to look at your little hobby shop. We are placing you under arrest for conspiracy to smuggle contraband into the United States." Dutch read him his Miranda rights as he sat in his chair, chin resting in his cupped hands, staring at the top of his desk. "If you want to give us any information as to the whereabouts a ship named Caribbean Gipsy, the captain named Cory Higgins and a woman known as Patricia or Trish Dixon or Wilson, it could help your case. But we need it immediately."

"What do you mean?" He asked.

"You know what the hell we mean." Dutch who had always been docile around the park superintendent, shouted with his face inches away from Leon. "Where the fuck is that ship, where are Higgins and his woman?"

Grasping at any straw which could lessen his future incarceration, he simply stated. "Try Bermuda, Savannah or someplace in between. Dixon, she works for a law firm in Atlanta. That is all you get until I get an attorney."

"Do you have one in mind?"

"Yes, Gretchen Hildebrandt. She is in a Charleston firm Called Friend and Fair."

"We will have her meet you at the county jail. Is she the cute little Florida chick you have been banging?"

He nearly whispered "yes." The word jail hit home with Leon, It sunk in. He knew lengthy incarceration was to be part of his future.

Chapter Fifty-Seven

At eleven knots, it would take ESCAPE three days to make Bermuda. Not having any further information on the whereabouts of Caribbean Gipsy, the skipper decided to head northwesterly and begin a patrol sector east of the mouth of the Savannah River. The move would put them on track to begin patrolling easterly towards the British island sooner and give them an extra day.

There was a level of excitement onboard as everyone who had been involved in a previous boarding of Caribbean Gipsy got a chance to look at the sketches and understand the complexity of the hidden compartments. Among the three organized boarding parties, the crews were shaking dice and competing for a spot on the team to finally take her down.

At noon on Thursday, the teletype sprung to life, spewing reams of reports describing the results of the three simultaneous federal raids in Atlanta, Palm Beach and Fort Sumter. There was also a report on the warehouse in Virginia Beach.

Ensign Beal was on watch on the bridge. All of the other officers gathered around the wardroom table with messages and charts of the Atlantic seaboard.

"It would be a spectacular way to finish off this patrol if we could bust this guy," Flood began.

"I have actually sat right on top of those frigging tanks filling out a boarding report," Buzz spoke up.

"I remember looking at them and admiring the construction and welding job. I wonder how many loads they have gotten through," Vince added.

"Whoever makes the boarding should ask the skipper to demonstrate the overboard discharge. When he does it, the boarding officer should then pull the handle out and ask him 'What happens if you do this?'" Sutton suggested.

The ship finally reached the Savannah River Buoy. Mr. Beal called the wardroom to inform the Commanding Officer he was about to make the ninety degree turn to starboard.

"No problem, go for it Mr. Beal."

Flood continued, "XO why don't you go make an announcement to the crew. We are on the hunt and everyone should keep their eyes on the horizon."

Chapter Fifty-Eight

Caribbean Gipsy's new skipper and his crew were in the wheelhouse working on a second beer when Leon's ominous transmission came across on the fax machine. "What we gonna do Jefe?" Manuel wondered.

"Well, there is a couple of Savannah numbers in this book. Why don't we spend the weekend seeing if we can peddle some or all of it in Bermuda? Things will die down in a couple of days and we will head west. I know a few of Chad's friends. They might buy if we can get it there.

"How about we go out into the community and see if we find anyone interested in buying a little coke?" Rob asked the crew.

"How we split money?" Manuel inquired.

"I will keep forty percent and you four split the rest. Manuel should get a bigger piece of the pie than the newer crew."

Manuel looked around the wheelhouse. Splitting sixty percent of anything was an unheard of portion for the Colombians. "Let's go see what we can do." Manuel offered.

They broke into two groups. Sammie who spoke better English took Hector and went with Rob. Caesar teamed up with Manuel. Manuel and Caesar took a cab to Castle Harbour to explore the bars. Rob and Sammie hit Somers's Warf where half a dozen drinking venues frequented by sailors and other blue collar workers stayed open until well past midnight.

In general, Bermuda boasts a conservative theme. There are no casinos, strip clubs and very little crime. Because of this attitude, law enforcement is lax. Often, successful criminals stop in one of the island harbors to conduct illicit trade. The banking system also provides a safe place for foreigners to keep money in offshore accounts.

Sitting at the bar in The Tavern by The Sea, Rob's attention was drawn to a CNN 'Breaking News' story on a story about the take down of a major drug smuggling operation. Implications from Virginia Beach, Atlanta, Palm Beach Florida and the National Monument at Fort Sumter were being explored by the press. The reporter was relating how the conspiracy included the monitoring of movements of Coast Guard ships on patrol from Fort Sumter and a sophisticated mixing and packaging operation in Virginia Beach. The suicide of a prominent Palm Beach attorney seemed to be related to the whole story. The story moved to a reporter in Atlanta interviewing Robert Whittaker.

"Whittaker, a candidate for a local city council position, seemed unaware of his brother's shenanigans. Allegedly, an accountant in this firm had been laundering drug monies through a trust account she managed in the basement. Robert has indicated his brother handled all oversight on the operation" she told the camera.

"In addition to whatever the government is doing, I am doing my own internal investigation and get to the bottom of this. Whatever the results are, I will make the report available to the press," he told the reporter.

Obviously shocked by the events, oddly he showed very little remorse over the death of his brother.

Byrd inhaled and exhaled deeply. He was happy all of the reporting disclosed nothing about a little blue freighter roaming around the Atlantic with a couple tons of cocaine and no place to take it.

Meanwhile, Sammie engaged a couple rough looking men who offered him a cigarette and bought him a North Rock beer.

He motioned to Rob. "Hey Jefe, these guys want to talk."

It took less than half an hour to make arrangements for ten-kilos of cargo for delivery to the buyers on a fifty-five-foot sailboat in the harbor. The buyers agreed to pay four grand per kilo or eighty thousand dollars for the stuff. This was about half the price they would have had to pay under any other circumstances. The two buyers also offered that they would alert an associate who was sailing east in a week. It was possible a similar deal might work with him.

Rob felt a little better about his future.

Rob and Sammie enjoyed a five-course lobster dinner before returning to the ship to dig out a package of narcotics to load into the skiff for delivery. Chester's Amex card took care of the tab and a generous tip.

When they arrived at the boat, Manuel, Hector and Caesar were waiting for them smiling. They had arranged for a twenty-kilo delivery to a small freighter anchored off Gibbons Bay. The delivery would happen when they left Bermuda on Sunday or Monday.

Manuel had also arranged for a local furniture warehouse to purchase all the furniture for ten grand. The truck would arrive at the moorings in St George's on Sunday.

Chapter Fifty-Nine

Channel surfing in his Hawaiian bungalow, Chad switched to the morning CNN news. He was alone. Debbi had gone shopping to buy decor for their new home.

"Wow! The shit has hit the fan!"

The reporter Shelly Knott was describing the takedown of a long running drug smuggling operation centered in an attorney's office in Palm Beach Florida. She related the connection between Chester Whittaker, the apparent leader of the operation, and a former Citadel Classmate, Leon Matthews, Chief Park Ranger at Fort Sumter.

"Whittaker committed suicide as federal agents raided his office. Leon was arrested for a number of federal and state felonies. Federal Treasury agents are reviewing accounting documents found in a trust department in Whittaker's brother's law firm in Atlanta Georgia."

She mentioned the city council election. Robert Whittaker had been leading for months in the polls. "Today, the city fathers are calling for him to withdraw from the election," she reported.

Photographs of Robert and his wife flashed on the screen behind the reporter. "Authorities are still looking for several other persons of interest. An accountant described as an 'Internal Auditor' named Trish Dixon and an American ship captain only known as Cory are being sought by a number of federal agencies." She went on. "Some officials believe this operation is connected with the two-day old discovery of a cocaine mixing lab in a vacant warehouse in Virginia Beach."

She turned, looking into another camera. "And now let's go to Fort Sumter in South Carolina to Dave Murphy who is covering the situation there. What's happening in Charleston, Dave?"

He was one floor below Leon's office standing in front of the teletype machine, fax transmitter and the status board. "Well Shelly, two DEA agents went undercover here for the past several months and look what they found." He pointed towards the equipment and went on to explain the discovery of antennae in the flagpoles, compromised Coast Guard patrol communications and the weather fax transmissions to smuggling vessels. "It is not known how long this operation has been going on but estimates are that at least three large cocaine shipments and dozens of marijuana and hash deliveries have been accomplished by the team."

"What's up?" Debbi walked through the front door.
"We left just in time, check this out."

.

Chapter Sixty

Early Saturday ESCAPE patrolled a straight line from the Savannah River channel entrance buoy to Hamilton Bermuda. The Two a Day report indicated that they were in sector Alpha sixteen and patrolling towards Alpha twenty-eight for the next twelve hours.

On the bridge, the mood was lighthearted. Skipper Dave was telling Vietnam sea stories to Buzz, the quartermaster of the watch and the helmsman.

Normally, Saturdays at sea were more relaxed than the rest of week. At noon the routine shifted to barbequing on the fantail, card games, letter writing and extra movies on the mess deck, chief's quarters and in the wardroom.

Vince and Phil gathered the two law enforcement teams after lunch for a chat on the fantail.

"We are going to get this guy this time, I just know it," Phil began. "There is a cute little hidden compartment below decks near the rudder post. I know, I have looked at it and leaned on it at least once."

"Jeeze, me too," added First Class Boatswain's Mate Oliver Mitchell.

"Yep, this guy has been boarded by every cutter from here to Cancun and no one has noticed these tanks." Phil continued. "The Intel says there is a high probability of encountering her within the next two days on this patrol track. All right gentlemen, go relax and get ready for some fun on the last week of our patrol."

The enlisted personnel joined others in the afternoon sun.

"Well OPS, what do you think?"

"It has been an interesting couple of days. The skipper got promoted, you have a command in Oregon. Say, isn't that where your wife is from?"

"Sure is, this will make her happy."

"And now, we have a good chance of bringing down a long running smuggling ring."

"Don't forget, you're getting an extra half stripe and just got orders for an XO's spot." Vince added.

"Yes sir, this old ship has some pretty damn good results lately."

Chapter Sixty-One

Leon was having a bad weekend. Being interrogated by Dutch and Emmett who, two days earlier were merely temporary US Parks Service employees, was more than he could handle.

On the second day of the questioning, he broke down and told everything he knew about Chester's operation. Aside from the details provided in Two a Day reports and payments provided by Trish several weeks after each haul, he actually knew very little. He had never met Cory Higgins, Robert Whittaker or any of the team operating the lab in Virginia Beach. He did lie about how much his cut was from each of the payoffs, reducing the actual value by better than fifty percent. He had called in Gretchen as his attorney. Actually, Nicholas Friend would be the defense boss on the case. She would assist. She assured him the cash he had stashed in the apartment in Charleston would remain safe until any incarceration was over. His gut feeling was that she would stick by him.

Leon was a first offender and an otherwise straight citizen. Nicholas assured him if he helped the authorities, four years was the most likely punishment. With good conduct, he might be out in thirty months. Of course, his career with the federal government was over.

It was after Gretchen told him of Chester's suicide, he decided to tell everything he knew.

The charges against him were Conspiracy to Smuggle Narcotics into the U.S., Misuse of Federal Property and Electronic Civil Espionage with the Intent to Distribute Classified Information.

Nicholas convinced him to plea for leniency in exchange for all he knew. Arraignment was set for two o'clock on Tuesday. After talking with the federal prosecuting attorney, the parties all agreed, Leon would plead guilty to the smuggling charges. The judge would dismiss all the other charges.

Chapter Sixty-Two

The delivery to the guys from The Tavern by the Sea went off without a hitch. The crew split the money Saturday afternoon. The twenty-kilo delivery was prepared and ready for a quick transfer on Monday morning.

Rob spent most of Sunday in a telephone exchange, calling numbers he found in Cory's book. It took about six hours to arrange a fire sale of the three thousand pounds of cocaine left onboard. One of Chad's friends agreed to take the whole load for a thousand bucks per kilo. That's about a third of what it was worth. All he had to do was get past the Coast Guard to a little fishing dock on Tybee Island on the Savannah River.

Rob chatted with Manuel about the possibility of getting caught. "Amigo, there is a good chance we might get caught."

"I know Jefe. How much time do you get for smuggling?"

"I don't know, one friend of mine got caught and spent a year in jail waiting for a trial then got locked up for another year and a half before they let him out. If you are good in jail, they let you out early. I guess if I had money waiting for me when I get out I could have something to look forward to."

"They will probably send you right back to Colombia once you are done."

"Fine with me."

"When we get done with the transfer to the freighter at Gibbons Bay, why don't we go to Flatt's Inlet and tie up for a few hours and go to open bank accounts?"

"I like the way you think, Jefe."

"We should make them joint accounts with someone you trust back home. Let's make a few calls then go to a bank."

"That works for me. If my brother steals it from me, I will get even when I get home. But let's hope we don't get caught then I think we retire like Captain Cory."

"I like the way you think Manuel."

Chapter Sixty-Three

In Atlanta, things had calmed down by Monday afternoon. It was clear to the federal investigators Robert Whittaker had been completely blindsided by his brother's criminal dealings. The Treasury Department had taken receivership of the pension trust account and would find a new administrator.

Political damage severe enough to knock him down twenty-five percent in the polls soon abated. With a month left before the election, damage control was in full swing. The Mayor, Governor and many members of the state republican delegations stepped up to endorse Mr. Whittaker for City Council. Even Assistant Treasury Secretary Schultz from Washington DC sent in an endorsement. Several associates with the firm were looking for work in other places.

The Peruvian Avenue building holding the Florida branch of the Whittaker Law Firm was cordoned off with yellow police tape. The city council wanted it gone but, the police chief demanded it stay until his investigation was over. The associate attorneys and paralegal staff were all looking for work elsewhere. Gina Whittaker left for Italy as soon as she could.

The FBI issued a warrant for the arrest of Patricia, aka, 'Trish' Dixon aka Patricia Wilson. DEA and Treasury agents searched her condominium in Buckhead. They found a neatly kept small home with simple but elegant furnishings. The three hundred thousand dollars she had in cash were in a safe deposit box she maintained in a South Carolina bank in the name of her deceased husband.

Tom Thrasher had vanished. The contents of his rented Palm Beach condo had been removed and were in storage in Texas. His borrowed Porsche was found in the Whittaker Building garage with the keys in it. Tom joined Chad Walgren in Hawaii to chat about their future.

Chapter Sixty-Four

By the time Manuel and Rob finished their banking, it was late Monday afternoon. They had to take a taxi all the way to Hamilton to find a bank with international connections.

Transiting across the northern reaches of the islands is dangerous cruising at best. Most of the navigational aids along the way are shipwrecks. They chose to leave on the high tide at four am Tuesday. It took five hours to clear Daniel's Head at Somerset Village. At nine knots, it was four days to the Savannah River. The buyers were not expecting them until the weekend.

Meanwhile, four hundred miles ahead on a collision course, ESCAPE was proceeding at a steady eight knots. Skipper Dave ordered the watches to zig zag along, moving five miles north and five miles south of the track line making a twenty-degree turn each half hour. This maneuvering diminished the cutter's speed of advance along the projected track to about six knots.

The daily routine onboard the cutter continued with underway watches, maintenance and repair of broken things, drills and meal preparation.

The lookout watches in the crow's nest high above the bridge were doubled up. The visible horizon from the bridge was about ten or eleven miles, while the lookouts one hundred feet aloft could see up to twenty miles. There was an air of tense excitement throughout the ship. In anticipation of new customers soon, the deck force made sure the three cells in the brig were ready for business.

An hour before sunset on Tuesday, ESCAPE crossed the currents of the Gulf Stream. Tanker and container ship traffic in the stream was busy with a northbound ship nearly every two miles.

At supper in the wardroom, all talk was about who was going to be the lucky one to turn the handle in the engine room and arrest Cory.

LTJG Ladner, scheduled for the twenty hundred to midnight watch stated, "If we run into them on the Mid Watch, make sure someone wakes me up."

Ops Boss Phil inserted, "I've got the mid watch so if we have a midnight boarding, you will be the man. You bet your ass we will wake you up."

Dave and Vince looked at one another enjoying the enthusiasm of their officers.

"Anyone up for a friendly game of poker." Vince inquired.

"Sure" the Skipper offered.

"OK then the game is on. I'm in until my watch." Buzz added.

There was a knock on the door and the messenger of the watch entered. "Captain, the OOD wants me to tell you we have a contact about five miles ahead. Not a freighter but a sailboat."

"Thanks, we will be up shortly." Dave looked around "Anyone up for a sunset boarding? I guess the game can wait."

The entire officer compliment with the exception of Vince went to the bridge.

The sailboat was an American flagged vessel heading north.

CWO Larry Jeffrey, ESCAPE's First Lieutenant, was standing the OOD watch. "Looks pretty touristy to me Skipper."

Let's see what they have to say to say, Smitty. Give him a call."

It turned out the sailing vessel Jolly Situation hailing from Nags Head North, Carolina was transiting home after a summer in the Lesser Antilles. A boarding found the wife of the owner was experiencing severe seasickness. The ships corpsman went over and administered to her. He started an IV of normal saline and instructed the owner on how to remove the needle when the liquid emptied. Anti-seasickness medication left onboard added to the family's appreciation of the Coast Guard. The inspection revealed a clean boat operated in Bristol condition.

An hour and a half after the first sighting of Jolly Situation, ESCAPE returned to her intended patrol pattern. Postponing the poker game to the next opportunity made sense and most off watch personnel retired for the evening in hopes that the mid watch would bring some excitement. To add to the possibility of sneaking up on someone, Flood ordered the ship to proceed eastbound without any visible lights. With all portholes with blackout covers, the ships status was now Dog Zebra.

The smoking lamp was out on all-weather decks and the bridge.

Chapter Sixty-Five

Just after two am, chugging along westbound, Rob was in the wheelhouse with Sammie as a lookout. Caribbean Gipsy ran on autopilot. Since leaving the western edge of Bermuda, they had only encountered one other ship, a southeasterly bound LNG tanker most likely headed from England to the terminal in Freeport.

"Pretty quiet out here Jefe."

"Si Sammie, but man it's dark. If there is a moon up there, we can't see it.

"Maybe darker is better Jefe."

"I don't know. It was easier when Cory made all the decisions. I just want to get this stuff off the boat and head for Montana."

"You think maybe I can catch a flight from Savannah to Colombia when we are done?"

"No, I think you probably need to go to Atlanta."

"I hope I can take a bus there. I don't want to stick out too much."

"Once we get into Savannah, I will help all of you find your way home."

"Thanks, Boss."

Fourteen miles west, the crow's nest lookout called to the bridge. "Contact on the horizon off the port bow, a white masthead light."

Phil went to the radar. "Yep, there he is." There was a small and faded blotch on the display.

Phil picked up the phone connected to the captain's quarters and cranked the handle once.

"What's up?"

"We are looking at a westbound vessel about fourteen miles out sir."

"I'll be up in five minutes. Meanwhile, turn a little south, stay dark and keep him at about eight to ten miles off our beam."

"Aye-Aye Captain."

"Right five degrees' rudder." Phil gave the command to turn south of the contact. A mark made by the quartermaster with a grease pencil on the display showed the first electronic signal of the other vessel. Five minutes later, another mark followed. The two marks were connected by a line extending westward on the screen. Using simple geometric positioning calculations, Phil and the Quartermaster quickly discerned the contact to be on a course straight to the Savannah River sea buoy.

Just as the line was drawn, the messenger of the watch shouted, "Captain on the bridge!"

"What do we have Phil?"

"Well, he is not huge and is showing running lights required of a ship of less than fifty meters. There is no aft masthead light."

The two officers walked to the port bridge wing and peered through their binoculars.

"This could be our guy. Let's get some night vision on him."

"Yes sir," Phil responded. "It's already here." The messenger of the watch anticipated the request and stepped onto the bridge wing holding two tactical night vision devices.

Both men strapped the night vision apparatus over their heads and looked eastward.

"It's the right configuration and size. The superstructure is about two-thirds the way down the hull. That's just like the Gipsy." The CO said. "Let's get everyone up, all engines on the line, and have the cooks make a lot of fresh coffee." He was directing his desires to the messenger of the watch. "XO first then Mr. Ladner and the boarding parties. And remind everyone we are still a 'darkened ship'."

"Aye-Aye Sir." The messenger saluted, turned and hopped down the ladder.

Dave turned towards the OOD. "OK Phil, let's put him on our beam then turn around and shadow him until we are ready. We will drop in behind him about half a mile, launch the boats and when we are ready, we will light him up."

"Got it Captain." Phil called the engine room to order up all of the available power then began maneuvering the ship in accordance with the CO's wishes.

"Pretty clear up ahead Jefe" Sammie half whispered.

"Si Sam, let's get Caesar and Hector up here for the four to eight watch. Then we need to be back up early when we cross the shipping lanes." Rob scanned the horizon with his binoculars seeing nothing of ESCAPE off their port beam.

"Ok Boss, I go get em."

Sammie left the wheelhouse and Rob stepped to the radar. The green cursor swept in its rhythmic circular motion every six seconds. Not as experienced as Cory at all things onboard this ship, since they departed Bermuda the radar had been set on the ten-mile range. The unit was capable of scanning accurately out to twenty-five miles. The radar antenna on the Gipsy was mounted on a bracket four feet forward of the main masthead. Each time the scanner spun around, the mast occluded an arc or 'shadow' of about twenty degrees directly astern. ESCAPE never appeared on Rob's radar.

Onboard ESCAPE the bridge was getting crowded. It took ten minutes to develop accurate night vision. In the total darkness, everyone moved slowly.

Vince stood next to his CO on the starboard wing. Both were wearing night vision devices showing the green fuzzy outline of the ship now ten miles ahead and just forward of the beam.

"So, when we get back in are you going out to Fort Sumter? I wonder what your chubby little photographer buddy will be telling folks when this story breaks."

"I would like to. I want to thank him for his contribution. We would be nowhere on this mission without those photographs. Just think, he's the catalyst that started to change our three-decade-old way of reporting daily ship positioning. I would also like to see the communication suite Matthews set up there."

"Excuse me, Captain," Buzz Ladner interrupted. "I have the boarding party and the gunnery team mustered on the mess deck. Do either of you want to chat with them?"

"Go ahead XO." Dave responded. "It's a pretty exciting morning. I want to get behind him by about a mile then launch the boats. Next, we will move up to his port quarter. When we are about fifty yards out, we will light him up with night sun and the siren. Put ESCAPE 1 on his starboard side and number 2, just in front of us. Keep everything dark."

"Yes sir." Vince responded.

"What do you think for timing?"

"We could be ready in half an hour." Vince looked at Buzz who nodded in agreement.

"Good. I want to do this while it is still dark and the further west we get, the closer to the shipping lanes we will be. I want to stay out of the traffic."

It was fifteen minutes after four am local time.

"No problem skipper, we will get busy. I'll have the First Lieutenant," the warrant officer in charge of the deck department

"Make sure the law enforcement detail is set without loud announcements."

Chapter Sixty-Six

Manuel and Hector relieved Rob and Sammie of the bridge watch. "Looks clear ahead." Rob spoke as he left. "Come wake us up around seven so we can all be on lookout when we cross the shipping lanes."

"No problem Jefe."

They moved along westward. Rob was drifting off to sleep. Suddenly, as if in a dream, he heard loud sirens and bright lights flashing outside his doorway.

"What the fuck!"

Hector knocked loudly on his door. "Jefe, Jefe! We're busted! We got boats all around and big ship right on our ass! What we gonna do?"

Rob was on his feet in seconds. His hands were shaking and he was sweating. Up on the bridge, he found Manuel with his eyes wide open and speechless.

"Manny, get your shit together! They don't know about our secret hiding place. They probably just do middle of the night stuff for fun."

"I hope so. We always see them down by Jamaica. What they doing way up here?"

"I guess they patrol everyplace. We don't get anything from Leon any more. We are on our own."

"Ahoy onboard the Caribbean Gipsy! This is the United States Coast Guard. Stop your vessel, heave to with your starboard beam to the wind and prepare for a boarding," Phil spoke into his microphone.

Rob keyed his microphone. "What is this all about? It's the middle of the night!"

"Yes Captain, you are an American flagged vessel. We are directing you to heave to immediately and prepare for boarding under Title 14 United States Code."

"Ok, ok! We are slowing down. Give me a minute."

"Roger, Captain. While we are getting ready to come aboard please answer a few questions. Where was your last port of call?"

"Bermuda." Rob's voice was quivering.

"What was your reason for stopping there?" Smitty was now on the radio gathering information.

"We delivered a load of furniture from St Thomas. It's what we do. We haul things. I have all the paperwork."

"Yes sir. Now where are you heading?"

"Savannah Georgia. We are looking for cargo to haul south."

"OK. Now, how many are in the crew?"

"Myself and four."

Smitty went on gathering information. Buzz and Vince were each in one of the small boats. The watch on the bridge was communicating with the two boarding parties on a secured VHF channel.

"ESCAPE ONE, ESCAPE TWO, he is stopping. When it looks right, begin the boarding. TWO you keep an eye on his upwind beam while XO and the team board." Phil gave the last minute instructions.

Smitty instructed Rob to place a ladder over the leeward port side to accommodate the boarding party. "Have one crewman at the ladder to assist then gather the remainder of the crew at the stern rail."

"Yes, sir."

Vince grabbed tightly the third rung of the ladder and stepped aboard. Manuel was waiting and offered a hand up. "Welcome aboard sir." He seemed nervous.

"You go to the stern rail and I will help the rest." Vince ordered.

Within three minutes, six crewmembers from ESCAPE were standing on the port side of the ship. Four walked towards the stern.

Two went forward to look for any stragglers. "Who is the skipper?" Vince asked.

"Me."

"We will all stay right here and Petty Officer Dix and Chief Logan will make a security check of your vessel."

Vince nodded seriously and the two men disappeared below.

In fifteen minutes they returned to the fantail declaring the ship secure.

"Ok Captain, why don't you, I, and Chief Logan here take a walk around. We will start with the engine room."

"This way." Rob pointed to an open metal door. A ladder led to the deck below.

"Are you a new skipper on this ship? Our records show a fella named Higgins as the master."

"Yeah, well he got sick and we left him down south. I've got a license. It is up in the wheelhouse." Rob spoke with a degree of uncertainty.

"We will look at all that in a while." Vince responded sternly.

It was hot in the mechanical space with the big Caterpillar main engine and a generator running.

Chief Logan shone his flashlight in every corner of the space. He leaned on the stainless steel water and sewage tanks. "Sure is a clean little ship." He shined his light on the sight glass indicating the sewage tank about two-thirds full. "You know Skipper it's OK to pump overboard way out here. No need to save this crap."

"I guess my engine guy forgot to dump it after we left Bermuda."

The chief looked at the valve designated 'overboard sewage discharge' and said, "Let's just take care of that now." He slid the valve handle and the tank drained in several seconds. The chief sounded surprised. "Man that was quick. It has to be a couple hundred gallons. Maybe this tank isn't as big as it looks." He looked towards Vince who nodded his head.

Rob was scared to death and was having a hard time controlling his own bodily discharge functions.

Chief Logan looked at the valve handle and said. "I wonder what else this little gadget does."

He pulled the handle towards him and once again turned it clockwise. The generator strained and accelerated, a hydraulic pump motor near the main engine began to whirl and two rams lifted up the water and sewage tanks like two opposing small dump trucks.

"Well, well, what do we have here?" Vince stepped over to the stack of ten kilo bags of cocaine. "It looks like you got yourself into a bit of trouble Captain Byrd." Rob wet his pants.

"Frisk him Chief."

"Really sir?"

"Yep, but not his crotch." Vince chuckled.

Chief Logan had Rob raise his hands and he felt down the sides of his body, found only a sailor's knife which he took and placed in his own lifejacket pocket.

Next, Vince spoke. "Ok Captain, here is what we are going to do. We will all go up to the fantail and I will send someone down to test this stuff and see what it is. If it is just flour or sugar, you will be on your way. If it is what we think it is you and your crew are in a lot of trouble."

Rob was silent. But, as Vince was talking, he slowly moved his foot and kicked the blue handled sea chest lever to start flooding the ship. Neither the Chief nor Vince noticed. The little freighter began taking on water at about four hundred-fifty gallons a minute.

"Let's go."

Chief led the way up, followed by Rob then Vince.

Once on deck, Chief led Rob to the rest of the crew and boarding party. Vince keyed his radio and told his skipper what they had found and how the secret compartment worked. Just as intelligence had said it would.

Gunner's Mate Second Class Billy Simpson approached Vince with Seaman Elliott. "Chief says you found about a ton of white stuff. Want me to go check it out sir?"

"That's what we came for, Gunny. And Elliott, go get a camera and take a lot of pictures of the false tanks and the pile of stuff. LT Sutton will be over in a few minutes to help document everything."

"Aye-Aye sir." Simpson responded. He, Elliott and Vince all joined the others at the stern of the ship. Simpson picked up a satchel containing a dozen field test kits and Elliott got a 35mm camera and two rolls of film from the Chief.

It had been about ten minutes since Rob and his escorts left the engine room. Elliott and Simpson headed for the ladder leading down.

"Remember gents, no one is left with evidence alone. Once we determine it is contraband, always two or more." Chief Logan reminded them of evidence custody protocol.

"Yes, Chief," they replied in unison in a friendly mocking manner.

By the time the duo reached the evidence, over four thousand gallons of sea water had invaded the ship. The two didn't notice the flooding immediately as the water was still just below the floor.

Simpson made a slit in the top of one of the bags. Interestingly he noticed that it had been opened and re sealed with duct tape. It was the same bag Rob had tested a week earlier.

"Hey El', take a shot of this."

It took Simpson just over two minutes to complete his test and verify that they were looking at pure cocaine. Another thousand gallons of the Atlantic Ocean was inside the ship.

"Let's go tell XO."

The two climbed up the ladder and poked their heads outside. Simpson yelled towards the fantail. "Test is positive for cocaine!" Phil was approached intending to join them below.

Elliott stepped down the ladder backwards and noticed his foot dropping in to about three inches of water. There was steam forming around the main engine as the water had touched the hot oil pan. "What the hell!" the seaman said loudly.

Simpson and Sutton also stepped down. Within ten seconds they both shouted: "She's sinking!"

Sutton told Elliott, "Go get the XO, tell him they have scuttled her! We will need pumps from ESCAPE and need them fast!" By now the water was ankle deep.

Up on deck Vince was reading Rob his Miranda rights when Elliott told him the news. "XO, this thing is sinking! Mr. Sutton says we need pumps and need them now."

"Shit! What the hell did you do?" he screamed at Rob.

"You just told me I had the right to be quiet." Byrd smirked.

Vince took a pair of handcuffs from his belt and clamped one on Rob's left hand and the other to the ship's rail. He took out a second pair of cuffs and secured Rob's right wrist to the ship.

"Ok, you can remain silent right here." Rob wet his pants again realizing if she sank, he might go with her.

At the same instant Caribbean Gipsy went dark as the water engulfed her generator.

Below, Phil was looking at the pile of cocaine.

"Elliott, take all the pictures you can in the dark, Simpson, we need at least two of those bags on deck as quickly as you can."

"Yes sir." He hoisted a bag to his shoulders and went to ladder. Chief Logan met him at the top and took the evidence. "Remember chief, always have two people with this stuff."

"Right." He laughed "Get two more."

"Sure Chief." By now, he was sloshing through a foot of water. The bottom of the pile of cocaine was soaked.

Vince got on his radio. "ESCAPE, they have scuttled her. We need a damage control team and pumps here ASAP."

Skipper Flood had assumed the deck watch duties while all the other officers were busy. He picked up the ships loudspeaker.

"Now hear this! This is the Captain. The ship we boarded is carrying cocaine, we have arrested the crew but they have scuttled her and she is sinking. Engineering department assemble all available personnel to board ESCAPE 2 on the starboard side in five minutes, bring pumps and hoses. Any admin crew, start taking pictures of the ship. We will buy you film when we get home."

The sun was rising on the eastern horizon and with light on everything, Flood could see Caribbean Gipsy sitting awkwardly lower in the water. As she rolled with the seas, each time she rolled it seemed to take longer to come back upright. She was losing her righting ability and her bow was digging deeper into the sea.

Ed Tarzano, appeared on the bridge. "What's up Skipper?"

"Looks like they have scuttled her. I bet he opened a sea chest when we approached. He is loaded with coke. Vince handcuffed the skipper to the rail and I guess he is scared shitty. But he won't tell anyone where the shutoff is."

"Well, we have two 250 gallons per minute pumps headed over but I am not sure we can catch up with it.

Vince also arrested Sammie, Hector, Manuel and Caesar. He quickly had them transported to ESCAPE to be placed in the brig. Rob, he kept handcuffed to the rail. Rob was crying and Vince ignored him.

Six engineers were onboard in the engine room. They started pumping and slowed the flooding but could not overtake it. Chief Logan came up on deck where Vince was on his radio talking to the skipper.

"Excuse me XO. The pumps are not catching up with the flooding. With the generator out, we can't use any of their pumps. We might lose her."

"How many bags did we get?"

"Three sir. We marked them with recording numbers before we took them off the stack. Elliott took three rolls of film. We have a ton of pictures and at least four witnesses to swear what was there."

"Let's give them three or four more minutes. If we don't get on top of the flooding, we will just have to let her go."

"Roger XO! I will go tell them."

Vince called his boss. "Yeah Captain, there is a good chance we will lose her. He must have opened a huge valve. I told them to keep trying to overtake it for three more minutes. If it doesn't work, we better get back home. We have three bags of evidence and dozens of pictures."

"OK Vince, she's not worth risking any of our people over. Keep that guy cuffed to his folly until the last minute. Try to get a few names out of him. Looks like you are enjoying that little part of this."

Vince responded, "Yes sir, I actually am." He went to the engine room door finding Chief Logan sitting on the top step of the ladder. "Let's wrap it all up and let her go. Get everyone back to ESCAPE then come get me and the dude last. I am going to go have some fun with him."

"I bet you are sir!" Logan smiled broadly and saluted his XO. "You're one badass cop, Commander."

Vince smiled and returned the salute then approached Byrd. "How ya feeling sailor?"

Rob was getting testy, wondering if they would really let him go down with the ship. He thought not. He spat on the deck between them. "How the fuck do you think I am feeling? You are gonna get me locked up for five years and I am broke."

Vince laughed out loud. "Did someone tell you that first offenders got five?"

"Yes. And I have good attorneys."

"If you mean that guy in Florida? Guess what? He's dead. And you weren't thinking too clearly when you flooded this beautiful ship with us onboard. That's an assault on a Federal Officer. Actually six Federal Officers. That will add ten years to your five. And this ship is owned by investors. Those folks will want a pint or two of your blood.

"Are you going to leave me here?" He began crying.

"What can you tell me about Higgins, Trish Dixon, Tom Thrasher and some guy named Chad?"

"I don't know where any of them are."

"OK. See ya later." Vince walked to the port side where ESCAPE 2 was approaching after returning everyone to the ship.

"Wait a minute! Please! Don't leave me here." Caribbean Gipsy's bow was nearly awash.

"Higgins and Dixon left the ship in Bermuda. I think they headed to Europe. Thrasher is my lawyer in Palm Beach and I don't know who Chad is."

Vince turned and came back. "Ok where did you pick up the cocaine?"

"Some French ship, rusty and old. It is called 'saint' something, about six hundred feet long. He headed south. He had French hookers on board. We were going to deliver this stuff to a guy on Tybee Island on the Savannah River. That's all I know."

"All right, I will mark you down as cooperative. We will talk to the US Attorney about the assault charges. Let's go watch your ship sink."

Vince released the cuffs and pointed towards the ladder.

Chapter Sixty-Seven

With three ten kilo bags of cocaine secured in a triple locked storage room and five prisoners sealed snugly in the brig, ESCAPE'S entire crew stood along the starboard rail. Many had cameras or video recorders in their hands. It was 0800 and the early fall sunshine reflected off of the stern of Caribbean Gipsy.

Vince and Phil had prepared half a dozen incident report messages for the district operations center where Susan Rico was on watch. Jessie Warburton stood smiling at her side as the messages arrived.

"Nice work Lieutenant. This is a big one."

"It sure is sir. Thanks again for including me."

"You have worked hard on this and contributed a lot. I wish I had as much experience as you have in my first five years. Keep your nose clean and you will have a wonderful career in this neat little club."

"Thank you sir. One of these days I will catch up with Cory Higgins and this case will be completely resolved."

"I hope you do Lieutenant. We don't always get to finish something so completely in this organization. But, he will be on the lam and you have quite a few years ahead of you. I hope your wish comes true."

The bow and cargo deck of the little ship were under water and she was pointing downward at a twenty-degree angle. Within ten minutes the angle increased to nearly vertical and the shiny blue stern of Caribbean Gipsy seemed to helplessly display her rudder and propeller as a drowning victim might wave an arm. Hissing sounds could be heard as air escaped the dead hull. In another five minutes she began a half mile journey to the floor of the Atlantic.

The speed of the impact caused the wheelhouse to separate from the hull as the bow slammed into the hard bottom of the sea. As the hull laid down across a large underwater ledge, her keel snapped and she broke into two fifty-five foot pieces to spend a century or two wasting away until nothing was left.

On the bridge, Skipper Dave, Vince, Phil, Ed Tarzano and all of the officers onboard witnessed the event in silence.

"What a sad misuse of talent and machinery. Every time I saw her down in the Gulf, I coveted the job Higgins had. And now for the rest of his life he will be looking over his shoulder on the

411

run," Flood remarked as bubbles continued to roil the surface. He turned to Vince and grinned, "So XO, where are you going for your family portraits this fall?"

"Don't know Captain, probably some indoor studio. That last setting was too damn stressful."

Everyone within earshot of the wheelhouse started laughing.

The skipper turned to his Operations Boss. "Phil, draw a line to Charleston. It's been a great patrol. Let's go home."

The End

About the Author

Pete DeBoer signed up for a four year hitch in the Coast Guard in 1964. Nearly twenty-three years later he retired. He served aboard three different cutters ranging from buoy tenders to high endurance ships deploying for months at a time in the Pacific, Atlantic, Bering Sea and the Caribbean. His three-year tour on the cutter ESCAPE in Charleston South Carolina 1981-84 is the inspiration for this story. Pete's fascination wiith the Caribbean, Gulf of Mexico and the Atlantic coastal waters and the people living there provideds the backdrop for this saga.

ESCAPE deployed on drug interdiction patrols thirty times while DeBoer served as Operations Officer and for a time as Executive Officer. His extensive travel in the western hemisphere includes every state in the union, all of Western Europe as far east as Poland and Central and South America.

After leaving the service, Pete built a house from top to bottom then took up real estate for half a dozen years. He created a small business providing office solutions to local customers. He served two terms as an elected Port Commissioner in the Port of Kingston Washington. During his commissioner years he produced monthly editorials for the local newspaper. A collection of his favorite "Down at the Port" stories will soon be released as a Kindle Book.

He is a licensed maritime captain and enjoys occaional employment taking anglers fishing for salmon and halibut in Southeast Alaska.

DeBoer lives in Kingston Washington, west of Seattle. He is passionately involved in his community and enjoys playing guitar and singing in the local pubs. His own boat *Jolly Mon* a forty-five year old classic yacht is always waiting in the marina to carry him off on his next adventure.